H M Bradshaw

Wind Over Tide

This book is a work of fiction. Names, characters, places and incidents are either products of the author's imagination or are used fictitiously.

ISBN: 978-1477481042

www.windovertide.net
author@windovertide.net
Tel: (818) 584 6814

For my grandparents who lived it:
Evelyn and Martin McWilliam,
Annie and William Bradshaw.

Acknowledgements

It is important for me to note that this novel would not have been possible without the encouragement and advice I received from my family, friends and many other marvellous people. So, first of all, thank you to my supportive husband, Sanger Robinson, and our wonderful children Hadley and Charles whom I love very much and who have had to put up with my constant daydreaming and strange moods as I lived through the emotions of this book. We love you too Angus and Eden Mary, and we dearly wish you were with us.

Thank you to my mother, Norma, and my brother, Duncan, for their unrelenting support, and for posting, at considerable expense by airmail, many books, stories and DVDs about Hull and trawling. Thanks also to my grandparents, aunts and uncles whose anecdotes over the years about the war, the trawling life and Hull, as well as their love and encouragement, have greatly contributed to the richness of this book, namely; the Bradshaws, the Coverdales, the Doys, the McWilliams, and the Nelsons. I wish my father, George, a former trawlerman, had lived to see this book. I think he would have liked it. He loved history. The same goes for my Uncle Bill who sat down with me over one of his home-cooked Chinese dinners to talk about his trawling experiences – a fond memory.

Thank you to my friend Audrey Kavka, M.D. for always believing in me. Your unwavering support and encouragement of my writing, as well as your moral and ethical fortitude, have guided me to where I am today. To the astonishingly successful and talented Linda

Woolverton who has gracefully embodied the role of both friend and mentor, I give my thanks. Without you, I might have forgotten at times to make writing a priority. Thanks to the ever-inspirational Trevor Southey, creator of breath-taking art, for showing me how to live and create as a dedicated artist. To writers Michael Blue and Hank Pellisier for their early encouragement.

To the late World War II pilot Martyn Jacobs for your friendship and for relating your war-time experiences of Hull before and after the Blitz. Martyn, I will be telling your incredible story one day too. To Amanda Bowden, thank you for your long friendship, and for taking the chance to read a work-in-progress. Also, a special thanks to your late father, the lovely Joe Bowden whose chuckle and warmth will always be remembered. Many thanks are due to Sean Evans for his assistance with editing and sausages. To Jean-luc Dieudonne, Stanley Jablonksi, and Sarah Hubbard, friends of more than twenty-five years whose honesty, humour and encouragement have helped pull me through the dark times.

For research, I heartily thank local Hull historian Alec Gill whose vast array of books and documentaries on Hull's fishing industry and the Hessle Road community, along with our meetings, were invaluable to the authenticity of this book, as was the tremendous experience of Skipper Dave Hird, whose knowledge of the industry and its history is unsurpassed. At 26 years old, he was the youngest Skipper out of Hull when he earned his ticket in 1968 (two years after I was born!). Yes, thank you Dave Hird and your son Chris for supplying me with information and beer down at The Bear in South Cave! Gratitude also goes to the *Hull Daily Mail* and to all the people of Hull who contributed their experiences to the series "The Fishing Years", which served both as encouragement and research for *Wind Over Tide*. And thank you to all those kind folk who responded to my request for information via a letter to the *Hull Daily Mail*.

Also, a special appreciation goes to the late World War II veteran and cowboy Jake Copass, a fellow scribe who shared his wartime experiences and talked about the cowboy lifestyle while teaching my friend Emily Hirsch and me how to lasso at the Alisal Guest Ranch in California. We miss you Emily.

As I write this acknowledgement list, I feel sad that so many of the men and women who experienced the war years are slipping away from us. What an incredible generation to whom we owe so much.

Last but not least, a thank you to those of you who have in any way large or small positively touched my life with kindness, understanding and forgiveness.

HMB

Wind Over Tide

≈ ≈ ≈

River Humber

Muddy eddy flowing fast
She dreams of falling in;
The sky is grey and overcast,
One slip and she'll go in.
Out o'er the wide brown river,
From here out to the sea,
The sun breaks through,
She smiles awhile,
Yet dreams of falling still.

Chapter 1

One grey, drizzly October morning in 1945 at St. Andrews Docks in Hull, a gigantic, black-haired man named William McKenzie Goodwell, first mate on the Ichthus, made his way in giant strides across the docks to a Norton motorbike parked by the filleting sheds. This handsome, devilish fisherman shared his father's Christian name, but his middle name came from the doctor who delivered him some twenty-five years before when William senior, so overjoyed by the presence of a protective caul covering his son's face, gave the doctor the credit.

Grabbing the keys from the front wheel, Mac sat astride his bike and took a moment to watch the bustling dock where the bobbers were busily unloading the catch from the trawler on which he had just come home.

Look at her, he thought proudly of the Ichthus, casting his black eyes from bow to stern, going up and down one mast, across the bridge and up and down the foremast. She's magnificent! When his eyes rested on the gun on the bow, leftovers from the war, his heart swelled with pride. They ought to pin a medal on her, he thought. For all the lives she saved, for all the ships she saved from mines. And now look, she's an unglorified civilian that has had to return to work like the rest of us. I suppose we're lucky, her an' me. We made it. Not like a lot of them poor buggers – boats and men alike.

An image of the dead body that had spilled out of the cod end along with the fish on this trip came to mind. Mac shook his head to free himself of it. The faceless body, half-eaten, half-clothed in a British navy uniform, was given a burial at sea by orders of the skipper, a very super-stitious man, who knew a dead body couldn't be kept on board without disturbing the crew. For his own peace of mind, Mac had been glad to see the body gone: he didn't need to be reminded of his father's fate and what became of a drowned man. But there would be more dead men in the net, and in his dreams every corpse they caught had his fa-ther's face. Shaking his head again, Mac pulled his mind away from such dismal thoughts and back to the activity on board the Ichthus and dockside, a sight which always brought him great satisfaction.

To Mac, everything about the fishing life was beautiful and rhythmic. Although only a spectator, he involuntarily played a part in the orchestra, by swaying his shoulders as he sat on his bike watching the dock workers swing and tip the baskets. For him, the whole performance began at sea played by the natural pitches, peaks and troughs, up and down like a musical scale, effortlessly tossing the boats therein and the men on board who swayed to keep their balance. Then there was the repeated trombone shooting and hauling of the trawl over starboard side, embracing the fish to their fate.

Once the catch was landed at Hull, the performance continued. Like this day, in the belly of the Ichthus, below-men sorted the fish into baskets ready to be winched out on deck where, in the cold autumn air, swingers, stripped to

3

their underwear because of the sweaty work, shouted out the species as each basket was swung ashore to the weighers-off who, in turn, hand-tipped the full baskets into wooden fish kits. Next came the whistling clog-clad barrow lads who transported the ten stone kits on wooden barrows to where the fish would be inspected for auction, arranging the kits in blocks of forty, ten by four, as they would be sold, with cod facing west toward the Iceland market, and haddock facing east toward the North Sea Market.

The buyers, big men but graceful as ballerinas, hopped and bounced across the rims of the kits inspecting the catch and noting the best-looking fish for which they would bid during the impending Dutch auction. Once the fish was sold, the filleters stepped in. Working in groups of four, they stood around freezing, water filled trays set on wooden boards balanced on wooden horses. Chatting to each other, and hardly looking down at the job at hand, each filliter employed swift and well-practiced skills when sharpening their array of fish knives (different species, different knife), scrape, scrape, back and forth the blade goes along the sharpening steel, and then filleting, which some claimed they could do blindfold.

Finally, there was the cleaning up, and even here a certain lyrical beauty could be found in the way the empty kits were spun, one after the other, in large barrels of hot water by an aproned man who bent over the barrel as if supplicating to the task. The clean kits were then stacked on the dock, awaiting the next day's catch while, on the trawler, the boards and pounds in the fish room were scrubbed and made ready for the ice delivery.

Apparently others felt the same as Mac, that their work should be a musical performance, since the workers were often driven to sing or whistle or stamp their heavy clogs as they worked, and this day was to be no exception.

"Hell-o-o," sang one bobber tenor.

The next man to him sang an echo, "Hell-o-o," but one octave higher, and thus it went like a wave along the dock cheering up all the workers.

The dock lasses liked to join in. Cheerful and flirty, wearing rollers, blood-stained aprons, and clogs, these working girls' cheeks and hands were red with cold. Mac scanned the girls' ruddy faces, looking for the prettiest one among them, but none of them were a match for Dolores who had been one of the gang before marriage and three children had stolen her away from the docks, and away from him.

Dolores - standing out from the rest with her long brown hair, creamy skin and luminescent eyes. Eyes that lit up only for him, or so he had believed. It used to be that he would look forward to seeing her on the docks when he returned home from sea, but then, afterwards, when she left to marry Jimmy Alford, he had dreaded not seeing her in the places where she used to be. Running a hand through thick hair that swept back in a V from his forehead, he rubbed the back of his neck. There would be no avoiding her now that the war was over, and he was a fisherman once more.

He was the first mate on the Ichthus, second in command to the skipper, which meant he was responsible for the crew and for bringing home the catch in the best condition possible for the market. There was a lot of responsibility on his shoulders but he had the breadth to carry the load. He was an intimidating presence at six foot four and around seventeen stone, with shoulders so broad he had developed the habit of turning slightly as he went through doorways and, at the same time, dipping his head.

With hands as big as shovels, he inspired fear and respect in his crew; all of whom would quickly know his wrath if they stepped out of line. Even the dock workers feared him: conscious of being watched by critical eyes set deep under thick black eyebrows, they toiled harder, taking extra care of every single fish landed from the Ichthus as if it were their first born.

Some catch it were an' all, Mac reflected. A record breaker I reckon. Well, we'll see, won't we, when the final tally is in.

Mac calculated there should be almost four thousand kits filled mostly with cod, then haddock, some plaice, catfish, coley, and a few reds thrown in. In all his life at sea he had never seen such beautifully big fish. The war had brought a reprieve: while man had turned to hunting man, the fish had multiplied and grown to full-size. It amused Mac to think that in the cod's opinion men should fight each other more often.

Nodding with great satisfaction at the honest industry of his profession, Mac's roving dark eyes counted ten gangs busy unloading the catch. Glad that's not my job, he thought. But then, they're as glad not to have mine, ruddy landlubbers.

He shifted on his bike; the kit bag full of dirty washing weighing uncomfortably on his shoulder. He should head home to his mother, to quell the uneasy feeling he had about her well-being; yet, he lingered.

An impatient growl emanated from his black wool coat. Mac chuckled.

"We'll be on our way soon, Monty," he told the Yorkshire Terrier snuggled against his cream fisherman's jumper. "I know you're as eager as me to see Mam. Or is it the chance of bacon, eh?"

He tickled the dog's ears then dropped the heavy kit bag to the floor. Squaring his large shoulders, he balanced the bike between his strong, muscular thighs, righted a parcel of fish on the fuel tank, then sat back more comfortably before taking a couple of rolled cigarettes from the tobacco pouch he kept in his trouser pocket.

One he put behind his ear, the other in his mouth. As he cupped his hand against the wind, ready to strike a match, his bike lurched sideways.

"Oy, watch out Ginger, you fat bastard, you almost knocked me over!" he snarled.

"Pardon me," slurred the red-headed cook of the Ichthus.

"Don't tell me you're pissed already!"

The cook grinned sheepishly, bearing his yellowed teeth and patting an empty flask in his coat pocket. As broad as he was tall, Ginger's clumsy gait gave the impression that with one slip, he could fall and roll overboard, which is probably why he chose to stay in the galley rather than on the deck, that and to be near the food and able to drink out of sight, of course.

At sea, he kept his curly orange hair suppressed under a knitted cap, out of sight of the skipper who would turn back for home if he knew one of his crew was a red head. Once ashore the skipper acted as though he didn't recognise the cook - at least he certainly never acknowledged him - perhaps because Ginger made the best hambone soup he had ever tasted.

"In case you're wondering, your missus and her trusty rolling pin are that way," Mac motioned with his thumb.

"Oh aye. Ta. Home sweet 'ome, here I come." Ginger belched, rubbing his temple as if anticipating a lump there.

Mac watched the cook amble away. He should have a word with him about the drinking before it started to interfere with the job. If Ginger were ever tardy with the hambone soup there would be no telling what the skipper would do.

"Bloody 'ell, 'aven't you left yet?" Bert Smith the bosun cried.

"Aye, don't worry," said Mac. "I've left. Reckon I left about twenty minutes ago."

"You bloody better 'ave. I heard a rumour that Butler was coming down this morning. And if you're not back by the time he gets here, there'll be hell to pay."

"Christ! Hand us me kit, will you? Ta. And keep your knickers on - I'll be back in time for the auction!" Mac shouted over the revving engine.

Bert rubbed his hands together. "Aye and it's gunner be a good un. Reckon we'll be millionaires after this load!"

"Aye, three day millionaires – that's us!" Mac yelled as he took off towards Hessle Road and home.

Chapter 2

All over the Hessle Road fishing community wives and mothers were getting their houses spic and span, making sure there was hot water on the stove for tea and a wash, a good breakfast cooking up, and clean, pressed shirts and trousers ready for the hunters returned to wear out to the pub.

For these women, the three weeks the men were away were filled with the half-expectation that, at any moment, bad news might arrive at the door via the bethel chaplain whose regrettable job it was to inform the families about lost trawlers and drowned fishermen. So once the men set foot on dry land, the women released a collective sigh of relief that eased out over the whole community like the tide coming in.

On the days the Goodwells knew Mac was coming home, good cheer filled every member of the clan as they awaited the roar of the Norton motorbike. And while today was no different in that all the usual preparations had been made; there was other big news that had recently arrived via a telegram.

"Well I never, our Vivian married," muttered Muriel Goodwell, for the umpteenth time, as she weaved her youngest daughter's hair into two long plaits.

Poor Winifred's hair had been plaited, brushed out and re-plaited several times that morning, and all because Muriel's hands needed to keep busy or she didn't know what she would do with them.

For the past thirteen years, Muriel had been both mother and father to her five children, that is, since her husband was lost at sea. Though she had once been an attractive woman, the hard life she had led being a fisherman's wife and a fisherman's mother, showed in the lines etched in her face.

Over recent years, she had also become thin; a change most striking to Mac given his weeks-long absences at sea. It wasn't only the locust years that had robbed Muriel of her former bloom: she simply never felt hungry anymore. There were more lost hair strands in the brush at night, and more grey: her once bounteous chestnut hair was thinning daily, revealing more pale scalp, so she wore her hair short and curled to hide the loss. She was very sick, she knew (to which the constant pain in her back could attest), but with what malady, she didn't know. She was waiting for Dr. McKenzie to tell her as, apparently, so was he.

An American! It can't be, Muriel sighed again to herself. But the telegram was still there, folded in her apron pocket. She stroked it for a moment, Winnie's hair forgotten. There was no need to read it again, she told herself, yet she found herself once more pulling it from the pocket, perhaps hoping that the letters had somehow rearranged themselves to form some other, more pleasing news.

Slipping on the glasses that hung on a chain around her neck, her eyes jumped from one word to the next, 'married,' 'American,' 'home,' 'train,' with today's date, and 'Queen Mary.' Muriel had heard all about the Queen Mary, she had even seen it on the news reels at the pictures, but to think that one of her very own daughters would be on it in two weeks, waving and smiling from the deck, on her way to a new life, was difficult for Muriel to comprehend. This war, she thought bitterly, has done us in in more ways than one.

"You're going to wear that thing out," remarked Prudence, whose sea grey eyes, set in a plain, pale face, appeared focussed on the darning task in front of her.

Her brow was furrowed and her lips were pursed, not in concentration at the task at hand, but more in a permanent disapproval of life itself. She was Muriel's eldest child.

"She did allus say she'd never be a fishwife, didn't she?" said Muriel. "Do you think this means she's going to live over there," she cleared her throat, "forever."

"Forever!" exclaimed Winnie.

"Shush," said Muriel. "Children should be seen and not 'eard."

"But I'm thirteen," said Winnie, shifting in the chair to appear taller. "An' you're allus telling me that you was working in a shoe factory at twelve, and that I should -"

"Shush," said Muriel.

"Who knows what's she's planning to do, Mam," said Prudence, reaching into her sewing basket for scissors. "You know our Vivian, she's allus been impulsive. Anyrode, we'll find out when she gets here, won't we?"

"Aye, I suppose so," said Muriel, scanning the telegram again. "I just can't stand the waiting and the not knowing. Our Vivian should have said more, or sent a letter."

"What time is it that she gets here, Mam?" asked Winnie.

The young girl reached behind with an outstretched hand, hoping for the telegram to be put in it, but Muriel quickly snatched it away, saying "Do you think I'm daft?"

"What?" asked Winnie, innocently blinking large brown eyes magnified by her spectacles.

"I know you only want to look at this telegram 'oping I'll forget you have it so you can take it to bloody school and show off. I've told you, you can't have it, so stop asking."

"But nobody believes me that our Vivian 'as married an American soldier!"

"Well they'll have to believe you soon enough won't they, when our Vivian gets here?"

But that wouldn't help Winnie get through that day's round of taunts and bullying at the hands of Dolly Collins. If only there were some other thing, just as special, that she could take instead.

"Now sit up. And stop whining. Shush."

Prudence winked sympathetically at Winnie, but the young girl seethed. It seemed to Winnie that everything that was important to her counted for nothing to everyone else. One day, I'll show 'em what I can do, she thought, jabbing her glasses back off the bridge of her nose.

"I don't know why our Vivian had to go to London in the first place," continued Muriel. "I knew no good would come of it. And now look what's 'appened. I'll bet he was one of her patients at that 'ospital she worked at."

"Oh Mam. It's not that bad, is it?" said Prudence in the best bored voice she could muster.

"Well, when you have children maybe you'll find out what it feels like having them scattered all over the place," Muriel retorted, though she quickly relented. "Oh, I'm sorry, love. I didn't mean owt by it."

But Prudence's shoulders remained stiff, and her eyes fixed on the fire. Her lips were thin and tight, and her slim body was so tense that even the glossy, black hair she kept wound in a bun, seemed to wind all the more tightly until it might pull from the roots like springs from an over-wound clock.

Muriel's eyes fell soft upon her.

"Look love, I can't help worrying about our Vivian. At least our Mac was born with a caul to keep him safe and you, well, you're the sensible one. You know 'ow our

Vivian is with her wild ways. Your dad allus reckoned she'd never settle down."

"She was still his favourite."

"And now this," Muriel went on. "I don't know 'ow to take it. I mean, should I be pleased she's found someone, or is it just another one of her ... ? Well, you know 'ow she is."

"Aye I know how it is," remarked Prudence.

"Oh, love," said Muriel, "Don't be like that. It's just that mothers allus worry about their bairns. It never ends no matter how old they are. I'll be worrying about you lot from the after-life, if I'm allowed. You'll see."

"Perhaps if my fiancé hadn't been killed at Dunkirk then I *would* be married with bairns of me own, and I *would* see."

The fire crackled.

"I know, love," Muriel said quietly while her thumbs traced the bumps in each of Winnie's thick plaits down to where the hair was held together with red ribbon. Not too many years would pass before Winnie would stop allowing Muriel to play with her hair, and, with this in mind, the mother sighed about all her children growing up.

"Mam," Winnie asked. "Do girls ever get born with cauls on their faces?"

"Girls? Oh, I don't know. I've never thought about it really. You do ask some daft questions our Winnie."

"It's allus the same when our Vivian's around," said Prudence. "It's all about her while the rest of us become second best, forgotten about."

"That's not true, love, and you know it. It's me mind lately. I can't think straight."

Proud shoulders sagged. Prudence couldn't stay hard against her mother; especially when the indignation she felt was wrapped in deceit. Really, she would prefer to avoid the subjects of fiancés, marriage and children, for neither her mother nor anyone else knew that she had written to Alec, shortly before he was killed, breaking off the engagement. Whether or not he had received the letter, Prudence didn't know, but the news of his death had come so suddenly, so unexpectedly that she hadn't been prepared with an appropriate response to the condolences.

"How about a cup of tea, love?" asked Muriel deliberately breaking into her daughter's thoughts. "Our Winnie, go get some fresh tea out of the pantry. Bloody hell!" she exclaimed noticing the empty chair in front of her. "Where'd she go? She were sitting right in front of me a minute ago. Winnie!"

"Maybe she's gone to fetch our Ted," Prudence said. "There, finished."

She hung the darned socks on the wooden clothes horse next to Mac's clean suit. Though there would be no appreciation from her brother that his socks were done and ready for him to put on, there would be plenty said if they weren't, which irritated Prudence. So sometimes she kept the pair under a cushion until after a few minutes of searching high and low, he was forced to ask for them and then she would hand them to him and at least get a 'Ta, love' out of him.

"I didn't hear our Ted, did you?" said Muriel. "Still, she likes to get him up to play with before school, doesn't she?"

"Aye, she's good with him," Prudence said. "She's going to miss him."

She looked at her mother for the effect. After a moment, catching a breath, Muriel said, "Aye, we all are." She busied herself pushing a chair under the table and smoothing the table cloth set for breakfast. "Anyrode, speaking of Ted."

"What about him?" Prudence said from inside the pantry.

"Well, he must have something about him, this American I mean, if he's taking on a girl with a bairn. Another man's child. Lord knows our Vivian's has her charms, to say the least, but still, to take on another man's son, he must really love her."

"Are you sure she's planning on taking Ted with her?" Prudence said, reappearing with the tea caddy.

"Of course she is! He's her son!" exclaimed Muriel. "What a thing to say!"

But her voice was shrill, betraying that she too had wondered the same thing.

"She left him once before," Prudence said. "With us."

"That were only temporary, 'cause of the war. This time, well, she'll probably be leaving for good. And I'm sure she couldn't bear it."

"Are you?" said Prudence. "I'm not."

"You're seeing things with green eyes," snapped Muriel. "Why can't you just be 'appy for her. What harm is it to you?"

"Did you call for me, Mam?" asked Winnie, back in the kitchen now, clutching her satchel; a hand-me-down from Prudence's school days.

"Where have you been?" asked Muriel. "And what's in that satchel? You're holding it like the crown jewels is in there."

"Nowt." Winnie swallowed and pushed her glasses back. "I mean just me books. They're heavy."

The caul, Mac's protective caul was in there. That was, the thin membrane that had been dried and wrapped carefully in linen some twenty five years before. Her mother would kill her if she knew. She ought to put it back.

"We thought you was fetching Ted."

"He's not awake yet."

"He could sleep for Britain that one. Bless 'im. He needs it. I could hear him last night, up coughing."

"Aye, I gave him some syrup," said Prudence. "It seems to 'elp, for a while anyrode. Bless 'im."

Muriel shook her head. The toddler's health was of concern to them all. He had been sickly since birth. Every cold he got went straight to his chest, and his breathing was continually laboured. To help clear his lungs, a square of fabric soaked in camphor oil was pinned to his vest every day. A medicinal odour followed him everywhere.

"Maybe the air's better in America," said Winnie, trying her best to be casual as she hung her satchel on a chair.

Muriel and Prudence both looked at her in surprise.

"Maybe it is," said Muriel, thoughtfully. "Drier. Anyrode, while he's here, let him sleep while he can. Winnie, love, will you feed the bird? Honestly, I'd forget we 'ad that thing if it weren't for the stink."

"Poor Houdini," Winnie said softly through the cage where a Mynah Bird sat on its perch. The bird hadn't spoken since their father was lost.

Muriel took a moment to confirm the time of the train on which the couple would be arriving later that day. She had decided not to take Ted with them to meet Vivian. It was cold and damp out, she reasoned, so it wouldn't be good for him to wait for who-knows-how-long in a draughty station. Besides, she thought, it might be a bit much for everyone to see each other all at once.

Prudence tutted upon seeing the telegram out again.

"Well, I suppose our Vivian's not the only one to fall for one of them American soldiers, is she?" Muriel said briskly, slipping the news back into her pocket. "War shakes things up a bit, doesn't it?"

The only Americans any of them had seen were on news reels or in movies. Muriel smiled recalling the times she and her husband had gone to the local picture house for the shilling matinee; but her smile faded when she remembered that the theatre had been bombed. She wouldn't be able to see William's ghost in the cafe anymore, sitting opposite in the same chair at the same table with the same ear-to-ear grin that had captured her heart all those years ago. There was nowhere for the ghosts to be anymore.

To cheer herself up, Muriel wondered if the American resembled James Cagney, or talked like him. Or maybe he dances like Fred Astaire. She amused herself at the notion

15

of him waltzing or tap-dancing around the parlour, perhaps suddenly grabbing her to dance with him as they do in the American musicals. Chance would be a fine thing.

The sound of a familiar engine came louder and louder, filling the room like an expanding bubble.

"It's our Mac!" yelled Winnie running down the hall-way and flinging open the front door hard enough that it slammed against the wall-paper.

The door shuddered to a halt; its decorative wrought iron rattling in protest while the net curtain billowed like a ghost. Among the iron swirls, curls and flowers was a design entwining in a heart Muriel's initials with her husband's. The wrought iron work had been welded by the elder William Goodwell, and then, during the war, hidden by the younger William Goodwell to save it from being recruited and melted down for munitions.

"How many bloody times do I 'ave to remind you not to slam the bloody door like that!" Muriel yelled. "And mind the bloody milk! 'Onestly, you'd think he'd been away for a year the way she carries on."

But in her own heart was the unbridled thrill of knowing that her son was safely home and, with her back turned to Prudence, Muriel shed the thankful tear she always did, for her and Mac and God alone.

Chapter 3

"Now then, Winnie," Fred Nickerson the milkman called from his seat on the horse-drawn milk cart. "I didn't recognise you without your shovel. Samson dropped one back there, in case you're wondering. I know your Mac likes a bit of manure on 'is roses."

"Ta, I'll fetch it later," Winnie replied with a wave. "He'll be here in a minute."

"Whoa, boy." Fred pulled on the reins to stop the cart, and listened. The ears on the great Shirehorse twitched too. Samson's head was lifted and his eyes were wide. He sniffed the air.

"Oh, aye," said Fred. "I can 'ear his bike, all right."

"Aye," said Winnie shooting a grin and a quick glance at the short, stocky milkman whose big ears and rough, red whiskers gave him a comical look.

By this time, all the milk had been delivered, and Fred's pockets were full of payment. Whistling an old show tune, the milkman was looking forward to making it home quickly for a mug of hot tea and a couple of bangers. Samson, however, seemed in no such hurry. The chestnut horse bearing the blaze of a white Yorkshire Rose, moved at the same slow, graceful gait no matter if the milk cans were full or empty, as if the heavy load was no heavier to him than the light one.

An old gypsy woman selling pegs door-to-door clucked at the horse. He pricked his ears, then snorted at the sound of the approaching motorcycle.

As the bike zoomed around the corner, Winnie grinned broadly. Jumping up and down, she waved, but Mac didn't slow down as he approached her, so she quickly hopped back onto the pavement out of his path. As he rode past, he flung his green kit bag next to her feet where it landed with a substantial thud. Then the fry of fish landed heavily in Winnie's outstretched arms causing her to step backwards with the momentum.

"Oh no, here he goes!" she breathed, hiding her face behind the fish parcel.

As Mac drove his bike up the street toward the horse and cart, Monty's black and tan head stuck out just above the open lapels of the fisherman's thick wool coat. The terrier's ears stood straight up, and his dark, bright eyes shone madly, catching and reflecting his master's excitement.

"Bugger!" shouted Fred leaping from his cart. "Not this again!"

Just when it seemed as though Mac was going to ride his bike straight into the horse, he laid flat to the tank and handlebars and, leaning the bike far over to the left, ducked his head and rode under Samson's great barrelled chest. He was so close to the ground he could have kissed it. Emerging on the other side of the horse, he righted the bike, which wobbled for an instant, but Mac soon regained control and, yelling and throwing both arms in the air, he rode victoriously to the end of the street.

Winnie cheered with pride, and relief, while the horse snorted nonchalantly before grabbing another mouthful of hay from the bag strapped around his neck.

"Ye mad alec, ye!" cried Fred with an old Yorkshire accent so thick his own people had trouble understanding him. "Drunk already, are ye Goodwell? No wonder they call ye Mad bloody Mac. There Samson. Steady lad," he said to soothe the horse, although he was the one unnerved.

"What on earth's going on?" asked Muriel, having come outside to see what all the commotion was about.

Breathlessly, Winnie turned to find her mother standing beside her, wiping her hands on her apron.

"Our Mac just rode his bike under Samson," she said excitedly.

"He what? I've told him to stop that nonsense."

"But it were brilliant, Mam! You should've seen it!"

"No, I shouldn't 'ave."

As Mac rode by, the milkman yelled and waved a horse whip in the air.

"I'll bloody see you tonight at the pub, ye daft bastard!" yelled Fred.

"Seven o'clock," responded Mac. "Mine's a pint."

He acknowledged Fred's two finger salute with a military one, and laughed. But later, when Mac was to recall the incident, something out of place struck him. In the motion of swinging his arm, Fred's coat sleeve had pulled back and Mac could have sworn he saw some lace. No, he was seeing things, surely.

"That must have been the first time old Fred's ever used that whip," remarked Muriel. "Not against his 'orse, mind you, had to be against my son, didn't it? Well, I never."

Mac pulled up his bike in front of the house, and Muriel couldn't help but smile at the sight of him.

"Hiya, Mam, Winnie," he said nodding to each, though his eyes quickly averted from his mother whom he noticed had lost even more weight since he had been away.

"What's this I hear about you riding your bike under Samson again?" asked Muriel. "You're going to give poor bloody Fred a heart attack."

Mac grinned, fluttering his thick eyebrows up and down.

"Anyrode, how come you're 'ome so early?"

"Glad to see me, then, are you?"

"You can't have settled up already."

"I thought I'd nip 'ome for me breakfast, like. An' warm up by the fire."

"You're going to get the sack if you carry on like that."

"Aw, Mam. Bert Smith's taking care of things. You know he's trying out for his mate's ticket. It'll do him good to learn on the job."

"Aye, but they're paying *you* to do it. Anyrode, he's been trying to get his mate's ticket for over three year. What makes you think he'll do it this time?"

Mac shrugged. Something was bothering her. He would find out soon enough.

"What's Butler going to say when he sees you gone?"

"He doesn't get there while 'alf nine," Mac said, making up a time.

"One of these days he'll surprise you and show up early. Then you'll be in for it."

"Bert'll tell him I had a family emergency."

"As if he would care. I'm being serious. When will you see that the same rules apply to you as they do to everybody else?"

"Not me," said Mac. "I'm one of a kind, me. Anyrode, whose side are you on?"

"The side of keeping food on our table. I don't want to see the skipper giving you the sack for larking about."

Talking with a freshly lit cigarette in the side of his mouth, Mac said, "Crostaff won't bother me, you know he won't. He can't." He tossed the match still burning. Muriel's eyes followed it then returned to Mac.

Strange how he would bring up Crostaff's indiscretion with Vivian now that she was on her way home and he was not yet aware of it nor the news that rode with it.

The gypsy was watching them; the basket of pegs swinging on the crook of her arm. Her colours so matched the golden hues of the fallen leaves that Muriel wondered if she was simply nothing more than a trick of the eye.

"Not today, ta," Muriel said firmly.

The gypsy shuffled away, whistling. Muriel looked up at the grey sky with a shiver. *A whistling woman and a crowing hen are neither fit for God nor men.* Perhaps she should have bought some pegs; pegs would have been cheaper than a gypsy's curse.

"You can stop that bloody racket, an' all!" Mac shouted, but the gypsy simply cackled and continued on.

"Leave her be," said Muriel. "Don't let her think she's got owt on you. You know what they're like. Best to stay away from them. All of them. Even the pretty ones."

Mac couldn't stay a grin.

"Tch, my son. Got a fag for your old mam, then?"

"Here," he said, handing her his tobacco pouch.

"Ta."

While she blew out smoke, Muriel examined the cigarette in her hand, held between yellowed fingers.

"You can only push Crostaff so far, Mac," she said in a low voice. "I've known 'im since he were a lad."

"I'll push him as far as I will," Mac said.

"He doesn't owe you nowt. What he owes, he owes to our Vivian and that bairn in there. You want to keep fighting? Then fight him and you'll get black-balled from fishing for ever. Never mind that you're all we've got to depend on right now until I get the chip shop going again. Mac, what's done is done. Let it go for our sakes."

She glanced up and down the street, drawing her cardigan around her with a shiver.

"Let's go inside," she said. "You never know who's listening around 'ere. Some of our neighbours have got better hearing than a blind dog at the dinner table. Park your bike round back and come in."

"Can I ride with you?" Winnie asked Mac.

"Aye, if it's all right with Mam."

"Can I, Mam? It's only round back."

"I don't see why not."

Winnie hitched up her skirt and threw a leg over the bike. Mac was too big for her to clasp her hands together in front of him, so she stuffed them into the pockets of his coat. The honorary wee dog growled jealously.

"Shut it, Monty," said Mac, pulling on the throttle.

He released the brake and let the bike jerk forward a few feet. Winnie fell back, screamed and scrambled for a better hold, digging her hands deeper into his pockets.

"Hey, I'll really give you some'at to scream about if you don't belt-up," Mac said with a grin.

"You did that on purpose!" exclaimed Winnie.

She punched his shoulder playfully.

"Right that's it. You've asked for it."

He revved the throttle again, and Winnie squealed with delight, trying her best to hold on.

"Be careful," said Muriel.

The revving stopped. Mac turned to Muriel.

"Why? Don't you trust me?" he scowled.

"Of course I do."

Their eyes met again. Already so much had been said between them, and he wasn't even supposed to be home yet. Wary of that look, Winnie turned away and pressed her cheek against the rough wool of Mac's coat.

It was always the same when he came home, as if Muriel and Mac were both happy and hurt to see each other. Winnie sensed that the tension between them had something to do with their father - the only subject Muriel and Mac never talked about directly. Trace scents of the North Sea had woven into the yarn of Mac's coat. Closing her eyes, the young girl took a deep breath and tried to imagine what it was like for her brother on the trawlers, as if the coat could tell her. She pictured a loud, grey angry sea, that was very cold. Once home, the men never talked much about their lives away but she had seen the power of the North Sea pounding the promenade at Scarborough.

"You know I trust you, Mac, love. That's not what I meant," Muriel said.

"Aye, well, some'ow I managed to get through a whole war in one piece without you looking over me shoulder every minute."

"Aye you did. And I'm right proud of you."

But her words were lost as he pulled away from the curb and raced up the road with Winnie clinging to his back. The bike pulled down the ten-foot behind the house where the close brick walls made the engine's roar seem even louder.

Like it's angry as well, Muriel thought. I should be more careful with what I say to him. He thinks I blame him for my William's death. Why won't he believe me when I say I don't. He were only twelve year old. He couldn't be expected to hold on to a fourteen stone man for long, especially one dragging in the North Sea, clothes made heavy with water.

Muriel bent to lift the huge kit bag but it was too heavy. She gasped at the twinge of pain in her back, which she had forgotten about for a moment. Breathing deeply, she waited for the pain to diminish to the dull ache that she tolerated like an irritating relative.

How am I going to get all this work done? she thought, studying the bomb-damage to the fish shop located on the ground floor of the terrace house adjacent to theirs. Being the end house, it had taken the brunt of the blast when a bomb landed and exploded across the street. Most of the windows had been blown out and then boarded up by Mac.

'If my William could see this,' thought Muriel sadly. 'It'd break his 'eart.'

The date the shop was opened was painted above the door; the very threshold William had carried her across all those years ago. Muriel felt a pang. How she wished she could feel that way again, just for a moment. Being a new-lywed girl seemed such a long time ago. But I'm lucky to have felt it at all, that young giddy love before the 'ard work sets in. Aye, there's more than time what's passed between me and that girl.

Thick black soot told the tale of flames licking up the front and sides of the house and around the windows. Muriel was glad she hadn't seen it ablaze. The house might be scarred for life, but the damage would have been many-fold had Mac not been persuaded, by an influx of rats scouring the fish shop and every other abandoned dwelling for scraps of food, to empty the deep fat fryers a few weeks before the blitz.

These days when it rained the dank odour of damp soot and rot pervaded their home, reminding them of the de-struction of the fire, and thus of the war itself.

Fixing up the shop would lessen their dependence on Mac, who, in turn, could move on with his own life, and maybe start a family of his own. With a nice girl. Perhaps the shop would bring in a couple of prospects, then he could finally get over that Dolores lass. Aye, she would keep an eye out for a decent, faithful girl, a bonny one, mind, since her son deserved nothing less and everything more. Things would work out one way or another. They always did, if she worked hard enough.

"Mam?"

Leaning against the door jam, there was George, her youngest, just now woken. Muriel liked to see him at this time when he still seemed vulnerable and in need of her. Pretty soon, fuelled by a full belly, he would be his cheeky self, getting into trouble with neighbours and teachers alike.

She brushed the top of his prickly head, a courtesy of his best friend Paddy's father who had so many kids who-ever was at his house, whether it was bed, bath, or de-lousing time, was corralled with the rest.

"You feel just like an 'edgehog," Muriel remarked. "An 'andsome one, though, ay?"

The boy grinned shyly, moving his head out of her reach. Though he rubbed the bristles himself to check.

"Come on love, give us an 'and with your brother's kit bag."

Chapter 4

The fish auction was almost over by the time Mac re-turned to the docks with the news about Vivian playing on his troubled mind, and breakfast unsettled in his belly. Fur-thermore, here parked was Samuel Butler's shiny new Aus-tin motor car, out-of-place against the rough and tumble of the dock. There would be trouble, then, if the trawler owner had noticed Mac's absence.

Sitting rigidly in the passenger seat was Mrs. Samuel Butler, Edith Bowles Butler, a handsome woman with ruby hair, who had married late and down to save her family from financial ruin. With her back to Mac, and eyes straight ahead, she resembled a well-bred horse wearing blinkers, seemingly unaware of the stinky business on the dock. Certainly, this was not the life she had imagined for herself when she was a young girl of nineteen studying art in Paris, was it? All those years ago; before she was brought home in disgrace, that is, and hidden away from the world, for a while.

The windows of the car were rolled up as tight as they would go. Not only against the cold but also against the nauseating stink, which nevertheless still permeated the car, as did the tendrils of poverty.

Rags! They dress their children in rags! she thought. Or worse! They should be ashamed allowing the children to go barefoot. And they wouldn't have to if they didn't spend all their money on cigarettes and drink. And, look at all the children they have. There! That pregnant woman with one in the pram and another one pushing it with her head no higher than the handle. That straggling girl - that's hers too. How does she cope? Not too well by the look of her, and the children.

It occurred to Edith that having so many children was quite a feat considering the men were away so much; whereas Samuel and she, who were together in the same bed almost every night, hadn't been able to produce so much as a smile between them in ten years. She sighed, but kept the painful emptiness in check, turning her attention once more to the docks.

Look at that woman greeting her husband. What a tiny baby. It must be a newborn – out in this weather! That blue blanket's thick wool, but still… I wonder.

The delight on the fisherman's face as he looked down at his child, stirred her heart. Perhaps that's the first time he's seen his son. Yes, I think so. How the women kiss those worn out men, I'll never know. Their appearance alone should serve as birth control. But they kiss with such passion…

And there he goes, that self-important little man, her husband Samuel Butler, striding about the dock in his expensive camel hair coat. To and fro he walked, behind a school of fishermen who, seemingly intent on their conversation, did not step aside to allow him through. Furious, he circumvented the group.

It's hardly Moses and the Red Sea, Edith thought, watching as her husband shook hands with the top buyers, taking in their congratulations about the quality and quantity of the catch.

A headache had taken over her well-being - a foregone result of the stink and muffled racket: workers stomping around in clogs, lorries and vans ready to take away the fish, men yelling "Cod", "Haddock", "Plaice" or "Copel", the auctioneer with his infernal hammer, women arriving in groups of chattering hens ready to smoke the herrings, and barrow lads rattling their wheelbarrows along the cobbled road.

Closing her eyes, she slowly counted to ten in English then in French. Feeling calmer, she watched a couple with five children leave the dock, swinging the youngest between them. She thought, No thinking man could do what they do. Oh, but look at that one. I've seen him before. Hard not miss. She noted how the men parted effortlessly as Mac walked through the crowd. They had to, for Mac didn't once pause in his stride.

Over the forest of kits of cod ready for auction, Bert Smith caught Mac's eye and nodded to him, mouthing the words, "Butler's here" to which Mac nodded back that he already knew. Smith nodded toward the back of the crowd to indicate the whereabouts of the trawler owner who was currently yelling at the skipper.

For his part, Butler was having difficulty making himself heard over the auction, so to get his point across he angrily pointed a finger in Crostaff's face. The skipper's muscular arms were folded in front of him, fists clenched. The thick forearms, which had earned him the nickname

Popeye, flexed. He shrugged stiffly in response to some question or other.

A man shouted "At!" and the last block of forty kits of cod were sold along with the oddments stacked in kits placed down on the foreshore of the dock.

Butler had calmed down, seemingly satisfied to have made his point, but as Crostaff looked Butler in the face, his blue eyes belied his subordinate demeanour. The look was not lost on Butler, who sometimes felt like prey in amongst the big, rough men. Only, luckily for him, it was as if they didn't know it yet but at any moment one of them might realize it, bark, attack and the rest of the pack would join in. This was one such moment: Crostaff looked ready to pounce. Perhaps, Butler felt, he had gone too far this time. The skipper, he knew, only pretended to respect him, but that was all right by Butler. In some ways it made the disparity of their roles more enjoyable.

He liked to keep the men in line, remind them who was the boss, but he didn't want to lose the man widely considered to be the best skipper both sides of the Humber, if not the whole industry. There were other good skippers, some great ones, and maybe now that the fishing was plentiful any one of those other good skippers would do, but, no, Crostaff always returned with a profitable catch. Butler couldn't recall the skipper ever completing a trip in debt to the company for the rent of the boat and equipment.

'Let him stare at me,' he thought. 'If it helps make him feel his life's worth some'at.'

To end the tension, Butler nodded and patted the skipper on the shoulder like a brother, then, spotting Mac in the back, he strode over as fast as he could.

"Where the fucking hell have you been, Goodwell?" shouted Butler.

"Family emergency," said Mac.

"Family emergency my arse," said Butler. "It's your job to manage my fish. That means gut it, pack it and sell it."

"I did manage it. I put Bert in charge while I nipped 'ome to see me mam. She's been feeling poorly."

"You're the ruddy first mate. It's your job, or 'ave you forgotten!"

"Bert's getting his mate's ticket. I trust him with me life, I do."

"Well, your life comes after my fish. Get it! I don't know why Crostaff puts up with you. I honestly don't."

"'Cause I'm the top first mate. He knows it and so do you. Have you ever known me to bring back a catch not fit for market. Have you? Look at this!" Mac exclaimed, grabbing a gleaming cod from a kit being pushed by a passing barrow lad.

"Oy!" exclaimed the fourteen-year-old lad with a red face filled with fury until he identified the thief as the fisherman much admired and emulated by the boys. Nodding respectfully he said, "How do, Mac."

Paying no mind to the boy, who admired the fisherman all the more for being ignored, Mac held the fish in front of Butler's face and squeezed it gently.

"See, firm to the touch, and," Mac said sniffing the fish with the same pleasure as if it were a rose. "Oh aye, get a whiff of this," he said pushing the large silvery body into Butler's face, less than an inch from the man's sharp little nose. Butler jerked back his balding head.

"Don't worry. She won't bite. Go on, then, give her a sniff."

Determined to stand his ground Butler tried, unsuccessfully, not to flinch but his nostrils flared angrily.

"Doesn't stink, does it?" said Mac proudly. "And look at the bright colour!"

He squeezed the fish so the gills opened, "See, the gills are as red as a Cox. Why, this fish is so fresh that if I threw it back in the water it'd start swimming right off. Tell me who else can do that for you, *every trip*."

Observing the exchange, the skipper pondered that if Butler fired Mac it would save him a lot of bother but also cost him a lot of fish, and therefore profit. It might even cost him a whole trip if enough of the men left with the first mate, which they might. Mac had an invisible grip over the crew. The men watched him as one, like a school of sardines moving this way and that as one body.

Despite what was between them, Crostaff greatly admired the young man. Mac ruled the crew, and they respected him. Crostaff had mused in the past that if Mac ever fell overboard the rest would join him rather than sail on without him. The first mate was considered good luck in a field where luck was a very serious matter. Butler too saw all this and coveted it.

"Well, I'll have more to choose from when the rest of our lads gets demobbed, won't I?" said Butler. "Then we'll see how cocky you are. You'll have to tow the line the way I want it towed, or else...," he motioned with his thumb over his shoulder.

Mac stared down at Butler with more direct threat than Crostaff would ever have dared. Some of the men were paying attention now, wanting something more to happen, but dreading it too.

"I've told Crostaff an' all," Butler continued gruffly, his voice breaking. "Any more of this larking about and you're out."

So Mac would not be given the sack, not today at any rate.

"Sorry, but can I have me fish back, please? This thing's really 'eavy," said the barrow lad whose cow lick hung down with sweat.

Mac tossed the fish back into the fray, and helped the lad get the heavy barrow going again on its over-blown wheels.

Butler conceded, "Three thousand six hundred kit, not bad."

"Not bad is the three thousand eight hundred I counted before we came through the gates," Mac said.

"Three thousand six hundred was landed. Ask Cro-staff."

The thieving bastard was always shorting the men on the final count. Mac wondered to whom Butler had sold the other two hundred kits, money that would be pure profit for the greedy git. He was probably going to buy that wife of his a new fur coat. But Muriel's voice cautioned him not to push his luck.

"Pardon me. My mistake," Mac said.

Edith marvelled at the social hierarchy of man as her husband bullied the physically stronger fisherman. There was no other pack animal , she could think of, where the weak towered over the strong. That's because we're the only species with money, she thought before a noise at the car window caught her attention.

There was a girl with large hazel eyes peering at her. The girl was holding a porcelain doll whose dead eyes also gazed at Edith, unblinkingly, as if just by will alone their eyes could take from her what they needed. Edith glanced away, but when she looked back the girl was still there. She was quite pretty really, with dark red hair and pale skin. In the rear-view mirror, Edith could see the girl's mother approaching. It was the pregnant woman Edith had spotted earlier. She hadn't come to meet the ship, then, she had been to the office to collect her husband's wages. Her husband must still be at sea, on a different boat.

Managing a slight smile to the girl at the window, Edith Butler gave a gentle shoo with a gloved hand, and mouthed, "Run along now."

But the girl and doll remained as they were, staring, un-blinkingly.

"Shirley!" Dolores Alford called. "Shirley, love! Get away from Mr. Butler's car!"

The girl's older sister ran up.

"Mam says get away!" yelled Sharon Alford, shoving Shirley to one side.

"Ow! Me arm!" complained Shirley. "You hurt Lizzie!"

"It's just a stupid doll," said Sharon.

Butler glanced over and grimaced, visibly annoyed by the girls standing next to his prized vehicle; but that would have to wait: he had unfinished business with Mac.

"And one more thing, Mad bloody Mac," he said. "Oy, are you listening to me!" For Mac's attention too was turned to the car but his eyes slid back to Butler. "One more thing, I 'ear your lads have broken that bloody winch again. I've a good mind to take it out of Crostaff's settlings."

"We can't keep mending it. We need a new one," said Mac. "It's a danger to the men the way it is   It's been a problem ever since she were hit on D-Day -"

"Don't bother, I've heard the sob story. New one my arse! It's been mended before, and it can be mended again. I'm not wasting good money on a new winch for that relic. She belongs in the knacker's yard, not out on the high seas. Don't forget she's mine, I own her, but Crostaff won't hear of me getting shut of her. Sentimental fool."

Mac too had a strong attachment to the Ichthus. She was the last boat on which his father had sailed. He said, "We're loyal to her 'cause she's loyal to us. She still brings in the fish, better than any boat here."

"Aye, she does that. But like any of us in this business, she'll be out on her ear once she doesn't. So until that day comes, my son, or until your skipper gets some sense into that thick head of his, get the bugger mended and see she's fit for Monday."

"Girls, get away from that car," Dolores cried again, calling the men's attention.

Old emotions stirred within Mac. A pain of longing filled his chest as if he had missed someone for a very long time.

"Get away, you mucky little buggers!" shouted Butler, scurrying toward the car. "If you scratch my vehicle I'll 'ave your father's wages docked. I will. What's your name?"

31

"Shirley Alford."

"Alford?" His demeanour changed. "Jimmy Alford, is he your dad? One of the stokers on the Wilberforce?"

Shirley nodded. Butler reached out to grab her arm but she was whisked out of his way, so very high and fast into the air that she caught her breath and screamed. Yet the screams soon turned into giggles when she saw it was Mac who had lifted her onto his shoulders.

"I'm sorry, Mr. Butler," said Dolores.

"No 'arm done by the looks o' things," Butler said congenially. "These all your kids then?"

"Aye."

Frowning, Mac looked at the trawler owner. He lifted Shirley to the ground where she ran to her mother, burying her face in her skirts. Part of Mac longed to gently push back the hair covering one side of Dolores' face, but he could tell by the way she kept her head slightly bowed so her hair stayed that another black eye was lurking: Jimmy's handiwork.

"Jimmy all right then, is he?" Mac asked.

Subconsciously, Dolores touched where she was hurt.

"Come on girls. We 'ave to get to the shops."

"But Mam."

"Go on then girls, listen to your mam," Butler said. "This is no place for kids anyrode, this close to the water. We've had one too many drownings this year as it is. Aye, in that mucky horrible water. Brrr! Run along now. No, wait." He rummaged in the pocket of his coat. "Here's a barley sugar each. Aye, go on, take them. I won't bite."

Shirley snatched the boiled sweets, stuffed one inside her cheek and handed the other one to Sharon. "Ta, mister. Ta-ra." The girls skipped off followed by Dolores pushing the pram. Butler watched them go, then turned to find Mac staring at him with an expression of disbelief on his face.

"What are you gorping at?" Butler said.

"Nowt," Mac said. "I'm off to see about that winch, then."

"Aye, see that you do."

After checking the car for scratches, and not finding any, Butler opened the door, but almost shut it again upon hearing his wife's complaining voice. Bracing himself, he forced a smile as he climbed into the driving seat.

"Edith dear, you know I've got to be here to keep the men in check or they'll run wild. They're just like dogs. You have to call them to heel or they'll end up biting the hand that feeds 'em."

He patted her knee.

"I thought dogs loved their owners," she said.

"That's where dogs are smarter, love," Butler said, flooding the engine with too much choke.

Chapter 5

One of the reasons Derek Stalworth, the pub landlord, was glad to see Mac walk through the doors of his pub was that the rest of the lads would probably stay longer now and, therefore, drink more. Stalworth, an amiable, well-liked fellow, was a bachelor in his thirties of reasonable looks but with larger than average ears and a bent nose that made him look a bit like a boxer, which he was not.

Nodding to Mac, he pushed the first mate's pint toward him as the fisherman walked up to the bar, himself exchanging respectful stiff nods and quiet greetings of, "How do," or "Now then," with the rest of the crew of the Ichthus who were by now thawed out and on their second or third pint of rationed beer.

A welcoming fire roared in the hearth, and Mac rubbed his hands at the sight of it. He took the drink gratefully, and gulped it down.

"Ready for another?" Stalworth asked.

Mac didn't need to reply as he leant against the bar with one big foot resting on the brass rail that ran around the bottom. When Monty's head stuck above the lapel of his coat, he grinned, and tickled the dog's ear.

"How's the family?" asked Stalworth.

"Fine. Ta for asking," replied Mac, supping the pint.

"Your mam and," Stalworth cleared his throat, "your Prudence all right then, are they?"

"Aye," said Mac, giving the landlord a look over the top of the glass.

"That's good to hear, then, that they're all right," Stalworth said. "I mean, since your Prudence came back from Scarborough, I've been seeing her out and about, like, going to the shops and the that. She allus waves 'hello' but, really, she still seems a bit melancholy, if you ask me."

"She does, does she?"

"Well, I mean, it's been difficult for her, losing her fiancé, and that."

"Aye it 'as," said Mac.

"So I was wondering if you thought she'd be up to making the costumes again for this year's pantomime."

"Pantomime?"

"Aye, I thought I'd get it going again, now that the war's over and we're all finding our feet again. Give us something to look forward to. Your Prudence allus made the costumes, so I thought it might cheer her up a bit, like."

"Aye, she could certainly do wi' some o' that."

"That's what I thought," said Stalworth. "So I was wondering, like, whether ..."

There was a pause during which Mac took another sip of his pint while the landlord looked at him hopefully.

"Do you want me to ask her?" said Mac.

"Aye," said Stalworth, relieved. "Aye, if you wouldn't mind. That would be grand."

Mac wiped his mouth with the back of his hand.

"And you 'aven't been able to ask her yoursen, then, when you've been seeing her 'out and about'."

The landlord flushed, not wanting to explain how he became tongue-tied whenever he was in the presence of the fisherman's sister. Those sea gray eyes drowned his nerve. Mac seemed to ponder an idea for a moment, then raising his eyebrows with a tip of his head as if in approval, he downed the rest of his beer in a couple of gulps, calculating the value of free beer, for life.

"You're all right, you know, Stalworth. You're all right."

"Tell her it's going to be *The Princess and the Pea*."

"I won't go that far."

Stalworth laughed then, vigorously polishing a glass, he changed the subject. "I hear you lads had a great trip."

"Aye, one of the best," Mac said with a grin.

This trip had made about sixteen thousand pounds in cash, but he wouldn't brag about it to Stalworth in case the landlord started charging him. Mac wouldn't cheat his mother though, most of the five per cent of the net he received would be going to her, which was gratifying to him. But he couldn't resist a little boasting:

"I tell you, Stalworth, them fish were fair flying into the boat. The men was up to their waists in the pounds gutting."

"Aye, so Bert was saying," said Stalworth, then, his voice dropping to a whisper, he asked. "Fancy a tot to celebrate and warm you up a bit."

"Aye I do, but 'ow about a tot of this?"

Mac pulled a bottle of vodka from his coat.

"Vodka? Where the bloody hell did you get that?"

Taking the bottle, Stalworth pulled his reading glasses from his shirt pocket to examine the foreign label.

"Where the hell is this from?"

"From this friend of mine who captains a submarine."

"A submarine!"

"Aye," said Bert Smith who had come to the bar when he saw the bottle being brought out.

It wasn't only that he was thirsting for a shot, he also wanted to be the one to once more tell the story of how they came by the vodka.

"You won't bloody believe this, Stalworth, but we was out there on the fish, like, when the water starts bubbling up port side. You should have seen Popeye's face. He ran right over to the gun and pointed it at the water. No ammunition, mind. Anyrode, then, lo and behold, this bloody Russian submarine comes up. We was shittin' oursens. We all thought we was done for 'cause we was in their water, like. Anyrode, the captain stuck his head out and - what was his name? Some'at 'inski'. Them Ruskies have weird names. Mac knows."

"Vladinski," said Mac.

"Aye, that's it, Lavinski. Any rode, like I said, we all thought we was done for and he started talking real serious and official, like, and using his hands to describe some'at. I thought he were talking about a torpedo. So then the skipper brings the galley lad on deck to translate (he's Russian tha knows). And you won't believe what the Ruskies wanted," said Bert, his small brown eyes wide with the question while the tip of his tongue touched his top lip, waiting.

Stalworth opened his hands as if to say he had no idea.

"He wanted some fresh fish for his men for their supper!"

"Why, the jammy sod," remarked Stalworth.

"Well, it were better than being arrested, and in return he gave us some vodka. Five bottles of it!"

"Bloody hell," said Stalworth. "Now I have heard it all."

"Skipper kept one for hissen and gave one to Mac."

Mac raised the bottle at Stalworth.

"And the rest of us got three to share for the way home. It was a real fucking treat I can tell you. We're usually dry by going home time."

Despite being the umpteenth time Smith had told that story since the boat docked, he was always ready for a new set of ears, and there, he spotted a pair on the butcher, Arnold Casing, who had arrived for his usual sup in exchange for some calf's liver, which he slipped discreetly behind the bar.

"Oy Casing," cried Bert, going over. "Get a load of this."

"Another one bites the dust," said Mac.

Stalworth chuckled, then held up his shot glass, "To the Ruskies."

"The Ruskies," agreed Mac.

The two men threw back the vodka in one greedy gulp.

"Hiya, Mac," said Mary, the barmaid, late to work.

To be polite, Mac nodded but without looking in her direction. He didn't want to get her hopes up. Ten children and how many men, including him, had each etched a weary line on her face like lovers in the bark of a tree. Once she said, "I should've charged you, then you might have seen some value in it. You Yorkshire men are all the same."

"So long as you don't charge by the pound, love," was his reply.

'Cup-o'-tea Mary' the men called her because of the way she held a man with her little finger sticking straight out. And that was how she held him when he was sixteen, and he had loved it, then, before he knew better, before he knew her affections meant nothing special about him. Now he saw her flirt with all the young boys that were just starting out and it made him sick to see them flattered and even sicker to see them days later with that grin of carnal knowledge on their daft, spotty faces.

Bert Smith's voice broke into his thoughts, "Oy, Mac," he said, "Didn't you hear us? I asked if you were ready for a game of dominoes. Or are you going to stand there all day dreaming about tits?"

"Oy, we'll have none of that," remarked the landlord.

The tidy, nipped-in features on Bert's thin face took on a look of slighted innocence. Putting a hand on his heart, he said, "What do you mean? I were talking about bird tits, you know the feathered kind, Blue tits, Great tits, any kind of tit tits. You're the one with the filthy mind presumes otherwise. You might not be aware of this but our Mac here is a bit of a bird fancier."

"Aye, well we all know the sort of exotic bird he fancies," said Stalworth. "But I'm trying to run a respectable h'establishment here, so you ornithologists better pipe down."

"Horny what?"

"Anyrode," continued Stalworth, suppressing a smile, "speaking of birds, this old twitcher here says he saw an Albatross at Spurn Point, and I says to him that's impossible 'cause them birds don't come north of the equator. It must have been a big seagull."

"I'm telling you, Stalworth, it were a Black Browed Albatross!" exclaimed Grandad, the chief engineer and oldest crew member on the Ichthus.

Except for his bald head, our Grandad was a rather hirsute fellow. Thick bushels of hair grew out of his ears and nostrils, and the hairs on his forearms and chest were thick and grey. To top it off he kept a beard, or rather the beard kept him since it was long and wild and in dire need of a trim. He hadn't been home yet to put in his teeth - but the crew were all used to his way of speaking.

"I saw it with me own eyes through these," he said holding aloft the bird-watching binoculars he always wore, even on shore where he spent most of his spare time at Spurn Point.

"Anyrode, if you won't take my word for it, it's 'ere in me book. Tell him Mac. You saw it an' all. Come on, I've got a pint riding on it."

The landlord took the proffered book, donned his reading glasses and examined the expert drawing of the Albatross in flight.

"Why, it certainly looks like one, I'll give you that," said Stalworth, flipping through the rest of the book which was full of pictures but no words. Grandad couldn't write, not even his name, Bernard Cutlass.

"You'll give me what?" sniffed Grandad. "That's as good as any photograph, that is. Tell 'em, Mac."

"Aye, we saw it all right" said Mac shifting uncomfortably in his seat at the domino table. He really didn't want to discuss the Albatross, not after what Grandad had said about it as they passed through the mouth of the Humber estuary and into the North Sea.

"See," spat Grandad. "Now you owe me that pint."

"All right, all right, keep your hair on," said Stalworth, handing back the book which Grandad carefully wrapped back in a square of wax paper. "I'll get you that pint."

"By heck she were a beauty an' all," Grandad reminisced. "Her wing span must have been about eight foot. What do you reckon, Mac?"

"Aye, reckon," murmured Mac.

"Aye, at least eight foot," sighed the old man, removing his flat, chequered cap and rubbing his bald head. "How they manage to get off the ground is amazing. They're right gooneys on land but once they get into the air, by heck, it's a privilege to see. The way they glide and soar using the wind. It's real smart that is." He demonstrated by weaving his old cap gracefully in front of him.

"Not that smart if she ended up at Spurn Point," remarked Bert.

"She'll find her way back!" Grandad retorted. "And be all the better for the experience an' all, like the rest of us eh? You didn't see her. She knew what she was doing. We watched her zigzag about for a bit, didn't we Mac? It were so ruddy beautiful, weren't it?"

Mac grunted.

"Seeing an Albatross is good luck you know," Grandad said loudly across the room to Stalworth.

"I thought one had to land on your boat for it to be good luck," Stalworth said from behind the bar where he was pulling the old man's bet.

"Close enough," said Grandad.

Stalworth smiled. The fishermen milked good luck out of every fable, no matter how farfetched.

"Aren't they supposed to contain the souls of dead sailors?" the landlord asked.

Mac's back stiffened. He clenched his fist around his beer. Would it be said again?

"Aye," said Grandad. "Funny you say that, 'cause when we spotted it, I said to Mac that it could be his father."

"Could be anybody," Stalworth said hastily.

"No, it had to be *somebody*," said Grandad. "A bird that magnificent could only have been someone as great as old Hambone. He were the best skipper I ever sailed with. I loved him. I really did. It's just that, when I saw that bird, I thought of him."

"Here's your beer," said Stalworth, thrusting a full pint glass into the old man's scrawny, weather-beaten hand. "Anyone else ready for another?"

"You know, I could die happy mesen, after seeing that bird," Grandad went on. "It's not a bad way to go on, is it?"

"You'll find out sooner than most," said Stalworth turning the old man in the direction of the dart board. "Now get back to your darts, these men have a serious game to play."

As they selected dominoes from the pile, Bert said, "So, do you think there's owt to it, then? What Grandad's saying?"

"You know I don't believe in ghosts," Mac said firmly, yet swigging his beer to wash away the lie.

Not really an untruth, though, more what he longed to believe. Wasn't he the one who avoided being alone on the deck of the Ichthus at night because once he thought he heard a splash like the sound of a lifebelt and rope being thrown into the water, then the heavy grunting and breathing as if a man was using the rope to scale the sides of the trawler and climb aboard? And that man he believed was his father come to punish him for letting him drown. No, he might not believe in ghosts but the ghosts appeared to believe in him.

Chapter 6

The train from London was running twenty minutes late, an occurrence which surprised none of the crowd waiting on the platform of Hull Paragon Station. Muriel didn't mind. She was never bored left alone with her own thoughts. Waiting for public transport was about the only time she could stand or sit without feeling guilty about housework left undone.

Anxious faces gazed down the railway line looking for signs of smoke. Ears strained for the sound of a whistle or the rumbling of wheels on the track. Each person wanted to be the first to hail arrival of the train, perhaps out of a desire to be the saviour who puts everyone's mind at rest.

Nervously turning her gold wedding band, Muriel felt the hard skin that had formed around it from all the years of washing and cooking and ironing and frying and filleting. She shoved her hands into her coat pockets, as if to hide them, even from herself, but then quickly pulled them out again. What have I got to hide? she thought. These hands reflect a busy life full of honest work. If your hands is the first thing St. Peter looks at then I'll be well in. Then smiling, she felt silly at her self-righteous thoughts.

Lately, it seems, I can't stop thinking about the afterlife and seeing my William again. I did love you, you daft sod. For all your faults, and for all mine. I really did. And we had passion, didn't we? Aye, we had that going for us, we did, right up until the last time you was home... She still fantasised about him, in dreams and day-dreams, wondering again if there was any of *that* in heaven.

"What are you thinking about, Mam?" asked George. "Dad?"

Muriel handed him a striped humbug.

"The train'll be along in a minute, love. Come 'ere."

She spat on a handkerchief to wipe a spot on his forehead.

"Stand still."

"What's our Vivian's 'usband going to look like, Mam?" asked George, speaking with the sweet in his cheek.

"How would I know? You'll 'ave to wait and see, just like I have to."

"How far is it to London?"

"Not now, George."

"Over two hundred mile, son," said the station master.

"Me feet are cold."

"George, please."

"Well, they are. What time is it?"

At last, the station master announced the arrival of the train and the atmosphere became charged as necks craned, hair was patted and socks were pulled up. From behind the clouds, sunlight spilled onto the track in warm welcome. Some pigeons shifted restlessly up on the rafters, and the building itself seemed to stand taller, bracing itself for the glorious arrival of the steam train.

"Bloody hell. Finally, here is it, then?" said Mac parting the crowd.

"I could say the same about you," said Muriel, doing her best to peer into each carriage window as the train roared in endlessly. "Why did it take you so long just to get baccy?"

"Aye, well I saw old what's-his-face an' we got to talking, like."

"Aye. I can smell old what's-his-face on your breath. Needed some Dutch courage, did you?"

Mac grinned. "I booked a taxi for you, Mam."

"A taxi! Bloody nora. It's our Vivian not the Queen of Sheba."

They fell silent watching the passengers disembark. The engine settled, and the noisy crowd jostled, giving off shouts of welcome and recognition. Spilling out of the train were men, mostly, wearing cheap, new civilian suits and carrying what was left, after the pub, of the few pound the military had given them when they were demobbed.

Women cried and children look bewildered, failing to recognize the strangers that swung them up in the air. Having heard about the terrible bomb damage suffered by Hull, the newly arrived smiled with relief that Paragon Station was still intact. There was hope, then, that their home might be too. Kingston Upon Hull was still here, bruised and battered but she had survived.

Anxiety plagued Muriel's features as she looked over the crowd hoping to spot Vivian's soft auburn hair. What if Vivian had missed the train or what if she had the day wrong.

"Can you see her?" she asked Mac who was taller than everyone else.

"Don't worry, Mam," said Mac, putting an arm round his mother's shoulders and squeezing her. "She'll be on this train."

"Why is it taking them so long?"

"Ay up!" said Mac nudging Muriel and nodding in the direction of the train. "Reckon that's our man?"

"I don't know. Maybe. Does he look like an American?"

There was something different about the man who jumped out, just two carriages down from where they were standing. Perhaps it was the way he appeared a little uncertain and out of place when he landed on the platform, or the way he glanced about the crowd searching but without knowing for whom or for what he was looking. Whatever it was, he just looked different. He was boyishly handsome, about five foot ten and wiry, with fair hair. He lifted a very large blue suitcase out of the train, then a kitbag, another smaller suitcase, and lastly a black guitar case, which looked as out of place on Hull's Paragon Station platform as he did.

Bless him, if it's him, he looks nervous, thought Muriel.

Passengers nodded and smiled in his direction as they talked about him, perhaps mentioning to their families that he was American, that they had seen him on the train, and heard him talk. A few people walked up to shake Jake's hand, a few slapped him heartily on the back offering their thanks to him and all American soldiers and their families for their sacrifices.

Jake Huggins appeared content to oblige their good intentions, yet for a time he had been resistant to the well wishes. When he was first discharged from the hospital, the onslaught of praise and gratitude from the British had overwhelmed him. In his case, he felt the admiration wasn't deserved.

A nervous, aw-shucks, kind of smile, lopsided and endearing, played across Jake's face. Muriel had never seen such brilliant white teeth. She smiled with pride observing the way some of the ladies, as they walked away from Jake, bowed their heads together and fanned themselves, laughing about how his accent had heated them up. But the smile vanished when Jake thought no one was looking.

Quite abruptly, many heads turned toward the train when an attractively dressed young, blonde woman appeared in the doorway. There were more murmurs from the people on the platform. "That's his wife." "No, she's English, from Hull actually," and that sort of thing were expressed. Dressed in a black feathered hat, red coat and red lipstick, she carried a brand new vanity case in one hand, and swung a black patent leather handbag, just as new, in the crook of the other arm. In fact, everything about her was new: her hair, her make-up, her clothes, even the expression on her face. She looked as out of place as the man they had been watching who, with a revitalised smile, held out his hand which the woman took as she stepped off the train.

As the woman's feet touched the platform, Muriel felt a flicker of recognition. It was Vivian! Her daughter looked very different, so much so that Muriel hesitated to call out to her. But when Vivian's bright blue eyes caught sight of Mac, her face broke into a more familiar smile, and her legs broke into a run leaving her husband and luggage by the train. That was Vivian all right.

"Mac!" she cried. "I wasn't sure. I thought you might be away! Mac!"

Pushing her way across the platform, she became stuck a couple of times by the sheer density of the crowd, so she jumped up, waved and called to Mac, who simply nodded and grinned in response. Mac also waved to Jake, who waved back, astonished to note that Vivian had in no way exaggerated her brother's gigantic stature.

Jake loaded himself up with the luggage as he surveyed the bustling train station overrun with people ebbing and flowing in and out of the building. Mostly he noted the drab, poor clothing relieved only by the odd bright head-scarf. The faces looked foreign, mysterious and somehow managed to look serious and cheerful at the same time. Reunited friends and family pushed and shoved each other. There was much laughter resulting from the obvious cajoling. He felt alone. There was no one to greet him with such familiarity. No matter how kind and friendly the Brit-

45

ish had been to him, he still felt like an outsider. There was a part of him that longed to be in a place where the scenery, the people and the food were all of his custom.

He missed the wide open plains of Texas and the days spent without seeing anyone, if that's what he wanted. For four years now he had been continually around people. How he longed for the freedom of solitude. England's narrow streets and cloudy skies made him feel caged and restricted.

Only two more weeks, then he and Vivian would be on the Queen Mary heading home to steaks and hamburgers and hot dogs, to apple pie and ice-cream, to pancakes and maple syrup. His stomach growled, wondering how many more turnip pies he would have to eat in the mean-time.

As Jake looked around the station for Vivian, he brushed at his upper right cheek as if to remove the black specks he could see out of the corner of his eye; shell fragments the doctors hadn't been able to remove and which he often forgot were there until they bothered a certain line of vision.

Spotting Vivian, he made his way in the same direction, catching glimpses of the red coat weaving through the forest of people like Little Red Riding Hood in the woods. Noticing Jake's awkward load, Muriel patted George on the bottom.

"Go on, then, give him an 'and," she said.

"Why do I have to 'elp him?"

"Just do as I say. Maybe he'll let you play his guitar, if that's what it is."

"Cor!" the young lad exclaimed, dashing off.

Although she found it tempting, Muriel resisted the urge to spit on her hankie and wipe off the red lipstick now smudged on Mac's cheek, and maybe her own, she thought touching her face. Instead, she studied her daughter who was beckoning for Jake to hurry up.

She looks different, older, thought Muriel. Look at her hair. It's almost white like Jean Harlow. And the way she talks. Who's she trying to fool by being posh? Not us. Not me, her own mother, surely. And it won't fly with anyone else around here neither.

"Well then, what do you think?" said Vivian, nodding in the direction of Jake as proudly as if she had won him at bingo.

"To what?" asked Muriel who couldn't take her eyes off Vivian's hair.

Feeling her mother's disapproving gaze, Vivian touched her hair absentmindedly.

"Not my hair, my husband."

"I haven't met him yet, have I?"

"Oh, Mam. You know what I mean. Don't you think he's handsome?"

"He'll do, I reckon."

"Do? Tch. Is that all you've got to say about him?"

"Well, isn't it a bit like closing the barn door after the horse has bolted?" said Muriel. "Asking my opinion, I mean. What difference would it make, now?"

"I know, Mam. I know," said Vivian, abashed. "Listen, Mam," she lowered her voice. "There's some'at I need to talk to you about. It's about our Ted. I have to tell you before –"

"It is a guitar!" George exclaimed to his family. "Hey Mac, I told 'im that you play an 'armonica like me dad used to."

Mac pulled said harmonica from his pocket and waved it.

"Oh, a *harmonica*," said Jake, who hadn't understood much of what the boy had said to him after he was greeted with the colloquial, "Now then."

"Aye, what did you think I said?" George asked.

"Erm," said Jake, scratching his head. "I'm not sure."

Vivian laughed and said, "Oh George you have to speak slowly so Jake can understand you."

"Understand me?" said the lad.

"Yes," she said. "He's not used to the Hull accent."

"Accent? But I talk normal, me."

How he sounded to others had never before occurred to George. To test himself, he talked to himself in his head. There was nothing wrong with it as far as he could tell.

"Pleased to make your acquaintance, Ma'am," Jake said to Muriel.

Why, he's the one what talks funny, thought George.

Muriel's knees went weak for being called Ma'am; she felt it was something she should live up to. At least his mam brought him up proper. You don't see much of that now-a-days.

It was easy to see why Vivian had fallen for him. He was handsome and quietly charming. Noticing the shell fragments in his cheek, Muriel considered for a moment how his mother must be feeling with her son so far away from home. She made a silent vow to that woman that she would take good care of him.

Jake extended a hand to Mac. Never had he seen such a giant of a man, despite the rough-tough jobs he had worked, either quicksilver mining, or as a cowhand through all kinds of weather and terrain that a man can endure.

"Pleased to meet you, Sir."

Mac nodded, said, "How do," and grabbed Jake's out-stretched hand, strongly shaking it like a terrier kills a rat while Jake tried his best not to wince.

Mad Mac, I see, thought Jake, remembering what Vivian had said about her brother's reputation.

For his turn, the fisherman was impressed by the way the American stood his ground, since most men, feeling challenged like dogs, looked away from his steady gaze. Still holding Jake in an iron grip, Mac noted the missing finger on Jake's right hand. So this was the man who was taking his sister away. I wanted to hate him but I can't, he thought. Though you ever know, I still might.

Monty's head suddenly popped over the lapel of Mac's coat and growled, causing Jake to exclaim and jump back in surprise. Muriel, Mac and George laughed.

"Get down, boy," said Mac. "Don't mind him, he's trained well. Go on, Monty, sic 'em, sic them Nazis."

The little dog growled viciously, baring is teeth.

"Gee," said Jake with a laugh. "Did he ever come face-to-face with any Krauts?"

"No, but he came with me on me ball bearing runs to Sweden, didn't you lad? He saw some action all right. Enough to 'ate them bastards as much as any man could."

"Don't worry, Jake," said Vivian. "His bark's worse than his bite."

"But the dog's a different matter," quipped Muriel.

"You what?" said Mac good-naturedly.

"Well come on, then. Let's get 'ome so you can tell us all about it," said Muriel. "By heck, Vivian, you must have seen some 'orrible things working in that 'ospital."

Jake looked past Muriel at Vivian with an expression of urging in his eyes while Vivian sought to change the subject. She wasn't ready to tell her mother that after only one day of nurse's training she had realised that bed-pans and bed-baths were not for her. Instead, she had dispensed a different kind of medicinal benefit over the counter, at a pub where she met Jake.

"Where's our Winnie and Prudence?" she quickly asked.

"At home making the tea," said Muriel. "Oh and wait till you see our Winnie."

"Why, has she grown a lot?"

'Not that. She came home from school today in a right bloody mood, wouldn't tell us what was up nor nowt. Then she went upstairs and came back down with short hair."

"Short hair?"

"Aye! Cut it hersen. I couldn't believe me own eyes!"

"Why?"

"Says she wants to be like Amy Johnson. Honestly, I don't know what they teach them at school these days. I went bananas but what can I do? What's done is done."

"Speaking of bananas," said Vivian, nudging Jake. "Go on, then. Yeah now. Why not?"

"Ah well," said Jake, "I was going to wait until we got to your house but ..." He reached into his kit bag and produced a bunch of bananas, which he handed to Muriel. "I thought you might prefer these to flowers."

"Bananas! Thanks lad, but I don't think we have a vase big enough," said Muriel who hadn't seen a banana for four years.

Jake smiled. He didn't know why Vivian had been so worried about his meeting her family.

"No really, ta, love," said Muriel with tears in her eyes. Over bananas, who'd have thought.

Chapter 7

Jake was stunned by the bomb devastation he saw as the taxi drove through Hull City centre then along Hessle Road in the direction of the Goodwell home. He hadn't expected such damage this far from London; even though Vivian had told him about it, he had believed she was exaggerating. The Luftwaffe had been aiming for the docks and missed, bombing homes and businesses instead. The destruction seemed random, destroying a couple of houses here, a theatre, a grocers, then there was a whole block of houses destroyed by ensuing fires. Looks like a tornado hit, he thought.

As they climbed out of the smoke-filled taxi, Vivian remarked, "See, I told you about the bomb damage and you didn't believe me, did you? He didn't believe me, Mam."

"Well, I'm sure he does now," said Muriel.

50

"It wasn't only me that didn't believe it," protested Jake. "It was the other fellas too –"

But Vivian cut him off with a cough and a glare because he had been about to mention the customers in the pub where she had worked. He would have to be careful. He didn't like misleading her family but she had promised she would reveal to them how she had really spent her time in London; as soon as the time was right, that is.

"Bloody southerners," said Muriel. "Think they're the only ones of any importance in England. We won't hear owt from that government of ours down there no more neither, now that they don't need our sons no more."

A horn sounded and a motorbike roared passed them before turning on the next street.

"I wish he'd slow down on that thing," Muriel commented.

Jake reached into his pocket for the fare.

"Mac already took care of that," said the driver.

"How about a tip?" asked Jake.

"I won't say no." He loved Yanks.

As the family milled indoors, Vivian hesitated for a moment to behold the front of the house and the damage to the fish shop. It wasn't the first time she had seen the effects of the war on their home, but the sight of it anew reminded her of the reason she had left. She felt like a different person to the girl who had been with Crostaff on the night the bombing took place. If only she could go back and make different choices … but she couldn't.

That night, while the bombs fell silently through the sky before exploding on the ground, she was at the skipper's house, taking advantage of his wife's being evacuated. It had been easy for them to sneak around back then, for apart from most of their neighbours being gone, there were no street lights, and all the windows were blacked out against the Luftwaffe. Vivian breathed in deeply at the memory. How would she feel when she saw him again?

"Glad to be home?" asked Jake who had waited with her outside the house, holding an umbrella, as she looked over the buildings, lost to her thoughts.

"Home? Yes," she replied thoughtfully, as if seriously considering his enquiry. "I'm glad to be home."

"What were you thinking about?" he asked.

"Oh," she looked away guiltily. "Nothing really. Just … I don't know."

"It was the expression on your face," he said, looking into her eyes. "You were smiling at first then you suddenly looked sad. What was it?"

Looking into his handsome, concerned face with its soft furrowed brow, she knew the time had come to tell him everything. "It's being home," she said. "It brings back memories, you know, some good, some bad."

"I know, honey," he said.

He touched her cheek, then slipping his hand around to cradle her neck, he kissed her on the lips. Their foreheads touched for a moment. Turning, he started for the door, but she pulled him back.

"Jake."

"What is it?" He frowned. "Look honey, whatever it is, I can handle it. I love you. Nothing can change that."

Vivian hoped that was true. "Oh Jake," she said. "I –"

Muriel stuck her head out of the front door, "Are you two coming in, then, or what? There's someone dying to see you! Come on, come on. We'll put the kettle on. Hurry up. It's cold and it's going to start chucking it down."

"Mind if I stay out here for a minute?" asked Jake, tapping a pack of American cigarettes.

"No, go ahead, love," said Muriel. "But our Vivian you come in. Come on."

Prudence was rinsing her arm under the cold tap in the parlour.

"What happened to you?" Vivian asked, removing her gloves and pretending not to notice her sister's eyes upon her, watching her every movement, and weighing up her appearance while Vivian's own eyes darted about the room like small fish outmanoeuvring a predator.

"Just some chip pan grease," said Prudence. "Splashed on me arm. Our Ted were pulling himself up near the stove, and as I reached over to pull him away I knocked the pan. Just glad none of it got on 'im."

"Does that mean our tea's not ready yet," Vivian said. "I'm starving."

"Sorry for the inconvenience," snapped Prudence.

"Oh, I'm just pulling your leg."

"Never mind. I know. Welcome home, then."

"Ta. It's good to see you."

Vivian felt nervous, desperate to keep talking and moving.

"But really, is there any chance of a cuppa?" she asked, pulling a pin from her hat and walking to the mirror to check her appearance. "I'm dying for some char."

"Hark at you," said Prudence. "What did your last servant die of?"

"I've been travelling all day. Is it really too much to ask?" Vivian pouted, returning to the mirror.

"Come on Ted, let's go outside," said Mac, swinging the boy up on to his shoulders. "You can have a go on me bike. Hold on tight," he said, making an exaggerated movement dipping and swinging the boy close to Vivian who pretended not to notice. Ted giggled, throwing his little arms around Mac's great head. "I can't see! I can't see!" Mac cried stumbling about blindly, ducking through the back door.

Vivian couldn't help but smile a little as she observed their reflection in the mirror. Of course, she had seen her son as soon as she had entered the room, but he wasn't the same newborn she had left, the baby she had pictured whenever she dared think of him. He was sitting up and crawling now, taking a few uncertain steps, perhaps even saying the odd word.

Vivian had missed the intervening months. There was the possibility she might not have recognised him on the street except there was no mistaking whose eyes he had. The old feelings she had for the skipper rose again in her breast. She hadn't expected to see him so soon, yet there he was living in her house, or rather it wasn't John Crostaff but a childish reflection of him from which there was no escape. Physically, he was more the skipper's son than hers, more a Crostaff than a Goodwell, which didn't make it any easier for her to accept that he really was the son to whom she had given birth. There was still a part of her that denied his existence as much as she had when she carried him in her womb.

Trapped within a maze of confused feelings, she heard her mother say, "Who left this bloody door open again? Coal doesn't grow on trees you know. Oh, it's our Mac and Ted," she said fondly, looking out the back door. All was forgiven. "I might have known."

As Muriel closed the door, Vivian's eyes shifted, meeting her mother's. She knew what those maternal eyes were asking.

"So?" inquired Muriel. "What do you think?"

"He doesn't know who I am," Vivian said.

"He will. If you let him."

"He's bigger."

"Aye. Time'll do that to a bairn. He says the odd word an' all now," Muriel added brightly. "You won't believe the first word he said. Go on, take a guess. We couldn't believe it, could we, Prudence? There's me and her taking care of him all the time, and who breezes in the door every three weeks and 'ardly pays any mind to the boy? That's right, your brother. You could have knocked me down with a feather when Ted said, 'Mac' as clear as anything. Of course, your brother was chuffed as owt an' that, but ..."

Her voice trailed off. They had told her all this in a letter.

"But of course, you'll see all this for yourself. It won't take long before he gets used to you, and Jake. Is Jake keen to meet him, then?"

"Mam, about Ted. I've been meaning to -"

Upon hearing the front door close and footsteps approaching, Vivian stopped talking. Muriel frowned. Jake poked his head into the parlour.

"Pardon me, ladies," Jake said. "Am I interrupting something?"

"No, Jake, love. Come in," said Muriel. "This is our Prudence. She's me eldest. Couldn't get owt done wi'out her."

Prudence's heart fluttered at the seldom given praise. She and Jake touched hands.

"What happened to your arm?" asked Jake. "It looks painful."

"Nowt to write home about," said Prudence, embarrassed. "Just a burn from the chip fat. Oh, I just realised, Vivian, you're a nurse. What should I do about me arm? It's quite nasty, really. I think it might blister."

"Erm," said Vivian. "I'm not really.... I mean, I don't have any ointment with me or owt like that."

"Well, do you think I should put a bandage on, or let it breathe?"

"I suppose you do best keeping it clean," said Vivian, avoiding a look from Jake. "You could put butter on it," she said suddenly, remembering a vague something or other.

"I'd rather save it for me toast," said Prudence. "Maybe Doctor McKenzie will have some'at. I sent our Winnie to fetch him."

"Oh, Doctor Mckenzie," Vivian said. "Of course."

Chapter 8

Dr. Duncan McKenzie was a short, wire-haired Scot with a white bushy beard and eyebrows to match. The eyebrows fringed friendly blue eyes that crinkled at the corners when he smiled. No one knew his age. For as far back as anyone could remember, his appearance and manner had remained the same. William used to joke that the doctor had been born that way: with white hair, a beard and a penchant for pie. Perhaps the only difference these days was the ivory-topped cane that accompanied him.

It was long past supper time Dr. McKenzie noted, slipping his silver watch back into his waistcoat pocket. By now Mrs. McKenzie would have put his supper in the oven to keep warm. He hoped it wouldn't be too dried out by the time he made it home. Friday night was Shepherd's Pie and neeps night, one of his favourite meals. His mouth watered at the mere thought of it. He grabbed his winter coat that had been warming by the fire.

"Me arm feels better already," said Prudence, gently touching the new bandage. "Ta."

"Och, it's my pleasure," said the doctor. "It's a good thing ye've got yer own nurse on the premises, Mrs. Goodwell."

"Aye," said Muriel.

Upon hearing the doctor's comment, Vivian took a deep drag on a cigarette. It was impossible, she thought, to have fooled the doctor too. She blew out the smoke wishing she was invisible behind it. The doctor opened his medical bag.

"So ye said ye sold yer kit to a student nurse," he said to Vivian. "Never mind, here's some ointment and a fresh bandage."

"Doctor, I couldn't take those. What if you need them later on?" she said, holding them out to him.

"Dinae worry, I have spares at home. Ye probably won't need them but just in case, eh? The main thing is to make sure she keeps the area clean, and if it blisters, leave it, don't pop it. But what am I telling ye. Ye already ken that."

"Aye, Doctor," sighed Vivian.

Resting heavy on his cane, the doctor said, "I'll let ye good folks get to yer supper, then."

"Ta for coming so quick, like, Doctor."

"No' as quick as twenty year ago, mind." He winked.

"How much do we owe you, then, Doctor?" asked Muriel.

"Och, there's nae charge for an old friend. But," he held up a small, chubby finger, "I wouldnae say nae to a wee dram of ... vodka."

"Bloody hell," said Mac. "News travels fast."

He poured the doctor a shot and then one for himself and one for Jake. They each raised their glass. "Cheers!"

The doctor threw it back and smacked his lips.

"How about another Doc?" asked Mac.

Holding up his pudgy hand again, Dr. McKenzie said, "Och, nae, thank ye, Mac. Just needed enough to take the nip out of the air. Ye ken, too much of a good thing?"

"I'll drink to that," said Mac, throwing back another.

The doctor chuckled but kept sober eyes on him.

"Everything in moderation is the key to a long, healthy life, wouldnae ye agree?"

"But what about a short, happy life, Doc?" asked Mac, pouring himself another drink. "What's wrong with that?"

Dr. McKenzie was used to the fishermen not planning for retirement, neither financially nor physically, evidently assuming they wouldn't make it that far. Those that did make it were unprepared and carried their bad habits with them.

Said the doctor, "*If you can look into the seeds of time, and say which grain will grow and which will not, speak then unto me.*"

"Don't waste your Shakespeare on me doctor. 'Specially that one. It's supposed to be bad luck, isn't it? Don't look so surprised. It's the skipper's wife, isn't it? She's a teacher tha knows, gives the old man all sorts of books for us to read while we're away. Poetry, plays, you name it. The lads prefer Westerns, like, but why, you'll read owt when you're bored, won't you? Aye, even us ignoramuses."

"Well, I've heard it's bad luck to mention Macbeth in a theatre but I'm not sure about a parlour," chuckled the doctor.

"Don't be cheeky to Dr. McKenzie," said Muriel. "He's right about moderation. Some'at we could all do to remember."

"Does that include nagging in moderation an' all? If so, I'll drink to that," said Mac.

"Lord 'elp us," said Muriel.

The doctor looked carefully at Muriel who, having lost against her son, had turned her attention back to the frying fish. She would never show it, but the doctor knew she must be feeling discomfort having stood at the cooker for some time.

"How's yer back treating ye, Mrs. Goodwell?" he asked.

"The same, Doctor, the same. Neither better nor worse."

"Your back's still hurting, Mam?" exclaimed Vivian. "After all this time! You never said nowt in your letters about it."

And you never asked in yours, thought Muriel.

"Aye, well, what can I do?" she said. "No use moping around, is there? Anyrode, it's not that bad."

"I hope ye're resting, like I told ye. No heavy lifting either. Ye've got enough help around this hoose noo with three able daughters and two strapping lads, not to mention an American." Jake smiled. "So sit back and take it easy for once."

58

"Aye, Doctor."

She wished he wouldn't go on about it. She didn't like her children looking at her as if they'd never seen her before. It was true she hadn't told them exactly how bad the pain was, but it wouldn't do them any good to be worrying about her all the time. She didn't like the fuss, and she didn't like any further reminders of her fallibility when the back pain served that purpose well enough.

"Be a good time to get a new mattress," said Dr. McKenzie. "That ancient feather thing ye have is nae good. What's it stuffed with anyway? Do-Do feathers?"

Muriel laughed. "Aye, I know doctor. It's old."

All the spare money they had would be going into re-opening the fish shop, which she didn't care to mention because the doctor would only consider the heavy work that needed to be done, and hence advise against it.

"See she gets that mattress," the doctor said to Mac who nodded and raised his fourth glass.

"I'll be away then. Let ye get to yer supper."

Noticing his eye on the Victoria Sponge Cake Prudence had made, Muriel asked, "Won't you take a piece of cake for yourself and Mrs. McKenzie, Doctor?"

"Och, I couldnae," he said with such insincerity Muriel almost giggled.

While Dr. McKenzie waited for the cake, he took the opportunity to find out more about the young man from America, as Mrs. McKenzie had so urged him before he left the house.

"So ye frae Texas," said Dr. McKenzie. "That's a big place I understand."

"Yes, Sir. Pretty big."

"Fit the whole of Britain in it."

Jake shrugged, "That's what they say, Sir."

"I see ye saw some action?" the doctor asked, tapping his own cheek to indicate the shell fragments in Jake's cheek. "Were ye seriously injured?"

"It wasn't too bad, Sir," Jake said.

He held up his right hand that was missing a finger. "The bomb took this off and I got shell fragments down my arm and in my chest. But I lived to talk about it."

"One of the lucky ones, eh?"

"And he got a bayonet wound in his side," said Vivian, pointing to his ribs.

"Like Christ, eh lad?" said the doctor who had seen, in the first world war, what hand-to-hand combat did to men, to boys.

Jake looked into the doctor's kind eyes, and felt the compassion there.

"Did you kill a German?" exclaimed George who had been dying to meet someone who had actually killed one of the enemy. "The feller that stabbed you? Did you kill 'im?"

"George!" Muriel reprimanded.

Mac studied Jake, enviously wondering the same thing. Aside from being shot at by U-Boats, the closest Mac had come to Germans was at Dunkirk when he had sailed with the Ichthus to rescue men from the water while they were being shot at from the beaches and the air. Their terror-filled faces still haunted him. Mac had often wished he could have squeezed his great hands around the neck of a Nazi; yet here was a man who had probably had that satisfaction, and who, seemingly, wasn't enthusiastic about it or even willing to admit to it.

"Sorry Jake," Muriel was saying. "You know how kids are. Allus so bleeding nosey."

"That's OK," said Jake.

There was an awkward moment of silence between them all until Dr. McKenzie said, "Well, if ye have any trouble with that old wound, ye ken who to come and see?"

"Thanks, Sir. I appreciate it."

Jake shifted uncomfortably in his seat.

"Is that your guitar?" asked the doctor.

"Yes," said Vivian. "He carries it everywhere with him. He's really good on it. Even makes up his own songs."

"I played better before I was hit," Jake said.

"You'll get your strength back, son. Me, I'm more a bagpipe man myself, ye ken. Mrs. McKenzie says it's no surprise given all the hot air that comes out of me."

Jake grinned.

Handing the doctor some cake wrapped wax paper, Prudence said, "Here you go, Doctor. I'll show you out."

The doctor thanked her and bade them all a good evening.

"Is that where you two met, then, in the hospital after you was injured?" Muriel asked Jake, as she served up heaping plates of fish, chips and mushy peas.

"Er-"

"I helped him a lot when he was wounded," Vivian said, quickly. "When he needed stitches."

Jake found it remarkable the way his wife could, quite deftly, say things that were truthful but not true. That is, it was true that he had needed stitches after a fight reopened the war wound. The fight, which had taken place in the pub where Vivian worked, was started by a drunk who called Jake "a big-headed Yankee stealing our women" and then punched him. Jake didn't fight back, so the drunk laughed and left him alone on the floor where he had landed awkwardly on a fallen bar stool. Fussing over him (they had flirted before the incident which had angered the drunk), Vivian put ice and a towel on Jake's cut and accompanied him to the hospital.

As they waited for his turn to see a doctor, they talked a little about their lives. Rather, Vivian did most of the talking. All Jake could think about was what he had seen of Vivian's cleavage when she had leaned over to help him at the pub. So he didn't hear much of what she said but the more he did get to know her, the more he realised her talent for double talk, and managed to fool himself into believing that her lies were meant for everyone else, not for him.

"You were his nurse? How romantic!" exclaimed Mac, impersonating an awestruck girl by flashing his eyelashes and wiggling his bosom. "Oh, Mr. –"

"Huggins," smiled Jake.

"Mr. 'uggins, it's time for your hourly bed bath."

"Don't be daft," said Muriel. "It *is* romantic. Go on, tell us all about it. I'll bet it's a good story."

"Not now, Mam," Vivian said blushing.

"Oh, if flannels could talk," said Mac.

"Stop it," Muriel said with a chuckle.

While the two of them bantered, Vivian cast a nervous glance Ted's way. Jake could have had any girl he wanted, not one saddled with a child. Ted looked so innocent. Not at all like she had borne him. How could someone so innocent be a lie? There was a nervous fire in her stomach. Why hadn't she already told Jake? Why hadn't she? It seemed so stupid now. She had mentioned Ted to Jake when describing her family, but it was only by saying, "And then there's Ted. He's the youngest."

She hadn't actually lied about Ted: she had only omitted the truth. But she could not delude herself. Perhaps, at the very least, she could fend off the revelation until later, after supper, when they were alone. It won't be that bad, it won't, she kept telling herself. After all, hadn't Jake smiled at Ted, put him in his high chair, and ruffled his hair, saying "so this must be Ted", not knowing his relation of course, but still he had responded well to the boy, and Ted to him. He'll understand, he will.

After the meal, Jake offered to help wash the pots.

"You what!" cried Mac.

"No, no, no," said Muriel, hastily taking the plates from Jake. "You don't have to do that. You're a guest."

Winnie giggled. Mac stared. Never in his life had he seen another man clean up after supper, not ashore anyway. George couldn't wait to tell his friend Paddy.

"That's women's work," Mac blurted. "I don't know how people do things where you come from, but here we let the lasses do the washing up."

"Oh you *let* us, do you? How kind." said Muriel. "Let's see, what else do you men *let* us do. Oh aye, there's the ironing, the floor scrubbing, the cooking, the –"

"All right, all right," said Mac, swatting her off with a big hand waved in the air.

But Muriel wasn't put off in the least. "Maybe the men are a bit more strict where Jake comes from and so they don't *let* their woman do any work at all," she added.

"It's just habit," said Jake, carrying plates to the sink.

"I bet your mam's really looking forward to your coming home," said Muriel.

"Jake's parents are dead, Mam," said Vivian so matter-of-factly that it took a moment to sink in.

"Oh, you poor love," Muriel said.

"Did them Injuns do it?" George asked eagerly. "Kill your mam and dad?"

"George! For heaven's sakes!" exclaimed Muriel clipping him around the ear with the swiftness and voracity of a moray eel. "That's so rude. Where's your manners? Sorry, love, but our George's been down at the picture house on a Saturday watching too many of them cowboy films. Him and that mate of his play a lot of cowboys and Indians. They're mad for it. When they're not playing footie that is."

Jake smiled at George to show he didn't mind the boy's comments. "Maw got bit by a rattler."

"A what?" asked George.

"A rattlesnake."

"A snake! Wow!"

Here was a boy who had never, ever heard of anyone he knew being bitten by a snake and never thought he would in his lifetime. Wait till Paddy hears this! he thought with glee, almost unable to keep his bottom on the chair.

"Yeah," said Jake, taking a deep breath.

"How big was it?" asked George.

"George, stop asking so many questions."

"Did you kill it?" asked Mac, almost viciously, imagining how he would feel if it had been his mother.

"You don't have to answer their questions, love," said Muriel, who was just as eager to hear all the details.

"It was already dead."

"But 'ow could it bite your mam if it were dead?"

"George, shush."

Jake shrugged. "They just can. It's a reflex. You have to sever the head on a freshly killed snake."

"Just like a vampire," George remarked knowledgably.

"What an evil animal," said Muriel with a shudder.

"It's their nature. The life they're born into. They can't help it," said Jake.

Just like Jake couldn't help running away when his mother cried out in pain all that night. It had taken his father two days to find him, hiding in the back of the woodshed, to give him the news of her passing, which he already knew, having heard the doctor leave.

"Well, I'm sorry, love," said Muriel. "It must have been very hard on you, and your father. He wasn't bitten as well, was he?"

Noticing a tear in his eye, she looked away, feeling a pain in her chest as she did for all suffering, as if the hot tear drops had fallen and scalded her own heart.

"No," said Jake. "He died later of…" He looked around the table at the questioning eyes, "of a broken heart," which was the truth in a way because his father was already dead to the world when he pulled the trigger.

"Oh my goodness. How old were you when your dad died?"

"Sixteen."

Muriel tutted. "How did you get by?" she asked. "Did you 'ave any family?"

64

"No, no family. I tried mining for a while, then got a job as a ranch hand. The money wasn't as good as mining but I liked being in the open air."

"You're a cowboy?!" George exclaimed.

"Yeah," Jake nodded. "I am."

"A real one? With cows and everything?"

Jake smiled. "I am. At least, I was before the war. And hope to be again but with my own ranch."

"Do you have a hat?"

"I do," Jake laughed.

"Cor!" exclaimed George. "Can I see it?"

"Sure."

"Tomorrow George," said Muriel, trying to tame her youngest son who looked about to burst with excitement, not just for himself but also with the thought of telling Paddy all about it. "Let the man get his rest tonight."

"Tomorrow!" George moaned, as if it would never come.

During the meal Jake was peppered with questions about the way their life would be in America. He explained about the plot of land his father had purchased through a newspaper advertisement, though at the time it had been a dream for the whole family to move there. Jake meant to see that dream realised in his parents' honour.

"You're certainly taking a lot on, moving to a new place," Muriel commented. "California. Well, I never."

"Two hundred acres," said Mac, a little wistfully.

"Sort of beats your allotment, doesn't it?" said Vivian.

"My allotment grows what we need," said Mac. "I've never 'eard you complain."

Muriel said to Jake, "Well, I really admire that you've turned your hand to owt to get by. It must have been very tough being on your own."

"Well, he's got me now," beamed Vivian, thrusting her arm through his.

"And us," said Muriel with such sincerity, that Jake realised he liked Muriel very much.

"Will you have a lot of cows?" asked George.

"Yeah. A few hundred to start with."

"Can we come and visit?" asked George. "And 'elp you fight them Injuns?"

"Sure," said Jake who didn't mind humouring the boy. "That'd be great. We'll need all the help we can get."

"Will you 'ave chickens?" asked Winnie. "I can take care of them. I collect the eggs from ours every morning."

She didn't mention that she was terrified, and dreaded sticking her hand under them because they always pecked her.

"Yeah, we'll have chickens," said Jake. "And geese and turkeys. So there'll be plenty for you to do. When you come visit."

"Gobble, gobble," said George.

Ted giggled.

"Gobble, gobble," said George again.

And Ted giggled even more. He was on the verge of one of his uncontrollable laughing fits, which would lead to an uncontrollable coughing fit. Encouraged by the receptive audience of one, George stood and repeated, "Gobble, gobble" in Ted's ear, which tickled his ear so he pushed his shoulder up to block him.

"Stop it, George," said Muriel. "You know he won't be able to stop once he starts, especially when he's overtired."

"He's such a happy little guy," remarked Jake.

"Aye, he's a bonny lad, isn't he?" said Muriel, pleased that Jake had accepted the boy so well. "We are going to miss him. But I think the change of climate will do him good. It's so damp here."

"Miss him?" asked Jake. "Where's he going?"

"Mam tell us about the chippy," interjected Vivian shrilly. "Prudence told me you were going to work on it and get it going again soon."

"Hold on a minute," Muriel said slowly, looking from Jake to Vivian to Ted and back again with a certain realisation unfolding in her mind.

"You 'aven't told him." Muriel clasped a hand over her mouth. "Oh, Vivian, how could you? I can't believe it."

"What about Ted?" asked Jake, looking first at the toddler then Vivian, then at each of them in turn. "What haven't you told me? Vivian?"

Vivian was sitting stiffly braced with her eyes closed and fists clenched; she wasn't breathing. Perhaps she hoped to suspend time by sheer will alone. She needed a break to prepare herself for the awful moments ahead. She wasn't ready to find out whether he would leave her over Ted, or over the lie.

Jake was at the point of awareness. He had only to leap across a chasm of disbelief to accept the truth. Impulsively, Muriel wanted to reach out her arms to prevent him from falling but the distance between them was too great. Prudence was horrified; whereas Mac was bemused. And, unfortunately, Winnie was so giddied up from her own excitement about being invited to America that she prattled on as if everyone at the table shared her enthusiasm.

"Teddy, you're going to have all them chickens and turkeys and cows to play with. It's going to be right grand living on a farm in America. There'll be lots and lots of gee-gees too. Do you have a small horse special for our Teddy?" she asked Jake who had his gaze fixed on Vivian.

"That's enough, our Winnie," said Muriel.

Of course, he was realising, Muriel was too old to have a son Ted's age; and, of course, her husband had died too long ago to have fathered the boy. He felt young, naïve and foolish to have fallen in love with Vivian. Should he tell her family about her other deception? He was tempted. He wanted to hurt Vivian, but he didn't want to upset her mother or the rest of the family. Vivian would trip herself up sooner or later, just as she had with Ted. I'll leave her

67

to hang herself, he thought. But I won't lie for her any-more.

He didn't know whether to run or stay seated. She's my wife. But I'm not her husband. I'm not a husband to her otherwise she wouldn't have treated me this way. And if I'm not a husband to her, what I am? Her meal ticket out of here? No. I don't buy that. She does love me. She does. You can't fake that, can you? Can she? He was con-fused as he went over their private moments together. In some ways, it would be easier for him if he thought she didn't love him, easier for him to leave.

Winnie, indignantly responding to her mother's telling her to be quiet, saw none of the agony in Jake's heart. "But Mam, our Ted is going to learn to ride a gee-gee!" she ex-claimed. "Aren't you, Ted? Aren't you?"

"Gee, gee," said Ted. "Gee-gee."

"That's right, Teddy!" exclaimed Winnie. "Gee-gee!"

"Winnie," Muriel said sternly. "Quiet."

George incited Ted's mirth further by galloping around the parlour on an imaginary horse, holding his hands out in front as if clasping reins.

"Giddy Up, Teddy! Giddy up!" he shouted while pre-tending to slap the rear of the horse.

Red-faced and near hysteria with laughter, Ted was banging his spoon enthusiastically on his tray.

But on his next circle around the parlour, George stopped dead in his tracks, having noticed that the grown-ups had fallen silent and grim-faced. Jake even looked like he might cry though he was fighting it mightily.

"Whoa!" George said to the pretend horse.

"That's enough, our George," said Muriel.

"All right, Mam," he said, dismounting and tying the horse's reins to the back of his chair.

Although Winnie didn't understand exactly what had happened between the adults, she was becoming nakedly aware, driven by the glares from Vivian, that she, Winnie, was the one who had said or done the thing that had caused the sinking shift in the mood at the table.

"I'm sorry," she blurted with a sob.

"Sorry?" said Muriel. "Oh, Winnie, love. It's nowt you've done. I'm not mad at you. Come 'ere, love."

The confused girl went to stand by her mother's chair where Muriel put an arm around her waist and pulled her close.

"Stop banging the spoon, Ted," Prudence said, putting a firm hand on his arm. A flood of tears ensued from the child, then a terrible hacking cough, making Prudence feel guilty for speaking too harshly. "He's tired. I'll put him to bed," she said, carrying the sobbing child out of the room, all the while saying softly to him, "Come 'ere, our Ted. There, there. I'm sorry. I shouldn't have spoken to you like that. You was only playing."

Jake clenched his jaw trying to keep his emotions in check. Perhaps the family's silence indicated they were waiting for him to speak, even the mantle clock seemed to have paused before it's next tick, or maybe it was the longest second of his life as he struggled to recoup some dignity from a situation in which he felt nothing but a cuckold.

Bile burned in his stomach, rising and scorching his throat. He thought of the merry boy, Ted. Is he laughing at me too? he thought. For being such a fool? No, the boy was innocent in all this. Jake made a vow not to allow the boy to suffer any of his wrath, not by look or by touch or by word, ever. That was, if he opted to stay.

"Vivian," Jake began.

Vivian started at the sound of her name, but it was too difficult for Jake to say more. He rubbed his tired eyes, trying to think of what to say, what to ask while at the same time wondering if it was worth hearing Vivian explain herself, yet again. Perhaps there would be only more lies.

As Jake rubbed his eyes, Muriel noticed the missing finger and her heart swelled with pity for him. The poor lad has been through so much already, she thought. And now this. She longed to chastise Vivian, whom she felt had betrayed them all - Ted most of all. She's worse the Judas. I know she's my daughter but … God help me I could wring her bloody neck like a Christmas goose. But it's between them now, 'usband and wife.

Jake found his voice, though it was dry and weak when he asked, "Vivian, what is it you didn't tell me about Ted?"

There was a long pause, during which Vivian reached with trembling hands for the packet of cigarettes on the table. The match failed to strike on the first go, then the second, so Mac lit one for her and she smiled at him gratefully, but he only nodded in such as way as to urge her to go on and to speak those words she had never yet spoken in her life.

"Is Ted your son?" Jake wanted her to say it. He needed to hear her speak so he could hear the remorse in her voice. He wanted to hear the words from her that he should have heard when they first met.

But all she could do was nod and take another drag on her cigarette, exhaling and hiding behind the smoke screen.

"Say it," said Jake, almost pleading now, which discomforted Mac enough he was driven to clear his throat and shift in his squeaky chair a bit. He needed a pint and was about to say as much when Vivian spoke.

"Aye. He is my …" But she had never before uttered the words, 'my son' and couldn't now. "He is that," she said, glancing up at Jake quickly before looking away again.

Jake's heart turned hard against her for more than just the deceit about her son; his heart became hard because he felt alone again, orphaned again, adrift, where just a moment ago he had felt connected to Vivian and this family. Tears boiled in the brims of his eyes. His first urge was to walk out the door and go far, far away from this stranger sitting next to him, but where could he go in this strange town. Where could he go when his leaden feet wouldn't budge even an inch. And running? Hadn't he vowed never to run again?

"I'm sorry, love," said Muriel, troubled by the face of the broken-hearted boy sitting at her table. "We had no idea you didn't know."

"Mam!" cried Vivian who felt they had all turned on her like a pack of wolves, hungry for the truth.

"This is your bed," said Muriel, unable, in the end, to keep herself from commenting. "You made it and you can bloody well lie in it. You've done a terrible, terrible thing. You've hurt this boy, this man. He's your 'usband. For God's sake why didn't you tell him! You've hurt Ted an' all with your deceit, though thank God he doesn't know 'ow you've denied him. I don't know what to say to you. I never did. You never learn, do you? You think you can do what you like to us, to everybody. You need to grow up, and I hope tonight's the night."

With their mother's words flying past them, Mac regarded the man seated at his right about whom, only moments ago, he had been so envious. The envy had been replaced in part by pity but also by a tinge of scorn. The poor lad seemed decent enough, but Mac now considered him a a bit of a twit to think he could tame his sister. As much as Mac loved her, she had given them all grief at some point in their lives. *I hope he didn't think he was her first when he married her. Maybe she pretended she was. I've had a few of those mesen. Well, he must have found out by now, anyrode. And he's still 'ere. Look at the wheels turning in Vivian's mind. She's in a real pickle this time. Her plan to escape Hull is in grave danger. Let's see what 'appens.*

Hand shaking as she smoked, Vivian said, "I tried to tell you loads of times. Honest, I did."

"But you didn't."

Had she planned it this way, to come out in front of her family like this so he wouldn't be able to react as strongly as the revelation demanded? If that had been her plan then she had been right. He felt muted when he wanted to shout and scream.

But what would be the point? he asked himself. What would be the point of my asking her why she didn't tell me. What would she say but words, words and more words meant to fill me up and move me further away from the hurt she's caused me. She's mighty good at that, spilling out sounds which leave no room for questions. Words that make you forget.

When they had met, he had enjoyed the gay chatter that pushed away his own darkness; a darkness that had prevailed since the time he had first killed a man. Vivian's bright voice had entered his ears and taken up space in his mind, idly engaging his thoughts so that other sad thoughts wouldn't make mischief. Without that voice, well, it was impossible for him to imagine how it would be. It would be like it was before. His mind would become like a garden untended by caring hands: the weeds would take over, choking the last vestiges of brightness, of pleasant memories that remained. I need that voice. I hate that I need it but I need it - but at what price? he thought.

Vivian was readying herself to say something important. She sat up straight and, rather officiously, stubbed out her cigarette in an ashtray set in the middle of the table.

"Anyrode," she said. "I didn't think it were necessary to say owt. Because, well, I mean ... don't you think ... that maybe Ted's better off ... where he knows everyone."

She said the last part quickly.

"Don't tell me you're suggesting you leave him 'ere!" Muriel gasped. "With us!"

"Well, he's 'appy here, isn't he?"

"God damn it, Vivian!" Jake said angrily.

This time he stood, knocking back his chair, looking as if he might strike her.

"I won't have it!" Muriel cried.

Mac jumped up ready to defend his sister who, shocked by Jake's reaction, had shrunk far back in her chair: the hard wood of which pressed penance-like in her back She had never considered that he possessed such depth of emotion. It was a moment of brutal honesty between them, and, surprisingly, she felt a little buzz of triumph because she knew then that he would rather stay and be angry than leave and be lonely.

"What have I missed?" Prudence asked, warming her hands by the fire after being in the cold upstairs putting Ted to bed.

"Well, you was right," said Muriel. "She were thinking of leaving him 'ere for us to take care of."

"I knew it!" exclaimed Prudence.

Annoyed that her sister had correctly predicted her behaviour, Vivian cried, "But Ted doesn't know me at all!"

"Ted doesn't know you because you've never given him the chance to," Prudence remarked. "You've 'ardly looked at him since you came through that door. You act like you're ashamed of him when," she paused, "when it should be the other way round."

"There's no need for that," Muriel said.

"I might 'ave known you'd be on her side," said Prudence.

"I'm not on nobody's side 'cept our Ted's, but we won't get nowhere sniping at each other."

"Just think, Prudence, how much Ted loves you," Vivian said. "It's clear he's much more attached to you than me."

"You what?" Prudence took a deep breath to calm herself, then said, "Don't you try it on with me, Vivian Goodwell. I'm not his mother and I don't intend to be. I've acted that part long enough as it is without a word of thanks from you. Don't get me wrong. I love our Ted with all my 'eart, but if you think I'm going to spend my precious life looking after your bast –" she bit her lip. What was it about Vivian that always made her say the worst thing? "Your children, then you've got another thing coming."

"It's Vivian Huggins now," Vivian said, glancing to Jake who politely excused himself and left out the back door, taking his guitar with him.

"Jake! Where are you going?" Vivian took a step as if to go after him.

"Leave 'im be. Let him cool off a bit," said Muriel.

"No, I'd better go after him."

"He won't go far," said Muriel. "Not without his coat on."

"He's a cowboy. He's used to it," said Mac.

"Don't you start," said Muriel.

"She doesn't want him to be alone 'cause then he'll 'ave too much time to think about what she's done," remarked Prudence. "Then what, eh, our Vivian?"

"That's enough, Prudence," said Muriel. "Sit down. We don't need no more fuel on the fire."

"Don't tell me you're going to let her get away with this one an' all? Just like everything else."

Prudence flopped angrily by the fire, enraged that once again Vivian had caused her to exchange words with her mother. Doesn't anyone else notice or care how conniving our Vivian is? Prudence didn't understand that her mother was old enough to know she couldn't change anyone.

"There's no need to be so mean," complained Vivian. "You always did like to throw things back in my face. I thought you'd be happy about keeping Ted."

"Throw things back in your face?" Prudence exclaimed. "We're talking about your son here! Doesn't that mean owt to you at all? And don't try to make me feel guilty by saying you thought I'd be 'appy to keep Ted 'ere. You must think I'm daft!"

"Winnie, George go upstairs," said Muriel. "Aye, go on, take your cake with you. Just this once, mind. You know I don't like you eating in your room."

The children took their plates and left the parlour but lingered in the dark hallway to eavesdrop.

"All the way upstairs!" Muriel called, going to the doorway to make sure.

Disappointed childish utterances were made followed by retreating footsteps and the creaking of the banister. Giggles.

"Go to your rooms and be quiet till you're called for."

The weary matriarch turned her attention to the older children, who were no more grown to her than the two younger ones upstairs. When will I get some peace? she asked herself. There's allus some'at. For the first time, she felt some relief that Vivian was going away and taking her troubles with her. Let it be her husband's burden, the poor sod, she thought. I've done enough worrying in my life. I can't take on no more. I'd forgotten what it's like when she's around. She's allus up to some'at. And now Jake knows it too.

But really, would it be so bad if Ted stayed here? I wouldn't mind. He's me grandson, and he's used to us. But no, I couldn't do it to our Prudence. The burden would be all hers, and she'd never forgive me. It's time for our Vivian to grow up and accept the responsibilities of being a wife and mother. Or will her 'usband, like the rest of us, save her from it?

"He's your nephew, you know," Vivian said to Prudence.

"A son needs his mother."

Yet, Prudence almost choked on the words. She didn't believe it so much in this instance, not with this particular mother.

"Do you realise," Prudence continued, "that you didn't even ask us, or me, if we would take care of Ted for you. You just buggered off to London to be Florence bloody Nightingale without a bye or leave and we was supposed to accept it because you was working for the war effort. Well, I accept it no more. The war's over and now it's time for you to be a mother to your son. And while you're at it, try being a daughter to your mother who's done nowt but worry about you and make excuses for you. And try being a sister to me and the others. Something other than being just good old you. Not to mention being a wife. You've got a lot of hats to wear but a head big enough, and then some."

Muriel opened her mouth to protest, but closed it again.

Being accustomed to blocking out what she didn't want to hear, Vivian appeared to be completely unmoved by her sister's words. Let her sound off about it a bit, thought Vivian. It'll soon be over then she'll just accept it, as she always does.

"I'm off for a pint," said Mac.

"How typical," said Prudence, now directing her anger at her brother. "Better not get involved in your own nephew's future. I'll be the only one to say owt, shall I? To stand up to her. You're all the same. You, Dad, Mam, you let her get away with everything and now look."

For a moment his black eyes studied Prudence's pouting expression, the firelight dancing in his eyes, then he turned to Vivian.

"Look our Vivian," he said. "Your son goes to America with you or else. There I said it. Does it make any difference? See, I can say the obvious like the rest of you, but owt I say won't change the outcome, will it? It's like pissing in the wind for me. Anyrode, I'm trying to relax after three weeks hard work. I don't need this racket."

In his view, the women ought to be left alone to sort out any family problems among themselves. There was nothing for a man to do but go for a quiet pint, then come back later and go along with whatever had been agreed upon by the lasses.

"Go on, then, 'ave your pint, Son," said Muriel. "It's best. And take the boy with you if you can find him out there."

When Mac left, a strong draught blew in; reaching around the parlour with icy, spectral fingers. Muriel shivered against the ill wind.

Chapter 9

The next morning Prudence lingered a while in bed with the covers pulled up to her chin. Curling her chilly toes, she rubbed her feet together to warm them. She felt some envy for the soundly sleeping sister next to her, but nonetheless pulled the eiderdown up over Winnie's exposed shoulder. As she did so, her heart lurched: Ted's cot was missing. So used was she to looking over and listening to that corner of the room that at first she panicked. Then she remembered that he had been moved to Vivian's room, and was no longer her responsibility.

Relieved, her head fell back on the pillow. He would be all right without her, wouldn't he? Doubt crept into her breast. She felt guilty about putting herself first. Yet surely his life would go on well enough without his aunt fretting and furrowing her brow over him all the time. She could look upon him with fresh eyes, eyes that could care but not feel ultimately responsible for his feeding and dirty nappies and whether he had slept or ate enough.

It's our Vivian's worry now. That's all there is to it. Oh, but our Ted. Her heart ached thinking about him and the life ahead of him. Oh, stop it! she commanded the thoughts swirling in her head. Her time would be better spent getting the morning's chores done rather than lolling about, thinking the same thoughts over and over again.

After quickly and quietly dressing so as not to wake Winnie, Prudence crept downstairs to the parlour where, as expected, her mother was already up, and it wasn't yet six o'clock. What was uncommon, though, was the unlit fire and no water on the boil. It was most unlike their mother to be doing anything other than bustling about. But today, dark circles cupped her eyes, and her rosary hung limply from one hand.

"Mam, are you all right?" Prudence asked.

"Oh, love, I didn't sleep too well, what with everything that's been going on and that, so I came downstairs to do some'at useful instead of tossing and turning in bed. But then I've just been sat here. I don't know 'ow long. Can't seem to get me engine started."

"Oh, never mind, Mam. I'll get us a fire going in no time."

Sweeping up the ashes from the night before, the daughter discreetly but carefully looked over at the mother. What she saw broke her heart a little. Her mother's whole being had been conquered by frailty; her skin was sallow and sad, and her dark eyes haunted; certainly more than one night without sleep could account for. The cold ashes in Prudence's bucket were as grey as her mother's skin. How could she not have noticed the slow decline in her mother's well-being? There was no doubt the stress of war had taken its toll, though mothers and wives were never accounted for as war casualties. The carefree feeling Prudence had experienced only moments before was replaced by a new burden; the need to take care of her mother.

Prudence smiled at Muriel, hoping to warm her mother up in any way she could. "Almost done, Mam. Got some good dry kindling 'ere."

"You're a good girl."

Watching the flames take hold, Prudence said, "It's all been too much. The war. None of us is eating proper. We're still trying to get by on rationing. Our stomachs have shrunk so we can't eat enough when there is food. There's no wonder you don't feel well. And what with our Vivian coming home with her new 'usband and all that stuff about poor Ted … well, it wears you down."

"It might be wearing us down, but it won't wear us out. We're made of stronger stuff than that. Anyrode, enough of the maudlin. Let's stick to talking about the weather like all good English folk."

"All right, Mam. It is pretty cold this morning. That can't be doing you no good neither."

"Aye, the cold makes me bones ache and me back's killing me this morning. I can't bend over."

"Sit closer to the fire. It'll soon warm up in here. Here look, let me rub your back for you."

Muriel straightened herself in the chair. "I'd rather have that cuppa, eh, love? I need some'at to grease the wheels. These days I'm like an old rusty bike that needs a lot of pedalling to get going. I've got a lot on me mind, that's all. You're right. It's all too much 'appening at once."

"Then one strong cup of scalding hot tea coming right up."

By the time the first pot of tea was brewing, Ted could be heard crying upstairs. Prudence heard him as she came in through the back door, her pink apron full of eggs.

"I'm tempted to go get him," she said. "But I'm not going to - or should I?"

Muriel smiled.

"No. Our Vivian has to learn sometime. Lady Muck is probably laid in bed wondering what the noise is."

Some floorboards squeaked above their heads. The baby quieted but it was a man's voice they heard soothing.

"Honestly," said Muriel. "If our Vivian landed in the dock she'd come up dry."

"Aye, she allus lands with her bum in the butter."

"So, what do you reckon to 'im, then?" asked Muriel in a low voice. "Vivian's feller?"

"He seems all right," said Prudence, deftly using one hand to crack eggs into a yellow bowl.

"Well, despite what happened, he slept in the same bed as 'er," said Muriel. "That says some'at."

"Nowhere else to go that late at night," Prudence remarked, whisking the eggs. "And drunk an' all."

"Aye, I know. Did you hear them two lads coming home last night? What a bloody racket! The noisy devils."

"I was awake anyrode," said Prudence. "Sounded like someone was dragging a dead body up them stairs."

Prudence sliced some bread for toast, enjoying the scent of the freshly cut slices.

"Unless you're 'ungry now, Mam, I'll wait for them to come downstairs before I start the eggs."

"I'm fine. Just a cup of tea and a biscuit will tide me over for now. Me appetite's not what it used to be neither."

More admissions, as if her shield was crumbling. Little by little she was letting down her guard, releasing the truth of how she really felt. To me, thought Prudence. Only to me. But I'm not ready. Me shoulders are weighted more and more with each ounce of revelation. But if it makes her load lighter, why shouldn't I bear it? I will and I can.

Taking a moment of respite before the entire household descended on the parlour, Prudence poured the tea and sat in the chair opposite her mother. Closing her eyes, she took an unhurried sip. The hot liquid burned down her throat. It was nice to have the time to enjoy things again, to take pleasure in the simple things she had denied herself throughout the constant mothering of Ted.

"Well, I'll go the top of our stairs! Will you take a look at that?" Muriel exclaimed, sitting up suddenly and not noticing the pain; for there was Jake, holding a quite contended Ted close to the checkered shirt he had quickly thrown on.

"You look a bit worse for the wear. Whatever 'appened ?" asked Muriel.

"Something called Old Peculiar," Jake said, squinting his bloodshot eyes.

"Oh dear," said Prudence. "I'm surprised Stalworth had any of that stuff left after the war."

"He'd kept it hidden in the cellar till he had something worth celebrating, he said."

"Why, what was he celebrating last night?"

"The groom," Jake said awkwardly.

"Oh. Of course."

"Anyrode, what's her upstairs up to?" Muriel asked him, raising her eyes to the ceiling.

"Sleeping with a pillow over her head."

"Sleeping!" cried Muriel. "I've a good mind to go up there and give her a bloody good hiding. By 'eck lad, you'd better watch out. You should start as you mean to go on."

Since, apparently, he did mean to go on.

"It's okay. I don't mind. I guess, this is something I have to get used to as well."

Muriel took a deep breath of love for her new son-in-law.

"Well, don't get too used to it or she'll let you do all the work. Mark my words, Son."

"Give 'im here," said Prudence. "He likes his milk first thing."

"No, I can get it for him. From what I understand, you've done enough. Where is it?"

"But," said Prudence, glancing at Muriel who was hiding a smile behind her hand.

"Have you done it before?"

"I've looked after plenty of calves. Birthed 'em, and fed 'em with a bottle when the mother didn't take to them. They're just as helpless as this little guy. How different can they be?"

Muriel laughed. "Well, I never," she said. "Did you hear that our Ted. You're just another little calf to this cowboy. I suppose you're right in a way, Jake. All young uns are the same. They just want feeding, cleaning and wearing out to make them happy. I wish things was allus that simple. Well, maybe they are. Mornin' Winnie."

"Mornin'. Moo, Teddy. Moo," said Winnie who had heard their conversation from the stairway.

"Moo," said Ted.

"Cows are lucky," said Muriel. "I much prefer mooing to the way our bairns whine. Oh George, I'm glad you've decided to join the land of the living. Put some coal on the fire for us."

"Tch."

"You don't get that sort of cheek from a calf neither," remarked Muriel, standing slowly, using the arm of the chair for support.

"Mam, what are you doing?" asked Prudence. "Sit down and rest. I'll get you whatever you need."

"I'm going to give our Vivian what for. The lazy cow."

"Please sit down, Mam. There's no point in getting yoursen all worked up now, is there? What good would it do?"

"She needs a good slap around the ear. Who does she think she is letting everyone else do the work?"

"She's a married woman now. Got an 'usband to sort her out," Prudence said, nodding in Jake's direction. "Relax, Mam."

Muriel sat.

"Mind if I make some coffee?" asked Jake.

"Not at all, but I'm afraid all we have is some of that camp coffee in the pantry. I don't know how old it is neither."

"No worries. I've got my own coffee grounds upstairs."

When Jake left the room, Muriel remarked, loudly enough, that if all American men were like that she would be taking the Queen Mary with Vivian so she could find one of her own.

Jake soon returned, arms laden with treasures for them all.

"Chocolate!" gasped Winnie.

"Yeah, a bar for you and one for George."

"Oo, ta."

The children greedily took the bars, unwrapping them.

"After breakfast," Muriel said.

"Mam!"

"After breakfast," she repeated. "Or not at all."

"Sorry," said Jake. "I guess I should have waited."

"They should be 'appy they got it at all," said Muriel, finding her own appetite stirred at the thought of chocolate.

"For you," he handed Muriel some fancy bars of soap and a box of chocolates.

"Well, I never!" exclaimed Muriel. "What a lovely surprise!"

He handed Prudence a box of chocolates as well, along with a slim package in a paper bag.

"For me? Real silk stockings! You're joking, aren't you? Ta very much. How on earth did you get these?" she said, embarrassed but delighted at the personal gift. "Oh Mam, look! I haven't seen a pair of these since, well, I can't remember."

She laughed as she ran the stockings over her hands, enjoying the luxurious feel of the silk. Too bad I don't have someone to wear them for, she thought.

"I really can't believe it," she said. "Ta, ever so much, Jake. The closest we've come to silk lately was making pillow cases and knickers out of fallen parachutes. As you may have noticed. I mean the pillow cases," she added, blushing.

"Can I see?" asked Winnie.

"Not on your nelly," said Prudence lifting the stockings beyond Winnie's reach.

"Please, please, please," Winnie jumped up and down.

"If I catch you anywhere near these I'll kill you."

"Mam, Prudence says she'll kill me if I touch her stockings."

"Then you'd better not touch 'em, ay?" said Muriel.

Jake boiled up some coffee as the kids sat at the parlour table mesmerised by the bars of chocolate.

"What's that stink?" asked Mac, who had enjoyed a lie in after kicking George out of the bed for moving around too much.

"Coffee," said Jake.

"It smells bloody strong."

"Wanna try some? It's the Old Peculiar of coffees."

"It's the same bloody colour," Mac said, peering into the pot. "No ta. I'll stick to me tea. I know me limits,

83

unlike some I could mention. By heck, just the smell of it'll put hairs on your chest. You'd better not have any, our Prudence."

"Ha, ha," she said.

"For you," said Jake, throwing a couple of packets of American cigarettes and some chewing gum Mac's way.

"For me? Ta very much."

After breakfast, George went to Paddy's house to share his chocolate bar, while Winnie ran upstairs to share hers with her doll, almost bumping into Vivian on the way.

"Oy, watch where you're going!"

Those in the parlour fell silent, listening to Vivian hum a tune as she descended the stairs. Her imminent presence felt like an intrusion, even to Muriel.

"What's for breakfast?" Vivian asked pulling her dressing gown tightly around her. Her hair and make-up were dishevelled. Mascara had run under her eyes. "I thought I smelled eggs."

"You did," said Prudence.

"Where are they?"

"Gone. You'll have to make your own."

"Tch. Jake, will you be a love and make an egg for me. I'm so tired," said Vivian slumping down at the table.

"Eggs in the pantry?" asked Jake.

"Bloody hell," said Mac, snapping his newspaper.

"Yes," said Muriel, unable to believe her eyes.

"Over easy," said Vivian, showing off now that she felt powerful with the secret out and her husband in acceptance.

That Vivian felt like a champion was an annoyance to Prudence, a fact she made known with disapproving eyes on Vivian who squeezed the last half cup of tea from the pot and nibbled on leftover toast.

"Tea's cold," she complained. "And so's the toast."

"Help yoursen. There's water boiling on the stove," said Prudence. "Unless you've forgotten where that is an' all."

"I'm on me 'oneymoon," said Vivian.

"So's Jake," said Muriel. "Here, love let me make her ladyship her bloody egg. A man's never cooked in my parlour, and it doesn't sit right wi' me."

"He likes it, Mam. Leave him be," said Vivian. "He's actually quite good at it. You should let him make tea for us one night." She yawned and stretched. "He makes this thing called meatloaf -"

"I'll do no such thing," said Muriel. "Gimme that egg. You're making a rod for your own back, Son, waiting on her. And I should know. I did it for eighteen year."

"Mam!"

"Don't 'Mam' me. It's just occurred to me that I've been too soft on you lot. No wonder me back hurts after all them years fetching and carrying. Tell me, our Mac, 'ow long would you wait before you cooked yoursen some'at, or would you starve to death first?"

Mac said, "Oh look, Hull's playing away at Leeds, today."

"Changing the subject, are you?"

"Aye, that I am, Mam," said Mac. "That I am."

"You're not going, are you?" said Muriel.

"Aye. Me and Bert."

"On your bike? With no road signs to go by?"

"Aye, on me bike. I'll find it. They must have put some of the signs up by now. I 'ave been to Leeds before, you know. Anyrode, I'd better get going, I've got to pick up Bert."

"But you've got plenty of time, the match doesn't start while ..."

Mac couldn't suppress a naughty grin.

"Oh save me," said Muriel, holding up a hand. "There's some things a mother shouldn't know, and the gypsy camp being on the way to Bert's house is one of them, I reckon."

Chapter 10

Mac was about to give the brass knocker a second, more impatient rap when the front door suddenly swung open and Bert Smith's step-daughter exclaimed, "William Goodwell, it *is* you!"

"Aye, 'tis me," he said. "Who else would it be?"

But what mischief was this that met his eyes? Gloria Baxter was no longer the skinny little lass he had last seen at the start of the war. Gone was the cheeky-eyed girl who always carried a skipping rope in her hand; instead, standing before him, was a beautiful young woman who gazed with uncommon directness into his black eyes.

"Gloria Baxter? By heck, I almost didn't recognise you."

"Aye, I know. Been five year or more since we evacuated to me aunt's in Whitby. But you look the same."

She smiled, parting voluptuous lips and showing off perfect white teeth, a rarity in those parts.

"Five year. You've, you're ..." his hands gestured her growth. "When did you get back?"

"Three weeks ago. I wanted to be back for me seventeenth birthday."

"Oh aye? Seventeen is it? Well ..."

"Well, aren't you going to wish me an 'appy birthday?"

If there was anything better to show the passing of time than a young girl blossoming from girl to womanhood, then Mac could not think of it in that moment. Through the chrysalis of war, Gloria's metamorphosis into a gorgeous young woman was almost complete. Yet there were still girlish things about her, the way she rocked forward on to her toes when she was saying something bold, and the slenderness and slight awkwardness of her white arms that seemed to move independently, belying a slight childish nervousness as they rocked the door to and fro. She had that youthful energy about her, the insatiable power that pushes a snowdrop through the snow in the first days of spring.

Wavy dark blonde hair fell just past her shoulders. The high cheek bones and wide smile she inherited from her mother, but the twinkle in those green eyes was all her own. This was the little girl he remembered who was forever counting her skips to the shops and back, to school and back, to the park and back. She was born with endless energy and a determination to be the best at everything she attempted. Her latest endeavour was bread-baking, and her hands were coated with flour to prove it.

Indeed, the scent of fresh baked bread (as fresh baked as she) hot out of the oven permeated the air, and all Mac's senses rumbled with irrepressible hunger. The willing girls at the gypsy camp now forgotten; perhaps never to be remembered.

Gloria brushed at her nose, leaving a trace of flour on the freckled end of it. He shifted his feet uncomfortably. This was his best friend's daughter, albeit step-daughter, a girl he had known for most of her life. I need a beer to clear me head, he thought. Bert would kill me.

Gloria smiled, dimpling her rosy cheeks, warm from baking. She knew there was something to his not being able to look too long at her.

"Bert said you was coming over. But if you want to see him, you'll have to go upstairs. He's in bed."

"In bed? What's he doing in bed at this time? We've got a footie match to go to."

"He's had an... accident," she said, trying not to laugh.

"An accident! He'd better be dead if he's going to miss footie!"

"It's worse than that," she tittered. "Hey, is your Winnie at home?"

"Aye, she is. What sort of accident?"

"I can't say," Gloria said coyly. "But can you give me a lift back to your house so I can see your Winnie? I haven't seen her since I got back. I bet she looks different an' all."

"I can't give you a lift you daft lass. Me and Bert are straight off to footie."

"I don't think so. He won't be able to ride your bike."

"Look, no more messing about. Can you fetch your dad or what? We're going to be late."

"I told you, I can't fetch him. I'll fetch me mam for you, if you like. Can I hold your dog? He's got more gray now, hasn't he?"

"Aye, but be quick," Mac said handing over Monty and catching a whiff of delicious perfume from Gloria. "But don't dress him up in that pink bonnet thing again."

"You remember!" said Gloria.

"Aye, how could I forget."

"Were you jealous? Do you want me to crochet you a matching one?"

"Now, now," he said, flustered. A young girl like that and she had the better of him.

"You'll have to wait your turn, mind, 'cause I'm making some'at for your mam."

"For my mam?"

"Aye, a shawl. I saw your mam last week and she looked a bit peaky, if you don't mind me saying, and I pictured her wearing a shawl of particular colours to cheer her up. It was like she had to have it. So I've decided to be the one to make it for her. It'll be the biggest thing I've ever made. I hope she likes it."

"Hm," said Mac, starting to feel cornered.

"I'll go fetch me mam. Come in, come in. Don't be a stranger. Mam!"

"What is it?" a voice called from the back of the house.

Gloria disappeared into the parlour, returning moments later with Monty who was now sporting a crocheted cap in Hull City colours.

"You said no *pink* bonnets. I made it just for him."

"Actually," said Mac. "It doesn't look 'alf bad."

He was about to to pat Gloria on the head like he used to, but then he pulled his hand away. She looked sideways at him, and smiled.

"Hiya Mac," said Mavis, drying her hands on a tea towel. "Look, you'll have to go up and see Bert for yoursen. He's in too much pain to come down."

"In too much pain? What 'appened?" said Mac.

"I think you'd better ask him yoursen. I'm so cross with him. He were supposed to wallpaper our bedroom this weekend an' all. I bought the rolls and scraped off the old paper and everything. He'll do owt to get out of it."

Then her shoulders shook and she clapped a hand over her mouth stifling a giggle. "I shouldn't laugh," she said, through her fingers. "Poor Bert. But it serves him right. Him *and* that ferret. Go on, go on. See for yoursen."

"All right, then. I will."

Mounting the stairs three at a time, Mac yelled, "Come on Bert! We've got a kick off to get to."

He burst into Bert's bedroom fully expecting to rally him for the game, but he immediately took a step back when he saw his friend prostrate on the bed wearing only his pyjama jacket. The bosun was naked from the waist down, except, that is, for some ice wrapped in a tea towel resting on his privates. Over on a chair by the window were a pair of trousers and several pieces of string all thrown about haphazardly as if removed in a hurry. Rolls of wallpaper were stacked in one corner of the room, and, as Mavis had said, the walls had been scraped bare of the old yellow patterned paper. A fire burned in the grate taking off some of the chill.

"I thought I 'eard you," Bert said miserably. "They closed the door 'cause they couldn't stand to hear me moaning. Mind you, I don't mind 'cause it means I don't have to listen to them cackling at my expense. Come in, come in. Oo, me bollocks."

"Sorry, I would have knocked, but," said Mac, trying not to laugh. "What happened?"

"It were Mac."

"Mac?"

"Aye, Mac, me ferret, he attacked me cock and balls. It doesn't half hurt, I can tell you. Them ferrets allus has to finish what they start. Tenacious little buggers they are."

"Hold on a minute, are you telling me that you named your new ferret after me?"

"Aye, well he's a fighter, you see, like you," said Bert, his features twisting in pain as he shifted his position. "It was out of respect you understand. Bloody 'ell, this hurts."

"So how is it that the ferret got anywhere near your wedding tackle, then? Lovers' quarrel was it?" Mac chuckled.

"No," Bert said firmly. "And this isn't no laughing matter. How would you like it?"

"Well, I wouldn't let a bloody ferret near me jewels, now would I?"

"That's cause you're too cowardly. Ferret-legging's not for the faint of heart, the weak-willed, the spineless, or the -"

"Ferret-legging! Don't tell me you stuck it down your trousers on purpose, you daft sod."

"Aye, I were trying to keep him down for over a minute, to get the world record. I thought it would impress my Mavis. No one's done it before."

"A minute! That's nowt! Bloody hell I could keep it up me arse longer than that."

"Oh aye? Well, I'll bet you can't keep it in your kegs for more than ten seconds. Go on try it. You think you're so bloody clever."

Mac glanced at his watch. "Sorry, I would but I can't. I suppose this means you're not coming."

"Not in this bloody state. I won't be able to sit on the bike. And stop trying to get out of it. It's only a minute. Go on. Let's see how long you can keep him down. Take off your kegs. No undercrackers, neither, mind. It's against the rules."

"Christ," said Mac, feeling obliged to put his balls where his mouth was.

So, with his back to Bert, he removed his trousers and underpants, then put the trousers back on.

"Jesus Christ you've got an hairy arse," exclaimed Bert. "Me poor ferret's going to have the fright of its life down there. Now tie your trousers round the ankle with the string. Aye, like that so he can't get out."

"I can't believe you've roped me into this. All right, ready. Where is the bloody thing, then?"

"Over there in its cage. You'll have to get him. I can't. It hurts too much to walk. Mind your fingers when you reach for him. He goes for owt that dangles. The bigger the better."

"Well, I suppose that's where I have the disadvantage over you for once," quipped Mac.

"Very funny," said Bert. "We'll see if you're laughing in a minute. Go on stick him down the front of your trousers, then you have to cinch your belt. Hold on, let me check the minute hand on me watch, all right go on, that's it. Now cinch your belt really tight. That's it. Ha!"

Mac pushed the ferret as far down his baggy trouser leg as it would go. There was no way out at the bottom so after scrambling for a second the ferret turned and scurried up his leg, circling his thigh like a helter skelter, scratching with its sharp claws and pulling on the hairs on his legs. Bert laughed, watching the small creature move up through the fabric. Then he winced, trying to hold his laugh so his body wouldn't shake.

"Ow! Shite, bugger, fuck!" shouted Mac through clenched teeth.

"Ten seconds," Bert said officially.

"You're lying," gasped Mac, his eyes watering.

He bit his knuckle.

"Jesus!"

The door creaked open.

"What the bloody hell are you two doing?" asked Mavis sticking her head in through the door. "I can hear you downstairs, swearing, you should be ashamed. Not the bloody ferret legging again! When will you learn? You boys never grow up, do you?"

But she couldn't keep the smile off her face.

"I just don't know how you can with that filthy animal," she said

"He's not filthy!" cried Bert. "Stop saying that!"

"I were talking to the ferret," she said, unable to stifle a laugh as she closed the door.

"Oy!," exclaimed Mac whose arse cheeks were fully clenched thwarting any chance to prove his prior claim.

Bert was no longer able to control himself. He was laughing hysterically while trying to keep his body still and thus his bits from jiggling, but not succeeding, so he was also crying tears of pain along with those of laughter.

"Oh, priceless!" he cried. "Priceless!"

By now Mac's face was bright red and his eyes were bulging with pain. His hips thrust back and forth trying to avoid the inevitable as the ferret scrambled this way and that.

"By heck. Did you see that?" cried Bert. "My Mavis smiling and making a joke. It's music to my ears, that is. I'd do owt to make 'er 'appy."

"Jesus, Bert!" Mac said. "How long has it been? I must have broken the record by now."

"Oops, sorry," said Bert, looking sheepish. "But I lost track of the minute hand when our Mavis came in. You'll have to start again if you want to time it proper."

"You bloody bugger!" exclaimed Mac, immediately unfastening the belt. "You did that on purpose. You sod."

The pain was obvious on Mac's scrunched face as he reached down the front of his wool trousers.

"Ow! shite! Ow! Come out you bastard. How the hell do I get him to let go? Ow shite, now he's got me finger.

92

Christ, but it's better than me todger. Ow, it's like a bloody vice."

Mac swung his arm into the air trying to dislodge the ferret whose sharp little teeth were securely embedded in his index finger. His trousers fell to the floor and he almost tripped over, which was more than Bert could stand.

Bawling with laughter but unable to take in the spectacle any longer, Bert rolled onto his front, crushing his injured parts. He yelped in pain, bit into the pillow and turned over again. Waving his hands in surrender, Bert pleaded, "Stop it! Stop it! I can't take anymore."

"What do you mean stop it. I can't get the bugger to let go. They're not teeth, they're bloody razor blades. Get him off me before I lose me finger. Hurry up or I'm going to start punching the little blighter."

"No don't hurt him! I have some rum here," said Bert, searching in the drawer of the bedside table. "Come here. This'll do the trick. Ow, oo, me bollocks."

Mac shuffled across the floor, tripped and fell. "Gerroff me you little bugger!" He squeezed the ferret's body between his thighs, trying to pry open its jaw with his other hand.

"Here, here, you don't have to do that. Drop some rum in its mouth. That's how I get it off. Whether it's because he likes it or not doesn't matter. Come here, closer."

"Only if you cover yoursen up. I can't be that close to you with your thing out," Mac said, shuffling over to the bed on his knees.

"Bloody hell, you'd think you'd have more to worry about. I know it must be intimidating, like. All right. All right. There's no need to get bent out of shape. Better? Here, hold him by the scruff of his neck, while I pour. Don't let go. As soon as he releases shove him back in his cage."

"Mac?" said Gloria, opening the door. "Me mam says to tell you -"

Her eyes flung wide open. There was Mac on his knees next to the bed with his trousers round his ankles and a ferret hanging from his finger while Bert, who was on the bed naked from the waist down, was leant over the fallen fisherman with a flask of rum in his hand.

"Oh shite!" exclaimed Mac.

Holding his breath to escape the pain, he grabbed the eider down and hid the lower half of his body under it.

"Doesn't nobody knock no more," said Bert. "Is that his dog? Oy, don't let it in here or it'll kill me ferret."

But his words came too late: Monty had spotted the ferret attacking his master. Letting out an excited yelp, the dog leapt from Gloria's arms. As well as the bonnet, he was now also sporting a frilly, white doll's dress on which his back legs got caught several times as he ran across the room toward the ferret. The dress slowed him down, giving the ferret a chance to escape, which it took.

"Ah. Thank fuck," said Mac, now released.

"Get him!" cried Bert.

"First things, first," replied Mac, who was still sore at his friend.

Using the eider down for cover, Mac pulled on his underwear and trousers, taking his time as the dog chased the ferret from one end of the room to the other until the ferret led the way out the door past Gloria.

"Stop your dog! Go get him!" yelled Bert. "He's going to kill my Mac."

"Maybe a bit of rum'll help me stop him," said Mac.

"Bloody hell. Take a swig then," said Bert.

Taking the proffered bottle, Mac took a long drink without hurry despite the crashes and Mavis' screams coming from below.

"Great," said Bert, flinching when his wife screamed "Bert! Come on get this bloody thing out of here before I kill it!"

"Now I'm really in trouble. Hurry up, Mac."

There was more crashing, more screams, and even swearing, to which Mavis was not prone.

"Please Mac," Bert whined. "Save me ferret. And me marriage."

Bert listened from his bed as Mac ran downstairs to sort out the fracas. "About bloody time," he heard his wife say. "They're in the parlour." He heard Mac giving commands to his dog, and hoped it wasn't too late. Moments later Mac returned to the room holding aloft by the scruffs of their necks the ferret in one hand and the dog in the other, both struggling and yelping to be freed.

"Got 'em," Mac said.

While the terrified ferret screeched and writhed its tiny body trying to escape its captor, the dog snapped and snarled at its prey with sharp white teeth bared aggressively. His tiny legs scrambled, seeking traction in the air. Alas, the bonnet was askew and the dress in tatters.

"Is he hurt?" Bert asked sulkily, not enjoying the pleasure he saw Mac derive from watching the dog's killer instinct against his beloved pet.

"No. He's all right, aren't you, Monty? A bit over excited, like, but-"

"I meant me ferret."

"Oh, of course. Well, Monty had it by the neck, but I got there before he killed it. As you can see. Here, I'll put it back in its cage."

Mac dropped Monty to the floor but the little dog kept jumping up at his leg, almost succeeding in running up it and getting to the ferret, which Mac swung out of the way.

"Off," Mac said firmly. "Down!"

The dog immediately obeyed by laying down on the floor with his chin resting on his paws; though his ears twitched and he kept his alert brown eyes on the ferret.

"Drop him in the cage backwards," said Bert. "So he can't see where he's going."

"Like this? There you go, Mac," said Mac, closing the door.

"Thank God," said Bert. "I'd be lost without him."

"Ta very much," said Mavis who had returned to the bedroom. "Perhaps you can train him to make your tea for you an' all."

"Look, I didn't mean owt like that," said Bert. "I'd be more lost without you, of course I would, love."

"Bert Smith, you should be resting not sky-larking about with your mates. You have to get well enough to paper this room before you go back to work. I'm not living like this for the next three weeks."

"All right, love. He's leaving aren't you, Mac? By the way, did me ferret get you then, you know, where it counts?" Bert asked raising his eyebrows.

"No, not really," said Mac. "What about yours? Does it really hurt that bad?"

"Only when I laugh."

Mac grinned but then his cheerful look turned to one of disappointment. "But what about footie? You know I don't like going on me own."

"Take Ginger."

"Not that fat bastard on me bike."

"What about your George?"

"No, I'll want to go for a drink after, and you know how it can get. He might get hurt."

"Aye, that's true. Well, there's slim pickings, unless … well, what about the American lad? Your new brother-in-law."

"Jake? But American's don't know nowt about football."

"Beggars can't be choosers," said Bert.

"Aye, I suppose you're right. There's no 'arm in asking. It's better for him than stopping in with the lasses all day. Ta-ra then. Don't let the bed bugs bite. Or the ferrets."

Outside, Mac gingerly straddled his bike. The pain was getting worse and needed a tot to quell it otherwise he wouldn't be able to make it to Leeds. Relax dads, he thought. I'm currently out of commission. Your daughters are safe tonight.

Kicking the bike to start was a lesson in endurance.

"Don't forget you promised to give us a lift to your 'ouse," Gloria said, all dressed up and ready to go with her coat and hat on, and a spot of make-up. "Seeing as though you're going there anyway, or so I heard."

He found her bold stare disconcerting, especially after the embarrassing incident earlier. She had transformed into something that scared him a little. And he wasn't usually afraid of anything. He reckoned she was more trouble than the rest of the lasses put together.

"If it's all right with your mam," he said.

"Aye," she said, swinging a bag of bread cakes over her shoulder. "It is."

Then she was on the back of the bike before he could change his mind. Throwing her arms about his waist, she shifted as close to him as possible. He shuffled forward a little.

"You don't have to hold on so tight," he said.

"Oh, I don't mind," she said. "Here, try this."

"What?" he said as she reached around and put a bread cake into his mouth.

"Huh?" he mumbled biting into it and tearing off the rest.

"Oh ta. Delicious. Now when we go round corners make sure you lean with me into the corner, not against it. Just follow my lead. Bloody hell this is good bread," he said, shoving the rest into his mouth before speeding off.

"Ta," she said, pressing her face against the broad back of the man she had longed dreamed of marrying.

Chapter 11

Grumbling about her husband's Homing Pigeons, Dolores Alford scrubbed angrily at the guano splattered on the front doorstep. She threw a venomous look up at the loft installed on their roof and shouted, "Pigeon Pie!"

The thought of food in any form, even pigeon pie, caused her stomach to grumble. To take her mind off it, she brushed vigorously with the worn donkey stone, feeling the same anger she always felt when she recalled how it had been her job to scrub the front door step ever since she was a child; whether it was this doorstep or the one at her parents' house just a few doors down, it was her job. Her dad made sure of it, and so now did her husband.

I'll be scrubbing the stone at the gates of hell, she thought, swishing the stone in a bucket of water and watching her two daughters play hopscotch on the path. Look how happy they are when Jimmy's away. I wish they knew more carefree days. I wish I did. Oh, look here's Mac, and Prudence. And me looking like I was dragged through an 'edge backwards.

As the bike pulled to the curb, Dolores knelt back on the heels of her slippers to wave a greeting. Her rounded pregnant belly showed. She brushed it self-consciously, sighing at the sad state of her attire. She was the poorest of the poor with a violent husband who drank and gambled everything he earned. Her self-confidence was so low she could wipe the floor with it.

Wiping gritty hands on her green housecoat, Dolores put on a smile. She knew green was an unlucky colour for fishermen but doubted Mac noticed her clothing these days. The housecoat had cost only a penny at the church jumble sale, so she had bought it reasoning that her own luck couldn't get any worse.

"Hiya, Dolores," said Prudence as she awkwardly dismounted the bike while Mac kept it steady, eyes straight ahead, the engine putting. He was already miffed with his sister for treating him like a taxi when all he wanted to do was get off to the football match. But in the few minutes it would take Jake to get ready to go with him, she argued, he could give her a quick lift to Dolores' house, couldn't he?

"Hiya," Dolores said, pushing a lock of hair behind an ear, exposing the black eye Mac had known would be there.

"Now then, Mrs. Alford," Mac said cordially, pretending not to notice the injury.

How she hated to be known by her husband's surname, whether it was Mac or anyone else addressing her. She always thought people were talking about someone else because it can't have been her that married that man, could it? How she missed the days when Mac would address her as 'Dol'.

Mac revved the throttle impatiently to show he was eager to get going, although there was nothing physically holding him in place. That was until young Shirley Alford ran up to touch his bike with her porcelain doll clutched tightly under one arm.

"Hey Mister, can me and Lizzie sit on it?"

"Where's your manners, Shirley?" said Dolores. "Honestly."

"Please, Mister. Lizzie really wants to."

The eyes, not as innocent as they should be at that age because of poverty and the brutality of the father, pleaded with him. But it was the cheeky smile playing on her small mouth that his heart couldn't refuse.

"If you like," he said.

"We do," she said cheekily.

Her spirit is not completely broken, then.

As he scooped up the young girl, one of her shoes fell off. The jumble sale shoes were much too big for Shirley's bony feet but she made do and didn't complain. It was better than going barefoot in October, like some.

"There you go, Lizzie," she said. "You sit in front of me."

Shirley squealed when Monty growled from deep within the Mac's coat.

"Quiet," said the master. "Don't mind him."

"Vroom! Vroom!" Shirley cried, pretending to steer the bike. The doll slipped to one side but Mac caught it.

"Careful Shirley!" called Dolores. "That's not very ladylike. Is she bothering you, Mac? I'm sorry. You can tell her to get down, if you like. Come on Shirley, stop bothering Mac."

It pained Dolores to see her daughter play with him. There was too much to think about what could have been if they were his children.

"It's no bother," Mac said curtly.

However, he dropped the girl carefully to the ground, and said, "Sorry, love, but I'm in an 'urry."

"Is it 'cause me mam said?"

"No, it's 'cause I said."

The girl shrugged and picked up her spare shoe, slipping it on like a clog. She was about to resume the game of hopscotch when she turned to Mac and tapped his great thigh.

"Hey Mister?"

"What is it, love."

"Will you take me and Lizzie to the seaside on it?"

"Shirley!" exclaimed Dolores. "Don't be so cheeky."

"Please. Me dad's allus says he's going to take us but he never 'as enough money for train fare."

"Shirley, don't say that, your dad -" Dolores began.

"Aye," Mac said. "When it's a bit warmer. I'll be glad to take you."

"Oo ta!" she exclaimed. "Ay, our Sharon did you hear that? Mac's going to take me and Lizzie to the seaside and we'll see the sea before you do!"

"No you won't," the older sister said sulkily. She had longed to sit on the bike too, but daren't ask. "Dad will take us, he promised."

"Dad never does owt nice he says he's going to," said Shirley who always spoke bravely against their father when he was away at sea. "He's too drunk and mean. But he allus keeps his promises to 'urt us."

"I'm going to tell him you said that."

"Don't!" cried Shirley with such terror Mac's heart froze.

"Girls, stop it," said Dolores, embarrassed. "Sharon you are not to say any such thing to your father. I don't want to hear another word about it, do you hear me? Do you?"

"I've brought some jam tarts," said Prudence. "You can 'ave one if you play nicely. And some extra bread cakes that Gloria Baxter made."

Dolores smiled gratefully.

"Oo jam tarts!" both girls exclaimed coming over to look in Prudence's shopping bag. "And eggs!"

"Mam, can we 'ave one now?"

"Aye, one each, mind. And no, you can't 'ave an extra one for Lizzie."

Dolores was close to the bike now. When he looked into her large, hazel eyes, flecked with green like Shirley's, his stomach tightened, responding to the ghost of beauty that graced her gaunt, oval face. It wouldn't serve either of them very well if she could see what he was thinking, so he looked away before she could read his thoughts. He wished she wouldn't look into his eyes so searchingly. He couldn't tell what she wanted from him. Forgiveness? But forgiveness wasn't his to give.

Mac recalled the feeling of going to sea and thinking he had the power to change the world because of a girl that loved him waiting faithfully back home. Yet, it was the world that had the power to change him. He should have learned that lesson when his father died, when the sea took him, when the world proved it had no special sympathies for a twelve year old boy. And it still showed no special

sympathy for him when Dolores eloped with Jimmy Alford.

'Arseford', was the name the lads had come up with for
Jimmy Alford. He was well-despised by anybody who
knew him. There was plenty of gossip about Alford's gambling and drinking, and the bullying. Consequently, Mac
had put word out to the local bookies to stop taking Alford's bets, but now Jimmy went to East Hull to gamble,
and there wasn't anything Mac could do about that since
even his charm did not extend that far.

Dolores lifted the thin infant boy, Shane, out of the old
pram, and rested him on her twenty-six week swollen belly.
The boy was a sickly baby and small for his age having
been born early weighing only four pounds. There wasn't a
scrap of fat on him. Dolores' mother had cruelly forecast
he wouldn't make it through another winter unless he
gained weight, so Dolores kept him wrapped up in extra
layers of wool to keep him warm.

No, there's no going back, Mac thought determinedly;
his knuckles tightening to white on the handlebars. But she
doesn't deserve those bruises no matter how it turned out
for me. The next time I see Alford, I'll -

Dolores touched his shoulder breaking him from his
thoughts. He realized he had been staring at the girls;
Shirley in particular caught his attention.

"Are the Tigers playing away or at home?" Dolores
asked.

"Away," he said.

"Hadn't you best be off, then?"

"Aye. Reckon."

Making a slow, wide turn in the street, he came back to
where Dolores was standing.

"You know that spirit, in Shirley," he said in a low
voice, fixing his gloves and looking, not at Dolores, but
down the road ahead of him. "You used to have some of
that fire in you, a long time ago. You're all she's got.

Don't let him put it out in her an' all or I'll 'ave to kill him. Do you hear me?"

"I wouldn't *let* him," Dolores snapped.

"I mean it," said Mac, gripping the handlebars of his bike as if he might snap them off with a flick of his wrist. "You made the choice to live with him. They didn't."

"Don't you think I know that!" she cried.

The bike roared away, drowning her words, as little Shirley ran alongside it on her fast, skinny little legs.

"Ta-ra, Mac!" the girl shouted, waving her doll. "Ta-ra!"

He waved from the top of the street before disappearing around a corner. Dolores didn't wave back. His words had stung her as much as his apparent indifference to her bruises. Prudence took Shane from Dolores and kissed his forehead. The infant whimpered and reached for her breast. "No, love," laughed Prudence, embarrassed. "You won't find owt there for you. Dolores, did you see what your Shane tried to do?"

But her friend's expression was wistful as she stared down the street after Mac.

"He does still care for you, you know," Prudence said.

"Got a funny way of showing it," said Dolores, getting back to work by emptying the dirty water down a drain. "Anyrode, doesn't matter if he does. I've made me bed."

"That sounds like your mam talking," said Prudence.

"That *is* what she said to me the last time I tried to leave Jimmy," sighed Dolores. "That and other things."

Her mother had less sympathy than anybody, saying that if she had been able to put up with it, with Dolores' father that is, then so could Dolores.

"It doesn't just rain on you, you know!" her mother had said that night before slamming the door in Dolores' face.

This was same door that Dolores had been so glad to close behind her when she left her parents' home to elope with Jimmy. The very door she wouldn't have believed in an eternity she would be in front of asking, begging, for re-entry through.

"Women do it all the time these days," Prudence was saying. "Everyone would understand."

"What? Divorce?"

Sharon was listening. Dolores had to be careful around her eldest daughter who blamed her for Jimmy's bad moods and would report anything she heard to her father to avoid trouble for herself.

"Here Sharon, take Shane inside and change his nappy. We'll be along in a minute. Go on."

"Not *that* many women do it," Dolores replied. "Not enough. How would it be for the girls, if I did that. They'd be taunted at school. Besides, he'd find me wherever I went. You know what he's like. He's said as much."

Prudence smiled sadly. She couldn't understand why Dolores wouldn't simply leave Jimmy. I would, she thought. I wouldn't put up with it for a minute. Mind you, *my* mam would take me back. And Mac, well, he wouldn't let it 'appen to me neither. Not to mention I wouldn't have married someone like Jimmy in the first place. I know Dolores was desperate to leave 'ome, but still. If only ...

"You know, Dolores, I wish you would reconsider moving into the flat above our chippy. You'd be safe there. It's a bit of a mess right now but we could clean it up in no time. I know we've talked about it before -"

"I couldn't afford it. Not on me own."

"You keep saying that but I'm sure we could work some'at out with me mam. You could work some of it off in the chippy."

Dolores shook her head, unable to believe it was possible.

"And you've got your net braiding," said Prudence.

"Aye. And look at me hands from that. People used to say I had nice hands. Long piano fingers. Smooth skin. Look at the blisters and the calluses from weaving the twine. At my age! Me 'ands was allus one of the things he'd compliment me on when we was courting. Before we was married o' course. He laid it on thick back then."

She clenched her fists, and held them to her bosom.

"No. I couldn't move in with you," Dolores said. "He'd only find me and cause trouble for you."

"Our Mac would sort him out."

"Aye, well, that's what I'm afraid of," she said with a half smile, "spreading me trouble around. Jimmy's still me bairns' father when all's said and done. And I'll never be able to escape that fact as long as I live."

Thunder clapped in the distance. Dolores looked into the grey sky wondering if there would be any lightning to follow. It was like that with Jimmy. There was always thunder, but she could never be sure if he would strike.

"He weren't like that before we was married, you see. I mean I wouldn't have married 'im, would I, if I'd known? While we was courting he brought me flowers, nowt expensive like, just daisies, but it were nice. He used to write me these daft love poems an' all," she sighed. "And I know it sounds silly, but the way he cared for his pigeons made me think he would be a good father. But that all changed once we was married. He doesn't even kiss me no more. Not that I mind, but," she paused, finding the admission difficult, "Not even on our wedding night. He just stuck it in. That ugly thing of his. Didn't care that he 'urt me, that it was me first time. Almost as if he wanted to be cruel about it. I reckon that as soon as he had me as his wife he didn't have to pretend no more."

She grimaced, but continued, ignoring Prudence's discomfort at her frankness. "And he's been sticking it in me ever since. Honestly, you're not missing much. I 'ate it but I'm going to end up with fifteen kids the way he goes on. And 'ow he expects to feed them all I don't know, what with all his gambling and drinking and carrying on."

Prudence didn't know what to say. This was the first time Dolores had broken down so completely about her marriage. Through the years, she had made the odd comment about Jimmy, and, of course, Prudence had seen the bruises, but she had never fully appreciated the desperation of her friend's life. The war had seen them apart. Prudence reached over to put a hand on Dolores' shoulder.

"I were desperate to get married, you see. I wanted to get away from me dad. And what did I do? I ended up marrying 'im," she nodded toward the house. "Jimmy Alford - a man just like me father. Out of the bloody frying pan and into the fire were written for me, you know."

Dolores' bitterness was rising. She fought it. She didn't want it to take over her soul and poison all that remained good in her life.

"No use in moaning though, is there?" She laughed bitterly. "We all say that after we've had good moan, don't we?"

"That's true," said Prudence. "We do. I suppose by the time we've moaned we've got it all out and feel better. But it 'elps, doesn't it, to get it off your chest?"

"Aye. I suppose it does. But don't you get sick of me moaning? I do. I get so sick of mesen sometimes I tune out me own thoughts."

"Dolores, you're me mate. You can talk to me any time, tell me owt, if it helps."

Dolores longed to spill the feeling that she wished Jimmy was dead. But she wouldn't tell her friend how jealous she felt when she saw the chaplain knock at her neighbours' doors to tell them their husbands had been lost at sea. She wished over and over again it was her house the chaplain was calling on. Not only did she wish it, she prayed for it, and she knew that was wrong, really wrong. No, she was sure Prudence wouldn't understand how deeply her hatred ran for Jimmy.

"Anyrode," Dolores said, "Me mam's right in a way. It doesn't just rain on me, does it? Look what happened to your feller and you don't go crying about it all the time. In fact, you hardly ever mention it."

Prudence's cheeks quickly flushed.

"Aye well," she said hurriedly. "We all have our crosses to bear, don't we? Let's forget all about our troubles, shall we? How about a cup of tea and a jam tart before we get started on the braiding, ay?"

"Aye," said Dolores. "But don't forget you can talk to me as much as I can talk to you. Well, almost as much."

"I will. Come on, let's get inside."

Prudence clasped her friend's thin forearm, aiming to steer her into the house, but when her fingers touched the ridged scar on Dolores' wrist, she couldn't help but pause. Both were reminded of the day Dolores had found out she was pregnant for the fourth time and how she couldn't bear the feeling of sinking further and irrecoverably into a mire of poverty and dependency on the man she despised.

"I didn't really mean it," said Dolores, responding to her friend's hesitant touch. "I stopped."

"I know," said Prudence. Then more brightly, "Let's have that cup of tea and I promise to tell you all about our Vivian's new feller and that."

"Oh good," Dolores said with relief. "I could do with a bit of lively gossip. I've been dying to hear about this American. Is he as 'andsome as they say he is?"

"Aye, not bad and –"

From inside the house one of the girls screamed. The women rushed into the parlour as fast as they could, squeezing by the nets hanging from one end of the hallway to the next ready for braiding.

"A bird, Mam! A bird!" cried Sharon.

"It's a lark! Look Lizzie, it's a lark!" yelled Shirley with absolute glee. "Poor thing, it's trapped!"

A panicked brown lark flapped against the window. Little Shane flapped his wings in imitation, accidentally walking into a makeshift easel, and knocking an unfinished painting of the milkman and his horse to the floor. Prudence picked it up, admiring her friend's talent and guessing correctly that Dolores had no money to pay for paint to finish it.

"Mam! Mam! get it!" screamed Sharon, dashing over to hide behind Dolores. "Get it before it gets trapped in me hair."

"It's not a bat, you daft ha'p'oth," said Shirley.

Soot trailed from the hearth across the floor.

"Poor thing must have come down the chimney!" cried Dolores.

"Daft thing more like," said Prudence. "I'll get it out. Stand back or you'll panic it! They can have heart attacks you know."

The bird flapped against the window; it's small beak tapping each time it flew into the glass. Shielding her face with her arm, Prudence tried to open the window under the bird, but the frightened lark flew through the parlour to the hallway where it became caught in one of the trawl nets hung for braiding.

"Oh, you silly thing, don't you know we're trying to 'elp you?" said Prudence. "That net is meant for fish not birds. Where's your broom, Dolores? I'll have to free it some'ow. Open the front door, Shirley!"

Shirley ran to the front door and opened it, calling, "Come on birdie! Come on! This way! It's all right."

Prudence jiggled the net, freeing the bird, but the lark, afraid of the people behind and the little girl in front, found the only way clear: up the stairs.

"Bloody hell," said Prudence. "This is no good. Fetch me a tea towel, Shirley."

"Why did it come in? Why?" cried Sharon, who was still cowering behind her mother, gripping her apron strings tightly.

"It's all right, love," Dolores said. "It's just a bird. It's more frightened of you than you are of it."

Shirley brought her favourite tea towel.

"He'll like this," she said. "It's got birds on."

Prudence smiled, realising that even in an emergency Shirley operated with a clear head. It was a good trait to have.

"Here we go, then," said Prudence.

She and Dolores headed up the stairs where they spotted the lark sitting on the landing banister. Prudence pointed to it and indicated to the girls that they should wait downstairs. The women advanced slowly upwards, but a creaky stair spooked the lark, and it took off again in the direction of Dolores and Jimmy's bedroom. Another creak on the stairs betrayed Shirley who was following them.

"Shirley love, stay there with Sharon," whispered Dolores. "There's too many of us scaring it."

"But Lizzie wants to see!"

"Lizzie can wait an' all. Now, do as your told, and shush!"

The bird flew into the bedroom where it hit hard against the dull glass window, and immediately dropped like a stone to a pillow on the bed below. Its head was bent awkwardly, and it jerked violently on Jimmy's feather pillow for a minute before becoming still.

"Oh no! Do you think it's dead?" whispered Dolores.

"No, it's probably just stunned," said Prudence, who lay the tea towel over it and quickly stood back expecting the bird to start flapping as it tried to escape the towel, but there was no movement.

"Oh no," said Dolores. "I hope we didn't kill it. That's bad luck, isn't it? Poor thing. It were right frightened. Maybe we should have let it be in the parlour. It weren't doing no harm."

"We was only trying to help it," said Prudence. "The thing's just too daft to know it."

Carefully scooping the towel under the bird, Prudence lifted it. The bird felt so fragile, so light, almost weightless in her hands, and still warm. Gently, she pulled back the top of the towel, half-expecting the bird to be gone as in a magician's trick, but it was there, limp and lifeless. It's head rolled back. She cradled it softly, trying to make the bird look whole for the girls' sakes.

"Look at the mess!" exclaimed Dolores at the small dusting of grey ashes covering the white pillow.

"I've just got done with me washing an' all." She shook her head. "Well, at least it's his pillow," she added. "And good thing he's away an' all. He'd go bananas if he saw it. It's bad luck having a bird in the house, you know. I hope it counts for bad luck past. I don't need no more in me future."

"What should we do with it?"

"Put it in the bin, I suppose."

Shirley pushed into the room and eagerly folded back the tea towel.

"It's sleeping," she said.

"Oh love," said Prudence. "I think it might be dead."

"No, it's not. It's just 'tending. If we put it outside, it'll fly away."

"No, love," Dolores said softly. "I think it's gone."

"You don't believe in owt," said Shirley, taking the bird carefully and going outside.

"I just don't want you to be disappointed," Dolores said quietly.

Shirley was about to lay the little bird on the grass next to the hopscotch game when she said, "I know, I'll put it in number three. Three's a lucky number. It's Lizzie's favourite."

"Good idea," said Prudence.

The little girl brought a chipped tea cup of water and placed it in the number three square near the bird. Then, dipping her tiny fingers in the cup, she sprinkled a few drops of water on the lark, saying, "We christen thee Lenny the lark. So wake up little bird. Wake up."

"Where on earth did she get that from?" Prudence whispered.

"Shane's christening, I expect," said Dolores, as much in awe of her daughter as was her friend.

Jealous of the attention her sister was getting, Sharon gingerly touched the bird with the toe of her shoe, but quickly jumped back lest it came back to life and bit her.

"Don't kick it!" cried Shirley.

"I didn't kick it. I nudged it. Mam, didn't I? I nudged it. Tell 'er!"

"Leave it alone, Sharon," said Dolores.

The older girl sat on the path sulkily while Shirley leant over the lark and gently blew across its beak. She stroked its wing with the doll's hand.

"I'm sorry, Shirley, love," said Dolores, squatting next to her daughter. "This is why I didn't want you to get your hopes up. We're going to have to accept that it's passed on."

But the bird's eyes fluttered open, drawing a shriek of delight from Shirley.

"Well, I never!" gasped Prudence.

Shirley clapped her hands as the lark got to its feet and hopped a couple of yards away from them. Then it flew to a branch on a nearby Oak tree where it ruffled and preened its dishevelled feathers, before breaking into a sweet morning song.

"Look Mam, look! He's all right! I knew it."

"Aye, love," said Dolores, giving Shirley a hug. "You did."

The young girl skipped ahead of them, back into the house, swaying her head, and wildly swinging her arms, lifting her knees higher than an angel's marionette.

"It's a good job Dad wasn't here," said Sharon.

At the mention of Jimmy they all paused on the doorstep.

"What do you mean, love?" said Dolores, uneasily, her own smile losing buoyancy.

Jimmy's mean eyes stared back at her, out of Sharon's face. Dolores recognised that look, the look that something horrid was about to be said or done out of jealousy or spite.

"'Cause he would have killed it," Sharon said viciously, using Jimmy's thin lips. "He would have stamped on that bird like he did my rabbit. Like this."

She stamped one foot on the ground then, seemingly possessed, jumped up and down with both feet while Dolores marvelled bitterly at Jimmy's omnipotent ability to spread darkness even when he was far away on a different sea. For a very short while, her mind had been free, exalted as the lark's song. Now, her anger reached for Sharon's bouncing arm, grabbed it, and held it like a vice. "Stop it! Now!"

"But he would have killed it! He would have! Ow! Let go! You're 'urting me!" Sharon cried. "He would. He would 'ave killed it. Just like he did my rabbit! And you wouldn't have done nowt about it! The same as you allus do."

The girl broke into wrenching sobs. Her little legs gave way and she hung limply by her arm, crying terribly. Dolores scooped her up and held on to her tightly with love this time instead of anger.

Prudence didn't know about the rabbit. "I'll put the kettle on," she said, trying to sound inviting. "We've got all those lovely treats to eat, don't we Sharon? I'd better go in and make sure Shirley doesn't scoff the lot."

The baby inside Dolores kicked.

"What was that, Mam?" asked Sharon, sniffing.

"Oh, you felt it too? It was the baby."

"Was it? Can I feel it?"

"I don't know if it'll do it again, but here put your 'and right there, a bit lower, that's right. There! Did you feel it?"

Sharon nodded excitedly. Dolores kissed the tear-stained cheeks.

"Will you hold me forever, Mam?"

"I would, love, but me arms are killing me," said Dolores, breaking the spell.

"Please, Mam, please. Please don't let go."

"I have to," said Dolores, releasing her hold, but the daughter clung on. "If you don't go now all the tarts will be eaten."

"I don't care," said Sharon burying her face in her mother's neck. "Carry me."

"I can't. You're too big."

Dolores reached around to release Sharon's arms from her neck, but her daughter's little hands intensified their grip.

"Come on, love," Dolores said uneasily. "You're too heavy. You don't want to hurt the baby, do you?"

After a moment filled with sniffing and wiping her nose on the back of her hand, the girl slid down her mother's body, and ran into the house. Dolores placed a hand on her womb, relieved to feel the baby moving again. But she thought, If you knew what was good for you, you'd stay in there, warm and safe.

Chapter 12

Vivian was pushing Ted's pram along a path in the direction of anywhere that led away from St. George's Road. After the stuffiness of the house and her thoughts, the fresh, cold wind and drizzle revived her. She felt she could walk for miles, forever, even in the heels she was wearing.

If she had slept at all, she couldn't remember: there had been too much on her mind. On top of which the howling wind and Jake's silence had done nothing to ease her into slumber. It was George who had finally driven her to the point where she felt she might go mad if she didn't leave the house at once.

For the umpteenth time he had told the same story in the same excited tone with even more excited interjections from Winnie: "So there was Jake leaning on our wall, like, smoking, like, and then our Mac came zooming up the road. He were going right fast. And then he slowed down and shouted 'Giddy up!' to Jake and made Jake run to catch up with him, and then Jake ran alongside the bike and mounted it just like a horse, just like in them films! 'Onest, Mam, it were just like at the pictures. And then he shouted, "Wahoo!" and waved his hat at us. You should have seen it, Mam!" "Aye, you should 'ave," confirmed Winnie. "Shouldn't she have, Gloria?" "Aye," said Gloria Baxter, proudly. "Just like at the pictures." "And he kept his cigarette in his mouth the whole time."

Before the story was told again, along with a possible reenactment, Vivian surprised them all by announcing her intention to take Ted for a walk. There was much fuss about the weather and what Ted was wearing, but eventually, she managed to escape.

Beneath her feet, the path was carpeted with damp red and golden leaves, one of which was spiked by the heel of her shoe. As she bent to remove it, Ted grabbed a chestnut tree leaf that blew into the pram. Giggling, he held it up for her to see, telling her what it was, but she wasn't attuned to his way of talking, so she didn't understand. Her mind was on other things, which was one of the reasons she had chosen to take the side streets rather than be seen on Hessle Road where it was as busy as a bee hive on a Saturday afternoon. Nosey bees an' all.

However, Ted wasn't one to be ignored. Vivian looked more carefully at the boy in the pram, trying her best to form the words, 'my son,' in her mind. But what does a mother's love feel like? she asked herself. What am I supposed to do?

"Don't eat that," she said snatching the leaf away from Ted who had no intention of eating the leaf but had only been admiring its colours and crisp sound.

His face crumpled.

"Now, now. There, there. Don't be a cry baby. It's for your own good," she said, believing that's what she should say, believing that if she said what she was supposed to say the love would fall into place.

The pram turned itself onto Pickering Road where the semi-detached lived. Here, the houses were bigger, with big gardens and lawns for the children to play on. Vivian had walked half-way up the road by the time she realised where she was - across the street from the skipper's house. She started; her heart beating. How did I end up here?

There was the Crostaffs' front door. Her stomach twisted tightly when she thought of who might walk out of it: the man she wasn't ready to face. Why had she come this way? A quick search up and down the street proved there was nowhere to hide. Then, as fate provided, there he was, standing in the doorway with car keys in one hand and in the other a large bag containing a blue tartan wool picnic blanket, a flask of tea, egg, tomato and cress sandwiches, and a couple of cold sausages.

"John," Iris Crostaff called from inside the house. "I can't find my handbag. Have you seen it?"

It was too late for Vivian to escape; she had been spotted and immediately recognised despite her white blonde hair.

Crostaff was in shock, afraid to step forward or retreat to the safety of his home. To him, the pram too stood out larger than it actually was. Deep panic set in his bones that now, now was the day his wife would find out when for almost two years he had lived with the torment and guilt of first the affair then the child. Sometimes he almost hated his wife for her not knowing, thinking she was stupid for not guessing and confronting him about it - hating her, then relenting and feeling sorry for her innocence. But all at once he realised how tenuous was the thread between her knowing and not knowing, between her trusting and not trusting. It became imperative to him that she retain that innocence forever, at all costs.

"John, love?" Iris called again from within the house. "Did you hear me? Have you seen my handbag?"

"No, love," he said. "Perhaps it's in the bedroom."

That would buy him some time. Iris was so absent-minded these days anything he told her was almost always forgotten. She lived life in a haze, often talking to herself, telling herself what she would be doing next. Half the time he wasn't sure if she was talking to him or the china cabinet.

"Oh, I don't think I would have taken it upstairs," he heard her mutter loudly. "I never do. I always leave it here on the hallway table. Did you move it?"

"No, love," Crostaff said.

Vivian had noted that there was no look of joy on his face when he saw her, only fear. Hoping to get away before an encounter was unavoidable, or worse, she was ignored all together, she started pushing the pram toward the end of the street. But the pram proved heavy and her arms weak and shaky. Her face was red. She could feel it burning. There was nothing she longed for more in that moment than to be in the arms of her simple, loving Jake whom, she couldn't forget, she had been stupid enough to betray. Never again, she thought. I'll be true to him always, even in my thoughts. I promise! I'll never lie again or keep owt from him. Please just let this moment pass quickly.

"It's all right, I have it," said Iris, her voice getting louder as she approached the front door. "It was in the fridge. I must have put it in there after I paid the milkman. Oh, look who it is!"

She had joined him in the doorway and seen where he was looking.

"Vivian!" she exclaimed, crossing the street. "Vivian Goodwell! Is that you? I heard you were back home - with a husband no less. Oh my goodness, and there I am calling you by your maiden name. How are you? How was London? It was very brave of you to go down there all on your own. Your mother said you were a nurse! You'll have to tell us all about it, won't she John?"

The skipper was putting the picnic items in the boot of their car. Once that was done, then what? He would check the oil. Yes, that's what he would do.

"Mrs. Crostaff," said Vivian. "Fancy seeing you here."

She could have bitten off her tongue with embarrassment. The woman lived there!

"Whatever's the matter, my dear? You look as though you've seen a ghost."

"Nowt. Nothing. I just felt a bit dizzy, that's all."

"A new bride feeling a bit dizzy?" Iris said, raising one eyebrow suggestively.

"No," said Vivian, blushing. "No, it's not that."

"All right, my dear. Mum's the word."

Vivian caught Iris Crostaff taking brief looks at Ted around the hood of the pram. Iris smiled at her. She had kind, brown eyes, and a soft, appealing face.

"So what is your new surname? Mrs. -"

"Huggins."

"Mrs. Huggins," said Iris. "Well, I never. Doesn't that sound super, John? Vivian Huggins."

The skipper nodded, closing the bonnet and fiddling with the oil rag.

"We should get going, love!" he called.

"Nonsense, dear. I'm sure we have a minute to say hello to an old friend."

Iris Crostaff smiled. Vivian smiled. Nothing was said for a few ticks. Then Iris' smile faded, which was a terrible shame because without that smile her features assumed a devastatingly sorrowful expression. In response, the Goodwell grin disappeared from Vivian's face too. It was as if they were playing a game of 'Simon Says', so when Iris' smile returned with more vigour, Vivian couldn't help but reciprocate.

117

Indeed, Iris Crostaff had this affect on most of the people she met. The gift she possessed of making people feel they must be in accord with her served her best in her role as school teacher. The children came to want nothing more than to see her radiant smile for when she wasn't smiling the classroom became morose and the days were long.

"So," Iris said, placing a gloved hand on the side of the pram so she could peer in. "Aren't you going to introduce me to this handsome young man?"

"Oh, yes. Sorry. Where's me manners? This is our Ted. Well, Edward but we call him Ted."

She had never spoken of him in this simple way to anybody.

"Edward. That's a nice name," Iris said straightening. She was smiling again at Vivian. "He's such a bonny lad. You must be very proud."

"Ta," said Vivian averting her gaze from the soft, pained eyes that searched her face.

"So you'll be taking him with you, then?"

"Taking him?"

"To America, I mean. Sorry, love. I don't mean to be nosey but you know how fast news travels around here."

"I do," said Vivian.

But she couldn't bring herself to say that yes they would be taking Ted with them. So the question remained unanswered between them. Iris frowned, not at Vivian necessarily, but inwards towards thoughts of her own.

"We lost our son, you know. He was two."

"I know. I'm sorry. It must have been … I can't imagine -"

"That's right," said Iris. "News does travel, doesn't it? The bad as well as the good. I thought perhaps you were too young at the time to remember."

"No." Vivian shook her head. "I mean I was but …"

She couldn't mention, could she, that while she was in their house, she had peeked into the boy's room which was decorated just as it was the day he died.

Iris called to her husband, "John, love, what on earth are you doing standing over there? Come and look at this bonny boy. Don't worry, he won't bite."

"I really have to get going," said Vivian. "I promised Ted we'd go to the graveyard."

"You must have missed him while you were in London," Iris said, ignoring her plea to leave. "Didn't you?"

Vivian nodded.

"John, I didn't call you over here just to stare at the pram's wheels," said Iris. "Look at the boy. Have you ever seen such a bonny lad? Look at his blonde hair and blue eyes! No, blue is too ordinary a word. I would say azure. Honestly, men and babies. They're just not interested, are they? I'm not sure where they think they'd be without them."

From the corner of her eye, Vivian discreetly watched the skipper lay eyes on his son for the first time. Her throat became dry and her hands tightened on the pram's handle. He quickly looked away to a place where neither she nor Iris could read his expression.

Involuntarily, Vivian's heart flipped when Crostaff's fine blonde hair was lifted by the breeze. She remembered how soft it had been between her fingers. The same fine hair, though a little darker covered his broad chest. Taking a deep breath, she recalled how it had felt when he laid his head on her belly after they made love that last time; the time she was sure Ted was conceived, at his house.

Guiltily, Vivian glanced Iris' way. Where would we be if we could read each other's thoughts? If she could read mine? Yet the skipper's wife did not appear to care for Vivian's thoughts, she looked to be reading her husband's.

"We're going to be late, Iris," he said.

"For what?" Iris asked. "Not for the seaside surely."

"You know what I mean," he said. "I'll be in the car."

"A few minutes ago he was telling me how much he *doesn't* want to go to the seaside when the weather's like this," Iris said. "But I'll take the seaside any way it comes.

Mind you, some days you don't know what it's going to be like till you get there, do you? So, you have to make the best of it. Anyway, I quite like being nice and cosy in the car with my tea and sandwiches, watching the wild weather do her worst, and then if the sky clears up, even better."

The car's engine turned over breaking into a gentle hum. Crostaff tooted the horn. Iris waved at him to be patient.

"Vivian, I would really like it if you would come by for a cup of tea the next time John's away."

"I'm sorry but we're not going to be here for very long."

"Oh," Iris said. "Well, try to make it, won't you, love? I'd like the company. I'm on my own a lot with only the furniture to talk to. Besides, I have something for you. Bye now."

As soon as the car door closed, Vivian recommenced her walk. She wouldn't watch the car pull away. Humiliated by Crostaff's seeming indifference to her and his son, she speedily made her way back home, bypassing the graveyard, which made Ted cry. But too many tears were streaming down her own face for her to notice. She felt young and foolish like she had been playing a child's part in an adult play.

Chapter 13

It was late in the evening and the men weren't home from the football match yet. A pair of knitting needles clicked and an iron pressed while Vivian was curling her hair by the fire; her mind on the events of that afternoon. Gloria and Winnie sipped at watery cocoa, dreaming of milk while the clock chimed the half hour. On the radio, *We'll meet again* began to play.

"Oh, Vera Lynn. This song doesn't half make me think of your dad," sighed Muriel, humming along, but she became melancholy and stopped. "The lads should have been back by now."

"Aye," agreed Prudence. "A couple of hours ago."

"I hope they're all right. I wish he wouldn't go so far on that bike of his. And where's our George? He's late an' all. He's usually home by now. Mind you, there's no rules at that Paddy's 'ouse. I don't know what we're going to do. It's all a shambles. Mac was supposed to give Gloria a ride home an' all. Here we are all waiting for him. Tch!"

"That fish and turnip pie's going to be dried up to nowt by the time they eat it," said Prudence, remarking on the men's teas keeping warm in the oven.

"Aye, and he'll have the cheek to complain about it an' all. Our Mac knows what time tea is. I'm sure it's his fault going into pubs and what not after the game. I hope he didn't get into no more fights. Not with Jake with him. He'll think we're a right bunch of 'ooligans. *But I know we'll meet again some sunny day.* Gloria, love, I think you'd better take off 'ome. Your mam will be right worried."

"It's all right. She knows I'm 'ere. I'll wait."

Muriel smiled inwardly. She had known Gloria all her life. The girl had always been sure of herself, as if she had known the kind of woman she would be. I wish I'd been more aware of all that when I was her age. I had no idea the effect my youth had on others. But then, I never looked like that neither. Muriel felt a pang of envy, then a pang of something else when she pictured Winnie at the same blossomed age as her friend.

"Anyrode, it's past our Winnie's bed time," she said firmly. "Our Prudence'll walk you 'ome."

"But Mam, we never got to play Princesses," whined Winnie.

"Perhaps Gloria is too old to play princesses now."

"No she's not! And it's not fair 'cause I wanted to be Elizabeth. I'm fed-up of being Margaret."

"That's because you're younger than me," said Gloria.

"But Princess Margaret doesn't do nowt."

"Don't worry, love. Princess Margaret's the prettiest," said Vivian. Then whispered, "The younger ones allus are." And winked.

"I heard that," said Prudence. "Honestly! You 'aven't said a word all night. I might have known it wouldn't be till you could find a way to insult me."

"Anyrode, Winnie," said Muriel. "You two girls have had plenty of time to play princesses. What on earth 'ave you been doing upstairs all this time?"

"Talking," said Winnie, blushing a little at what she had told Gloria about the caul and the way Dolly Collins had snatched it, and taunted her before flushing it down the toilet at school.

Gloria had a way of getting Winnie to reveal her innermost secrets, which Winnie often regretted and swore never to do again. But she had been so sullen that Gloria had worked especially hard to coax the story out of her, and when Gloria learned what had happened to the caul she had become so enraged that Winnie had been forced to shush her lest her mother hear them. "What if he drowns? What if he drowns now?" Gloria had cried. "It'll be all her fault! How could she!" Her eyes had narrowed with hatred for Winnie's enemy, and Winnie had been glad to see it. Finally, she had someone on her side.

Muriel misread the blush on Winnie's cheeks. "And I bet I can guess what you was talking about an' all: boys."

There's no stopping it, Muriel thought. They all grow up eventually. And, in a way, there's something so normal about it, it's a relief after the war and that.

"Go on, then," she said. "Five more minutes, then our Prudence'll walk you home."

"Ta Mam!"

122

Examining the nail she had broken while helping to clean out the fryers, Vivian sniffed her hands. They stunk of animal fat, despite a good scrubbing. It was a foul odour she had hoped never to smell on her hands again. She felt the pull of being back in Hull and working in the shop, as though she was struggling to walk through the thick muddy banks of the River Humber, with each step sucking her deeper into the mud until soon she wouldn't have the strength to free her legs at all.

She sighed heavily.

"What is it, love?" said Muriel, unable to keep quiet any longer. "You've been quiet all afternoon. Is there some'at you want to tell us."

"Like what?"

"Well, we was wondering like," said Muriel. "I mean, it doesn't matter now that you're married, does it? You've been off and you didn't touch your tea. Are you, you know?"

"Pregnant?" said Prudence.

"Pregnant! Oh, you think I had to get married, is that it? Bloody nora! You make one mistake and everyone makes sure you keep paying for it for the rest of your life! I hate it here! I can't wait to leave."

Shocked by her outburst, Prudence and Muriel exchanged a puzzled glance while Vivian sat gruffly in a chair.

"No, I'm not *pregnant*. Nor will I ever be again."

"What does that mean?"

"Nowt. Just you won't be getting no more grandchildren out of me. So don't hold your breath."

"Doesn't Jake want children?"

Vivian paused. Jake did want children.

"He'll have to like it or lump it," she said.

"Like he had to with our Ted," said Muriel. "You're asking an awful lot of that poor boy."

Vivian shot her a look. "Maybe I am. Well look what's happened, he's decided to like it after all, hasn't he?"

"So he's definitely staying?" asked Prudence.

"It's none of your business!"

"You're lucky finding a feller like that," said Muriel.

"Me, lucky?"

"Well, there aren't that many fellers left after a war. I remember there were a lot of lasses couldn't find one after the Great War. So you'd better look sharp our Prudence or you'll be an old maid before you know it."

"I'd rather be an old maid than marry someone I don't love just to escape me troubles."

"Are you talking about me?" asked Vivian.

"Not if you love him, I aren't," said Prudence. "But, if the cap fits on your big 'ead then wear it."

"You what!"

"Have you 'eard you two?" said Muriel. "Love? Love is some'at that's built slowly over years, many years. It deepens with age and experience, through ups and downs and everything life throws at you. Aye, there's laughter but there's plenty of tears an' all. You know what they say, for better or worse, for richer and poorer, that's meant to tell you to expect hard times and stick with it. It's not until afterwards that you know it was love. Real love. I know that flighty feeling you're talking about. Don't forget, I was young once," she pointed to her chest. "Real love, lasting love is the bulb that needs an 'arsh winter before it can absorb water and sunshine to grow right and blossom. The harsher the winter the brighter the bloom. Love needs to be tested, or you'll never know whether it was love. I had love with your dad. We built it together, like he built everything in this house, 'aphazardly, but with dedication and care.

"However, you," she said pointing to Prudence, "Did not have that sort of love with that fiancé of yours. You 'adn't even begun. What you're mourning is the life you think was snatched away from you when everything was fresh. The real memories were yet to be made. It's time to stop moping around and make a life for yoursen. Go on, get on with it. Like your sister here."

Sometimes the only way to push Prudence was to compare her to Vivian. Muriel knew a lot would now be said between them but there would be some truth in it, and each would have to go away and lick her wounds in private, with no choice but to ponder what had been said.

"Like our Vivian? You've got to be joking, Mam! She's not getting on with life. She's running away from it, and she's using that poor feller to do it."

"I'm not using him," said Vivian. "Not anymore than he's using me, than anyone uses anyone. Remember, I didn't force him to marry me. He wanted to. He asked me. You're just jealous because I've made my dream come true. That's what I've done. I'm not going to end up a fishwife like you. If you end up a wife to anyone. Besides, I thought you liked playing Mrs. Goody-two-shoes. I remember that look of smug satisfaction on your face when you found out I was pregnant. You thought I was going to be stuck 'ere with all of you, living out me days scrubbing and stinking of lard and fish."

"How dare you!" retorted Prudence. "I supported you! You've no idea how it's been having to clean up your mess and fend off all the looks and comments from everyone. I've defended you."

"I didn't need defending. You did it for yoursen, for your own pride."

"What are you talking about?"

"You know full well what I mean. All these things you do pretending to help others is nothing other than to keep yoursen feeling needed. Helping Mam all the time when she can help hersen. Looking after our Winnie and George, who are old enough to take care of themselves -"

"Don't forget Ted," said Prudence. "Again."

"How could I forget? You want me to be so bloody grateful to you all the time. You want everyone to be grateful to you all the time. Well, no one asked you to help them. You're just afraid not to be needed, so you make yoursen needed. You want us all to think we couldn't get by without you. But we can. We can all get along without you very well if you'd just give us a chance. But no, you stick around suffocating us."

Vivian's voice had risen to a high pitch.

"How dare you?" Prudence said seething.

"How dare I? I dare because you've been looking down from your high horse at me for all these years and it's time someone shot that horse out from under you. If you were out living a proper life you'd be too busy to be tut, tut, tutting at me all the time."

"I don't do that!"

"Yes you do. You do! And now look, you're going to go and make yoursen even more indispensable with the fish shop. Keep busy living other people's lives for them and you'll never have to dream one of your own!"

"That's enough," said Muriel.

"Mam, why do you let her go on at me," said Prudence.

"Why do you?" asked Muriel.

The women fell silent although their passion filled the air. Then Prudence said quietly, "But I like it 'ere, in Hull. I like being in the fish shop and seeing the people I know every day. I've got nowt to be ashamed of, so I've no need to run away. I can look them in the eye. I'm not afraid that they know everything about me."

"That's because you don't see what I see in their eyes when they look at me," said Vivian. "When you and Mam look at me."

Muriel and Prudence glanced at each other, not without a little shame. Prudence longed for some fresh air. The argument with Vivian had left her drained, and a little sad.

"I suppose I'd better walk Gloria home," she announced. "Then I'll see about our George on the way back."

"Oh, aye, love, ta. I'd forgotten about them," Muriel said briskly. "No point in waiting for the lads any longer. I 'ope they're all right."

"I'm sure they are, Mam. They've probably forgotten about us and are in the pub having a last pint. I'll walk by there and see if our Mac's bike is parked in front."

"Aye love. You're probably right."

"I hope they didn't get in an accident," Vivian said.

"Vivian, shush," said Prudence.

Muriel thought, I've got the one daughter that tells me not to worry because everything will be all right, and I've got the other one what scares me half to death. Which one should I believe, I wonder.

Chapter 14

After dropping off a very chatty Gloria Baxter at her home, Prudence enjoyed the silence of the night as she made her way to Paddy Crumblewell's house to fetch George. That evening, there was a strong wind that gave resistance when she walked, blowing away a lot of the cobwebs on her soul. Autumn was her favourite season. She loved the blustery weather and drawing in of the nights.

The streets were very dark and cold and silent as she walked. She heard only her footsteps, but she didn't mind that, knowing there was a warm hearth and company waiting for her at home. As she approached the pub, she could see that Mac's bike was not there. He's out late drinking somewhere else, that's all, she thought.

Lights from the pub shone on the path in front of her. Voices, some shouts and laughter, breathed out through an open window, and drifted through the night air wrapped in circles of cigarette smoke. The pub seemed so inviting. She wished she could go in. Well, why shouldn't she? She could just pop in and say she was looking for her brother. But the men would look at her and see only that she was a woman, not a woman to be attracted to or to dance with, but a woman nuisance encroaching upon their man-time. They would feel annoyed and uncomfortable. They would wish her to leave.

Well, bugger them, she thought. Who cares what they think. They'll never have the guts to say owt. Not to me. All I'm going to do, is go in and ask about our Mac. It's possible I just missed him.

So she opened the door and stepped inside. The whole place went quiet, almost guiltily, as if she had caught the men in the throes of some surreptitious endeavour. The pub wasn't as welcoming as it was inviting, and she wished she hadn't gone in. She had known Mac wouldn't be there. It was so unlike her to stir the pot. What I am trying to prove? Well, now look I've got mesen in a right pickle. I can hardly turn tail and leave or they'll think I'm daft.

"Why it's Prudence Goodwell!" exclaimed Stalworth.

"Hiya, Mr. Stalworth," she said, smiling gratefully.

Stalworth looked around at the men, all still frozen in place like statues - some with pint glasses less than an inch from their mouths, as if Medusa had walked in.

"I was looking for me brother," Prudence explained.

Relieved, the pub patrons returned to their drinking. It wasn't bad news, then, that had caused a woman to breech their quarters.

"Sorry, love, but he isn't here," said Mary.

"I'll handle this, Mary," Stalworth said.

"Oo, pardon me for breathing."

"Didn't he go to the match in Leeds?"

"Aye, Mr. Stalworth, but he's late back so I thought maybe he'd be in here 'aving a quick pint."

"No, we haven't seen him. But you never know, he might stop in afore last orders."

"He probably couldn't find his way home in the dark," said Mary. "That happened to me eldest. He's probably sleeping it off in a field somewhere."

"Don't you have some work to do?" said Stalworth. "You could start by polishing some glasses."

"Aye, you should polish them knockers while you're at it," said one of the patrons. "They're looking a bit rusty."

Some of the customers laughed.

Said another, "Let me give you an 'and, Mary. I bet I could get 'em gleaming in no time!"

More laughter.

"Oh, piss off," said Mary.

"Now, now gentleman. There's a lady present. Prudence, why don't you come and sit down on this stool right here and have a drink?" suggested Stalworth. "It's on me."

A murmur of disapproval wove through the pub.

"No, ta," she said, sitting down on the stool anyway. "I'm on me way to pick up our George, from your house actually," she said to Mary.

"What? At this hour?" said Mary. "They'll be in bed."

"Aye, well, George 'asn't come home yet. So he must still be there."

"That's my useless 'usband for you," said Mary. "Keeping the bairns up at all hours. All right, all right, I'm coming. 'Nother pint of bitter, is it?"

With Mary safely down at the other end of the bar, Stalworth smiled easily at Prudence.

"Listen, love, are you sure you don't want that drink? A glass of sherry perhaps to ward off the chill?"

"Ta, Mr. Stalworth, but I'm positive. I've got to go fetch our George. Me mam's got enough to worry about

129

without me coming 'ome late and tipsy with the rest of them."

"Another time, then."

"All right," she said, getting up to leave.

Stalworth came out from behind the bar.

"If you don't mind, I'll walk you to the door. Mary, take over for us. I'll be back in a jiffy."

Once outside, Prudence was about to thank him and take her leave when he said, "Would you mind if I walked you all the way, Miss Goodwell? It's a dark night and a respectable young lady such as yourself shouldn't be wandering around on her own."

"That's very kind of you, Mr. Stalworth, but I'll be all right, and, besides, it's a few streets over."

Stalworth cleared his throat. "I don't mind at all. I could use the exercise and fresh air. And it would make me feel better," he said. "To know that you'd got 'ome safely."

"What about the pub?"

"Oh, it pretty much runs itself."

They were already walking together on their way to the Crumblewell house, as if his words had taken hold of her arm and guided her gently along without her realizing it. He asked how she was and so she told him about the fish shop re-opening. He seemed very interested to hear everything she had to say about it. It was a while since she had shared a conversation with anyone other than her family or Dolores who was always complaining, and not really listening anymore. For someone to be interested in her thoughts and ideas felt refreshing, and a man at that.

They talked about the upcoming pantomime rehearsals and how much fun it would be for everyone to go to the theatre again. It was dark on the streets but the sense Stalworth had of her walking next to him was warm and wonderful. Occasionally, their elbows tapped into each other, and they each apologised at the same time, then laughed both feeling self-conscious. He had always sensed an intelligence about her that set her apart, and he satisfied this theory by talking about books and current events, all the while imagining that he would be extending the conversation beyond the evening.

The Crumblewell house was in darkness, as were most of the houses on the street. Apparently, everyone was asleep.

"We must have missed him," said Prudence. "I came all this way for nowt."

"Really for nowt? You don't mind too much, do you?" said Stalworth.

"No, Derek," she said, flushing in the darkness. He had asked her to use his first name and she had reciprocated in kind. "But don't tell our George that or I can't be mad at him. I'm gearing up for a right good telling off."

Stalworth chuckled.

Just then, an upstairs window slid open noisily. They looked up to see a small head pop out and a familiar voice call, "Prudence! Prudence, is that you?"

"George? What are you doing up there, and why are all the lights off?"

"He wouldn't let me come 'ome."

"Who wouldn't?"

"Paddy's dad. I kept trying to leave but he told me to go to bed with t'rest of them."

"Why would he do that?"

"I don't know. But he got really angry about it and threatened me with his slipper. So I did what I was told."

"Why don't you come down now and I'll talk to him if there's any bother?"

She was glad to have Derek by her side.

"I can't get out, the door's locked."

A light flicked on in the bedroom and a gruff voice shouted, "How many fucking times do I have to tell you to get to sleep! I'm going to give you a bloody good hiding in a minute! Where's me fucking slippers?"

"Mr. Crumblewell!" Prudence called. "Mr. Crumble-well!"

"What the fuck?" he said, coming to the same window that George was leaning out of. "What the hell do you want at this hour?"

"I've come to pick up our George."

"Who?"

"George. George Goodwell, me brother. The lad standing next to you."

Crumblewell looked at George in surprise. Grabbing one of the boy's ears, he held him up on his tiptoes. "You mean this one is yours?"

"Ow! Me ear!"

"Aye."

"Oh shite." Crumblewell laughed, embarrassed. "So that's why he kept trying to leave. Sorry, love, I thought he were one of mine. It's hard to keep track sometimes. All right, lad. Come on downstairs. Why didn't you tell me?"

"I did!" protested George as the window shut.

"Poor George," Prudence said with a chuckle.

"I've never heard owt like it," said Stalworth. "Mind you, they've got quite a litter in there."

"Aye, twelve or thirteen I think."

"No wonder he can't remember which ones are his or not."

"I don't think they all are, are they? Oh, I shouldn't have said that," she said, clapping her hand over her mouth.

Stalworth laughed. "That's all right. Mary does have a bit of a reputation, doesn't she? All her own doing, mind." He paused. "Never with me, though, mind. Never with me."

Prudence blushed, admitting to herself that she was re-lieved to hear it.

"No, definitely not with me," he was saying. "I don't believe in fraternising with the staff. By heck, thirteen's a bit much, isn't it?

"Unlucky for some," said Prudence.

"Aye. Like I said, thirteen's too many. I reckon three's enough. One each and one for the world. What do you think?"

The question was unsettling. Prudence wasn't really sure what she was being asked or why she was being asked it, but anyway, she wasn't committing to anything when she said, "Yes. I think three children is the right amount."

Drawing himself up with pleasure, Stalworth felt he was making headway in the matter of Prudence Goodwell whom he had long since admired from afar for her quiet seriousness and sense of duty. He thanked God he had jumped on the exceedingly rare opportunity to be alone with her.

The constant furrow in her brow amused him; she looked as though everything around her was a puzzle that she was in the process of unravelling. He longed to hold her hand, but since the boy had joined them, no more could be said on the matter of the future, or, more precisely, their future.

Revelling in his new found freedom, the boy ran off into the darkness, dribbling an imaginary football. "He shoots! He scores! And the crowd goes wild! Yay! Georgie Goodwell! There's only one Georgie Goodwell!"

A single headlamp and the sound of a motorbike. Mac and Jake were home too, then, and the rest of the evening would be filled with the telling of their adventures. Prudence smiled, feeling a sense of well-being. Everything was in its rightful place.

Chapter 15

A farewell party for the newlyweds was quickly organised. On the day, the smell of baked pastry filled the air. Canned-salmon sandwiches were stacked neatly under a tea towel, as was a bowl of mashed potato salad made with grated carrot and onion all grown on the family's allotment. An apple pie, baked by Gloria, cooled invitingly on the parlour table. There were devilled eggs and pickled vegetables; cauliflower and carrots, a surfeit from Mac's garden the year before.

It wasn't quite the spread Muriel would have liked to put on but she knew people would be expecting less. That can of salmon had remained sealed all through the depression and the war. Goodness knows how old it was, but Muriel thought the party was a fitting time to eat it.

Of course, Muriel and Prudence had done most of the work while Vivian kept herself busy looking busy, which had exhausted her as much as actual work might have. Thankfully, Jake had pitched in to help. Bless him, thought Muriel.

"How's your lip, love?" she asked.

Gingerly, Jake touched his swollen lower lip, a consequence of the fight he was in with Mac after the football match.

"Better. I think."

"I'd love to know how our Mac comes away without a scratch on him. All because someone called his dog a cod-headed rat. Honestly, that dog'll be the death of him."

"Bugger," whispered George to the Mynah bird while tapping its cage.

Muriel spun around.

"Our George I hope you're not trying to teach Houdini to swear again, are you?"

"It'd be nice if he said some'at," moaned George. "Paddy's canary sings all the time."

"Aye well," she said, "let's hope Houdini's first word in more than a decade is some'at a bit more profound than 'bugger'." George giggled. "I'm not joking. And stop banging his cage."

"I weren't banging, I were tapping. I were just trying to get his attention."

"Don't be so daft," she said, slapping George across the top of his head.

"Ow! Why did you do that?"

"I stand corrected," said Muriel. "It does make you talk."

"But I didn't hit his 'ead," George complained, touching the side of his head and finding it floured.

"You deserved it. Now go and get ready."

The lad slouched up the stairs, passing Winnie who had borrowed one of Vivian's dresses for the party. Her hair was still short and boyish but it had been fashioned into an actual hairstyle by a local hairdresser, and, all in all, Winnie felt quite grown up and sophisticated. The dress nipped in at the waist and had seams in the bust line, drawing the eye to her developing womanhood while Gloria, who was behind her, was every inch a fully fledged woman in a dress of her mother's.

Angry at being slapped across the head, George managed to nudge Winnie as he passed by her.

"Mam! Our George pushed me!" Winnie yelled, hurrying into the parlour.

"I've already told you two. I don't want to hear it. Not today of all days," said Muriel. "We've too much to do."

"But Mam!"

Muriel swiftly tapped Winnie across the top of the head.

"Ow! Why did you do that?"

"Because it makes me feel better" said Muriel. "It's up to you whether you give me cause or not."

"Just do as Mam says," said Vivian as she applied red lipstick in front of the parlour mirror.

135

Winnie's cheeks burned. With arms folded she slumped into a chair by the fire. It wasn't fair that her mother had hit her. Not when she was dressed up for the party and certainly not in front of Gloria. Only a moment ago, she had felt so grown up. Well, she wasn't going to let them get to her. Winnie sat up straight, put her knees together and clasped her hands delicately on her lap, oblivious that she also had flour in her hair from Muriel's hand.

"There," said Vivian turning from the mirror.

Her make-up was perfect, as always. Winnie pouted. She wasn't allowed to wear make-up until she was sixteen, which, to her, was ages away.

"Bit bright for daytime, isn't it?" Muriel commented.

Vivian pressed her red lips together.

"Jake likes it," she said. Or, he used to.

With most of the work now done, Jake had gone to sit by the window and watch the rain slide down the glass. It had rained almost non-stop since they had arrived. He was ready for some sunshine, for a hot day, for a cloudless sky. He hadn't seen a day over seventy degrees for months. All the greyness was depressing to him. What he wouldn't give to see a big blue sky stretching as far as the eye could see.

"Don't you, Jake? You like it when I wear this red."

"Maybe it is a bit bright," he remarked.

Her smile faded.

"You know, it's a shame you don't like it anymore," she said applying a defiant second coat, then blotting her lips on a piece of newspaper. "'Cause I've got loads left."

Separating her eyelashes with the tip of a finger, she said "I reckon it's true what you've allus said, Mam."

"Oh aye, and what's that?" asked Muriel.

"Whatever they like about you in the beginning, is what turns them off in the end. Jake used to love the way I look, but since we got married he complains that it takes me too long to get ready. And now, apparently, I'm too bright. But it's the same colour I was wearing when we met. What do you want me to do, start going around looking like our Prudence with no make-up at all and me hair looking drab."

"Ta very much," said Prudence, entering the parlour. "The rest of me might not be up to much, but me ears work just fine."

"Well, don't you look nice," said Muriel, remarking on Prudence's effort for the party.

Dressed in a flattering flowered frock, Prudence had styled her hair into a side part with quite glamorous waves. Nudging Vivian aside, she used the mirror to position a hair grip.

Vivian laughed. "Aren't those Great Aunt Lily's clothes?"

Prudence flushed.

"Aye," said Muriel. "I said she could wear them. They're of no use to our Lily where she's gone. And stop being so nasty. Like new they are. Aunt Lily were alive when she wore them. And she had style."

"I'm not being nasty. I were just asking."

Muriel sighed and shook her head.

"Aye, the words. If we just looked at the words you said, it's allus just asking but we was also privy to your laugh and your tone and the way you was standing all cocky like."

"The way I were standing! I'm nasty because of the way I were standing!"

"Aye, with your nose in the air and one hand on your hip, and your other hand stroking that new fur stole. Where did you get that from anyway? And that new red coat you've been parading around in like a bloody peacock?"

"Mam, it's all right," said Prudence.

"No," said Muriel. "It's not all right. I want to know. I want to know where she got that stuff from while the rest of us have been rummaging through jumble sales and patching our old clothes. Did you buy it for her Jake? I didn't think so. So, you're not going to answer us, then, our Vivian?"

"It's nobody's business but mine," said Vivian, who couldn't understand why they cared so much. "I went without so I could have this. Clothes last longer than a slice of bread."

"And to think I saved all that money for you." said Muriel. "And you didn't send us a penny to help with Ted but you managed to get yoursen what was important to you, by hook or by crook, didn't you?"

"All what money?" asked Prudence.

Oh dear, so the time had come. Muriel's eyes went from face to face, each one waiting for her to explain the comment. Even Winnie had come out of her sophisticated trance to pay attention. Muriel sighed, pulling on her bottom lip. Then she went into the pantry, climbed the stool, and reached along the top shelf until her hand found the old toffee tin.

"This money," she said, prising open the lid and placing the box on the parlour table for all to see.

The box was full of pale blue envelopes, all marked, 'For Edward'. Two of the envelopes had been opened.

"After the first two came I knew what was in them so I didn't bother opening the rest," Muriel explained.

Vivian grabbed one of the open envelopes and looked inside.

"It's money!" she exclaimed. "Five pounds!"

She looked inside the other opened envelope. "And the same in here!"

"Aye. Reckon they all contain the same thing. Those envelopes came through our letterbox once a month, as regular as clockwork but I never saw who delivered them. And, honestly, I thought it best not to."

"But it must have been...," but Vivian's voice trailed off.

She couldn't say *his* name in front of Jake.

"Mam, we could 'ave used that money," said Prudence.

"It wasn't ours to spend," said Muriel.

"I mean we could have used it for Ted. For his clothes, and the doctor."

"If we'd needed it, really needed it," said Muriel, pausing. "But we didn't, not really. So I saved it. For you," she said to Vivian. "For when you came back. I thought you'd need it for you and Ted to start your lives together."

"How many envelopes are in there?" exclaimed Vivian, leafing through the tin. "Maybe there's more in some of them."

"Maybe there's less," said Prudence, looking into the tin.

Vivian said, "Trust you to allus think of the worst."

"Trust you to be greedy and not happy or grateful with what you've got but allus wanting more," said Prudence.

"You don't understand," said Vivian. "I –"

But the right words failed her. They didn't understand that here was proof she hadn't been totally cast aside by Crostaff. The envelopes proved he did care what happened to her, and his son, their son. The money also made her feel a little independent, as if she had a say in her own future.

"Now, now," said Muriel. "Don't you girls start. I didn't mean to bring it up now. I knew it would cause problems. Money allus does. Anyrode, it'll 'elp you both out when you start your new life in America. But for now let's put it away and sort it out later, after the party."

"OK, Mam," said Prudence, reaching for the tin.

But Vivian pulled it away, smiling. "I think I'll take it upstairs, to my room," she said.

The doorbell rang, announcing the arrival of Dolores and her children. Prudence let them in. Sharon placed a small homemade pie on the parlour table.

"Pigeon?" asked Prudence.

"No," Dolores laughed. "Rhubarb."

"Well, thanks, love," said Prudence. "We've enough to feed Harry Tate's Navy. Wasn't that nice of Dolores, Mam?"

"Aye. Ta," said Muriel, though her lips were pursed.

Prudence introduced Dolores to Jake.

"And Dolores you know Gloria Baxter," she said.

"Aye, I do," Dolores said with a nod and a smile. "Though I wouldn't have recognised you. I don't think I've seen you since the war began. You've certainly changed quite a bit."

"That's what everyone tells me."

Thanks to Winnie's loose lips, Gloria knew all about Dolores' history with Mac, and so she had considered Dolores a rival for his affections. She needn't have worried though, she thought. There's no competition from that shilling dinner. She looks twenty year older than me, not ten.

She said, "You've changed a lot, too, Mrs. Alford."

And Muriel smiled, thinking, I do like this lass. I do.

"This is Lizzie," Shirley held up her doll to Jake. She wanted to hear his voice, and she wasn't disappointed.

"Hi, Lizzie."

"She likes you."

"Oh, gee, well, tell her I like her too."

"Why don't you girls go outdoors and play," suggested Muriel. "The rain's let up a bit and it'll be good for you to run around and get some fresh air. Go on. You an' all, our George."

The sounds of the children playing *Oranges and Lemons* drifted into the parlour. Dolores pulled her cardigan close.

"Pity our Mac's away, missing the party," remarked Vivian. "I can't believe I won't see him again before we leave."

"Aye, fishermen miss a lot, don't they? Births, weddings, funerals, the lot. But then who doesn't mind missing a funeral? I wonder if he'll miss mine."

"That's a bit morbid, Mam," said Prudence.

"I'm only being practical. Just remember, I want to be cremated and a bit of me scattered at sea to be with your father. Mac can do that part, can't he?"

"All right, Mam. We know," said Prudence. "But let's not dwell on such things today, eh?"

"Hark at you, wanting to stay on the bright side. Well, I just want to make sure. It has to be talked about, you know."

Only half paying attention to the conversation, Jake watched as Ted was being impatiently dressed by Vivian. She was pulling his little arms roughly through the sleeves of a red cardigan, then buttoning it uncomfortably to the top of his scrawny neck, but the toddler seemed to understand her limitations and didn't complain or hope she could do any better.

That kid's smarter than me, thought Jake.

Chapter 16

By late afternoon there were about forty friends and neighbours bustling inside one nine nine St. George's Road. The front room was full of chatter and clinking tea cups and saucers, and a fire roared in the hearth.

Busybody Elsie Waggin greeted Muriel with a warm smile.

"I brought some of me pies. Mind you, it looks like everyone brought something. We're all starved for some company and good cheer. I've haven't seen some of these folks since the war started. I can't wait to catch up. I'm so glad you decided to have a shin-dig for your Vivian. Bring us all together, like." She nudged Muriel. "I must say that son-in-law of yours is rather 'andsome, isn't he?" she whispered. "Even with a cut lip. A real American in our midst! Fancy!"

"Aye, fancy," said Muriel who didn't have the energy to listen to Elsie Waggin.

Muriel was terribly exhausted after the week's comings and goings. Her legs felt shaky and weak from holding up an aching back all day. She needed a sit-down, and the vacant chair by the fire seemed to be beckoning her. But she hesitated, overwhelmed by the awful feeling she might not make the short distance to the chair. She reached out to the parlour table for support.

"Hiya Vivian!" Elsie was saying. "None of us have seen you since you got back. What was it like in London? Oh and don't forget we want to 'ear all about your new life in America an' all. Never a dull moment for you, is there?"

Vivian been dreading the inevitable interrogation by Elsie Waggin; a woman who seemed to suspect everybody of something or other whether there was anything to hide or not.

"Excuse me, Mrs. Waggin, but I need to - Tea anyone?" Vivian called, though she had no intention of making any.

"That sounded like last orders," remarked Derek Stalworth, striding into the parlour, carrying a large bouquet of roses and fern wrapped in yesterday's newspaper. "I'll take a cuppa. Here, Prudence, I brought some flowers for your Mam."

"Oh, she'll like those," said Prudence, not without a little disappointment.

"Oh, and these are for you," he said, producing another bouquet from behind his back.

A warm flush radiated through Prudence.

"Oo ta. Thanks for coming," she said.

He was dressed up, Prudence noted, clean shaven and wearing aftershave.

"Mam, look who's here."

"Now then, Mrs. Goodwell," Derek said. "These are for you."

"Thank you very much indeed, Mr. Stalworth," said Muriel, taking the flowers. "That's very thoughtful of you."

"My pleasure. I say, are you alright? You look a bit pale."

"Mam?" Prudence asked.

"I'm just a bit hot, that's all. It's right stuffy in here. You go on and get some'at to eat. I'll be all right. I just need to take off me cardy."

Muriel was afraid to let go of the table. Her legs still felt a bit wobbly, and her forehead was beaded with perspiration. Out of nowhere, a hot cup of tea was thrust at Muriel so she had to let go of the table to take it.

"I put a drop of brandy in it for you," Elsie said. "You look like you could use it."

"Hm," muttered Muriel, then, "Oh, ta," when a plate of sandwiches came at her. She had to shove the bouquet under one arm to take the plate.

"Prize ham," said Theresa Casing, the butcher's wife, opening her little piggy eyes as far as they would go. "And made with puh-lenty of butter."

"Ta," muttered Muriel. Plenty of butter was the last thing she wanted to think about. The table swam in front of her. The air was stifling in the parlour with the fire going and all the hot bodies closing in around her. For a brief moment she felt disconnected from the room; all the voices faded into the background for a moment before coming back again louder.

Jake came to her side.

"Let me take those, Muriel," he said, taking the cup and flowers.

"Ta, love. You're a saviour. I'm sweating in this cardy."

The hive of ladies emitted a buzz of approval for Jake's thoughtfulness. Putting one hand to her chest, Elsie fanned herself with the other.

143

"Oo I do love the way you talk Jake! Sounds so polite. I don't know how you can stand it, Muriel."

I'm wondering how I can stand at all, thought Muriel, her hand shaking as she took her tea and sandwich plate from Jake.

Some tea spilled in the saucer.

"Oh dear," she said, "I think I need to sit down."

"Are you sure you're feeling all right, Mrs. Goodwell" Stalworth asked again.

"Aye, love, just a bit tired. I'll be all right after a sit down. Would one of you two fine gentlemen give us an 'and?"

"Aye, love."

Not sure how much of a hand she needed, Stalworth gently cupped her elbow to guide her to the chair, but when she took the first step her legs gave way. The landlord caught her around the waist and managed to break her fall, but the good china slipped from her hands and broke, spilling tea and the ham sandwiches on the floor. A collective gasp arose from the room.

"Mam!" cried Prudence.

"Muriel!"

Winnie started to choke on the flaky pastry from a sausage roll. She waved her hands in front of her face while her eyes watered and her face turned scarlet. It was Mrs. Casing who came to her aid, slapping Winnie hard on the back between the shoulder blades, until the piece of chewed roll shot out of the girl's mouth and into the trifle, where it sank slowly into the cream.

"Let that be a lesson," said the butcher's wife.

"What happened, Mam?" cried Prudence. "Are you all right?"

Muriel's forehead was hot and clammy to her touch.

"Mam! Can you hear me? Mam?"

All the ladies had gathered around and were asking Muriel if she was all right, could they get her anything, and what had happened.

"I don't know what happened," breathed Muriel slowly. "But I do know I need some air."

She sounded scared, and she was. She was in shock, badly shaken from the weakness that had overwhelmed her just before she fell. If she tried standing, she was afraid the same thing might happen again.

"Everyone stand back a bit, and give me mam some air."

The guests complied, then with some effort, Prudence and Jake, with help from Derek Stalworth, lifted Muriel from the floor and sat her on the chair.

"What happened? Did you faint?" said Prudence. "It is hot in here. Vivian open the door. Let some fresh air in here."

"Mam?" asked Vivian.

"Go on," said Prudence. "Open the door."

"It's me back. Me legs went weak," Muriel said, wincing as she tried to sit up. "I feel so tired." Then, managing a weak smile, she said, "Sorry. I didn't mean to cause such a fuss."

"A fuss? Don't be so daft, Mam," said Prudence.

Prudence looked around at the shocked faces, then back at her mother for whom she felt not only the pain of her fall but the embarrassment of it occurring in front of all their neighbours and friends. Muriel Goodwell, who was always so strong, vital and dignified in the community, had fallen with her dress riding up showing the tops of her stockings and threadbare suspender belt. This is not how she would want to be remembered.

"I'll get shut of everyone," Prudence whispered.

Muriel nodded. "Aye. It's best."

"Everybody out," Stalworth ordered, as if he was shooing out the last of his customers at closing time. "Come on, they don't need our help."

Quietly, respectfully, the guests grabbed their hats and coats and made their way, shepherded by Derek Stalworth, down the hallway and out through the front door. Prudence threw the landlord a grateful smile, surprised at how well he fit into the house, and how calmly he handled the situation.

Muriel was breathing with difficulty.

"Oh Mam," said Prudence. "What happened?"

"I don't know. You know I've 'ad this pain in me back. It's got so I can't stand it anymore."

"It's that bad?"

"Aye, love. I'm afraid to say it is."

"Oh, Mam. I wished you'd said some'at."

"I didn't want a fuss."

Prudence closed her eyes for a moment to quell the irritation she felt not only with her mother for not telling them how bad the pain was but also at herself for not noticing.

"Mam, I'm sorry I pushed you into getting the chippy up and running. I should have -"

"Pushed me?" said Muriel. "You've got an 'igh opinion of yoursen, 'aven't you? Opening the shop again were my decision, and don't you forget it. Pushed me indeed. I wanted to see it done before I – I mean we need the money."

"Aye, Mam," said Prudence. "But from now on, you'll 'ave to let me do *all* the work. When I think of all the cleaning you've been doing in there." Clasping her mother's hands, she asked, "What did you mean? Before you what?"

"I don't know," Muriel replied weakly. "I really don't. It just came out."

Their eyes locked. Prudence shook her head, knowing but not knowing, feeling tears come to her eyes.

"What should we do, Vivian?" she cried. "What should we do?"

"How would I know?"

"'Cause you're the bloody nurse. What should we do?"

"I'll go fetch the doctor."

"God you're a great help," said Prudence. "Is that all they taught you? I could have worked that one out for mesen. Winnie, go fetch Doctor McKenzie."

"But -" said Winnie.

"Don't you dare 'but' me," Prudence said. "Just do as you're told for once without the need for questions or explanations. Please."

"Come here a minute, love," said Muriel.

"Mam?" said Winnie.

"It's all right. Come here."

She hugged Winnie tightly.

"Now go on. Fetch the doctor."

"I'd best be going too," said Dolores. "I'll walk with you, Winnie."

"Take some food with you, Dolores," said Prudence. "There's too much for us to eat in a month of Sundays. It'll only go to waste."

"Ta. I will."

"I wouldn't mind a bit of that brandy now," said Muriel.

"I'll get it," said Elsie who, like an errant sheep, had somehow managed to escape Stalworth's shepherding arms when he had corralled the others.

"Thanks, Elsie, but I think we can manage. You've been ever so kind."

"Oh, I don't mind," bleated Elsie Waggin as she poured the last of the brandy into two tall glasses. "I could use one mesen."

Glasses in hand she manoeuvred past Stalworth with her double-chinned head leaning to one side as if she was half-expecting to be caught by the crook of his staff and thus steered away home. Handing one of the glasses to Muriel she said, "Cheers," and threw back her own tot.

"Well, I'd better be off then," she said as if her absence would be regretted. She was eager to get on the Road and share the day's events with whomever's path she crossed. "Sorry I can't stay longer to help but I have to get home.

There's a mountain of ironing to do. I'll come and get me plates tomorrow, Prudence. See 'ow your mother's doing."

"You don't have to," Prudence said hastily. "Our Winnie can drop them off since there's others to take back an' all."

"It's no bother," said Elsie Waggin.

"The cheek of that woman drinking the last of our brandy," Vivian commented after Elsie Waggin left.

"Not to worry," said Stalworth with a wink and the subsequent production of a full bottle of brandy from the pocket of his rain coat.

"I wondered what that thing was sticking in me leg when you 'elped me up," said Muriel.

"Mam!"

"Well I did."

Derek chuckled as he set the bottle on the table.

"I'll leave it here for you ladies to take care of, then," he said. "And, if you're no longer in need of my services, I'll be off too. Not long till opening time. No, no, I'll see mesen out."

"Hold on, Sir, if it's okay, I'll come with you," said Jake. "I'd like to get some fresh air. If that's OK?" He turned to Muriel and Prudence.

"Actually, Jake I think you should stay –" Vivian began.

"Course, it's all right, son," said Muriel who preferred not to have the men around when the doctor came. "Only, bring some of that fresh air back with you, will you love?"

Jake smiled, nodded, and then with a respectful tip of his Stetson he left with Stalworth.

The brandy brought some colour to Muriel's cheeks. Prudence pressed the back of her hand to Muriel's forehead.

"I feel a bit better," said Muriel.

"Do you think you have the strength to make it upstairs?"

"No. Don't put me up there," Muriel said with a shiver. "Make me a bed down here. I don't want to be shut in on me own. It's warmer down here. Just bring in the settee from the front room, and some sheets and an eider down and I'll be all right. We can put it along that wall by the fire."

By the time they set up the bed for Muriel, Dr. McKenzie had arrived. His expression was grave, and Muriel could sense there was something he had been withholding from her. Keeping her eyes fixed on him as he retrieved a stethoscope and other equipment from his bag, she gave instructions to the others:

"Put on a pot of tea, Vivian. You younger kids go upstairs for a bit. No, I won't hear any arguing about it. And take Ted with you. Aye, all right, take a couple of jam tarts with you. This is becoming an 'abit. And no listening at the top of the stairs neither!"

"What's this all about, Doctor?" Prudence asked.

The doctor held up a finger to motion for her to wait. He was listening to Muriel's breathing. Then he asked Muriel to breathe while he pressed on her stomach, which she found very uncomfortable. After completing the general examination of his patient, he put away his equipment. His expression was grave.

"Come on, Doctor," said Muriel. "Don't keep it from us any longer. I know you had your reasons for not telling me the crux of the matter, but if you think I didn't know some'at serious was up – well, all I can say is that while a woman might not know the scientific name of things, she knows her own body, better than any doctor."

Doctor McKenzie glanced at Prudence, then Vivian. They were so innocent of the knowledge that he alone held.

"Oh I don't mind them knowing when I know," said Muriel. "They're me daughters."

"Mam, I don't understand," said Prudence, her heart becoming heavy. "Doctor McKenzie, what's me mam talking about?"

The doctor's kind blue eyes, set under heavy white brows, drifted from one to the other as he stroked his white beard. Their faces were expectant of bad news, but they would change to dismay when their worst fears were soon realised. There was nothing he could do to prevent their knowing any longer. At least they hadn't had to live with the horror for years; it would only be for a matter of months.

"Aye," he nodded as if responding to a question that had been asked. "I'm afraid, it's ovarian cancer."

"Cancer!" gasped Prudence and Vivian.

Prudence felt the word spread through her being as if the disease had infected her too.

"Aye," he said.

"Oh Mam!" cried Prudence.

The banister creaked upstairs.

"Winnie," said Muriel, tears coming to her eyes.

Until the moment the doctor had actually said it, Muriel had hoped he would tell her she was an hysterical woman full of nonsense and that there was nothing really wrong with her other than her being tired and stressed from the war. Yes, she had hoped, she had hoped with all her heart that the dread she had been feeling had all been a silly figment of her imagination.

"You knew?" asked Prudence.

The doctor nodded.

"But why didn't you tell us?" Prudence raised her voice. "We could 'ave –"

"Shush," said Muriel, putting a staying hand on her daughter's arm.

"There was nothing that could have been done, not for this type of cancer," he said. "Other than worry and fret. I couldnae bring myself to tell ye. I thought it best ye didnae know."

Tears pricked his merry eyes causing them to twinkle all the more, as he continued, "Muriel, ye've been through so much in this life, I wanted ye to look forward to living instead of to more sorrow, ye ken. At least for a while."

"So all that talk about a new bed was," Muriel paused while she collected the strength to speak, "to make me last days ... more comfortable?"

Head bowed, the doctor rubbed his eyes and nodded.

"But is Death really supposed to be comfortable?" she asked.

"Why should ye have to suffer more, Muriel Goodwell?" asked Doctor McKenzie. "Ye're one of the best people I ken."

"Oh, I'm not special, Doctor, though I appreciate the sentiment. I really do. But there's nothing wrong with suffering. Life's not all gin and roses, is it? Suffering's a part of it, and we would do better to accept that instead of asking, 'Why me?' and 'What did I do to deserve this?' Christ suffered on the cross, didn't He? God understands human suffering."

"Then why does He allow it?" Prudence asked wearily. She had been staring into the flames, dabbing her eyes with a damp handkerchief. "Surely, He could make it all go away, if He wanted to."

"Love, if we didn't suffer we wouldn't know what to be thankful for," responded Muriel. "We wouldn't have hope."

"Och," said Doctor McKenzie whose job it was to ease the suffering in the world.

Muriel continued, "We take so much for granted. Suffering is God's way of reminding us that we should be thankful, and that we should take joy in what we have because none of this," she waved a hand around the parlour to indicate the physical realm, "lasts forever. Life is a gift, and I'll thank God for reminding me."

Doctor McKenzie cleared his throat. "Och, well, talking of gifts. I'm not sure if I should mention it now, it was Mrs. McKenzie's idea, ye ken, but we have a spare bed that's as good as new. Ye're welcome to it. There are a lot of changes coming along with the new National Insurance Act and as ye ken, I've been strongly in favour of free health care, and not just because I'm aboot to retire," he chortled. "Once the National Health Service is established here, which I believe it will be despite some of my colleague's attempts otherwise, Mrs. McKenzie and I plan to retire to somewhere smaller, down south, ye ken because of her rheumatism. So, if ye'd consider taking the bed off oor hands, we'd be grateful."

Muriel cast her eyes over the settee which had been made into a bed for her convenience. The question remained: for how long.

"Ta, Doctor, it'll be a tight fit in here but I'll take it," she said. "Just to ease your burden, mind."

The doctor chortled.

"Aye," he said. "Mrs. McKenzie will be pleased."

Muriel felt the first twinge of pity coming her way, and it stung. She thought, The doctor was right not to tell me because then I would have had to endure months of pity from mesen and others and he knows me well enough to know I couldn't have borne it. I would have suffered more pain from pity than cancer. Even the pity in this minute is killing me.

"Some nurse you are," Prudence spat at Vivian. "How come you didn't know?"

"How on earth was I supposed to know that!"

"You've seen how Mam winces and how slow she's got —"

"Now, now," said Muriel. "I'm too tired for this sort of talk. Come on, Prudence, you know better. I know you're upset but there's no one to blame but fate. You two need to put aside your differences now and come together. There's a family to run."

"A family to run?" asked Vivian. "What do you mean?"

"Well, love, you can start by getting our Dr. McKenzie here a cup of tea," Muriel said. "Maybe you'd like a drop of brandy in it an' all, Doctor?"

He showed his pleasure with a nod. Beckoning to him, Muriel lowered her voice to make sure the younger children couldn't overhear.

"Let's not beat about the bush any longer, Doctor McKenzie, how long have I got left on this earth?"

Scratching his neck, he blew air to soften her bluntness. These Yorkshire folk don't mince words.

"It's difficult to say," he said.

"A year? Two years?" she asked.

In one mouthful, he gulped half of the spiked tea. Their expectant, hopeful eyes were upon him, but he was about to dash that hope the way an errant wave smashes a ship against the rocks.

"Any time frae noo to six months," he said quietly.

"Six months!" Muriel gasped in a whisper.

"Oh, Mam," said Prudence.

Vivian let out a giant sob. Her hands shook as she pulled out and lit a cigarette. Then she poured another tot of brandy for herself, spilling some on the white tablecloth. Holding the bottle, she glanced around to see if anyone else wanted brandy, but her voice wouldn't come so she gave up and placed the bottle back on the table.

"Six months at best," Muriel said. "Well, that is a shock. So this time next year ..."

Maybe I won't see another birthday, she thought. May? No, I might not make it.

Fear and panic gripped her. She had thought herself prepared to hear the worst, but hearing it, actually hearing the sentence was so final. Me time's up. It's over, for this life anyrode. If there is another life. No, I won't have any doubts about that. I won't. Not now. That's the devil's work. God help me. It matters more than ever now. This is it. This is what my faith comes down to. I've been tested before many times and I've proven myself to be true. Can I do it now, now when it matters the most? Christ help me. I'm lucky. I'm lucky. At least I have that much. Some people don't know. I 'ave the chance to make me peace with everyone. And soon, sooner than I could ever have imagined, I'll see my William once more.

"I'm sorry," said Doctor McKenzie, "but I didnae want ye to suffer in mind as much as body."

"I understand," Muriel said. "I don't blame you or hold it against you. You are right in a way, knowing would have added nowt but more worry for us all. Life's been difficult enough as it is."

"At a different time, if there was no war, I mean," the doctor said. "I might have acted differently."

"I know, I know," said Muriel. "You did what you thought was best. I know that. All good people do. Here give me some more of that brandy, Vivian. It's bloody good stuff. I hope that Derek Stalworth's got an unlimited supply. Will you give us a prescription for it, Doctor?"

"Should you be drinking that much, Mam?" asked Prudence.

"Oh, don't you start. Bloody hell. Imagine if I'd have had to listen to that for the past few year."

Gently, the doctor touched Muriel's cheek, saying to Prudence, "Your mother should have whatever takes her fancy."

"Oo, careful doctor. I've allus had a thing for you, you know."

Doctor McKenzie laughed. "Och! I daresay there's been a time or two that Mrs. McKenzie would have been glad to have me off her hands."

"Just pulling your leg, Doctor."

"More's the pity for me, then," he said, looking thoughtful as he tried to assess Muriel's pain level. "I can give ye something for the pain, ye ken, as much as ye'd like. At this stage of the game, that's my job. It's what I can do for ye."

"I could have done with some'at a while back," she said.

"Och, I really thought ye'd tell me when it got that bad."

Muriel shrugged. "I've become so used to me aches an' pains over the years, I could hardly tell you whether it's worse or worser."

"Ye Yorkshire folk," said the doctor. "Ye'll work till ye can't work anymore. Ye're the hardiest lot I've ever come across. It's a hard life fishing or being married to fishing. I've seen it all, all the years I've been here. Ye husbands are gone for weeks while ye wives are raising the children on their own with no ken if ye're husband is going to make it home or no. And oft times, too oft, he doesnae." He put a sympathetic hand on Muriel's shoulder. "I admire how ye survive. Ye've all been an inspiration to me and Mrs. McKenzie, and I thank ye for that."

He raised his tea cup.

"Cheers," said Muriel, raising her own teacup. "Well, ta for the eulogy, Doctor. You'll have to do me the honour of speaking at my funeral with your silver words. Maybe folks'll think more of me, then."

She took a drag on a cigarette she had cajoled from Vivian.

Dr. McKenzie laughed. "Still got the spirit, then?"

"And why wouldn't I? It's only me body that's dying, not me soul."

"Mam," said Prudence. "perhaps you should be resting now."

"For what? I've got nowt to save me energy for. Why sleep anymore? The eternal sleep's going to get me soon enough."

"Mam, don't," said Prudence.

"Ah, sod it," said Muriel, bitterness creeping into her voice.

Prudence was working hard to stem her tears. The doctor put a comforting arm around her shoulders. She rested her head briefly on his lapel as he reached over to squeeze Muriel's foot through the blanket.

"Don't worry yoursens," said Muriel. "I'll have me moments, won't I? Prudence, I am going to heed your advice and take it easy. Why not? I've earned it. I'm going to lie here and watch you two lasses do all the work and wait on me 'and and foot. It's going to be bloody brilliant. I'll feel like the Queen of Sheba."

She laughed.

"Mam, it isn't funny," said Prudence.

"Isn't it? Who said it isn't funny? Why can't death be funny? Eh Doctor? You've seen enough of it. It can't all be sadness and misery, can it? Why should it be? We should be happy we're going to finally meet our maker. The greatest mystery of mankind is about to be revealed to me, and I can decide whether or not to enjoy it. I never pitied mesen in life, so I shan't pity mesen in death neither."

Trying to laugh again, she sobbed instead.

"Life is just so... relentless. There's never a respite. Until now. The final respite."

Vivian sat heavily at the table, resting her head in her hands. Her plans to leave Hull were drifting out of reach like smoke up a chimney.

"Doctor, I'm sorry. Me mind's all over the place. I don't know what to say," said Muriel, drying her tears.

"Ye've had a nasty shock," said Doctor McKenzie, fastening his coat. "I'll be back tomorrow to check in on ye. I could set ye up on the Morphine noo. I brought a couple of vials with me."

"Morphine?" asked Muriel. "I don't think I'm ready for that sort of thing yet. I'll just stick with me paracetamol and brandy for now."

"As ye wish. But they still aren't giving out medals for bravery in the face of cancer yet, ye ken. Although they should."

"How about some bramble pie for you and Mrs. McKenzie, Doctor?" asked Prudence.

"If you can spare it," he said, patting his portly stomach in anticipation.

With the pie in hand, the doctor bade them a whispered farewell. Muriel had dozed off.

"I think I'll go for a walk an' all," whispered Vivian, standing. "Get some fresh air."

"No, you won't," said Prudence. "You and I 'ave to talk."

"We can walk and talk, can't we?"

"And who's going to look after Mam?"

"Our Winnie and George."

"They're too young. And I'm not ready to tell them why Mam needs looking after. I've got to sort out me own feelings before I can handle dealing with theirs. They are going to be devastated. I wish they was older but it can't be 'elped. Here, we can talk and clear up," Prudence said, quietly collecting the tea things and putting them by the sink. Though she was in no mood to wash the pots, they wouldn't wash themselves. She leant heavily against the sink.

"Can't we talk when I get back?" whined Vivian, slipping on her red coat. "I really need some fresh air. I'll only be a minute."

"Sit down," Prudence said.

"Who are you to tell me what to do?"

"Please," said Prudence. "We need to work out what we're going to do."

This was not a conversation Vivian wanted to have. However, she sat down and lit a cigarette with shaking hands.

"I have to get out of here," she said with a cigarette in her mouth. "I can't stand it. I feel like the walls are closing in on me."

"I know the feeling," said Prudence.

"You do?"

Vivian stared into the crackling flames, picking a piece of tobacco from her tongue. The noose was tightening, she could feel it. Any moment now, she was going to be hung by her ties to this place. Glancing over at Muriel, she sighed, then leant over to pull the blanket up.

"I never knew Mam snored," she said.

"So do you."

"I don't! Do I?"

"No. I'm just pulling your leg."

Prudence picked up her knitting needles and wool. Settling into the chair opposite Vivian, she cast on the required number of stitches to knit a bed jacket for Muriel.

"But we're leaving on Saturday," Vivian said, hopelessly.

"You mean you were," said Prudence.

"I'm not staying here!" cried Vivian.

"You'd bloody better," whispered Prudence.

"Why? Why? Why should I?"

Prudence violently stuck the needles into the ball of wool.

"Because my dear you're a nurse, and Mam needs full-time care, or she will soon. Winnie and George are in school, and are too young besides. And I have the fish shop to run. We haven't even finished getting it ready but we need the money, especially with all the extra medical care Mam might need. I know in your mind you've already designated me to stay and look after *our* mother on me own: to watch her die while you go gallivanting."

"Stay?" said Vivian in a loud whisper. "What do you mean, 'Stay'? How can you be 'designated to stay' when you weren't planning on going nowhere in the first place. I'm the one with all the dreams and ideas. Mam knows that. You just want to keep me here, so I can be as miserable as you; wishing I had a life instead of having one."

"Miserable?"

"Aye. In a way. But you're happy in your misery. You feed off other folks' troubles. You've got none of your own because you don't have a life."

"That's because I haven't had a chance to have one! I have a sense of responsibility to this family. Mam needed me after Dad died. That sort of thing allus falls on the eldest child. Then there was the war, remember, in which my fiancé was killed!"

She stopped abruptly, feeling deceitful for invoking Alec's memory to make excuses for herself.

"That were years ago," said Vivian. "You can't tell me you haven't met another feller in all that time. There's plenty more fish in the sea you know."

"If I had a shilling for every time someone said that to me I'd be able to buy all the fish in the sea never mind marry them," Prudence replied. "Anyrode, what makes you think I haven't met another feller?"

"'Cause there isn't none here for starters."

"Depends where you look."

"I've looked," said Vivian.

"But the best ones are already taken, is that it?"

Vivian threw a darted glance. "Aye, that's it," she said.

As Prudence counted her stitches, she said, "So you think I want to stay 'ere and raise our George and Winnie and care for Mam while she's dying?"

"Yes, I do. In a way, I think you do. "

Prudence let out a noise of disgust. "You have no idea what it's like to feel responsible for someone else, do you?"

"It's excuses all of it," said Vivian. "You're so inside yoursen, you're afraid of stepping outside the front door. All your life is lived in your head. You should get out a bit, go dancing, get some different clothes. Men like a woman who takes care of hersen."

"I thought men liked women to take care of *them*," said Prudence, already with three rows of knitting done and she hadn't looked down once.

Vivian laughed. "That's after the wedding. But that's why you have to look further afield than Hessle Road. You think I want to spend my life cooking and cleaning after some dirty fisherman coming home from sea full of fleas? Not bloody likely. And you shouldn't settle for that neither."

"Why d'you think I would?"

"'Cause what else is there around here?"

"I'm going to tell our Mac you said that."

"I love my brother, but I wouldn't wanner marry him."

"I'm sure the feeling's mutual," said Prudence.

Vivian laughed. Prudence smiled.

"Fancy a cuppa?" she said, sticking the needles into the ball of wool, more gently this time.

As she put the heat on under the kettle, Prudence mulled over the way it seemed impossible to sting Vivian with words. Why can't I be more like that? she asked herself. Because I believe there's a truth in what people say about me, whereas Vivian doesn't. She has her own opinion of herself and sticks to it. And maybe it isn't even a good opinion but it doesn't matter.

"You haven't said yet whether you'll stay," said Prudence.

"I didn't know I had a choice."

"Choice! You didn't give us any choice when you left Ted with us, did you? And now, if I hadn't said owt, you'd have left again with no thought to us."

"I never asked for nowt from nobody."

"No, you never ask, you just presume. And it works so long as there are people around willing to pick up the pieces for you. But it's time for you to pay us back a little. You're in debt to a lot of people."

"But I have to go," Vivian said, more weakly.

"Why are you always running away?"

"I'm not running away!" said Vivian. "I've never run away. I was sent away."

"Sent away?"

"Aye. No one wanted me here. Not you, not Mam. I was just an embarrassment to you all. So I left."

"Is that what you tell yoursen?"

"Aye, it is."

Was that true?

"Aye, well," said Prudence. "You say that I'm the one that's 'iding, but it's you that's doing the hiding, not in your head but in a different country, that's all. You can't keep running from your secrets and your mistakes."

"There you go, rubbing my face in it again! What do you want from me? Do you want me to stay here forever with you, lurking about indoors? It's too late, Prudence! I'm married! And, by the way, I don't count Ted as a mistake."

"You know I didn't mean that," Prudence said quietly.

"I know you didn't. Ta."

She took a brimming tea cup from Prudence.

"I guess you've got me all figured out," Prudence said. "At least you care that much."

"Bloody chalk and cheese," said Muriel who had been listening. "You two are as different as chalk and cheese."

She pulled herself up to a sitting position.

"Mam!" said Prudence. "You're awake."

"I've been awake. Honestly, you two make enough noise to wake the dead. I hope you're going to cut it out when I pass on because I'd really like to rest in peace. I think I've earned it. But if I have to come back from the dead to bash your heads together I will."

"Mam!" Vivian cried.

"I mean it. If you two don't settle down, all the dead will come back to haunt us."

"Sorry, Mam," they both apologized.

"While I'm still here, and I am still very much here, Prudence, before you take over …"

"I were just trying to organize things."

"You was trying to organize me," said Vivian.

"For crying out bloody loud, both of you shut your gobs right this minute and listen to what I have to say!"

Still mindful of their mother's wrath, even in her weakened state, the two girls sat to attention.

"And where's my cuppa. I'm gagging."

"Here you go, Mam."

"And I wouldn't mind a bit of bread and butter to go with it," said Muriel. "I haven't had owt to eat since this morning. It's a pity about them ham sandwiches I dropped."

"Hold on. There's a couple left."

But Muriel stayed Prudence's arm.

"No let Nurse Vivian get 'em for me while she's topping up her tea. She's been complaining about being bored."

Vivian sliced a piece of Gloria's Yorkshire parkin to go on the plate with the sandwiches. The cake felt fresh and the ginger scent made Vivian's stomach growl, so she sliced some for herself and Prudence as well.

"Here's how it's going to be," said Muriel. "Ta love."

"But we were going to leave this Saturday," Vivian reiterated glumly.

"Sorry love, but you're going to have to stay and help out now that we know what's what. It's not for me I'm asking. It's for the others. I've done enough running after you in my lifetime. Now you can return the favour."

Vivian was crestfallen.

"Look, love, I know you have your plans and dreams," said Muriel. "I'm glad you've got your ambitions. Really I am. And I want you to fulfil every dream you've ever had but wait a while for me, please. Don't you think I dreamed of far off places when I was a young girl? Not even that far off. Dover would have been nice. I allus wanted to see them white cliffs. But it's too late now, for me."

She gazed into the fire for a moment.

"It doesn't have to be too late, Mam," said Vivian. "You'll feel better tomorrow. I know you will. Then you can come and see us off at Dover."

"I wish we could do it like that," said Muriel.

Muriel chewed the sandwich, despondently staring into the red and orange flames. Then she gathered herself together, brushing some crumbs off the nightdress she had changed into, and smoothing the sides of her hair. She said, "I must look a right state. I don't know what happened. Why I suddenly feel so wiped out. I suppose being busy with everything kept me going, planning for the next thing, and when there was nothing left to plan for –"

She handed the plate to Prudence.

"Here I can't finish this. I'm not so hungry after all. But I wish I was."

Prudence's eyes traced the bite taken out of the sandwich, evidence that their mother was still alive. Soon there would be only photographs and memories.

"Vivian, I want you to go to America and have your own life, just not yet. Do this for us. You can't leave our Prudence to do everything again. It's too much with the bairns and the chippy, and the biggest bairn of all, Mac to look after."

"But Jake ..."

"But Jake nothing. I 'aven't known the lad long but I think he'll understand. He seems nice enough. What he's doing with you, I'll never know."

"Mam!"

Muriel chuckled.

"But what if..." said Vivian.

"What if? Oh, don't worry about having to stay too long. You heard the doctor. I promise I'll be gone in six months."

"Don't say it like that. You make me sound 'orrible."

"Look Vivian, the good part of it is, it'll give Ted and Jake a better chance to get to know each other. Come to think of it, it'll give Ted and you a better chance to know each other an' all before you whisk him off to a strange land. Oh, speak of the devil."

Jake had returned from his walk, looking refreshed. He flashed a lop-sided smile, and the women were relieved for a change of subject. Everything they needed to say to each other had been said, for now.

"Brrr! It's cold out there," he said, standing by the fire and rubbing his hands.

"You were gone a long time," said Vivian.

"I walked all the way to," he thought for a moment, "Walton Street, is it? Looks like there's gonna be a fair. I watched them setting it up. Rides and side shows. Looks like fun."

"Hull Fair!" exclaimed Vivian, happy at once. "I'd forgotten all about it."

"The fair usually comes every year," Prudence informed Jake. "But this'll be the first time in six year 'cause of the war and that. We all like to go. Maybe we could get you a wheelchair, Mam, so you could come with us."

"A wheelchair! I'd rather not go! I'm not going to have folks seeing me as an invalid! I won't go if I can't get there on me own two feet. It's funny how you never think when you're doing some'at that it might be the last time. Just shows you, you've got to make the most of every minute. I mean, we made the best of it with your dad and that, but that's because there was always the possibility he might not come home, being at sea an' all. But I never have gave much thought to me own demise or to making things special just for me."

"We'll do our best for you, Mam, over these next few months. Won't we Vivian?" said Prudence.

"These next few months?" Jake asked. "What do you mean?"

Chapter 17

Hull Fair! Eager to get to Walton Street, the younger girls and boys skipped ahead; pennies jangling in their pockets and excitement jangling in their eyes while the adults trailed behind enjoying the crisp, star-filled night and wondering when was the last time they had felt such childish delight.

After many assurances from Muriel that she would be fine on her own, Prudence had promised to return with the biggest bag of fudge for her. But still, as Prudence pushed Ted along in the pram, side by side with Dolores who was pushing Shane, Prudence's mind was on their mother at home alone. It was painful to think that next year, at the next Hull Fair, their mother would be gone. She fought the urge to turn back. All she wanted to do, for the time they had left together, was to sit and hold her mother's hand, but she knew her mother would be cross if she returned home fudgeless and full of pity.

"Sorry, I'm having trouble keeping up," said Dolores.

"Oh, that's all right."

"I've never had an easy pregnancy, and this one's t' worst of all. I'm so tired all the time. Look at me ankles. I look like I've got elephant legs."

She didn't mention the minor cramping she felt from time to time during which she held her breath, waiting, praying for one outcome or the other. But the cramps always passed, and she could breathe again. If she mentioned the cramps, Prudence would insist on getting the doctor, and Dolores didn't have money for false alarms.

Prudence smiled down at Ted, realising he had no idea what was about to befall him. There had been some seaside fun and games at Scarborough but nothing like Hull Fair. The fair had been coming to Hull for almost seven hundred years and here they were but a speck in its history and its future. Prudence felt insignificant, lost in it but then an important part of it like one of the vital cogs in the merry-go-rounds. There would be no fair without the people who went to it. She and the thousands of people from all over the country who attended every year, bringing their laughter, smiles and pennies, were just another attraction at the fair to be enjoyed as much as any of the rides or bazaar stalls.

Slowing her pace to stay abreast with Dolores, she said, "I can get our Winnie to push the pram for you."

"What, and spoil her fun? No, ta, I'll manage."
Dolores smiled sadly. "Oh, I shouldn't moan, should I? I
mean I've got me 'ealth. Me children are healthy, skin and
bones but healthy. I've got you. There are people worse
off."

"You can moan to me," said Prudence. "I don't mind."

But then perhaps she did mind. Despite her worries
about Muriel, Prudence had been looking forward to the
fair. All day, the children had talked non-stop to Jake
about how he wouldn't believe this or that when he saw it,
as if the poor man had never been to a fair before. So she
quickened her pace a bit, distancing herself from her friend
and her problems, without getting too close to Jake and
Vivian who were walking ahead, together, but in silence,
and not touching.

I'm in no man's land, thought Prudence.

Bright lights and loud music loomed in the sky - beckoning them forth. Happy children with sticky smiles
passed them going the other way with their exhausted parents close behind carrying the requisite spoils of the fair:
toffee apples, candy floss, a coconut, a pomegranate, and
the odd goldfish. The smallest children, being too exhausted to walk, slept in their parents' arms, heads lolling
back and forth with each step.

With the excitement too much to bear, Winnie, George,
Shirley and Sharon broke into a run while Gloria quickened her step so she wouldn't be too far behind.

"I like hooking the ducks," said Winnie, breathing hard.

"So do we," said Shirley. "Don't we Lizzie?"

"That's for babies," said George.

"Is not," said Winnie.

"Is too," said Sharon and George together.

"It's not just for babies, is it Gloria?" said Winnie.

But Gloria didn't answer, she was too busy absorbing
all the looks from the boys. Aloofly, she smiled, letting
them know she was saving herself for someone special. She
had perfected a seductive walk and had taken to coyly

glancing over her shoulder to see if any of the boys turned to look, which invariably they did, their eyes almost popping out of their heads.

"Uncle Jake and me are going to shoot some ducks with a pop gun," said George, aiming in the air and squinting down an imaginary barrel. "He's a real cowboy," he informed Sharon and Shirley. "And 'e's me brother-in-law. He has a real gun that he uses to defend hissen against Indians."

"Does not," said Sharon.

"Does too. He showed it to me!"

"And me! I was there an' all," said Winnie.

"Aye, but he only let me touch it. Girls aren't allowed."

"They are allowed!"

"No, they're not. It's a cowboy rule. Jake said the gun belonged to his dad. *And* he said he's going to show me how to lasso a cow."

"What cow?" asked Paddy. "There aren't any cows around here."

"Jake'll teach me an' all," insisted Winnie.

"No, he won't," scoffed George. "Girls aren't allowed to do that stuff."

"Yes they are!"

"D'you think he'll let us borrow his stuff to play cowboys and injuns?" asked Paddy.

George hesitated, remembering he had sworn to Jake that he wouldn't tell anyone about the gun, then he said, "Sure," in the manner he had heard Jake say it.

"What about his hat?" asked Paddy.

Looking back over his shoulder at the American, George said again, "Sure any time. He doesn't mind."

"Wow!" said Paddy. "We'll be well in. It'll be like the real thing. Has he ever killed any injuns himsen."

"Yeah, loads."

"Don't be daft," said Winnie. "Injuns was years ago."

"Well, he killed Germans. Loads of 'em. And they're worse."

"We're here!" exclaimed Vivian.

"Wait for us!" cried Prudence. "Come on, Dolores!"

Turning the corner onto Walton Street, the sounds and lights and savoury sweet odours hit them like a giant wave. Prudence laughed as Ted's head nearly span out of its post as he looked left and right with eyes wider than coconuts. People were milling about from one stall to the other laughing and eating. Children whined and complained of stomach aches from the variety of foods consumed. It was as if rationing had been excused for the night in this magical place, and the lucky fair-goers were living in the land of plenty. The savoury scent of frying onions filled the air mixing with the sweetness of the candy floss machine, which the children ran to and watched wide-eyed as pink fluff grew and grew on a stick that whirled and twirled around in a machine operated by the grubby hand of an experienced gypsy boy.

Jake bought the children each a candy floss, which they eagerly bit into, enjoying the feeling of the fluff turning back to sugar in their hot little mouths. Vivian leant over and took a bit out of Winnie's.

"Oy!" the young girl cried. "That's mine!"

"Do you want your own cotton candy?" asked Jake.

Vivian laughed and shook her head; pushing the sticky pink stuff into her mouth and licking her fingers. He loved that laugh.

"Come on, Jake!" Vivian cried as she ran up to a crudely built, wooden sweet stand.

Her eyes feasted on the rows and rows of square, brown fudges and toffees all laid out neatly under bright lights. The sugary treats gave off a strong, pleasing caramel aroma.

"Whitby fudge!" cried Vivian. "And toffee! Bloody hell, I haven't had this in ages!"

"If I had a penny for every time I've heard that tonight," said one of the kindly-looking women behind the counter. "I could give this away for free."

The stall holders, both elderly women, might have been twins. They looked identical in their matching white aprons and caps, and as sweet as their wares. Prudence handed over money to pay for two bags of fudge, and she fancied that each of the stall-holders would taste of vanilla if licked.

Vivian urged Jake to try a piece. He popped a square into his mouth. The rich sugar-butter-vanilla mix melted on his tongue, too sweet for his tastes but nonetheless appreciated.

"Isn't it heavenly!" said Vivian, thrusting an arm through his crooked one.

He nodded, accepting her arm.

"Reminds me of maple syrup," he said.

"What's that when it's at home?" asked George.

"It comes from the trees in New England," said Jake. "We have it on pancakes. I didn't realize how much I missed it until now."

"Don't worry, it won't be long before you'll be having it again," said Vivian, patting his arm.

"What's New England?" asked George. "Are we in Old England?"

"Oh George, don't be a pest!" exclaimed Vivian.

"Me and Lizzie want to go on the merry-go-round!" cried Shirley.

And they did. They also went into the haunted house, without Dolores who said she would stay and take care of Shane and Ted who were too young for the scary ghosts and skeletons. But when the offer was made to take turns, she still refused to go and finally confessed she was too afraid to go herself. Next they visited the hall of mirrors where they laughed and pointed at each other's distorted reflections. They shook hands with the tallest man in Britain, the bearded lady, and the fat lady, who had somehow managed to retain her folds despite rationing. And the children screamed at a two-headed foetus pickled in a jar, which almost caused pregnant Dolores to faint, but luckily she had the pram to help keep her upright.

Offering George and Paddy advice on how to shoot the pop guns, Jake helped Paddy shoot five ducks and win his own cowboy hat, which he proudly sported as he jaunted alongside the American. George, who was less amiable to advice and insisted upon holding the gun himself, shot one duck and won a small bouncing ball, which after only one bounce became lost in the crowd. He was so jealous of Paddy, he kept pretending to accidentally knock off his friend's hat. After the fifth time, Paddy became so incensed that Jake lent George his hat for the rest of the evening, which suited the hierarchy of the boys' friendship splendidly.

The girls successfully hooked enough ducks to win small wooden dolls made out of clothes pegs and dressed with lace. Despite the late hour, the children kept pleading to stay five minutes more and for one more ride, but when Winnie threw up on the big wheel Prudence made the decision to go home.

As they walked back down Walton Street, they approached a brightly coloured caravan, decorated in red, gold, green and blue. There was a large advertisement on the side proclaiming that the "World Famous Gypsy Rosa Lee," resided within. The door to the caravan opened and out stepped a beautiful dark-haired gypsy girl who beckoned our ladies with a crooked finger and big brown eyes that flirted with Jake on the side.

Vivian giggled, "So how about it, then, Sis?"

"Why not?" said Prudence.

"Hark at you!" exclaimed Vivian. "Being so daring."

"I 'ave me moments," said Prudence.

"Count me out," said Jake.

"We never counted you in. How about you, Dolores?"

Dolores hesitated. She had only saved up enough for the girls to have some fun.

"I'll pay," Prudence whispered in her friend's ear.

"Ta, love, but I know my future, don't I?" said Dolores, patting her swollen belly.

"But you don't know if it's a boy or a girl. Go on, it'll be a laugh."

"I can watch the kids," Jake said.

"But I want to go an' all," whined Winnie.

"You're too young," said Prudence.

"That only means I've got more of a future than you do."

"Why, you cheeky devil," said Prudence.

"Don't you want to do it Gloria?" asked Winnie.

"No," Gloria said. "No need. I know my future an' all."

A comment that pained Dolores.

"I'll do yours for free, our Winnie," said George, grabbing his sister's hand. "Oh, look here, it says you've got a lot of cooking, cleaning and ironing in your future, and six bairns to look after while you're at it."

"Bloody hell, our George, you are clairvoyant. You should set up a stall here," said Vivian.

Snatching her hand away, Winnie said, "Really? Well, I can see a broken neck in your future, George Goodwell."

"Come on, let's do it," said Vivian. "I'll go first, then if it's no good nobody else has to do it."

And with that decided amongst herself, she strode up the wooden steps and into the caravan.

"Are you sure you don't mind staying with the bairns, Jake?" asked Dolores.

"I can help an' all," said Gloria. "I'm almost seventeen, you know. Go on Dolores. I'm dying to hear what she tells you."

Dolores wasn't sure she liked the girl's tone.

"She's right," said Jake. Go on have some fun. We'll walk them over to the ring toss. Winnie can push Shane."

"So can our George," Winnie said hotly, but nevertheless obediently taking the reins of the pram.

"All right, then. Ta," said Dolores. "Wait for me Prudence. We can go in together."

Prudence and Dolores stepped inside the candlelit caravan. Vivian was already behind the curtain in the back, having her fortune told. They could hear her voice, low and eager.

"She didn't waste no time, did she?" whispered Prudence

"Wait," said Cezar.

The heavily accented voice surprised them because they had thought themselves alone. But sitting shirtless in the corner drinking beer from a dark brown bottle was the young gypsy's brother. He gazed unwaveringly at them through thick, dark lashes, licking his lips. Like the rest of the girls who had ventured into the caravan that evening, they fought to suppress giggles of embarrassment.

Vivian should have warned us, thought Prudence. Though it's just like her not to. I mustn't look at him. It's so beastly.

Cezar had been enjoying himself all evening watching the giddy girls file into the caravan. He particularly relished the part when the girls first saw him, the way their eyes grew wide as they took in the sight of his lean, muscular body; perhaps some wishing a touch of his chest was in their near future.

The girls he recognised as more willing, he might follow around the fair and, if he kept receiving invitations via continuous backward glances, he would eventually grab a hand and pull the girl away from her friends and into the shadows behind a stall or ride and say pretty things to them in his native Romanian tongue before venturing a kiss and if the response was warm, venturing further with his hands, and sometimes more.

He preferred girls with some weight on them, but such tastes were hard to satisfy during war time when food was scarce. Skinny girls reminded him of hard times. There was no harm in toying with these two, he thought, even

172

though one of them was pregnant. He rubbed his chest as if nonchalantly, and was satisfied to see the women exchange an embarrassed look.

"I don't like the look of yours," Dolores whispered, and they giggled.

A small basket of wooden peg dolls, like the ones the younger girls had won, was in the centre of the table, along with an assembly line of scissors, lace and pegs. Rosa popped her head through the curtain and noted their presence.

"Soon, please wait, sit," she said, before disappearing once more behind the red curtain.

Cezar pointed to the seat opposite him, and the young women sat down, giggling and trying not to look his way, as he drank and smiled and winked at them.

After a while, the back curtain pulled aside, spilling soft light into the living area. Vivian came out beaming.

"Oo, she's ever so good," she gushed. "You won't believe what she said to me! She said I'm going to travel to far-off lands! I mean 'ow would she know that! Anyrode, I'll tell you more after you've 'ad your turn."

"Go on, you turn," said Vivian, pushing Dolores through the curtains.

The curtain closed behind Dolores but not before Prudence caught a flickering glimpse in the candlelight of a shrivelled old woman in black juxtaposed against the voluptuous granddaughter who was colourfully clothed in red skirt and bodice, and white petticoats. The grand-daughter acted as translator.

"See you in a mo," said Vivian. "I'm dying to tell Jake."

"No, please stay," said Prudence.

But Vivian closed the slim door behind her leaving Prudence alone with the gypsy man. Using the beer bottle, he drew aside the lace curtain and watched the blonde plant a kiss on the cheek of the man he had seen with them. Another man, whom he recognised as one of the pub's landlords, joined the couple and exchanged greetings. Hopefully, they would be engaged for a while. He would have to work fast in the little time he had.

Behind the curtain, Dolores cut the tarot card pack as instructed then handed the pack to the old lady, Rosa Lee, who kept her eyes on her customer's face, studying every moment of the eyes, hands and mouth. The old woman noted the over-worked hands, swollen belly and over-tired features with the remains of a bruise over one eye. She read into the slouched shoulders and Dolores' inability to meet her gaze.

Lighted mainly with candles, although an oil lamp hung in the corner at low flame, the back room was small, the bed having been folded up out of the way to make room for a small table that was covered with a stained red and gold rose cloth fringed in black silk. Shadows from the candles played games with the old woman's wrinkles and large Romanian features, rendering them eerie and sinister and wise. Nothing she said could be doubted.

The cards were laid face down then turned over one by one to reveal strange and mystical drawings that were the key to Dolores' future. The old lady spoke in Romanian as she crossed her fingertips across the cards.

"You future have great sorrow, great joy," said the gypsy girl, translating what had been said.

Same as last year then, thought Dolores, thinking of the joy she had experienced when Shane was born, and also the tiny joys she caught as fragile as butterflies from her children and friends. Sorrow? She wore sorrow's cloak well.

The old woman muttered some more, turning over a card with two hearts, but she moved on without commenting to Dolores until she turned over the next card.

"You joys and sorrows be same," the young Rosa translated.

"The same? What does that mean?"

"You know," said Rosa. "When come."

The next turned card showed a skeleton.

"Death," whispered Rosa.

The old woman shushed her, and spoke in Romanian.

"Death?" exclaimed Dolores.

"Death sometimes end," said Rosa, translating. "Sometimes beginning."

"But which is it for me?" cried Dolores.

The old lady cackled, tightly grabbing Dolores's hand with gnarled fingers and yellowed nails. Dolores was repulsed and longed to draw away but was held as if hypnotised. Gold and silver bangles jangled against each other as Rosa Lee pulled Dolores' hand closer to her side of the table. Turning the hand, she lifted Dolores's clenched fingers, and traced her bony finger along the lines of the exposed palm, down, up and across.

"But I don't have enough money to 'ave me palm read an' all," Dolores protested.

"No money," said Rosa.

The fortune teller smiled revealing blackened and missing teeth.

Rosa translated, "Is possible you marry again."

"I will?" exclaimed Dolores, immediately thinking of Mac as her second husband.

The old woman muttered something.

"Grandmother see two weddings, but -"

The old woman muttered again and pointed to a break in Dolores's lifeline.

"Grandmother say you have two destinies. You find right one you happy."

"But when?" asked Dolores, unable to conceal the hope in her voice. "When is this going to happen?'

The old woman shrugged and rattled on.

Rosa translated, "Not possible know. One year, twenty."

Rosa Lee's voice rose as she wagged a finger at Dolores.

"Grandmother say warning. When you pray death, death want this:" She rubbed her thumb against her fingers to indicate payment.

"I don't know what you're talking about," said Dolores, getting up to leave. "This is nonsense."

Her pregnant belly knocked the table, wobbling the candlestick, which she righted with a shaky hand. She was scared to think someone might know her innermost thoughts about Jimmy: how she had, at times, wished him dead. But the gypsy could only be guessing, she told herself. What beaten down wife didn't sometimes wish her husband dead?

Rosa put her hand on Dolores' shoulder. "We say warning. Be careful. We have charm can help."

"That's not a surprise, is it? I already told you I don't have any money. Can't you see that in me cards? I don't need your charms, I have this?" Dolores said, patting the tiny, gold crucifix she wore, the one Jimmy had bought her while they were courting, and which she was afraid to take off in case he pawned.

Rosa Lee cackled.

"God no here, why you here?" asked Rosa.

"It were just meant to be a bit of fun."

"Fun?"

As quick as an adder, the old woman leaned forward and put her hand on Dolores's swollen belly. The room was so cramped, Dolores couldn't back away. Muttering, Rosa Lee shook her head.

"A girl," said Rosa, strangely, without any of the usual joy people had when they spoke of babies.

Gypsy Rosa Lee spoke again, but Rosa shook her head, refusing to translate what was said. The old gypsy shrugged and touched the cards on the table as if hoping to derive more information from them.

"Another girl," said Dolores disappointed. "Me 'usband's not going to like that at all. What's her life going to be like? Is it going to be better than mine? I 'ope so."

After a pause during which the elder Rosa Lee kept quiet, Rosa eventually said, "Your baby, she know only love."

The heart inside Dolores swelled, and her eyes teared up.

"Why, that's beautiful," she said, dabbing her eyes with a handkerchief retrieved from her coat sleeve. "The lucky thing. Could anyone want more for their children than that?"

Rosa smiled, but not joyfully.

"Ta," Dolores said to the older gypsy. "Ta very much. You've put me mind at rest, about this one anyrode. Here, I've only got a penny but I'd like to tip you. Oh no. Clumsy me!"

She had knocked over the candlestick. The lighted candle broke away and rolled across the table. Jumping up, the old woman hissed angrily, and said in English, "Fire."

"Sorry. It's just that I'm so clumsy these days," said Dolores. "You know, being pregnant an' all. Here let me."

"No, I do," said Rosa righting the candle. But the flame had touched one of the cards, burning it. Rosa waved it in the air and blew on it to put out the fire. "Look, fire burn card. Is two hearts. Grandmother, is no good?"

Cezar's gaze made Prudence uncomfortable, so she turned away from him, shuffling closer to the safety of the curtain where she could overhear the low murmur of women's voices, young and old. Behind her, a wireless turned on, and its volume was raised. She heard a creak of a seat, then him whistling along to the tune of the big band sound, coming closer to where she was sitting. But she didn't realise how close until he whispered, "Boyfriend fish'man?"

"No, I don't have a ... I mean, me brother's a fisherman. A big one an' all. He's two of you."

"Big fish'man? Yes. Big fish'man on motorbike?" He made bike noises like the engine of Mac's Norton.

He was so close, his hot breath moved her hair as he talked. Her heart raced. She felt danger. Should she call out?

"Aye, that's him," she said. "The real big bloke with a bad temper. You know him, then?"

She hoped thoughts of Mac's wrath were deterrent enough.

"My sister - she know many fish'man. She like fish'man. I no like fish'man."

Prudence moved out of the way, so she face him. Speaking foreign words to her, he smiled, but there was menace in his demeanour. She felt entirely alone, like a rabbit in a hunter's sights. Only the hunter knew whether or not he was going to pull the trigger. The hairs on the back of her neck prickled.

"Look, I've changed me mind about having me fortune told. I'm sorry but I 'ave to go."

He blocked the exit with his body so quickly she bumped against him.

"Do you mind! I said, I've changed me mind. Let me go!"

Panic rose in her. She glanced toward the curtain but a muscular arm blocked her there as well. She was about to cry out when a strong hand covered her mouth, silencing her. Her muffled cries could not be heard over the radio, nor could her futile struggling. Wrestling in his strong arms proved useless, and only expended her energy. Thinking she would do better to lull him into believing she had given up, she relaxed. He chuckled and said something Romanian, then repeated himself in English, "Good little bunny."

To him she had no more strength than the rabbits he caught that writhed and kicked in his embrace before he broke their soft, warm necks.

The door burst open. Stalworth had spotted the duelling shadows through the net curtains and had immediately sensed what was going on. Roaring with rage, he had charged at the caravan door like an angry bull, smashing it open with such force he fell to the floor but straight away sprung to his feet and grabbed Cezar, pummelling him into the ground.

Alarmed, Dolores darted through the curtain in time to see Cezar laid on the floor trying to defend himself against the landlord's fury. Jake tried to intervene but, for his trouble, received a punch on the mouth re-splitting his lip. He doubled over with pain, spouting blood. Dolores could guess what had happened, especially when she spotted Prudence sitting still on a chair with her hair a mess, and her lipstick smudged: she was in shock after being kissed by the gypsy.

A torrent of Romanian spewed forth from both grandmother and granddaughter as they pushed by Dolores and joined the fray, working to save Cezar from the landlord's relentless punches. The old woman jumped on Stalworth's back and bit his ear. The landlord yelled and staggered back in pain, with a hand covering his bleeding ear. Then he fell into a chair, trapping Rosa Lee under him. She bit him again and he jumped up as if shocked, while she scrambled out of the chair to see to her grandson.

"You dirty bastard," Stalworth said pointing at Cezar. "I ought to kill you for touching her."

Cezar stood and hissed at the landlord, but didn't take any steps toward him. As young and strong as he was, he was no match for the landlord's valour.

"Come on, let's get out of here," said Vivian, helping Prudence to her feet.

"I'm all right," said Prudence. "Just a bit shaken up. Nowt happened. Nowt serious anyrode."

But as they reached the door, Cezar laughed and said, "She like it."

Upon which George yelled, "I'm gunner kill you!" and barged at the gypsy knocking him from his feet again.

Cezar fell winded which the young boy took to his advantage, raining more blows down on the gypsy's face.

Vivian hurried Prudence out of the caravan as Jake stopped the fight by grabbing George's haunches and pulling him away, the way two fighting dogs are separated. The young boy's arms flailed and his teeth gnashed as he was carried outside and dropped to the ground, tears of rage stinging his eyes.

"You did good lad," Stalworth said, patting George's head. "Oo, I'll be feeling this for a few days," he added, rubbing his sore shoulder, and moving it around in its socket to gauge the damage. "Me ear an' all. They're like animals them gypsies."

"That door wasn't locked, you know," Vivian said to him. "You went barging in like Dambusters."

"Should I have knocked first? Come on, Viv, you can't rescue a damsel in distress by simply opening a door," responded Stalworth. 'There has to be more excitement than that, ay, Prudence?"

But Prudence was far too embarrassed by the evening's events to comment. She was horrified to think of the whole community finding out about it.

"Oh come here, love," said Vivian, putting an arm round her sister. "You've still got your virtue. Let's get you home and have a lovely cup of tea."

"Don't tell Mam, though. Or Mac. There's been enough upset as it is."

Chapter 18

Eyeing the newly installed shiny brass bell that hung portentously above the door to the fish shop, Muriel remarked, "That thing'll drive us bloody crackers at tea time when we get them big crowds."

Jake slipped a screwdriver back into Mac's tool box, closing the lid with the finality of a job well done. With all of them working hard they had managed to make the shop shipshape in just a few days, and once the fish and chip money started coming in they could work on repairing the rest of the house. Glass for the large front window and door had been replaced, the floor had been cleared of all rubble and brand new linoleum had been installed. The ceiling had been repaired and repainted cream, along with the walls, and all the equipment had been scrubbed cleaned and filled with fresh lard for frying. The shop was ready for customers.

Outside, Dolores was painting the final lettering on the window, listing the menu and the shop hours.

"Oh, go on, Mam, it'll be nice to hear customers again," said Prudence, swinging the door to demonstrate the effectiveness of the bell. "Weren't it nice of Derek to give us a new one when he heard the other one got broke."

"All right. All right. But please stop it," said Muriel. "It's already giving me a bloody 'eadache."

"A headache, Mam? Shouldn't you go and sit down?"

"No, I should stick me knickers in that bell to stop it ringing," said Muriel, tired of the fuss.

Muriel hid her pain well. She had made a considerable effort to be on her feet to see the shop completed and ready for customers - customers who hadn't crossed that threshold for almost six years.

"What do you think to Dolores' handiwork, Mam?" asked Prudence.

Dolores was putting the finishing touches to the lettering in 'Plaice'. The white words, outlined in gold, looked backwards to the women standing inside the shop. Dolores waved to them when she noticed they were watching her.

"Not bad," conceded Muriel. "You've all worked really hard. And God bless you, Jake. We needed a man to help us with the heavy stuff. If we'd have had to wait every three weeks for our Mac's help ..."

"You're welcome, Ma'am."

Muriel ran a hand along the shiny fryer, then she touched the stack of newspapers that were ready to wrap up the fresh fried fish and chips.

"It would be nice to wait for Mac for our grand opening," she said.

"I know but we need to start making money, Mam. And we can make money hand-over-fist with fish and chips not being rationed. Look how busy we was in Scarborough."

"Aye, I know," said Muriel with a sigh.

Nodding with approval, she took a long-lasting look around the chip shop, unsure if it would be the last time she would see it. The tremendous pain inside her seemed to wash over her anew each time she completed an important task, like a boat going through successive locks of a canal. Eventually, she knew, the pain would be complete, whole, never to wane again, and she would be one with it and they would die together. But it wasn't here yet in its entirety, she knew, because she could still endure it.

"I'll say it again. You lasses, and lads," she nodded to Jake, "'ave done a grand job. The shop looks smashing. Your dad would be so proud."

"Ta, Mam."

Muriel coughed. "You know there are times I can't believe he missed the whole bloody war. He were lucky in a way. I know the daft sod would have tried to sign up again. He would have been there, wouldn't he? At Dunkirk and D-Day, I mean, with Mac. He would have loved it, you know, having a chance to be a real hero like the rest of our fisherman, like our Mac. Well, if he 'asn't heard owt about it where he is now, I'll be sure to tell him when I get there."

"Mam," said Prudence. "I wish you wouldn't –"

"Oh, don't mind me," said Muriel. "I've come to accept it. I'm all right with it, really. Me fate's been decided. And as far as wishing goes, I wish I could stop worrying about what's going to happen to you lot. Although it looks like you're all taken care of, even you Prudence."

Prudence blushed, and grinned that famous Goodwell grin.

"Aw," said Muriel. "Me eldest daughter in love."

"I don't know about that! Let's not get carried away!"

"Don't be daft, lass."

Suddenly overcome, Muriel reached over to squeeze her oldest daughter's cheek.

"Mam," laughed Prudence, who hadn't been touched in any way affectionately by her mother since she was a girl. And even then she couldn't remember it, but only knew it must have happened by watching the way Muriel was with the younger children.

"What? I were only putting some colour in your cheeks. You look so bloody pale. Here, let me get the other one an' all. Oh, that didn't hurt! There. Now you look alive."

Muriel's eyes were shiny with tears of some sort or another, happiness and sadness. What she daren't speak of was the regret of not living to see her youngest children reach adulthood. Grandchildren, she thought sadly. I'll miss meeting you. Thank goodness for our Ted; he's the only one I'll ever know. And to think of all the upset when our Vivian got pregnant. How silly it was of me to care what other people thought. I did stand by her though. I did. But I could have done better. I was so hard on her at times. By and by, though, I've taken good care of them all.

Muriel had accepted that she was dying, and though she was looking forward to being reunited with her loved ones, she had difficulty imagining the world turning with no place set for her at the dinner table. Her birthdays would no longer be celebrated with happiness, and the forecast of Christmases without her fretting over a roasting goose almost sent her into a panic. And when those that remember me die, what then? It will be as if I never was. Except in God's eye.

If this was going to be her last Christmas, she was re-solved to make the absolute most of it. Rationing be damned, she was determined to have a goose and all the trimmings, a Christmas pudding with lots of brandy and real custard, and maybe even a Christmas cake with thick marzipan and drifts of icing set like snow.

"Well young man," she said to Jake, "may I take your arm so you can see me back 'ome? I know it's only next door but our Vivian, your Vivian, should have the tea brewed by now, and I'm ready for a lie down."

"Yes, Ma'am."

"Oo, Jake, son," said Muriel, "I'll never get used to be-ing called that. You've spoiled me rotten. I hope St. Pe-ter's going to greet me like that at them pearly gates. If he was from Hull, it'd be more like, 'Oy you! Aye, you Mrs. Whatsit. Get yoursen through them bloody gates. I need to close 'em right quick 'cause there's a bugger of a draft coming from down below!'"

Jake laughed, showing his white teeth, and Muriel's heart fluttered.

"Maybe you shouldn't say things like that," said Pru-dence. "It's sacrilegious."

"Oh, wind your neck in. Let me have me fun for good-ness' sakes. Don't you think God has a sense of humour? I reckon he must have otherwise he wouldn't have put our bums so close to our hows-your-fathers."

"I beg your pardon!"

"Stop!" Muriel held up a hand to Prudence's gaping mouth. "No more chastising me."

Smiling broadly, Jake held out his arm for Muriel, who smiling too, was about to take it when she gasped, "Oh, no! Look who it is!"

The trawler owners' chaplain, Mr. Throth, dressed in his customary dark suit and white collar, was riding his old black bike toward the shop. He swung a long, spindly leg over the bike ready to dismount, making it obvious he was paying a call to them.

"Oh no!" cried Muriel. "Not our Mac! No!"

Her legs gave way, but Jake caught her and guided her to sit on a small step ladder.

"Mam, go home. I'll see to it," said Prudence.

"No, I want to hear it," said Muriel.

I wish I'd died yesterday, she thought.

A sick feeling tightened inside her. This wasn't the first time the chaplain had paid a visit to her house. She remembered clearly the day he had informed her about her husband; though upon being pressed, the chaplain hadn't known which William Goodwell was lost, and she couldn't be convinced that it wasn't her twelve year old son until together, she and the chaplain returned to the head office of Butler's and telegraphed The Ichthus. How clearly she re-membered the office where she had struggled to retain her dignity, not giving the staff the satisfaction of her bursting into tears so they could tell their friends and family about the fishwife that had come to the office and carried on so. She knew the office staff considered themselves superior to the fishermen because they touched paper and pens instead of the raw flesh on which their livelihoods depended. She could recall each and every face in that room watching her expectantly, waiting. She had disappointed them.

"Mam, stay here," said Prudence. "I'll see to it. Jake watch her, please."

"I'm not a bairn!" cried Muriel

The bell tinkled as Prudence opened the door and went outside, thinking, Our first customer: Death. But her heart jumped, and she gripped the door handle more tightly when she heard the chaplain say, "Mrs. Alford?"

So he hadn't come for them, the Goodwells, he had come to see Dolores. Prudence's heart lifted a little, be-cause Mac must be safe. She looked back through the open doorway at her mother who had also heard. Muriel broke into sobs, her whole body shaking. Prudence indicated to Jake that he should take Muriel back to the house. He nod-ded and helped Muriel to her feet.

"Yes?" said Dolores, turning, surprised to hear her name called.

When she saw it was the chaplain, she fell with a gasp against the window, smudging the lettering. She had been concentrating so hard on the painting, she hadn't heard the telltale creaky bike crossing the street, or the chaplain's song: he was often singing or whistling *Sweet Molly Malone*. Mr. Throth parked the bike, removed a bicycle clip from his trouser cuff and brushed off the front of his black shirt. His fastidiousness made Dolores aware of her own shabby appearance. Hadn't Vivian poked fun at her earlier for the paint in her hair?

What a sorry sight I am to receive such news!

Resting the paintbrush on top of the can, Dolores wiped her hands on her apron, then smoothed the sides of her hair with her forearms. Her mind was blank, waiting for whatever news was to be delivered. She glanced at the smudged lettering.

"Dearest Mrs. Alford, I do apologise," said Mr. Throth in his thick Devonshire accent. "I didn't mean to sneak up on you like that. I went to your house first of course but your neighbour said you'd be here."

"She was right. I am," said Dolores.

Go on! Go on! her mind urged him. Out with it!

"Grand opening tomorrow, then?" said Mr. Throth, eyeing the two white placards that stated such in large red lettering.

One was for outside the shop and the other would be placed on the pavement at the corner of St. George's Road and Hessle Road. The women had also made leaflets and posted them in the local shops. Derek Stalworth had taken a few for the pub.

"Aye. That's right. Tomorrow."

During the pause in which Dolores could see the chaplain searching for the right words to explain his ominous presence, she braced herself for bad news. A dozen scenarios of Jimmy's demise raced through her mind, and her heart pumped so fast she feared she would faint. She held the window ledge for support.

Even after all these years, it was never easy for the chaplain to be the bearer of bad news. People hated him for it, he could see it in their eyes, and it was always difficult to be met with such dread each time he knocked on someone's door. He was the last person people wanted to see; their expressions of shock and fear always gave him a start. Which was why he sang his song - to alert people to his approach. At least, then, his knock was half-expected. But poor Dolores Alford hadn't heard him coming at all.

He flexed the meagre muscles in his gangly arms ready to catch Mrs. Alford if she fainted or to embrace her if she simply cried. His arms may have been thin and long, and unlikely to break a cobweb, but they had surprisingly physical and healing strength: over the past twenty years they had offered support and comfort to many a new widow.

Mr. Throth nodded to Prudence whom he noticed was standing in the shop doorway. He knew her as a sensible girl who would take care of the situation if need be.

"Mr. Throth, please tell me, has some'at 'appened to my Jimmy, then, or what?" cried Dolores. "I mean, that's why you're 'ere, isn't it?"

"Yes," he said, swallowing hard so the movement of the Adam's apple in his scrawny neck was exaggerated.

A jumbled assortment of emotions fought for position inside Dolores: joy and fear raged against each other like demons. At first she thought of her children being fatherless, then she thought of their lives being monsterless.

"Well, is he dead?" she asked. Dare she hope?

Possibilities spun and spun tighter and tighter on the spindle of Dolores's mind, making her dizzy. They had no money, what would they do to survive? However awful Jimmy had been, at least there had been some pennies on which she and the children could depend. Struggling to regain her composure, she closed her eyes.

187

"No," the chaplain said carefully. "He's not dead."

Dolores gasped. A cry of protest almost slipped from her mouth, but she stopped it with her hand. Fate had once again deceived her. Tears burned in her eyes. But the way the chaplain had said 'dead' was hesitant and without finality, almost as if he should have added 'yet'.

"I don't mean to be rude, Mr. Throth, but why are you here, then, if my husband isn't, hasn't ...? I don't understand."

If Mr. Throth were a gambling man, he would have bet that Mrs. Dolores Alford was more disappointed, than relieved to hear that her husband was not dead. She wouldn't be the first. In his long career, he had seen it all, and had learned not to judge. Actually, he had become a better husband, father and friend because of the glad-women: he didn't want anyone to be relieved by his death.

"Mr. Alford had a bad accident," said Mr. Throth. "There was some sort of fire in the engine room of the Wilberforce."

"A fire!" Prudence and Dolores gasped together.

"Aye, I'm afraid, he's badly burned all over, from head to foot. I was at the docks when they brought him in. He was delirious, in terrible pain. There was quite a commotion about it. They took him straight to Hull Royal. He's very badly burned. Unrecognisable, I'm afraid."

"Unrecognisable?" An image of a burned thing flashed in Dolores' mind. But alive, she thought bitterly.

"Do they think he'll make it?" Prudence was asking.

"It's too soon to tell. But there's a long road ahead, if he's to recover."

Recover? Dolores was angry. Angry at God and Jimmy and the chaplain for not giving her the news for which she had longed. Oh, it was wrong of her to wish him to die, and she felt sorry to God for it, but why, why couldn't he have had the decency to die and leave her and the children be. Now she would have to take care of him, bathe him, dress him, and feed him while he convalesced.

The thought of him burned repulsed her. The very being she hated to touch would now be dependent *on her touch*. And his tongue, vicious scorpion tail, would lash out at her, criticizing and commanding but mostly despising that he depended on her.

He deserves it, she thought. He was going to burn in hell anyrode. So I wonder, did he make a deal with God to pay his debts now, on earth, burning here instead of hell?

Until that morning, she hadn't realised her life could get any worse. The medical bills mounted in her mind.

"He's at Hull Royal?" she asked.

"Aye."

Dolores nodded. Then, feeling dizzy, she fell against the window again, smudging more lettering. The chaplain reached forward to steady her.

"No," she said, "I'm all right. Ta."

Respectful of her wishes, he stepped back. His angular limbs, almost too long to ever be completely straight, hung from his body like spider legs. Dolores imagined she had seen four sets of arms reaching for her when she stumbled.

"He was asking for you," the chaplain said.

"Aye," Dolores sighed.

"I'll go with you to the hospital," said Prudence.

"Ta, Prudence, but there's some finishing up to do 'ere. And I know you're eager to get it done."

"Oh, I don't mind. Another day won't make much of a difference. Still, if you'd rather go on your own."

"I would, but ta. Mind you, I will have that cuppa afore I go, though. Steady me nerves a bit."

"I wouldn't mind one mesen," said Prudence. "Father?"

"Thank you but no," said Mr. Throth. "I must be off. Oh, and one more thing, Jimmy was asking for the children as well."

"Oh, I don't think they should see him like that!" Dolores exclaimed. "The way you described it. It would frighten them too much."

189

"He sounded desperate," said the Chaplain. "And, well," his voice turned to a whisper, "it might be the *last time*. I can't impress upon you enough what a terrible state he's in."

Dolores and Prudence exchanged a glance.

"Can Lizzie ring your bell, Mister?" asked Shirley who had quietly approached to see what the big people were discussing after their deadly serious expressions had ignited her interest. Her mother looked even more grim than usual, and Shirley wanted to be the first to tell Sharon about whatever it was.

"Not now, Shirley. Go back to playing elastics."

"But we're out, Mam. Look at me knee."

She lifted a leg to reveal the skinned knee cap that never seemed to heal; only scabbing over temporarily until the next game scraped it again.

"Please, do as I say, Shirley, and go on. You'll get another turn in a minute."

"*England, Ireland, Scotland, Wales, Inside, Outside, Inside, On*," chanted Winnie as she successfully completed her turn.

A sympathetic smile from the chaplain moved Shirley to go to her mother and put her arms around her waist, burying her face in the apron strung across Dolores's swollen belly. Absentmindedly, Dolores stroked her daughter's head, feeling the smooth, clean hair and the warm scalp beneath it. She gathered up the long hair, wavy from plaiting, and, with one hand after the other, stroked the fine, dark tresses; the dreamy motion of which soothed troubled child and mother alike.

"I'll be off, then," said the Chaplain mounting his bike.

Needing all his effort to pedal, the chaplain only nodded in response to Prudence's farewell. The old bike was as stiff as him, and it took a few turns to get them both going.

"Well, I never," said Dolores. "Did you hear that? In tears? My Jimmy?"

"Sounds 'orrible, what happened," said Prudence.

"Yeah, 'orrible," said Dolores, though she didn't feel an ounce of pity in her chest. "I'll bet he was drunk."

"Are you talking about me dad?" asked Shirley.

"Oh, I forgot you was there."

She let go of the hair.

"Now, I don't want any fuss. Go wash your hands and face. We're going to go to the 'ospital to see your dad. He's right poorly. There was an accident. Tell Sharon to get ready an' all. And tell her I don't want to be bothered with no questions till we get on our way. Go on. I'll tell you both all about it once we're on the bus."

She picked up a cloth to correct the smudged lettering.

"In tears," she said again, shaking her head and taking a deep breath.

"Strange things happen to people when they nearly die," said Prudence. "Look at Norman Nettles after he fell of the keel drunk and me dad had to use a boat hook to get him out of the dock."

"Aye, I remember," said Dolores. "It were years ago, mind. I remember what they said an' all: that the dock water's so mucky they had to treat him for poisoning before they treated him for drowning."

Prudence laughed.

"Aye well, Norman said he saw angels. Swore he'd never drink again, and he never has. His wife says he's a changed man."

"Aye, I know. She says he's a bloody nuisance at home all the time bothering her, instead of being down at the pub having pints with the lads. He drives her mad allus telling her how to make gravy and polish the brasses and what have you. She told me she was planning to take up drinking just to get away from him!"

Prudence laughed again, "Well, you know what I mean."

"Aye. I suppose so. But Jimmy. Well, he's told me before that he's going to give up drinking, and he means it in the moment, but he never sticks to it. Anyrode, it's been ages since he made any promises like that. I think even he gave up on 'imself." Dolores shrugged. "No, there's been too much between us. He's been too vile, too cruel at times. I can't even bring mesen to tell you 'alf of it. No, there's nowt he can say to me now that would make me believe he could change."

"Hadn't you better get off? The window can wait," said Prudence. "They know what we've got. Fish, fish and more fish."

"I know, ta. But I'd like a few minutes to get mesen together and I allus find painting calms me soul."

"All right. I'll get the lasses cleaned up and ready to go, and get you that well-earned cup of tea an' all."

A few minutes later, the lettering was finished, and Dolores, her nerves now calmed a little by the concentration of the work, stood back to admire it. She wondered if it could be seen clearly from the other side of the street, so she crossed and looked, and yes, it could. She was pleased with herself about the work. She was really quite talented, but always, in the back of her mind, was the needling self-doubt that had been so generously sewn by years of abuse from her parents and further nurtured and matured by her husband.

"That looks right grand," said Prudence, handing Dolores a cup of tea.

"Oo ta."

"Winnie's seeing to the girls."

As Dolores took a sip, Prudence admired the shop front with great pride. The wood frame was now cherry red with gold edging; formerly it had been black. Painted above the large window in bold gold lettering was, "St. George's Fish 'n' Chips" - the new name upon which they had all agreed. Prudence smiled recalling Mac's comment on the new name: "Good name that, 'cause there'll be a couple of old dragons running it, anyrode."

"Ah, that tea hit the spot. Strong and sweet," said Dolores. "I hope you didn't use up your sugar ration on me."

"No, don't worry. I didn't use up my ration, I used up our Mac's," quipped Prudence.

Dolores laughed, but at once her face turned serious.

"I shouldn't be laughing, not with Jimmy in the hospital."

There was a moment's silence between them during which Dolores suspired heavily, contemplating what lay before her. The feeling of pride and accomplishment she had felt at completing a task so well quickly vanished, living in its stead only dread of the events to follow.

"Time to round up the troops," she said. "I expect your Winnie's tired of my lasses arguing with her by now."

"Aw, she's all right," said Prudence. "You can wait another minute or two, if you'd like. Finish your tea."

"Oh no. I'd best be off. Believe me, those girls would try a saint's patience. Look at me, I've got more paint on me than on the shop. Looks like I used me dress instead of a brush. Tch. And in me hair an' all."

She squeezed the hardened paint in her hair.

"You can borrow one of my frock's if you like."

"Ta, but that would only cause more problems. It'd be like the Spanish Inquisition. Where did I buy it? How much? All that. He'd probably think I have a boyfriend that bought it for me. Or worse, he'll think it was Mac. He never believed it was over between us. It's hard work trying to avoid trouble with him, and now he'll be in bed all day with nowt to do but think about what I'm doing wrong."

Folding the ladder, she said, "Prudence, do you really think I should take the girls? I mean, it won't make no difference to Shane. He's too young. Although, Jimmy will want to see his son, his blue-eyed boy. Shane's the only one he really cares about. The only one he hasn't hit."

193

Not yet at any rate, Prudence thought, but she said, "What will Jimmy do if you don't take them?"

Dolores looked away. "Well, that is the question, isn't it?" As she lifted the ladder, her voice strained with the effort. "He'll be mad, won't he? And then there's no telling what he'll do if he gets his strength back. He's like an elephant when it comes to remembering. And it'll be worse because he'll brood on it all the while he's recovering. I can't win. Sorry, I sound a bit like a broken record, don't I?"

Prudence touched her friend's arm.

"Why not take them to the hospital, but have them stay in the waiting room. You can decide then, when you get there."

"I suppose so," said Dolores. "I don't feel right about it, but … Oh, it does me 'ead in trying to imagine all the whys and wherefores of Jimmy Alford's mind! Imagine if he was dead and I only had me own conscience to think about."

She winced, holding her breath.

"What is it?" asked Prudence.

"Oh, just some of the usual aches and pains of pregnancy. Don't look so concerned. I'm all right."

"At least this one doesn't know what's going on," smiled Prudence as she rubbed Dolores's pregnant belly.

"Lucky devil isn't it," said Dolores. "For now at any rate. Whoever you are stay in there for as long as you can! I keep telling her that."

"You think it's a girl?"

"That's what the gypsy said. Oh, sorry, I didn't mean to bring that up."

"Don't worry. It was nothing, really," said Prudence, blushing slightly. "Here let me take that heavy ladder. Come on, let's go back inside."

As she walked with Prudence, Dolores held her belly, feeling guilty about bringing another innocent being to share her penurious life. All her children brought her joy, yet she often wondered about the struggle and hardships they would have to endure throughout their lives. They were born so innocent, but it was taken away from them, almost immediately for some such as hers. Was life really worth living for those rare, precious moments of pleasure and laughter? It had to be. It was all they owned.

Chapter 19

Bracing herself, Dolores stood back a little from the entrance to the ward, in a place where Jimmy couldn't see her. She needn't have worried; he wasn't looking in her direction, but nevertheless she wanted to have the chance to look him over first, that is, the patient she assumed was him - the heavily bandaged one lying on his back, staring up at the ceiling. Shirley's warm little fingers slid into her hand. Dolores smiled down at her daughter. Shirley was gripping her doll tightly.

Drawing a deep breath, Dolores closed her eyes. When she had first arrived, she tuned out the rest of the ward, but now she took a moment to look around it. Most of the other patients were sitting up, chatting to each other or to visitors. Some read the newspaper, those that could read. Others listened to the latest hatches, matches and dispatches being read to them by a visitor, commenting, smiling or shaking their heads solemnly when the dead was someone they knew.

When a nurse breezed past them out of the ward, Dolores felt the nurse's independence push her aside like a gale force wind. She experienced a moment of jealousy before remembering that it was the same independence she wanted for her daughters. She looked to see if the girls had noticed and admired the nurse but their eyes were fixed on their father.

The burden of where she was and why she was there fell again on Dolores. She didn't want to be there, in the hospital or in her life. She was tired of feeling trapped by circumstance. Now there was this to get through. She wished she was somebody, or somewhere, else.

The notion that there was a better life just out of reach never left her, though she knew such thoughts were futile. She felt the other life taunted her like the ghost of a choice unmade. She wished it was possible to be living that happier life somewhere alongside this one, so she could drift into it whenever she wished to see what it was like. She had spent her childhood, then her marriage, always dreaming of a kinder life. Was that the way she was made up? To never be happy? To always be filled with longing and regret?

Nurse Evans bustled back into the ward carrying a glass of water and a straw to Jimmy's bed. Quietly saying something to him, she drew the curtain to take the sun off his face. Jimmy lifted his head a little to take the straw, managing a few sips. Dolores saw how pathetic he was, and pity fought for a place inside her. She was so used to being afraid of his physical strength, she couldn't imagine being close to him and not waiting for him to strike.

The nurse patted his hand reassuringly. How shocking it was to see someone being so gentle with him. Perhaps Prudence was right, that this experience would change him now that he needed people. He needed her.

"Wait here girls," she said with a sense of purpose the girls didn't recognise.

Forcing a smile, Dolores approached the bed as the nurse was popping a thermometer into Jimmy's mouth.

"Hiya, Jimmy. Nurse erm…," Dolores said.

"Nurse Evans. Good afternoon. Come to see our Mr. Alford, then have you?" said the nurse in a sing-song Welsh accent.

"I'm his wife."

The nurse checked the watch pinned to her uniform. Without looking up she said, "I've been taking care of Mr. Alford since he came in this morning. In a really sorry state he was. That was some time ago."

With strong, green eyes, the nurse took a measurement of this Mrs Alford who presented particularly shabbily standing next to her own crisp, clean uniform. The disapproval the nurse felt in defence of her patient was quite apparent. A flick of her eyebrows showed her distaste in regard to the children's attire too, as all those women who have never had children of their own expect impossibly high standards of those who do.

"I came as soon as I could," Dolores said. "I were painting, you see, and I didn't 'ave time to change. Me girls too."

The urge to express how much she wanted her daughters to be just like the nurse, independent with a career, came over Prudence, but she said nothing for fear of appearing foolish.

"See you don't tire him out," the nurse said crisply. "Mr. Alford's in a lot of pain and needs his rest. And," she paused as if taking pains to be sensitive, "sanitation is an important part of his recovery. His wounds must not get infected. Perhaps the children could keep their distance? Right you are."

Dolores was accustomed to having her poverty remarked upon, but never her cleanliness. She wished she could shrivel up and disappear.

The nurse removed the thermometer and shook it.

"Ninety-nine point eight. Don't stay too long and don't excite him. He needs plenty of rest."

"Yes, Nurse."

Nurse Evans went on to complete her rounds, singing gaily in her native Welsh. Dolores was surprised to hear singing in a hospital. It didn't seem professional, but she supposed it cheered the men. And it wasn't the only thing that cheered them given the way their eyes followed the nurse's bustling, busty body around the ward. Again, Dolores felt a stab of envy for the way the nurse handled herself. She looked down her nose at me, she thought. Whereas, there's no one for me to look down on, is there? I'm right at the bottom looking up.

Jimmy patted the bed near to his waist, indicating that Dolores should sit there but she wasn't ready to be that close to him. Turning, she smiled reassuringly at her daughters. Their father must look scary to them, she thought, like a mummy.

"There's not enough room, Jimmy. I'll get a chair."

She pulled a chair close to the bed. Jimmy's hand seemed to cry out for touch, but she clasped her hands in her lap, slowly gathering the strength to look into his eyes, or rather eye. The sight of the hideous sealed lid where his right eye used to be caused her to gasp involuntarily. His injuries were worse than she had imagined.

"They won't let me have a mirror," he said. "But your face works just as well. Ta."

"I'm sorry, Jimmy. I told mesen, I mean, I tried to be prepared. I'm sorry. It's just such a shock seeing you like this. You must be in terrible pain."

"Shocked are you? How do you think I bloody feel? I'll bet you was more shocked when they told you I weren't dead. I'd like to have seen your mug when you saw that chaplain coming for you, and then to be told I'm still alive, well," he paused. "I am still alive, aren't I? Sometimes, I'm not so sure."

"No, Jimmy. Don't say that. It's not like that. I am sorry to see you like this. To have the girls see you like this. I want to make a fresh start, really I do. I were hoping -"

"A fresh start?" he scoffed. "Bloody nora! Have you heard you?"

Without warning, he snatched her hand. Despite his injuries, he hadn't lost any of the strength in his grip. She winced as he pulled her close to his face where the stench of burned flesh and thick ointment turned her stomach.

"Listen you stupid bitch: when I get out of here, and I will get out of here, don't think for a minute I won't, I'm going to knock your fucking block off. Do you hear me?"

"Jimmy!" she cried, recoiling. "Why would you say such a thing?" she whispered. "Here of all places? In front of all these people."

Retaining a firm grip on her hand, he kept her close.

"Don't think I don't know how you went whining to your cat's paw and sent him after us. I know your manipulative little games."

"What are you talking about?"

"What are you talking about?" he imitated her. "You must take me for a right fucking git. Mad bloody Mac. Thinks he's some sort of fucking 'ero, doesn't he?"

"What? *Mac* did this to you?"

"Oh aye. As if you didn't know."

"But you was at sea. How could he have done it?"

"Our boats was laid up together in Iceland 'cause of bad weather, and he jumped ship, didn't he? Came charging down to the engine room like a bat out of Hell. Straight out of Hell. Didn't give me no chance to defend mesen. There were witnesses. He's going to hang for this."

Dolores thought back to the other morning, when she had last seen Mac. He hadn't reacted at all to her injury. And he may be hot-headed at times, she considered, but to set fire to someone was too cruel and criminal an act for him. This was probably another of Jimmy's stories, she thought. The chaplain had said he was delirious.

"Jimmy, I swear I didn't say nowt to Mac."

"You didn't 'ave to *say* owt, did you, love? I know what you're like with them big, sorrowful eyes of yourn, making everyone pity you. You might not have said it with words, but some'ow you let him know you wanted rid of me."

"Jimmy, I wouldn't. Him and me, we don't talk like that."

"Don't look so innocent. I can see the guilt in your eyes. If it weren't for him, I wouldn't be lying here and that's the truth. You've him to thank for it."

"'Thank'?"

"Well, who knows when I'll be able to work again. And there's the hospital bills needs paying for. Aye, you've already been thinking about that, 'aven't you? I can tell. Would 'ave been cheaper to have a funeral, wouldn't it? Aye. Aye. Well, next time tell your boyfriend to finish the job he started. He'd be doing us all a favour."

"Calm down, Jimmy. You're getting yoursen all worked up. Look what the nurse said."

Half-expecting the nurse to come barrelling down on her for getting Jimmy agitated, Dolores glanced around the room to see who might be listening. Fortunately, the nurse was busy with another patient. When Dolores turned back, she caught Jimmy looking at her slyly. She could guess what was coming, and, as always, his expression made her feel guilty but for what she didn't know.

"You've been shagging him behind my back all along, haven't you?" he whispered with tight, white-spittle lips. "That's 'ow you got him to do it. I'm not going to blame him. It's you. You're like a succubus with your wiles."

This time Dolores dare not look around to see if anyone was eavesdropping. Foul language has a way of travelling light and far on the wind so she was sure she would be met with disapproving and accusatory eyes.

"Jimmy, please. Keep your voice down."

"Go on. Admit it."

"No," she said. "I won't. I have not been ... fooling around with Bill Goodwell. How many more times do I have to tell you? I've only ever been with you. You know that."

"I know no such thing."

"Jimmy you was me first and me only."

He scoffed. "Bloody hell you say it like it was some sort of prize. Lucky me. God, was I a gullible twat."

"Jimmy, you know you was me first - on our wedding night."

Her eyes were full of meaning.

"Tch. All you women are witches. You can fake owt."

"No, Jimmy."

Full of anguish, Dolores hung her head in her hands. People were all around and the children were only a few feet away.

"You can't fool me," said Jimmy. "I wouldn't be surprised if them kids weren't mine."

"How dare you!" she retorted angrily.

He had never gone that far before with his accusations. Yes, he could deny her, but never the children, never. She wouldn't have it. Oh, but how convincing could she be when there was nothing she wished more than to have borne her children to another man.

"How dare I?" he said, enjoying the rise he had finally got out of her. "There's only the eldest one looks like me. But the others, and that one you're carrying, I bet they're his."

Dolores glanced over to the children where Shirley was keeping Shane entertained by making Lizzie perform a silly dance, but Sharon met her eyes as if she had always been watching and listening. How Dolores despised having her eldest daughter's accusing eyes on her. They always seemed so critical. Look, now I'm the one what's been ridiculous, Dolores told herself. She's too young to have them sorts of feelings.

To Jimmy she said, "Don't say those things, you'll hurt the children."

He scoffed. Dolores lowered her voice even further.

"I *was* a virgin when we married. You know that. Or maybe you can't remember."

"Remember? Remember? I remember all right. I had a bit to drink, if that's what you mean, but I remember all right."

Dolores was alerted by the reference to his drinking that night, something to which he had never before admitted. He started coughing, and the heaving dry cough made his eye water. The cough was painful, evidenced by the way he winced each time and held his stumped bandaged hand to his chest. Dolores watched him, disgusted at the sight of the burnt, bandaged man struggling for breath. Even his lungs sounded charred; she half-expected smoke to be released with every cough.

Wildly gesturing to the glass of water the nurse had left on the bedside table, he coughed uncontrollably. Dolores held the glass for him while his lips gripped the straw and sucked. Apparently sated, he nodded. She took a tissue to dab his eye.

"Got any fags?" he asked.

"Do you really think you should be smoking?"

"Who gives a fuck? Just give us one."

"Tch."

"Come on, hurry up and light it for us. That's it. Ah."

He blew smoke circles up to the ceiling.

"I'll tell you what I remember from our wedding night," he said, lifting his head and awkwardly putting an arm under it. "I remember the look in your eyes."

He glanced at her, and then away, but it was enough to spread fear like ice water through her veins. She felt the way a child feels when it is found in a lie and thus knows it will be punished, except, in this case, the punishment had already been meted out.

"It's funny really, the way you act like butter wouldn't melt in your mouth." He laughed cheerlessly. The sound was vulgar to her. She felt her body folding, shrinking. She had been found out.

"Go on, let's 'ear it, then," he said. "Why don't you put on a straight face and tell me that you weren't thinking of

Mac when you was walking up that aisle to marry poor, gullible Jimmy Alford."

So, he had known all along.

"Aye," he said. "I knew it. You wouldn't look at me as you was walking up. Then when it were time to kiss, you closed your eyes and I knew then, you'd never stop thinking of 'im. Though I soon put a stop to any fantasies you might have had while we was doing it, didn't I? I made sure you knew it were me and only me doing it to you."

Hot tears welled in her eyes; tears of shame, guilt and discovery.

"You know, I kept thinking while we was courting that it would be different once we was married. That you would forget about him. But when you closed your eyes, I knew it wouldn't be no different. I mean, right up until that moment I had 'oped. I thought once you said, 'I do' you would believe it. You would become *my wife* and *forsake all others*. It meant a lot to me to ask you to marry me. I was serious about it. Do you understand? I lost the biggest gamble of my life. And that hurt. I can't tell you how much that hurt me."

Tears dripped off her chin. With difficulty, because Jimmy wouldn't release her hand, she used her teeth to pull a handkerchief from the sleeve of her cardigan. She didn't care who was listening now. It was all out in the open: the truth of their feelings for each other. There were no more lies between them. She felt the weight of his words on her conscience. She couldn't deny what he said.

Dabbing her eyes, she said, "But you didn't have to *hurt* us, Jimmy. The girls anyrode. They was innocent."

"*Forsaking all others*," Jimmy said again, firmly, before he closed his eyes and sank back onto the pillows, releasing her hand.

There was a long silence between them. Yet all around there was bustling activity, to'ing and fro'ing of which Dolores was slowly becoming aware, as if she had been unconscious and woken up to find herself in a hospital.

Patients and visitors chatted, some laughed, others cursed, and nurses were called. Healthy looking girls wearing starched uniforms bustled in and out of the ward as if simple walking weren't enough and they had to make their whole bodies busy with each step.

It was tea time on the ward, and Dolores gratefully accepted the cup and saucer thrust toward her by a pair of over-worked hands. The tea was weak but it was warm and welcome nonetheless. Dolores marvelled at how life was going on around her while her own was standing still. When she looked back at Jimmy she had no idea that he was struggling to keep his voice straight, since, for so long, she had not credited him as being a person with feelings, only thinking of him as hard and cruel and bitter, striking out coldly like a snake.

"It were the only way I could get you to feel some'at for us," he finally managed to say, but still with his eyes closed. "By being like that. By being like him, your dad."

"Like me dad?"

"D'you think I'm daft?" he said, flicking his eye open. "It didn't take me long to work out why you married me. To get away from him. You was desperate. Any port in a storm sort of thing. And Mac wouldn't 'ave you, would he? Smart lad. So it were down to me, poor Jimmy Alford. Maybe you're thinking, 'Why would he decide to be like me dad? Why not like Mac?' Well, I knew *how* to be like you dad, you see. It came easy to me. But I didn't know about the other. And besides, why should I have given you what you wanted. Why? Don't you think that while we was courting I had dreams about our wedding night. About wanting to make love to you. The times I'd thought about how soft your skin would feel." He paused. His chin quivered. "You was so beautiful.

"I wanted to cherish you but in the end, when I couldn't hide from the truth no more, I wanted to defile you. I cried afterwards. Aye, on our wedding night. Don't look so surprised. No, you don't know about my tears, only about your own. I went to the pub to get drunk, to hide what I did. But you can't hide from yoursen, no matter how much you drink. I know that now. I also know that you can't make someone love you. I learned that one on our wedding day an' all."

The culpability of her own actions was settling on Dolores' shoulders. How could all those years have passed without her once asking herself why Jimmy had changed so much on their wedding day? She glanced over at her bedraggled brood, their children who were still waiting in the hallway. Sharon was leaning against the wall while Shirley sat on the floor, cradling the doll on her crossed legs. The girls looked tired and worn out, not the way children should look. It's true, Dolores thought. I never gave him a chance.

Yet her heart remained hard against him for his deliberate cruelty against her and the children. All the years of abuse had been his revenge, and here he was trying to justify it, lay the blame with her. Maybe she deserved his anger but she did not deserve his wrath. The kind of cruelty Jimmy had exhibited over the years had to have already been a part of him, a dormant seed like a cancer planted at birth, that had waited for the right circumstance, then waxing, took over, killing the host.

"And then," continued Jimmy. "I forgot there was a reason for me to do it, to hurt you. I just did it. It's not what I'd wanted for mesen, starting out. When I started out as a barrow lad, I had me dreams of a better life. I came from so little, well, from nowt really. Me mam gave me up, yet I dared 'ope for so much, for a family of me own, for children -"

He stopped abruptly, coughing and gesturing for the water again. She obliged him. Putting the glass back, she was suddenly overcome.

"Oh Jimmy, why?" she cried.

Closing her eyes, she reached forward and took his hand firmly in hers, all the while fighting the urge to recoil.

"I could 'ave loved you, Jimmy. If you'd just given me a chance."

"I wish you believed that," he said.

She hung her head, wanting to believe she could have loved him. Could she still? The thought sickened her.

"I'm sorry," she said, thinking of the blurred years that had passed between and around them.

She saw the broken man before her. He was just a man. She realized she had not given much thought to his feelings when she married him. She hadn't allowed for him to have any. It had all been at her convenience, for her own survival. Maybe that's what happens when your dad hits you and your mother, for her own sake, doesn't defend you, or worse, turns the father against you, she thought. You're allus scared and you don't know how to be owt else 'cause trouble comes your way no matter what you do.

She felt wasted. Yet, at one time, she must have been whole: surely her heart must have been born in one piece. Perhaps there still existed an unsullied part of her heart, so deeply hidden and protected that she had forgotten what it felt like to feel pure.

We have destroyed each other, she thought simply.

Like two black holes colliding.

"More tea, love?" asked Dot, the canteen lady, pausing at the foot of Jimmy's bed.

"Aye, yes please," said Dolores. "Jimmy, do you want one?"

"It'll be too hot," he said.

"What about a biscuit, then?" asked the canteen lady.

He shook his head.

"I'll have one, please," said Dolores. "And his too, if you don't mind."

The lady raised her eyebrows, "I don't know if I can …"

"They're not for me," said Dolores nodding toward her children.

"Oh I see, love," said the lady who had thirteen children, eighteen grandchildren and two great-grand children, and had yet to see sixty years of age.

She poured a cup of tea for Dolores and one for Jimmy.

"If he doesn't want it, you can have it," she with a wink.

"And 'ere," she said, handing Dolores five Digestive biscuits. "One for each of you."

Dolores smiled gratefully, tears pricking her eyes at the small kindness.

"My pleasure, love. We have to stick together during these times, don't we? More tea, love?" Dot asked, moving on to the patient in the next bed.

"I shouldn't have done what I done to you and the girls," Jimmy said emptily.

He shouldn't have, so why did she find herself thinking of a way to excuse all those years of brutality. But then, no. She wouldn't let him off that lightly. She took a sip of tea, exceedingly thankful for the hot brew. She needed the strength, a lot of strength for what she was about to say to him now.

"What's done is done," she said.

Her hands shook, and the chipped, yellow tea cup rattled in the saucer as she placed it on the side table. They looked at each other for the first time. They knew each other now like never before.

"Jimmy," she began, but she didn't know where to go from there.

She knew what she wanted to say, but didn't know if it was true. After all these years of Mac slipping in and out of her thoughts and her dreams, he was going to be a difficult habit to break. Yet, she had to erase him once and for all, forever, if there was to be any chance of saving her family's future. She had been very young when Mac and she courted, and so had he. Her feelings for him had never been fully realized. She couldn't say anymore whether those feelings were real or just what she kept around for hope's sake, a silly fantasy. Whichever it was, no matter, Mac had to stay in her past. This was her present. Here in the hospital ward with Jimmy, and their children twenty feet away, was real and important. She told herself, Jimmy's my children's father. I've got nowhere else to go. I have to make the best of it. He's opened up to me like never before. If we can keep being true … maybe it will work.

Taking his hand in hers, she said, "Jimmy. We can't change what's 'appened, but we can change what's going to 'appen from now on. We've hurt each other, but that can stop. We don't have to hurt each other no more."

"Oh no?" he said.

The bitterness had crept back into his voice.

"What I mean is we could try to find a way to work it out. Start again, like."

"I can't start again," Jimmy said.

"We can try," she said.

"Look at me. It's over for me."

"No, Jimmy. I can help you. Once you're 'ome, we'll take care of you. Me and the girls. And when you're better –"

"When I'm better?! Look at me!" he raised his voice. "You still can't see me you, can you, you daft cow!"

He lunged forward, and Dolores jumped back out of her chair, knocking the tea cup and shattering it on the floor. The room quieted and the other patients and visitors looked their way with unreserved interest.

"First it was convenience, now pity," shouted Jimmy. "You feel everything for me except *love*."

Hurrying down the ward came Nurse Evans, calling, "Heavens above Mr. Alford. Please calm down. You're disturbing the other patients."

"Jimmy, please," Dolores said softly, putting a hand up to calm him; but he knocked it away.

"Use your eyes," he said. "'Cause this isn't no fairy tale with no happily ever after. When are you going to accept life for what it is?'"

"Mr. Alford. Please calm yourself," said the nurse, reaching over and grabbing his wrist to check his pulse while Dolores picked up the broken tea cup as inconspicuously as she could. But there was no avoiding the rustle of raised eyebrows and the feeling of many pairs of eyes boring into her slumped back.

"I advised you *not* to excite your husband," the nurse said sternly, drawing the curtain around them.

"She didn't excite me," said Jimmy. "It's me. I've been a rotten husband and a rotten father. And now she tells me it's all right. We'll start over. Well, I started out a bastard and I'd like to keep it that way. I'm going to die a bastard an' all."

"Jimmy, please don't talk like that, the girls'll hear."

"Yes, Mr. Alford. It doesn't do any good to talk that way. We want to think about your getting all better and going home to your own bed. Now won't that be lovely? Try to cheer him up," the nurse said in an aside to Dolores. "His head's in his feathers."

A passing thought came to Dolores of the unconscious lark on Jimmy's pillow. She shivered.

"There is no cheering me up," said Jimmy. "Why is it so important for everyone to be cheered up all the time?"

"Oh come now, Mr. Alford, be patient," said the nurse. "Things can only get better, can't they now?"

As she plumped the pillows, her bosom pressed against the side of his head moving it sideways and back in time with her movements. The time was past when he would have made a lewd joke or turned his face pretending to bite her breast. Now his head just moved like a buoy bobbing on the sea. Tears brimmed in his open eye and seeped through the sealed lid of the damaged one.

"All I wanted was for someone to love me," he sobbed.

"Now, now, Mr. Alford. There's no use in feeling sorry for yourself, now, is there? There are those worse off than you."

"Oh aye," he said, "I'd have to go to the graveyard to meet him that's worse off than me. Oh no, I take that back. The dead are better off than me. The dead feel no pain."

"Jimmy, don't!" Dolores admonished him in a loud whisper.

"You've got your wife and children," the nurse reminded him. "Bear in mind that because of the wars a lot of young men never lived long enough to have a family. You've a lot to be thankful for."

"Well, I'm bloody not."

Dolores recognised the bitterness rising in his voice again. Her nerves went on guard waiting for the explosion. How many years had she spent with that feeling of dread in the pit of her stomach, with that tenseness across her neck and shoulders as she waited for him to explode with rage. Her head was bowed constantly because of it.

"Things'll be all right Jimmy, you'll see," said Dolores. "Just give it a chance."

Softly, she squeezed his leg through the blanket.

"Stop saying that." He kicked his leg angrily. "It's not you lying here on this bed, is it? Me fucking cock's burned an' all you know! They didn't tell you that, did they?"

A tidal hush swept over the ward. Everyone wanted to hear more.

"Really Mr. Alford. Show some decorum," chastised Nurse Evans.

"Show some fucking decorum!" He grabbed at the bandages on his head. "I'll show you," he said to Dolores. "Then we'll see if you still think 'Things'll be all right, Jimmy'."

"Don't!" cried Dolores.

"Why not?" he sneered. "You might as well see what you'll be waking up to for the rest of your miserable life, or the rest of mine!"

The nurse tried to stop him but he pushed her away, hard enough that she fell through the curtain onto the patient in the next bed causing his winched broken leg to swing painfully. She called for assistance, her voice now urgent and angry. Never in all her career had she lost control over one of her charges. And to be pushed so viciously! It was the wife's fault, she decided. He had been a model patient until she arrived.

When Dolores saw how badly Jimmy's head was burned, she covered her mouth so she wouldn't cry out and frighten the girls. Jimmy's red raw and peeling skin seemed to roar in pain as if it were separate from the man whose good eye stared out triumphantly from the burnt flesh.

From somewhere far away Dolores heard a child screaming. She turned abruptly. Sharon was standing at the end of the bed staring, terrified, at her father. Fortunately, another quicker nurse had succeeded in preventing Shirley from the terrible sight by scooping her up just as the little girl was about to come through the curtain after her sister. Dolores made a grab for Sharon, but her daughter wrestled free.

"Me dad!" She screamed. "Where's me dad? I want me dad! What have you done with me dad!"

More purposefully, Dolores caught hold of Sharon. Gripping the sides of Sharon's face, she urged the girl to look away from her father and into her eyes. But when she did, Dolores saw that something inside Sharon had snapped and was broken forever.

Jimmy couldn't be reached either. He was staring infinitely at a place where he couldn't hear his daughter screams or his wife's entreaties. He couldn't even hear God. Never having felt more alone in his life, he experienced the serene surety that there was no Heaven or Hell. Once he died it would be the absolute end of him. And good riddance, he thought. I won't be missed, not even by the devil.

211

Pressing Sharon's tear-stained face against her hip, Dolores walked back to the corridor where Shirley waited with the pram and the God-sent nurse to whom Dolores smiled appreciatively.

But in reply the nurse said, "You shouldn't have brought them here. It's a disgrace."

Dolores nodded. "I know."

Chapter 20

Early the next day, in response to an urgent knock, Dolores opened her front door and was surprised to find Dr. McKenzie standing there. Behind and above him, the sky was overcast with huge grey clouds churning like the North sea. The doctor was tucked up in his usual winter attire, though the buttons of his coat were unevenly fastened, denoting haste. Shivering against the morning chill, and gripping Shane more tightly to her hip, Dolores sensed bad news coming her way:

"Has some'at happened to Jimmy?"

"Ye mean he's no here?"

"Here?" she cried in astonishment. "Why would he be here?"

"Matron called and said he left the hospital in the wee hours this morning."

"Left the hospital?" Dolores felt faint.

"May I come inside? It's a wee bit cold oot here."

"Of course. Where's me manners? Come in, come in."

She stepped aside and the doctor entered the dim hallway with his walking stick in one hand and his black bag in the other. The girls, seated for breakfast at the table in the parlour, craned their necks to look down the hallway, and see who it was who had disturbed their household at such early an hour.

"But how could he leave?" said Dolores. "He was too poorly. I saw him yesterday. Who said he could leave?"

Unfastening the top button of his thick coat, the doctor shook his head, "Nae one. He must have taken it upon himself. He was in nae state to be gallivanting aboot. I was certain he would come straight home."

"Home," said Dolores, feeling nervous that Jimmy might show up at any moment when the house was so untidy. Shane tried to stick a piece of rusk biscuit into Dolores' mouth, so she cocked her head to one side out of his reach. He chuckled and tried again. "Not now, Shane. Mummy's busy."

"Mam, what's going on?" asked Sharon. "Is it about Dad?"

"Sharon, finish your breakfast like I said. And stop asking so many questions. Go on. Sit down."

Pulling a face, the girl did as she was told.

The doctor saw how worn down Dolores was with three children to care for and one on the way. And now, a husband too injured to work but alive enough to be a terrible burden.

"Would you like a cup of tea, Doctor? Please, come into the parlour where it's warm."

Shane was placed in a shabby high chair close to the table where Shirley and Sharon were eating watery porridge.

Stirring the leaves in the teapot, Dolores said, "I just don't understand how he was *allowed* to leave."

"There were only the night nurses on duty, and he was pretty determined, apparently."

"He can be," she said, slipping the tea cosy over the pot. "So you really think he's coming here, then?"

"Aye. Of course, where else would he go?"

"To the pub, or the bookies."

The doctor chuckled, "It's not opening hours yet. Besides, he's in nae fit state or attire. He left dressed like a ghost - wearing a sheet."

"A sheet!" Shirley and Sharon exclaimed.

"Children should be seen and not heard," Dolores said. "Finish your porridge."

"But it's 'orrible," said Shirley. "Lizzie doesn't like it."

Dolores sighed impatiently. Sometimes, she got really fed up with that doll. "Just do as I say. You an' all Lizzie."

"All his clothes had to be cut off," the doctor explained. "so he had nothing to wear, except his bandages."

"Woo, woo," sang Shirley, who had put a tea towel over Lizzie and was walking the doll around the room, holding her arms outstretched like a ghost.

"Stop it," said Sharon. "Mam, tell her to stop it."

"Both of you shush, and sit down, Shirley. Stop scaring your sister."

"I daresay he looks a sight," said the doctor. "I drove up and doon Hessle Road and Anlaby Road for a wee bit hoping to catch up to him. He wouldnae be hard to spot noo, would he? But, alas, I didnae see him."

"I suppose it makes sense that he would come here," Dolores said, twisting a handkerchief and repeatedly glancing at the door as if Jimmy might burst through it at any minute. "But he would have been here by now, wouldn't he?"

"Aye, if he'd walked straight here, that is. The nurses were quite definite about him saying he was going *home*."

"Well, it's a good thing you're here, then, Doctor, in case he does show up and -"

But she didn't want to say in case Jimmy came home angry. She hoped the doctor took her to mean just in case her husband needed immediate medical attention.

"Do you take sugar, Doctor?" she asked, allowing a teardrop of milk to fall into each cup.

"Aye, but hold on."

Reaching into the breast pocket of his overcoat, which he had hung on the back of a chair, he retrieved a small brown bag of sugar he carried with him to homes such as these where sugar would be in short supply. He didn't bother at the Goodwells: he was aware of their dabblings in the black market, which he wasn't too shy about himself.

"Don't ye take sugar, Mrs. Alford?"

She was caught between lying and avoiding embarrassment.

"Here. Two is it?" he said, spooning two heaps of sugar from his bag into her tea. "That's what I have in mine."

She smiled, gratefully.

"Ye provide the tea and I'll provide the sugar, eh?"

"Ta, Doctor."

"Oh, here, ladies, would ye like a bit sprinkled on yer porridge?"

"Yes please!"

As the doctor heaped generous amounts of sugar over the girls' oats, their eyes waxed wider than the bowls in front of them.

"Oo ta," they said, digging into their porridge with unaccustomed enthusiasm.

"I ate porridge every day when I was a child," he said. "It makes ye smart."

Although Dolores was glad for her daughters to enjoy a bit of a treat, and grateful to the doctor for his kindness, she felt embarrassed for herself, and couldn't escape thinking about the next day when the girls would have to go back to eating plain porridge that would perhaps taste all the more plain because of the sweetness of today. Oh, but the extra-sweetened tea tasted heavenly, and she closed her eyes, allowing the tea to soak into her parched tongue for a long moment before swallowing it. I should have learned a long time ago to savour the good times. Perhaps if I'd known they would be so few and far between …

"Och, ye don't mind if I wait here a wee while, do ye?" asked Dr. McKenzie. "Just in case."

"No," Dolores said. "I don't mind."

The girls were sent off to school but not without Shirley protesting that they too should wait.

"What if he's mad?" Shirley whispered. "Really mad."

"I'll be all right," said Dolores. "The doctor's here."

"But he's old," Shirley whispered. "I'll leave Lizzie to watch over you, just in case."

"All right, love."

The doctor shifted uncomfortably in his seat - both because he knew the family's history and because he didn't like to be reminded of his advancing years. He pulled on his grey beard thoughtfully. This family needed help, and he knew just where to ask for it.

The front door shut as Shirley joined her sister on the path. Sharon had made no argument about leaving. She was convinced her father was coming for her because of the way she had screamed at him in the hospital.

Through the front window, Dolores watched the girls make their way to school. Chattering all the while, Shirley skipped up the street then back to Sharon who said nothing but looked furtively around, grasping an old umbrella over her shoulder. Dolores hoped they wouldn't run in to Jimmy.

"Dolores," said the doctor, alerting her to a shadow at the back door.

Dolores started, half-expecting to see a ghostly figure enter the house, but the door opened and a familiar voice called, "Hello! Anybody home?"

It was Prudence Goodwell poking her head around the door.

"Hiya. It's only me. Oh, goodness, Dr. McKenzie, I didn't expect to see you here. Is everything all right?"

"You didn't half give us a start, Prudence. We thought you might be Jimmy."

"Jimmy? Why?"

216

"We dinae ken where he is," said the doctor who went on to explain what had happened.

Slumping into a chair, Prudence declared, "What a palaver."

"Cup of tea, love?" Dolores asked.

"No, ta. I don't have time to stop. I just popped round to see if you wanted to work in the chippy at dinnertime for us, but it looks like you won't be able to in case Jimmy shows up."

"No. I suppose not," said Dolores, though she could certainly use the money.

"I wish I could wait with you, love," said Prudence. "But I've got tatties to peel."

"Here, Prudence," the doctor said after consulting his pocket watch. "If it's all right with Mrs. Alford, I'll give ye a lift. I really ought to get back to my surgery. There'll no doubt be a long, impatient queue waiting for me, even this early. And noo I'm wondering whether Jimmy might have returned to the hospital. He can't have gone very far before realising he needed oor help. I'll give the hospital a ring as soon as I get back."

"I really hope so," said Dolores, relieved at the notion.

"And when I drop ye off, Prudence, I'd like to pop in and see how yer mother's faring."

"She'll be pleased to see you, Doctor. She's doing as well as can be expected. You know me mam, never complains. Wish I could say the same for our Vivian, like," she added.

The doctor chuckled as he wrapped a warm maroon scarf around his neck.

"I'll take the long way back to look oot for Jimmy," he told Dolores. "If he shows up here, make sure he returns to the hospital straight away."

"I will. Oh, doctor, don't forget this," said Dolores, holding up the brown bag of sugar.

But he held up his hand to refuse it.

Standing in the doorway to wave them off, Dolores held Shane as close as she could.

"My son," she said lovingly, nuzzling the soft hair at the nape of his neck. "Let's go back inside where it's warm."

Dolores waited all day for Jimmy to come home, keeping busy by braiding nets at record speed as she sang over and over again to Shane:

"Who would like a fishy
On a little dishy
Who would like a fishy
When the boat comes home?

Dance to your mammy
Dance to your daddy
Dance to your mammy
When the boat comes home."

Shane never tired of hearing it, clapping and giggling along, but Dolores sometimes tired of singing it. And, on this day, she found it more difficult with each rendition to sing the line, "Dance to your daddy." The words became stuck in her throat, and she could barely hold back the tears. Shane noticed the change in her mood, and stopped giggling.

"Oh don't mind me," she said. "I'm just a silly moo."

When she sang it again, she repeated, 'Dance to your mammy' three times, leaving 'daddy' out all together.

At dinner-time, the front door burst open letting in the two girls back home for their mid-day meal. The suddenness of their arrival gave Dolores a fright.

"Did he come back, then?" asked Shirley, breathlessly.

They had run all the way home. The girls had spent the morning at school waiting for news of their father; their day-dreaming leading to repeated admonishments from the teachers. But they couldn't help it.

To Dolores, it was as if no time had passed between the girls leaving that morning and their return just now. Looking at the nets, she was astonished at how much she had completed in just a few hours. She couldn't remember any of it, tying the knots, threading the needle, getting more twine, which she must have done several times. She touched the completed nets imagining fish stuck in them, struggling to be free like the lark.

"No, love. Your dad didn't come home."

"Did you call the hospital?" Sharon asked hopefully.

"No, not yet love. I suppose I should," said Dolores. "Listen, will you two be all right here with Shane, while I go to the phone box and ring the 'ospital?"

"Aye, Mam," said Shirley.

"Are you 'ungry? I'll make some Bubble 'n' Squeak before I go. It'll only take me a minute."

She went into the parlour to fry up a batch of mashed potato and cabbage patties.

"What if he comes back while you're gone?" said Sharon.

"I don't think he will, love. He would have been 'ere by now. The doctor thought so an' all. Any'ow, I'll only be gone a minute. Here, get some plates out."

The phone closest to their house had been bombed, along with most of the houses on the street. She cursed the Germans under her breath as she hurried along. If she had been friendlier with her neighbours she would have known if one of them had installed a telephone. But she was too embarrassed to make new friends: making new friends meant making new excuses for her bruises and penury.

She was panting by the time she reached the telephone box, so she rested for a moment before calling. The last thing she wanted to do was sound hysterical and incoherent to the hospital operator. Her heart beat nervously, and still more when the nurse confirmed her true gut-feeling - that he had not returned to the hospital. Then, where was he?

Pushing around the pennies in her palm, she wondered if she should call the doctor to see if he had heard any news of Jimmy, but no, surely he would have let her know by now. Thinking of Jimmy being down at the pub or the bookies made no sense. First of all he had no money or clothes, and secondly, neither the landlord nor the bookie would serve him in that state. Quite possibly, he was disorientated, wondering the streets lost, or, perhaps, he had collapsed somewhere and was suffering debilitating pain. Dolores didn't like to bother the police, Jimmy despised them, but there was no alternative.

The police, however, fared no better in their search. Jimmy Alford had disappeared without a trace. He hadn't been spotted anywhere by anyone. The police were at a loss to explain his whereabouts, offering the suggestion that he might show up the next day, that perhaps he had found shelter in one of the many abandoned houses along the way.

"Don't worry, love," Constable Popple said, "I'll go door-to-door and find him for you."

Dolores smiled weakly in response. She couldn't fight the feeling that she didn't really want Jimmy to be found. The truth was, she wanted him to be lost and gone forever; not to end his suffering, but to end hers.

The news of Jimmy's disappearance travelled fast. The concerned and nosy neighbours who came over with their cups of tea and fresh baked pies had no idea what was in her heart. How the people now crowding her tiny two-up, two-down would recoil in disgust if they could see the tumult in her soul. Well-meaning hands, attempting to convey solidarity and alleviate worry, squeezed her shoulders while tears of frustration streaked her cheeks. If she heard, "He'll be all right, love," one more time she would scream, and, perhaps, worse confess her true desires: "But I don't want him to be all right! I want him dead!"

As she thought this, she inadvertently raised her fists wildly in the air and let out an anguished cry, alarming everyone in the room. Prudence immediately ran to her side, seized her arms, and tried to comfort her. Fortunately,

Winnie had put Dolores' children to bed, and was reading to them, so they were not witness to their mother's fit.

Dolores heavily resented Prudence in that moment. She resented her friend's freedom and composure, her capabilities and control, while her own life was lived in torment and seemed as impossible to extricate herself from as a fly from masking tape. She did not want to be calm; she flailed her arms again, this time in protest of her friend's restraint. The hysteria was building in her and she hoped the madness would soon take over so she didn't have to fight or think anymore. She screamed Jimmy's name but was rendered quiet by a slap across her cheek delivered swiftly and firmly by Prudence Goodwell.

A moment of stunned silence filled the room. Some of the onlookers nodded, relieved, as they too had been about to step in and dispense the same remedy to the hysterical woman. Her loss of control was viewed with annoyance. Anybody could lose control given the same situation, but not anybody did; otherwise people would collapse one after the other like falling dominoes, and the whole world would go mad. Thus Dolores received no sympathy for her lack of self-restraint.

"I'm sorry, love," Prudence said, her voice shaking, "But I didn't want you to disturb the children. They've finally fallen asleep."

Numbly, Dolores allowed herself to be directed to a quiet spot by the fire. Prudence glanced anxiously at the mantle clock. With Muriel incapacitated, Prudence had been left with no choice other than to leave Jake and George in charge of the fish shop. Of course, she had first asked Vivian to take over for her, but Vivian had complained that she had enough to do taking care of Muriel and Ted, which Prudence should have known would exhaust Vivian's limited durability.

Vivian had then suggested closing the shop for the evening, to which Prudence responded angrily that good fish would go to waste, and besides they couldn't afford it, and how typical it was of Vivian not to think of that. Which in turn had led to Vivian storming over to Prudence and shouting that she was merely making a suggestion that would make all their lives easier but that Prudence had to make everything a struggle and hard work. "But life *is* 'ard work," Prudence had replied. "It's supposed to be. Not everyone's like you allus trying to shirk your responsibilities and get everyone else to do your work for you."

At that point, Jake had volunteered that he and George could manage the fish and chip shop, and though she tried her utmost, Prudence could not think of a reason why they couldn't, especially when Jake supposed that if they had any questions they could always come next door to ask Muriel or Vivian. Vivian was triumphant and Prudence was annoyed that, once again, Vivian got her way.

However, Prudence had to admit, the boys running the shop was a reasonable solution to their problem. Jake had proved himself quite capable in the parlour making the Goodwells pork and beans and biscuits, and chilli and pancakes. But the whole business of leaving the running of the shop to others was a worry gnawing at the back of Prudence's mind like a mouse nibbling on cheese, so Prudence considered Dolores' loss of control a personal betrayal, a selfish disregard for the sacrifices she had made to be with her.

She was beginning to view Dolores as a burden. She tried to dismiss such thoughts, though, by arguing that good friends are there for each other in times of need. But something sly slipped into her mind, a bit of devilment that asked, But what does she need from you? Not your advice because she never takes it. Then what? Just someone to cry to, who'll bother to listen, while she moans, moans, and moans on. For a brief moment, Prudence actually felt some dislike for Dolores and her relentless neediness. But immediately, feeling terribly disloyal, she tried to rid herself of such trespassing thoughts. Thank goodness the doctor was there; a calming body for both of them.

"Och, calm yourself, young lady," Dr. McKenzie was saying to Dolores. "It'll do the baby nae good if you're hysterical."

"I know. I'm sorry," she said.

"Perhaps if everyone left," Prudence suggested to Dolores' mother; actually hoping to enlist her help, but she should have known better.

"Do you mind! I'm her mother. I can stay if I want to."

"We should all take Miss Goodwell's advice," said Dr. McKenzie. "Let's leave the poor woman alone to collect her thoughts. Dolores, I'll drop in tomorrow to see you unless I receive word from Constable Popple that Jimmy has been found."

"Ta, Doctor."

"I'm going to stay over," said Prudence, hoping to regain, with buttered fingers, a grasp on her role as a good, dependable friend to Dolores.

That was how they had related to each other for all the years they had known each other, and that's the relationship Dolores still needed. Prudence imagined that if she turned her back on Dolores, her fragile friend would somehow float away, untethered, into the abyss where she would be lost forever.

"There's no need for you to stay," said Dolores whose cheek and pride still stung from the slap.

"Nonsense," said Prudence, with forced cheerfulness. "You rest while I make us a cuppa, when this lot finally clears out. If I put the kettle on now we'll never get shut of 'em."

"I did me best," cried Dolores's mother. "It's not my fault she landed hersen in this spot of bother! She wouldn't listen to me, her own mother. No. She won't listen to nobody. Allus got to do what she wants. And look what 'appens! She's brought it all on herself."

"Madam, please allow me to escort you home," volunteered Constable Popple, slipping his notebook and pencil into a breast pocket. "Then I'll continue with the search of all the properties between here and the hospital."

Taking the arm of Dolores' mother, the policeman guided her out of the house and up the street to her own front door. The neighbours, who were also encouraged to leave, made promises of bringing more food the next day. Of course, Dolores realized, that the offers were driven by the need to know the latest news, but she didn't tell them not to come: extra food was welcome at any time, if not for her sake, then for the bairns.

The last to leave were Dr. McKenzie and Winnie, who, Prudence made promise against her will, was to have all the potatoes peeled in the morning, ready for the shop opening at half-past eleven.

"You can get George to help you."

"But he won't want to."

"Tell him if he doesn't, he'll get the biggest clip 'round his ear he's ever had," said Prudence.

"And we all know what that's like, don't we?" Dolores said.

Prudence squirmed. Her hand would sting forever with that slap. Dolores would see to it.

Chapter 21

As soon as the last customers left, Jake happily locked the door and turned the sign from *Open* to *Closed*, deciding to himself that he would rather deal with cattle than people. All the talk had been about Jimmy Alford. Many theories abounded concerning his whereabouts with some of the customers planning to form parties to conduct their own searches of the area the next morning.

There was also conjecture about Mac's involvement and how the fire actually started on board the Wilberforce. Someone who knew someone who knew someone said it was several minutes after Mac left that Jimmy Alford was seen running across the deck on fire before jumping into the sea. "No one faults your brother, mind," said the customer. "Arseford had it coming."

Hopefully, Jake thought, Prudence would be back at the helm the next day. A tired smile from George echoed the sentiment. Jake ruffled the boy's hair.

"Job well done," he said.

"Aye, we did all right, didn't we? Let's go and 'ave some of that cocoa me mam promised us," said George. "And don't forget I want to show you me war collection."

"I wouldn't miss it," said Jake.

On the blue candlewick bedspread draped over his bed, George had laid out his entire war collection for Jake to admire. Carefully arranged in order of size, the extensive treasure trove impressed Jake who had expected to see just a few bits of shrapnel, of which there were plenty of pieces, but there were also other more interesting treasures too. Standing to attention, the shiny pieces of metal glinted proudly in the lamplight.

"Where d'ya get all this stuff?"

"Around 'ere and in Scarborough, where we was evacuated to."

"Where's that?"

"About sixty mile up the coast. It's a seaside town. Used to be real posh in Victorian days with a promenade and that."

"Oh boy, this is great," said Jake picking up a port hole and looking through it.

"Aye. It's from a German U-boat. I found it on the beach. There was a lot of stuff washed up there. I used to go every day looking for stuff. Early in the morning, before anyone else, like. That port hole was one of me best discoveries. I used to think about who was looking through it right before they was torpedoed. Here look at this," he said, picking up a weathered black leather boot.

He stuck his foot in the boot.

"This belonged to a Nazi," he said. "With small feet," he added. "Look it almost fits me. The foot was still in it when I found it."

"Still in the boot?"

"Aye. There was crabs all over it and it stank."

"How'd ya get the foot out?"

The boy shrugged, "I used our Vivian's curling iron. It were right squishy. I reckon the crabs finished it off 'cause it weren't there the next day. I looked for it an' all. No bones neither."

Taking off the boot, so Jake could get a closer look, George said, "If you put it to your ear, you can hear the sea."

Jake brought the boot to his ear, sending the boy into peels of laugher.

"You sure got me," smiled Jake, giving the boot back to George who took a discreet listen himself just in case, but there was nothing, not even the echoed screams of blown apart sailors.

"Do *you* have any souvenirs?" George asked, getting to the business he really wanted to discuss.

"Souvenirs?"

"It's all right if you don't. I were just wondering, like from that feller that stabbed you."

Jake took a deep breath.

"Oh no, I didn't take anything," he said. Except his life.

There was the letter, but he didn't count that as a souvenir. Besides, he hadn't taken it, the letter had been given to him, entrusted to him.

"You killed him, didn't you?" George whispered eagerly. "Go on, you can tell me. How did it 'appen?"

How *did* it happen? thought Jake. How did a cowboy end up in France? There, at the Battle of the Bulge, terrified, he had run, tried to escape, but there was no place safe to go. He had tripped over God-knows-what (another frightened soldier, another dead one?), and had fallen, and was curled in the foetal position when the German caught up to him.

With his hands over his face, Jake had sobbed and rocked, and called for his mother whose lovely face he had struggled to evoke but all his memory would serve him was her pale hand reaching out to save him from the snake. He cried out and begged for mercy when the bayonet struck his leg but the second stab of the bayonet, in his side, snapped him into action. Rage came. He was embroiled in a battle for his life. The whole war had come down to just him and the soldier in front of him. Whoever won that private battle, would turn the tide of war to his country's favour. Out of bullets, they resorted to hand-to-hand combat. Jake scrambled to his feet and lunged at the German with his bayonet. The enemy with crazed blue eyes knocked the blade away with his own rifle, but Jake was able to follow through with the butt of his gun, smashing it into the face of the *feind*. Over and over again, he smashed at that hated face. The beast had been unleashed. Soon, all that existed was the thud of his rifle, the splinter of bones and the splitting of flesh. The coward had become a hero.

When Jake came to, he found himself astride the felled German whose face now resembled hamburger meat. Both men still gripped their bloody rifles. Chest heaving, Jake dropped his gun to the ground, and sank slowly back on his heels. Bloody spittle bubbled on the German's lips. The poor guy was still alive, but barely. Jake was in shock. 'I did that,' he thought. 'That was me.' He sobbed, wretched.

His adversary had been brave, had sought out the fight, chasing Jake down until there was no choice for Jake but to fight. This soldier would take to the grave the secret that Jake had run. Jake was afraid to meet the dying man's eyes, but when he did, he saw that the fading blue eyes were not afraid to look at him. One eye socket was broken.

The young soldier, Jake's age, tried to lift his head, to speak. He was beyond pain but exhausted. Jake didn't hate him anymore.

"I'm sorry," Jake said. "I'm sorry."

Tears streamed down his face while the war went on around them. He had never felt so alone, so naked before God.

"*Sie haben mich getötet,*" the German slurred.

One side of his mouth twitched, perhaps attempting to smile. He reached over to unfasten the buttons of his tunic, so Jake snatched up his rifle, but the soldier held up a hand to show peace. He had trouble with the buttons, so Jake helped him. The soldier then reached inside his tunic and pulled out an envelope, which he pressed into Jake's hand.

"*Bitte,*" he said.

"Yes," Jake said. "I'll take care of it. Don't worry."

Then, as if waiting for angels, the German turned his clear, now peaceful blue eyes to the sky.

Jake was touched by the civility of the gesture of trust. Only moments before, the German had sneered while stabbing him with a bayonet. But the patriotic killer was gone, only a dying boy remained. Death had brought them together, reminding them that they were two men who out of uniform might have done kind things for one another. But civil men wear civilian clothes. Dressed in their colours, there had been no choice but to fight.

Through his tears Jake said, "It was you or me, pal. It was you or me. Why'd ya come for me? I wouldn't have killed ya on any other day."

To which the soldier, with yet another attempt at a wry smile, struggled to reply, "*Alles hat ein ende – nur die Wurst hat zwei.*"

The young German seemed content to have his life taken away. The war was over for him, and he died believing his was an honourable death. Touching his own wounds, Jake became jealous of the German's new found freedom. His arm and side hurt like hell, reminding him of their struggle and how he had run.

That's my blood on his bayonet, he thought.

"That's my blood!" he shouted, making a grab for the rifle still in the soldier's grip. But the dying man was strong and unyielding, so Jake let go and picked up his own rifle to finish the job.

On that crisp January Day, under Heaven's blue, there upon white-frosted grass spilled fresh with blood, was where the young German died, and where Jake vowed to never run away again.

American soldiers ran toward him, shouting in urgent voices. One of them stepped on the dead man's head with the same indifference as if it were nothing more than the ground beneath his combat boot. The same soldier yelled, "Son of a gun, this one's alive! Fucking kraut almost got another one of our boys. He killed three before he got to you. Ran through us all like a rabid dog. It's all right. You're gonna be okay, son." Then shouting, "He's lost a lot of blood! Hurry up with that fucking stretcher! Jesus Christ!"

The envelope was addressed to a woman in Dresden: Fraulein Elizabet Klaus. Two bloods, Jake and the dead soldier's, were mixed and smeared over the address. One blood dead and one blood still alive. Inside the unsealed envelope, Jake discovered a folded, unfinished letter written in strange, foreign lettering with odd marks scattered above some of the letters. The letter started out simply to, '*Mutter*' which stalled Jake from reading further. With heavy heart, he read the first word over and over again.

There were only two paragraphs. The letter was unfinished and unsigned. Jake would never know the soldier's Christian name; he would know only that his surname was Klaus. What sort of boy had Klaus been? A scallywag? Had he climbed trees, played soccer, gone fishing with his father? Yes, he had been one tough cookie, Jake was sure of it, probably the leader of his gang. And when the war came along he had eagerly signed up to become a hero for his country. A hero to the very end.

Reading again the name and address on the front of the envelope, Jake thought of what he had done to that woman's son. He tried to imagine what she looked like and what her expression would have been when she was finally told, as she had always feared, that her son was dead. Would she think of me? Her son's killer? Though it wasn't me that killed him. It was the war machine. I was just grease on the wheels. Would she think of the boys her son had killed, the three before me? Or would she feel proud holding his medal of combat? Strange that there had been no one to mourn my death, and yet I survived. Perhaps that's why. Perhaps there would have been no lesson learned, no pain, from my death. So it had to be him, Klaus.

Jake considered adding some words of his own to the letter, a postscript. He didn't like that it was unfinished. The letter ended as abruptly as the soldier's life. Anyway, he wasn't sure what he would write in English never mind German, which he didn't speak or write. Yet, he delayed posting the letter. After a while the letter became a terrible burden to him. He couldn't stand to think about it or be in possession of it anymore. Twice or more he threw it away, only to retrieve it, full of remorse, minutes or hours later while vowing to post it the next day.

As soon as he recovered from the bayonet wounds, Jake went back to the front to fight or die, he wasn't sure which, but he always carried the letter with him ready to pass it along when his final moment came. Let it be someone else's burden, he had thought, not feeling worthy of anything but dying.

In some ways, he thought of himself as already dead and had lost some fear because of it. His actions became as he imagined Klaus would act, bravely. It wasn't long before Jake was injured again, more seriously, and back in the hospital. Though this time he was discharged for good, with a recommendation for the Purple Heart, and the hope that he would have no more opportunity to kill another human being.

"How did it happen?" George asked again, not sure if his question had been heard.

Jake sighed, rubbing his chin thoughtfully. "I ... don't know."

George frowned, noticing the seriousness of Jake's mood. He had heard the fishermen swap stories from their adventures at sea, and, once they got talking, a ripple of relaxation would spread through the group. Soon they would be joking. But it's like getting blood from a stone, trying to get him to talk. Perhaps, George reasoned, if he shared one of his own war stories, the American might follow suit.

So he said, "We was shot at once."

"Really? Where?" Jake asked, genuinely surprised.

"In Scarborough. Me and some lads was beachcombing and this plane came flying low at us firing his gun."

He stood, motioning as if he were holding a machine gun and making the rat-a-tat-tat noise as he did so.

"It were one of them Messerschmitts. We knew all their planes, even just by listening you could tell what it was. We knew ours too. The spitfires."

A broad grin cracked his face in two, and his eyes grew wide with pride.

I wish I could have come out of the war as innocent as I went in, thought Jake.

"That were the best sound ever – our planes," said George. "That and the all-clear, of course. Aye, we could tell the planes apart,' he said, playing the different engine drones in his head, remembering the fear of one sound against the joy of the other. "But anyrode it were definitely one of theirs, we could see the black crosses on the wings and on the sides. It were grey with yellow bits on it. I can remember it very clearly. It were right scary."

"What was he doing in ... ?"

"Scarborough," said George. "I don't know, but it were around the time they was bombing York, or trying to, more like it, so maybe he was taking a gander around before he went 'ome. Pretty dangerous. It were early morning. I mean dangerous for him to be out in the daylight anyrode. That's what Mac said."

"Did he hit any of you?"

George shook his head, "No. We was too fast for him."

Jake smiled. The boys would all have been killed if that had been the intention of the pilot. Jake opined that the pilot had been toying with them for a bit of fun to tell his friends back at base.

"I found one of the bullets he shot at us," said George.

"Oh yeah? Where is it?"

George nodded to a locked box on the corner of his bed. "In there."

Jake sensed he was being baited.

"What else d'ya have in there?" he asked, folding his arms.

"Well, that depends."

"Depends on what?"

"I was wondering, like," began George, playing with his fingers and pausing to take a bite out of a fingernail.

"Go on," said Jake.

"I was wondering if you'd show me your gun again."

"Again? I didn't show it to ya last time. Y'all just happened to see it my bag while I was picking out an undershirt."

George gave off a cheeky grin.

"I know, but could I hold it? Just for a minute?"

"Your mom didn't seem too happy when ya mentioned the gun."

"She won't know. I won't tell nobody."

Jake looked doubtful.

"Then I'll show you what's in my box," George said.

Jake smiled again at the boy's naive attempt at manipulation. Well, what harm would it do to show him the gun?

It was true Muriel had been nervous about it, but that was generally the feeling in a country where most people did not own guns unless they hunted. He had seen the big piles of guns when the British soldiers had to turn in their weapons, man by man.

"O.K."

"Smashing!"

"Come on. I keep it in our closet."

George felt as though they were on a military manoeuvre the way they crept from his room to Jake's so the ladies downstairs wouldn't hear them. As soon as Jake retrieved the gun from the top shelf of the wardrobe, George reached out for it, but Jake said, "One sec." And George could not hide his disappointment when Jake spun open the chamber of the Colt and dropped the bullets into his palm.

"No way," said Jake in answer to George's complaint. "I shouldn't even keep it loaded here. There's no need."

Jake put the bullets in an ash tray and handed the gun, butt first, to George who hesitated until a reassuring nod from Jake bolstered his nerve enough to take it.

"Wow! It's heavy."

"Here, wanna try the belt and holster."

"Can I?!"

George could hardly breathe; he was so excited.

He slipped the gun into the holster. The belt was so big, he had to keep his legs spread so it wouldn't slide down his legs. Then, just like in the westerns he had seen, George pulled the gun out as quickly as he could and aimed it at a photograph of a nameless aunt that had hung on the wall for over forty years.

"Hey there little gunslinger, ya did that pretty darn quick," said Jake.

George's finger was tense against the trigger.

"Never pull the trigger unless ya mean to kill something."

Spinning the chamber, Jake explained how many rounds could be held in the gun. Feeling pretty tough,

George stuck his finger through the trigger, and tried to spin the gun. Jake laughed, but kindly so.

"Here let me show ya. I'll need this."

Jake took the holster from George. He fastened the belt around his waist and a thin leather lace around his thigh. The lad couldn't believe he was looking at a real cowboy. Noticing George's admiring look, Jake reached into the dark wardrobe to get his ten gallon hat. The cowhide hat had the scent and feel of Texas, and it fit just like home too.

"Whoa!" whispered George in awe.

Jake smiled as he slipped on the hat, casting his eyes into shadow. The hairs on the back of George's neck prickled, and goose pimples ran up and down his arms.

"You're a real cowboy," he gasped gleefully, wishing Paddy was there to witness the event.

Jake pulled out his gun so quickly, George jumped, holding up his hands in defence. Jake laughed, and twizzled the gun forwards three times then back three times before slipping the Colt back into its holster. His hand stayed poised above the gun, ready to pull it out.

"How did you do that?" asked George, sick with excitement.

Jake performed the gun trick again for his young admirer.

"Will you learn me?"

"Sure. Any time," said Jake. "Oh-oh, we've been found out."

At her mother's insistence, Winnie had brought up two mugs of cocoa and a plate of biscuits for the boys. Through the crack in the door, she had been watching the goings-on for the whole demonstration.

"I want to have a go!"

"Shush Winnie or Mam'll find out. It's still my turn. I haven't finished looking at it yet," said George. "Have I, Jake?"

"Yes, you have," said Winnie. "It's my turn, isn't it Jake? Tell him, it's my turn or I'll tell."

"Winnie, there's no need for that," said Jake.

"Are them real bullets?" Winnie asked, fingering the bullets in the ash tray on top of the chest of drawers. She picked one up and examined it closely. "Where does it go?"

Jake showed her.

"In there?" she asked. "This way?"

"No, like this," Jake said, closing the chamber and spinning it.

"Wow!" said Winnie. "Can I try it?"

"Now then, cowboy," said Vivian who was leaning, provocatively, against the door frame. "Say, why don't you come up and see me sometime?"

Jake cleared his throat.

"I was teaching Winnie and George a couple of tricks."

"Well, don't let me mam catch you or she'll have your guts for garters."

"Please don't tell," said George and Winnie together.

"I won't," Vivian said staring right at Jake. "For the right price."

It was a look he hadn't seen in a while. He couldn't help but feel the heat from it. They hadn't been together since coming to Hull. He had shrugged off her touch and slept with his back to her since finding out about the boy. But ... she was so goddamn gorgeous.

"You haven't worn that stuff for a while," she said. "I used to like it."

Jake said, "Sorry kids but the lesson's over for today."

"But I want to show Paddy."

"And I want to shoot some'at."

"Paddy can wait," said Vivian. "Go on you two. It's past your bed time."

"Do we have to?"

"'Fraid so, kids," said Jake.

Vivian closed the door firmly on the slow-moving children. Man and wife stood ten feet apart, neither making the first move, like a duel. It was a while since Jake had looked at her with eyes that didn't feel cheated. The right curves gave the black dress she wore a sensuous shape, which his eyes drifted over in waves. My wife, he thought.

Then anger rose within him over memories of her deception. Yet the anger merely served as impetus to the desire to have her again. There she stood, red lips poised in a knowing smile, daring him with her blue eyes. After what they had been through she had hoped he still wanted her, and she could see that he did.

He reached for his belt to unfasten it.

No," she said. "Let me."

His hands fell helplessly to his sides. Their eyes locked. Without looking down, her hands reached forward and touched his belt. She ran her fingers over the thick leather and the broad, metal buckle. Her cheek was against his as she stroked the holster. He was angry, but he wanted her.

She pulled the gun from its holster.

"This reminds me of something," she whispered.

He didn't respond but breathed heavily. She ran the barrel across her lips but he turned his face when she tried to get him to do the same. She smiled. The mother-of-pearl buttons on her dress slipped easily through the buttonholes as she unfastened them one by one. The open dress revealed the peach silk slip he had bought her the day they left the courthouse as man and wife. The slip was delicately edged with cream lace that drew down to a point between her breasts where his eyes rested, as always. Smiling again, she slid the gun barrel up and down her cleavage. It was more than he could stand. He reached for her, but she held him back with the gun pointed at his chest.

"There ain't no bullets in it," he told her, forgetting.

"Let's pretend there is."

Her dress fell to the floor and she stepped out of it. As she lay back on the bed, still pointing the gun at him, she lifted her slip to reveal matching silk knickers. She ran the gun up her thigh. It was as if his eyes were tied to it, following the barrel's path to where she pressed the gun against herself. Watching her, Jake could scarcely breathe.

Soon, they were both without clothes and she was on top of him. Strong perfume clung to his nostrils and soft bleached hair rubbed against his cheek. Red nails dug into him, and it was her same motions back and forth, and her same breathing in his ear. She was no longer looking at him. Was she thinking of someone else? Angrily, he pushed her off.

"What is it?" she cried, awakened from her trance.

Without a word, he turned her over onto her front and roughly pulled up her hips. He slapped her.

"Ow! Jake! What are you doing?"

Rage drove him on. He finished quickly.

"You bastard," she said, sitting up and touching her messed-up hair. "You ruined me shampoo and set."

Make-up was smudged on her face and the pillow. Jake slipped on his pyjamas, pleased that she was the one angry for a change.

"Pass us me nightie," she said sulkily.

He picked a blue one from the drawer.

"Not that old thing. Me new black one."

Ignoring her, he tossed the old nightdress on the bed. Too cold to argue she passed it over her head. The nightie was old-fashioned, flannel, and had belonged to their Great Aunt Lily.

"It's bloody freezing in here," she complained.

"Cigarette?" he asked, lighting one for himself.

"Yeah," she said, up now and securing the belt of her dressing gown.

"Where's me slippers? Me feet are fit to drop off."

"Here," he said, pulling them from under the bed.

"Ta."

The end of her cigarette glowed brightly as she sucked at it. She looked over, studying him as he fell onto the bed. She hadn't seen that aggressive side of him before, and she wasn't sure what to make of it.

"Ya done look like a raccoon," he said with his eyes closed.

"A what?"

He indicated her eyes, so she looked in the square mirror that hung by a ribbon above the chest of drawers. Black eye liner had smudged under her eyes, and her eyebrows were no longer smoothly drawn in.

"Bloody hell! Look what you did to me! I look a right bloody picture."

"Like I said, a raccoon."

"What's a bloody raccoon when it's at home?" she said, taking a brush angrily to her hair.

She glared back at him from the reflection in the mirror, but his eyes remained closed.

"I suppose you think it's funny, do you?" she said.

He didn't reply and, before she had taken the lid off the jar of cold cream, he was snoring.

"Bloody typical!" she snorted, digging her fingers into the white stuff and smearing it over her face with indignant fury.

Using short, violent strokes, she wiped the cream and make-up from her face, but, after a moment, her shoulders sank and the will to fight left her. With her head in her hands and tears in her eyes, she wondered what had happened to the boy soldier who had once loved her like a puppy dog. She stared into the mirror at her reddened eyes and tear-streaked face.

Look at me, crying over a bloke again.

Sniffing and wiping her nose on the back of her hand, she thought, It were me that happened to him. Good old Vivian Goodwell, that's what it is. I'm no bloody good to nobody. Not Jake. Not Ted. Not me mam. And especially not mesen. It would be best if I just went away, somewhere where I wouldn't be no more bother to no one.

"Angel?"

His tone was gentle, conciliatory. Her face was scrubbed free of make-up. He had been watching her with one eye which he quickly shut whenever she had glanced back at him in the mirror. She did look like an angel with a clean face.

"Come to bed, honey. Come on."

"That's not how you're supposed to treat a wife," she said, straightening the silver brush set, making sure the brush, comb and mirror were aligned.

"Then let me show you how I treat an angel."

Chapter 22

Wondering why she had offered to spend the night, Prudence pulled the overhead cord to turn off the light in Dolores' bedroom. As she lay her head back on the pillow, on Jimmy's side of the bed, Prudence brought to mind the lark that had lain unconscious there just a few days before. Hopefully, Dolores had washed the pillow-case since then but Prudence sniffed the pillow anyway. There was nothing but the scent of starch. Satisfied it was clean, she settled back with the intention of wishing her friend a good night's sleep, but Dolores's breaths were already even and deep. She was asleep, but not peacefully: the occasional furrow that crossed her brow belied the unsettled mind beneath.

After the excitement of the day, Prudence had expected Dolores to toss and turn all night, worrying about the whereabouts of her husband, but, seemingly, the sleeping draught the doctor had prescribed had proven effective. Prudence was a little envious and wondered if there was enough left for her to take some, but she couldn't be bothered to go downstairs in the cold, dark house, nor had she the nerve. The day's strange events had left her a little jittery.

The Alford's house did not rest untroubled, and Prudence imagined that every creak and squeak was the sound of Jimmy Alford coming home. Some mice scampered along in the attic above, and Prudence's heart skipped a beat. She tried to focus her mind on something safe. Derek Stalworth came to mind, and she smiled. Her eyes drifted close and soon she too was asleep.

While Dolores' body slept, her mind dreamed on, and in her sleep she felt something flutter against her face. Subconsciously, she brushed at it with her hand, but the thing persisted. To escape whatever it was, she turned on her side, but once more something tickled her ear. She brushed at it again, still too asleep to care too much. But when she heard a menacing voice whisper, "Home at last." she screamed and bolted upright, her wild awake eyes catching a glimpse of a wispy cloak of white floating in the darkness at the foot of the bed.

"Jimmy?" she cried, frantically reaching for the light cord that hung low above the bed.

But her efforts to switch on the light were thwarted by the back of her own hand that kept tapping away the cord the faster she tried to grab it. And all the while the familiar fear of him was rising in her. She could taste it. Her stomach knotted and her heart beat rapidly. Her chest was tight and she couldn't breathe. Gasping, she thought she might drown in terror.

"What is it?" Prudence asked sleepily.

"It's Jimmy; he's 'ere," Dolores whispered.

"What? Here? Now?" cried Prudence.

"Shush!" said Dolores who finally caught hold of the light cord and tugged it.

Click. Saviour light spilled forth, as welcome as it was on Earth's first day. Forced to retreat, the darkness now existed only in the corners of the room, where it waited black and crouching like a panther.

A giant moth fluttered against the light bulb. Singed, it flew away then, unable to help itself, flew back. Prudence blinked. The light was bright. Jimmy's pigeons cooed eerily and scratched in their loft on the roof above their heads as if something had disturbed them too.

Sitting up, Prudence whispered, "Did you just say that Jimmy's here? Here in the 'ouse?"

"Aye. I saw some'at. There, at the foot of the bed."

"What was it?"

"Shush!"

Prudence's heart beat fast. She pulled the covers up to her chin.

"Jimmy, are you there?" Dolores called. "Prudence Goodwell's 'ere with me. We was worried. Are you all right?"

A gurgling noise startled them but it was only Shane, disturbed by the light and voices, stirring in the drawer he slept in on the floor close to the bed. Prudence peered into the darkness where she couldn't see or hear anything, other than blood thumping in her ears. The door to the bedroom was open, but it could have been left that way when they came to bed.

"Dolores, tell me exactly what happened?"

"I felt some'at on me face, then I 'eard him, his voice. And, and," she stammered, whispering too. "Then I saw him."

"Where exactly?"

"There! I saw him there! Wearing a sheet!"

She was pointing to the foot of the bed. There was no one there presently, though it occurred to Prudence that Jimmy might have dropped to the floor and was hiding behind or under the bed. He certainly hadn't expected Prudence to be there.

"Jimmy?" she called. "I'll go back to my house, if that's what you want."

At this suggestion Dolores shook her head vehemently to which Prudence mouthed, "I won't really go."

"Jimmy, say some'at," said Dolores. "Prudence was just here keeping us company till you got 'ome. We've been expecting you, you see. We've been ever so worried."

Not a sound came forth from the darkness.

"Are you sure it wasn't a dream?" Prudence whispered. "It could have been that moth you felt."

She indicated the large grey moth that was still making futile attempts to endear itself to the light bulb; perhaps each time hoping the light would be kinder to it than the last. Its shadow fluttered large and menacingly on the ceiling and walls.

"It wasn't the bloody moth," whispered Dolores, annoyed at the suggestion. "It's Jimmy. It makes sense. Don't you see? He probably waited outside, hiding somewhere, till everyone left. Then he snuck in the back door."

"You said you were going to lock it, precisely so this wouldn't 'appen. You wanted to make sure he would have to knock to come in," said Prudence.

"I meant to, but after I took that stuff Dr. McKenzie gave me, well, I might have forgot. I can't be sure."

The very real prospect of the door being left unlocked and Jimmy sneaking in, truly scared Prudence. Her mouth ran dry. She longed for a drink, but the jug of water on the chest of drawers seemed a very long way from her side of the bed. The thought of putting her feet on the floor when Jimmy might be under the bed terrified her. She was sure she could feel his presence lurking, as if there was pure evil under the bed and the bed itself might levitate out of fear. Closing her eyes, she reprimanded herself, *I'm the rational one, remember? But that doesn't mean he's not 'ere …*

"You said you 'eard some'at, his voice, what did he say?"

"He said, 'Here I am. I'm 'ome.' And it were real scary, the way he said it. Sounded more like a threat than owt else. Mind you, so does everything he says. Even when he asks for a cup of tea, he makes it sound more like a death threat than a request. Anyrode, then I screamed.

Probably frightened him off, like. Or maybe he saw you was 'ere an' all so he ran out."

Prudence shuddered at the thought of Jimmy standing over her without her knowing. Though she hadn't seen him in his current state, Dolores had described his appearance so vividly, Prudence was quite able to evoke a horrific image of him burned with only one eye and his skin red and peeling.

Pointing down at the bed, Prudence mouthed to Dolores whether she thought he could be hiding under the bed. Dolores shook her head.

"No room," she whispered, then her eyes flew open. "Oh, the girls!" she exclaimed. "I 'ope they're all right. What if he's gone in there?"

"We'd 'ave probably heard some'at from them."

"Aye, you're probably right," said Dolores. "But I 'ave to make sure." She took a deep breath. "Will you come wi' me?"

"Aye, all right."

A look between them offered no courage: there was nothing but fear in both of their faces. Nonetheless, they got out of the bed, quietly. Prudence had borrowed a threadbare nightie from Dolores, but there were no extra slippers, except Jimmy's and those were downstairs by his chair, which was where they would remain: not only would Prudence not have wanted to wear his slippers, Dolores was too afraid to move them from their designated spot in case Jimmy did come home.

Bare feet it had to be. The linoleum floor was cold. Since there was no spare dressing gown either, she slipped on her cardigan. Together, the two women crept toward the open bedroom door, carefully peering around the end of the bed in case he was crouching there. He wasn't. Then they stood in the doorway to the landing bracing themselves for the next step

"Jimmy?" whispered Dolores. "Are you there? It's me Dolores."

If he was there, surely he would have laughed at that daft remark. Bracing herself, she reached around into the hallway half-expecting her hand to be grabbed in the darkness as she felt along the rough wallpaper for the stiff landing-light switch. She flicked it on. Instantly, the hallway went from black to bright. Some cockroaches scattered quickly into the cracks and crevices of the house, leaving the narrow landing bare. A faded multi-coloured rag rug Dolores had bought at a jumble sale the year before waited to be stepped on.

"Jimmy?" Dolores whispered again, not at all relishing the thought of a reply.

She couldn't understand why he would still be hiding. Surely he knew Prudence well enough that he would have made himself known by now. The notion struck her that maybe it was his appearance that kept him hidden. It was likely he didn't want Prudence to see him so disfigured, or perhaps he didn't want to see her reaction to his disfigurement. Dolores whispered this thought to Prudence, who nodded in agreement.

"Perhaps it would be best to leave him be," Dolores whispered. "I mean, if he wants to 'ide, he can. Let's just check on the girls though."

Prudence was in agreement. She was not eager to lay eyes on Jimmy Alford at this time or any other. They crept down the landing until they reached the door to the girls' room. Dolores sighed with relief when she saw that Shirley and Sharon were still sound asleep on the single bed they shared. They looked so peaceful, facing each other. She felt silly for thinking they would be in any danger. Perhaps she *had* been dreaming. Perhaps it *was* the moth or the pigeons she had heard, or that stuff the doctor had given her was playing tricks with her mind. It had seemed so real though, hearing his voice and seeing his already ghost-like figure at the foot of the bed.

"Well, at least they're all right," she whispered, closing the door.

244

"Do you think it would be best if I did go 'ome," whispered Prudence. "So he could come out."

"Oh no," whispered Dolores, alarmed at the possibility of being on her own. "Wait while morning. He'll be all right till then. If he's 'ere at all. Sometimes I can't tell no more what's me imagination and what isn't. I'm sorry. I'm still a bit shaken up mesen. You don't mind, do you? Just while morning?"

"No, I don't mind," said Prudence. "Anyrode, I'd much rather stay 'ere than walk home in the dark on me own after this."

By the time they climbed back into bed, after brushing off the dead moth and picking up Shane to sleep with them, Dolores was completely convinced she had imagined hearing and seeing Jimmy. Even so, she strained to listen for sounds from downstairs or outside. Yet it was only the wind whispering at the windows and down the chimney that she heard, not her sick husband. Then it was only the pigeons on the roof scratching for food. She couldn't remember when she had last fed them. Scratch, scratch, coo, coo. But what was that creak? Did it come from downstairs? Perhaps he was sleeping in the chair by the fire as he had done on many other nights when he was too drunk to make it up the stairs. In the morning, she would go down and there he would be, waiting for his cup of tea and his breakfast, like always. She hoped he wasn't angry that Prudence had slept over.

She jerked away when Prudence's feet touched her calf.

"Oo your feet aren't 'alf cold."

"Sorry," murmured Prudence.

As Dolores settled on her side with a protective arm around Shane, she felt cramping in her lower back. Holding her breath, and with one hand on her belly, she waited for the pain to pass. "Sorry, love, I hope you don't feel fear where you are," she whispered. "I hope you only feel me love."

245

Chapter 23

Two weeks or so passed, and Jimmy Alford was still missing. The curtains at the Alfords' house remained drawn, day and night. Dolores kept them closed for fear she would see Jimmy's sneering, rotten face pressed to the window. There was no sign of where he had gone or when he would be back. Abandoned houses in the area had been searched by neighbours and the police, signs had been posted and a picture of him (happy after winning a pigeon race) had been published in the Hull Daily Mail. Everything that could be done to find Jimmy Alford was done. His disappearance and injuries were the talk of the community. Everyone enjoyed the opportunity to postulate about the local mystery. The gossip was a relief from their own troubles.

About Jimmy's fate, Dolores had so many conflicting feelings and ideas washing around in her head that she couldn't isolate just one and claim it as *the* gut-feeling. All she really felt was constant fear and anxiety. She found herself spending hours in a daze. Every ordinary thing from getting out of bed, to getting dressed, to sweeping the scullery floor became monumental and insurmountable tasks that she thought about doing long before she made the move to commence them. The unfinished chores were piling up.

Outside, the girls were playing with Shane, or otherwise occupying themselves while, by the dying fire, Dolores was huddled in the chair that faced Jimmy's wing-backed, empty chair. She shivered but the cold air wasn't the cause of it. There had been many an evening whence they had sat, she and Jimmy; evenings of which she had no fond memories.

Dolores and the girls had collectively held their breaths whenever Jimmy was home, as if Jimmy was the only one permitted to move freely through time until he left again, which was never too soon. And when he did leave, their collective breaths would release in one long suspiration. Once again, they too could move freely.

Now, as she stared into his empty chair, Dolores found that if she looked hard enough at the cushions she was sure she could see them move to allow for someone sitting on them. The urge to urinate was strong in her but she dare not move.

He was in the house. She knew this, even if she couldn't see him. She knew he was there. His brown slippers, on the floor in front of the wing-backed chair, had the shape of feet still in them, suspiring upwards to create the whole being, so much so she half-expected them to walk towards her to mete out punishment as they often had in the hands of Jimmy.

The hairs on the back of her neck rose. She dare not turn around. Every draft she felt was a door opening somewhere in the house through which Jimmy was walking. A very ancient and fish-like smell mingled with beer and lost money wafted its way to her in waves until she thought she was going to be sick from it. Yet, when she made the effort to sniff the air and seek it out, she could smell only the damp of the house.

He was playing a game of hide and seek with her, chuckling, she knew. She had stopped calling out his name because it scared the girls whose chanting voices and clapping hands billowed in through the cracks under the doors and around the windows. The sounds of their play puzzled Dolores for a moment because she had been sure it was night-time but it couldn't be if the girls and Shane were outside. Dolores covered her ears, trying to block out the words they were chanting:

"A sailor went to sea, sea, sea,
To see what he could see, see, see
But all that he could see, see, see
Was the bottom of the deep blue sea, sea, sea."

Dolores daren't move. She had become convinced that if she put a foot on the floor, her leg would be grabbed by Jimmy whom she was sure was waiting behind her chair. She could hear him breathing, a monstrous familiar sound that was growing louder, but then it stopped, suddenly, along with her heart. Too afraid to move her head, her eyes shifted left and right as she waited for Jimmy to appear.

Water broke and spilled from between her legs, yet still she was afraid to move. The front door opened and heavy footsteps came down the hallway toward her.

A man's desperate voice called out, "Dolores!"

As soon as her name was called, she screamed and collapsed into a dead faint. Mac ran to her side, alarmed to find her pale and sweaty. Constable Popple had instructed him to wait outside until he arrived on his bike, but Mac had been too eager to break the news that Jimmy Alford's drowned body had been found at the docks, snared by the hook at the end of George's fishing pole.

Gently saying her name, he touched the pale forehead beaded with sweat. But she was out cold. Cradling her limp body, he carried her up the stairs to her bedroom where he gently lay her on the bed. Again, he called her name and stroked the side of her face, but there was no response. He ran to the window over-looking the street and yelled for the girls to fetch the doctor, throwing change from his pocket. "No questions," he told them as they started in. "Just do as I say. Now!" The coins clattered on the path and into the road, scattering everywhere.

Frantically, he searched the bedroom for some brandy or such with which to revive Dolores. He pulled out drawers. He looked in, behind and on top of the wardrobe but with no success. Surely, Alford had a stash somewhere. Then Shirley came breathlessly into the room.

"Why's me Mam in bed? What's wrong?"

"Did Sharon go for the doctor?" he shot at her.

"Aye. She's the eldest," Shirley said, wringing her little hands. "Is me mam all right?"

"Aye, she just got a little dizzy. Look, love, do you have any brandy in the house? Owt at all? Whiskey? Rum?"

Shirley hesitated before answering, "Sharon said not to tell me mam about it 'cause me dad'll kill us. He made her promise not to tell."

"Please Shirley. Your mam needs it. Your dad's not going to care anymore."

"Why not?"

He caught himself. "He just won't. Now, please. Your mam's not feeling well. She needs that brandy."

By the time Shirley returned with the drink, measured carefully into a glass, Dolores was half-awake, moaning and clutching her swollen belly.

"Where's the bottle?" asked Mac, needing a drink himself.

"Me dad's not going to like it."

"Your dad -" He was interrupted by a loud wail.

"It's coming!" Dolores cried. "It's too soon! Jimmy!"

Hearing her call her husband's name stung Mac, and reminded him of why he was there. But now was not the time to tell her that Jimmy was dead. Gently grabbing the stunned young girl by the shoulders, Mac slowly said, "Fetch the brandy, Shirley."

"It's rum."

"It's rum. Well, all right, fetch the rum, then, all of it, believe me your dad won't care. Then after that, fetch some hot water and some towels or whatever the midwife asked for when Shane was born."

"Mam's having the baby?"

"Aye. We need your help, so 'urry up. Fetch some'at, owt."

"It's too soon," moaned Dolores.

"Aye, I know," said Mac, who didn't know much, if anything about such things. "The doctor's on his way. Everything's going to be fine. Here, 'ave a sip of rum."

"Mac?" she asked, after taking a sip.

"Aye, it's me."

The pain and fear in her eyes softened.

"But what are you doing here? Where's Jimmy?"

"Never mind him. Here, 'ave some more, it'll do you good."

She took a huge swallow, wincing as it burned a path to her stomach. He finished it off. His hands were shaking.

"Help me wi' me knickers," Dolores said, struggling with her undergarments. "Sorry," she half-smiled.

The baby was coming whether he knew anything about it or not. Keeping his face averted, he helped to remove her soaked underwear. For all the times he had imagined such intimacy between them, this was not one of the ways. He took her hand, hurting every time the pain came to Dolores in waves.

"Here's the rum," said Shirley.

Mac took a swig.

"I thought it was for me mam."

"Shush," said Dolores.

But Mac felt ashamed, and placed the rest of the bottle on the bedside table.

"Where's Shane?" asked Dolores, her voice tight with pain.

"In his pram. I brought him inside."

"You're a good girl."

"There isn't no hot watter," Shirley said. "Fire's out."

"Shit," said Mac.

"I've got the towels though," she said, holding the bundle forward for him to see.

"Aye, good lass. Here, I'll get a fire started and put some water on. You stay here and take care of your mam."

She nodded, full of importance as she took her mother's hand. Dolores squeezed hard.

"Ow!"

"Sorry, love," said Dolores through clenched teeth. "That one came fast after the last one. Hurry up Mac, it's coming!"

"Jesus Christ!" she heard him exclaim from below, along with a lot of clanging of pots and pans from the parlour.

Taking the stairs two at a time, he arrived with a pot of cold water.

"I've started a fire," he said to Shirley. "Keep it going and put some coal on."

"But I want to see the baby coming."

"You will," said Dolores through clenched teeth. "Just be a good girl and do as your told. And take care of Shane."

"Do as your mam says," said Mac. "And I'll take you for a ride on me bike. To the seaside!"

Reluctantly, the girl left. There were more contractions. Mac felt helpless. A man can do nowt but be here, he thought. I can't ease it. I can't move it along. To think this is what me mam went through for me. I'm surprised she still talks to me.

His shame forgotten, he reached for the rum, and swallowed a gob full with every contraction. Dolores refused to take anymore spirit; she would only sip water. Time passed but Mac would never know how long, whether it was minutes or hours.

"Get ready," said Dolores, breathing hard.

"What?"

"I can feel her. Here she comes."

"Oh God," said Mac. "I can see its head. Keep pushing," he said instinctively. "Hurry up!"

"Oh my God!"

Mac could not believe he was seeing a baby be born. It was so tiny. Its head and neck came out, then he could see the tops of its shoulders. Dolores let out a yell as the whole body slipped out into his hands. Mac exclaimed too with surprise at his catch. The baby was as slippery as a cod in his hands but warm and bloody and unrecognisable as a human being.

"Here," he held it up for Dolores to see. "What do I do with it now?"

"The cord!" Dolores cried. "The cord is round her neck! Get it off! Get it off! That's it! Oh, is she all right? Give her to me. Let me see. Oh, it is a girl. The gypsy was right. She's so little. Oh, she's so little. Give me a towel. Cry, baby girl, cry. Come on! You can do it!"

Using the damp towel Mac handed her, she wiped the baby's face and mouth. The baby let out a quiet cry.

"There!" Dolores exclaimed with a tired smile. "There, she cried. It wasn't much of one, though, was it? Oh, she's so little. She looks like a baby though, doesn't she? I was so worried. That's why I sent our Shirley out. I wasn't sure, with it being so early. My angel."

Sobbing, Dolores quickly cleaned off the rest of the tiny body, "What time is it? We have to know what time she was born. Oh, she's so little."

"Five and twenty past eleven."

"Another girl." She smiled at her daughter but then her expression saddened. "Jimmy's not going to like it. Well, never mind. Let's wrap her up and keep her warm. Poor little thing. Why, she can't weigh more than a bag of sugar. Come on cry little one," she said, giving the baby a little pinch to which the baby responded with a whimper.

"Five and twenty past eleven? Morning or night?"

"Morning."

Dolores unbuttoned her dress and brought the baby to her bosom. She noticed Mac's awestruck face. Jimmy had never taken pleasure in the birth of his children, and yet here the man she might have married was full of wonder like a new father should be. She took the towels he held out to her and tucked them around the baby. Her face scrunched up with more contractions for the placenta.

"Has Jimmy been found?" she asked, her voice tight with pain. "Is that why you're here?"

The news he had come to impart had been temporarily put aside, but once again it was foremost in his mind. He wiped his blood-stained fingers on a towel as if trying to wipe away the memory of the dripping, shrouded corpse he had helped pull out of the dock. He reached for a cigarette, lit it and started talking, "We came in this morning. Our George and Paddy was there to meet us with their Guy for Bonfire night. They was hoping to make some money off us, like. Anyrode, they was fishing, even though me mam's told 'em not too 'cause it's too dangerous at the docks, and …" The image of Jimmy's bloated body flooded his mind, ghastly to behold. "They found him."

"They found him."

"Aye. He's dead, Dolores. Drowned."

"Oh."

He wasn't sure whether she had heard him. The baby whimpered. Dolores soothed her with a soft tone and by stroking a finger on the baby's cheek. Discreetly, under a shawl, Dolores brought the infant to her nipple. "Come on," she whispered to her. "There is milk. Your brothers and sisters like it." She dripped some milk onto the baby's lips. "She's like a miniature from a doll house. I think Lizzie's bigger than she is."

"Lizzie?"

"Shirley's doll."

"Oh, aye," but Mac couldn't remember it.

"I heard what happened on the Wilberforce," Dolores said quietly. "If that's why you can't meet me eyes."

The fisherman walked to the window and looked out. The sky was grey, constant grey, hiding the sun for a long, long time.

"Why? Why did you do it?" she asked.

After a moment, he turned from the window and said, "You know why."

"But to set fire to him!"

"Set fire to him! Is that what he told you? I didn't do that, he did that to himself."

"Come on, Mac."

"I'm telling you he did! Look, I'm not saying I weren't involved but when I heard our boats was laid up together me only thought was to go teach him a lesson."

Dolores looked at him, and their eyes met briefly. To dispel some emotion, Mac ran a hand through his hair, and shifted his gaze out the window.

"Go on," she said softly.

He found an ashtray and tapped some ash into it.

"So, I went over to the Wilberforce, to the engine room, like, and I started having a go at Jimmy, telling him what I thought of him and what I'd do to him the next time he laid an 'and on you or your girls... And that's all I was intending to do, 'onest. I didn't touch him, I swear. Not then, anyrode."

He took a drag on his cigarette.

"Then the Chief told me to stop causing bother and to sod off back to the Ichthus. I had to respect him, mind, he were a good mate of me dad's. But when I turned to leave, Jimmy hit me on me back with his shovel. So I took it from him, and, aye, I were about to whallop him on the 'ead wi' it when he fell backwards over some coal. Right smack on his back, the daft twat. Anyrode, when he fell, his flask of rum fell out of his pocket, so, of course, I picked it up, took a swig and poured the rest over him."

"His precious rum!" she scoffed.

"Aye, washed most of the coal dust off him at any rate," Mac said with a humourless chuckle.

"But the fire?"

"Well, I chucked his shovel into the furnace, didn't I? And then, as I left, I heard the chief tell him to fetch it, so I reckon that's when it must have 'appened."

There was a pause as they both had their memories of Jimmy's demise.

"I never asked you to do owt on my account."

"It's only your pride what stops you."

"Me pride? I lost that long ago. Go on, blow your smoke, like you're an 'ero or some'at. Your life carries on the same as it allus does, doesn't it? No matter how you tear mine apart."

Her raised voice caused the baby to whimper, so she shushed her, and held her close, rocking. Mac sat heavily in a wooden chair that creaked under his weight. He put his head in hands. Dolores relented. She could see his struggle.

"Listen, Bill," Dolores said, for that's what she had called him while they were courting. "I know you was trying to help me but you only made things worse. Before all this 'appened, we was barely scraping by, but at least we *was* getting by with the tiniest 'elp from whatever I could scrounge out of Jimmy's pockets. But now I don't know what I'm going to do."

"I'll help you with the bills." His voice cracked.

"That's not what I'm after. You know me better than that. I'm saying that per'aps we should stay away from each other for a while. Stay out of each other's lives. I know I loved you once ... but that were years ago."

"You left me," said Mac.

"No, Mac, no. *You left me.*"

He looked surprised.

"Not physically, I mean," she continued, "I don't think you ever would have *left* me. You might have even married me if I'd waited. But ..." Their eyes met. "But you had this way of, oh, how can I say it, I felt that you pitied me."

"Pitied you?"

"Aye. Because of me dad an' that. Oh it's so 'ard to say."

"Say it."

"Sometimes you made me feel like you was rescuing me, as if our lives was a fairy tale, and I was Rapunzel. You wanted to be my knight in shining armour. You wanted me to be grateful."

"What? You bloody women and your fairy stories. What a load of codswallop! It's all in your 'ead. And so what? So what if I did want to rescue you. Wouldn't that have better than the life you chose? Better to be pitied than beaten."

Dolores squirmed as more cramping took hold.

"Look, I know I hurt your pride when I married Jimmy, but in a way you hurt mine. I know it sounds silly now but I allus had this idea you would lose any feelings for me when I didn't need rescuing no more."

Mac shook his head. "You lasses do me 'ead in. Why can't you be more straight forward like a bloke. If you'd talked to me about this before … I mean what is love based on if it's not because we want to help each other."

"I don't know," she said. "Maybe yours was the right love, but I didn't know it, so instead I went for some'at I did know."

Minutes passed. With his forearms resting on his knees, Mac stared at his large boots on the bare floor. What was it Jimmy had screamed at him as he left the engine room? *'She would have made you as miserable as she's made me!'* Was there any truth to that? Exhaling a mouthful of smoke, he walked over to the doorway, wishing the doctor would hurry up.

Another severe cramp caused Dolores to squeeze her eyes shut. More blood gushed from between her legs, but she kept it hidden.

"Jimmy's dead? Really dead?"

"Aye, love," he said gently. "They reckon he must have gone straight to the docks from the hospital. His body … he'd been in the water a while."

"Drownded," she said.

A prickly sensation swept over her scalp. Blood drained from her head. She went pale on pale, and sweaty.

"But that's not possible. He's been here. I feel sick," she said. "Pass us that rum if there's -"

She slumped back, unconscious, dropping the baby, but Mac was swift enough to catch it. The baby looked cold so he wrapped her up tightly, leaving the umbilical cord coming out through the open end of the towel. He held the tiny one close to him while he tried to revive Dolores, who was unresponsive to his touch or words, as well as to the rum being passed under her nose. The baby cried softly, mewing. He jiggled her up and down to soothe her but his motions were awkward and unnatural and the baby cried more. She was smaller than one of his great hands. He was afraid he might hurt her.

From nowhere it seemed, but much to Mac's relief, Dr. McKenzie appeared in the bedroom. He quickly clamped the cord and cut it, freeing the baby from the mother. Mac tried to pass the baby over to the doctor's care, but all Doctor McKenzie did was open the towel to examine her. The doctor gave a pinch, and the baby squirmed and squeaked a protest.

"Och, well, her reflexes seem all right but her colour's not so good. She's breathing on her own, but not well. Och, she's such a wee, wee thing. Ye take her downstairs by the fire and keep her warm," the doctor said gravely to Mac. "That's all we can do for her. She's come too soon. I'm sorry but I've got to see to the mother. She's still bleeding. Best leave me to it, son."

"But the baby? Will she be all right?"

"She's very premature. I can't say for sure. I'll be down as soon as I get Mrs. Alford stabilised. Oh, bring me some hot water as soon as you can."

Mac stumbled downstairs with leaden legs, his eyes on the little thing in his hands. His heart swelled. "You'll live," he told her. "I promise you. Your mam'll be right as rain an' all, you'll see. She can't wait to take care of you proper. But in the meantime, you'll just have to trust this fisherman."

"Is that the baby?! Can I hold it?" asked Shirley who was sitting with Sharon at the parlour table with Monty on her lap. The girls' thin legs swung to and fro beneath them.

Constable Popple was there too. He had been showing the girls a magic trick or two.

"Sorry, Shirley love," said Mac. "but she's too small. Here, is that water hot yet?"

"Not another girl," said Sharon. "Me dad's going to go mad when he finds out."

Mac and the constable exchanged a glance. The girls too would have to be told. But their eyes agreed to wait. Dolores should be the one to tell them.

"What's her name?" asked Constable Popple.

"She doesn't have one yet," said Mac, as he went through drawers looking for something with which to carry the hot water.

Shirley spoke up, "Mam told me Sheridan for a girl and Shaun for a boy. So it must be Sheridan 'cause it's a girl. Sherry for short, she said."

"She didn't say owt to me about it," Sharon retorted. "You're fibbing."

"No, I'm not!"

"What about ...," Sharon began but she had to pause while she thought of more names. "Sheila!" she cried triumphantly. "Sheila's a nice name."

"Or Shannon?" suggested Constable Popple.

"No," said Shirley, calmly, coolly. "You're both wrong. It's Sheridan. Sheridan Mary Alford."

The middle name couldn't be argued with since both the girls and Dolores shared the same one, as had Dolores' mother before her.

"Is not!" cried Sharon.

"Let's wait for your mam, ay, girls," said Constable Popple, sorry he'd asked. "As soon as she's better I'm sure she'll tell us what the name is."

"But I already know what it is," complained Shirley.

The constable shot her a stern, official look, so she clammed up immediately, while Sharon, who had given up the argument for now, rested her chin in one hand and drummed the table with the fingers of the other. Having seen all her siblings be born, she didn't know what the fuss was about this one.

"Is there owt I can do to help?" asked the constable. "I could pop to the shops to get some milk and what not."

He had noticed the bare cupboards.

"Can I come?" asked Sharon, who felt safe with Popple.

"Is that all right?" asked the constable, directing the question to Mac.

Mac was confused. He wasn't sure why he was the one being asked for permission. It was too much of a burden to be responsible for somebody else's children. Surely it was enough that he was taking care of the newborn.

"Don't worry," said Shirley, pulling her chair closer to where she could see the baby. "I'm going to stay to 'elp you."

Mac couldn't help but grin at the reassuring smile young Shirley had put on her sweet, thin face.

"I think we'll be all right," he said, with a nod to the constable. "Go ahead."

"Aye, we'll be all right," said Shirley. "I'll make us a cup of tea. Go on Monty. Get down."

The big fisherman felt at a loss cradling such a small creature in his arms, but he had the notion to unbutton his shirt and keep her there against his strong chest where she would be kept warm. Holding her this way, he carried the heavy pan of water upstairs to the doctor who was seeing to Dolores, trying to stem the haemorrhaging tide of blood. Mac was uncomfortable, acutely aware of Dolores's lack of privacy, so he dare not look, but he could sense what was happening.

"The poor lass has lost a lot of blood," said the doctor, dipping his hands into the water and wiping at his blood stained hands. He tutted, these days finding it more difficult to get the blood off old skin than new. Finally satisfied, he wiped his hands dry with a towel, handed to him by Shirley who had sneaked upstairs after Mac. "Thank ye, young lady, now shoo. Ye shouldn't be in here. And the dog too."

259

He waited for her to leave, though he guessed, correctly, that she would be listening from the landing. Never mind, he thought. She's the strongest character of all of them.

Nevertheless, he lowered his voice. "Mrs. Alford has lost a lot of blood, but I do expect her to make a full recovery as long as she gets plenty of rest and iron. I'll talk to Casings about getting some liver for her. Mrs. McKenzie can cook 'em up. I'm not one for prescribing it raw like some others. Mrs. McKenzie makes a wonderful pot of liver and onions. A bowl of that every day and Dolores will be back on her feet in no time."

His mouth salivated at the thought of a bowl for himself: the thick savoury gravy was his favourite for dipping bread.

Mac nodded and smiled, but it was only a poor relative of the usual Goodwell grin. As he turned to leave the room, Shirley ran downstairs, relieved to hear that her mother would be all right.

"Son, wait a minute." The doctor rose from the bed and came to Mac, escorting him onto the landing. "May I?"

Mac nodded and the doctor pulled back his shirt to take a look at the baby. He pinched her leg again, angering Mac who looked like he might strike the doctor down. But the way the doctor shook his head and looked saddened, hurt his chest, and his eyes felt hot with sorrow. Though the pinch had been hard; this time, the baby had shown no reaction.

"Poor wee thing," said the doctor. "Even if she lives... Och, do your best to keep her warm. There's not much more we can do than that, I'm afraid. I have to stay here and see to the mother. She's not completely out of the woods yet, ye ken."

Back downstairs, Mac took Jimmy's chair. The baby was still tucked inside his shirt. Shirley copied him by stuffing her doll down the neck of her green cardigan.

Then she handed Mac a pink and white, crocheted blanket, which he took and folded around the baby's head.

"That's me dad's chair," she said.

"Your dad won't mind," said Mac.

"Why not?" she asked.

When Mac didn't answer, she asked, "Is he dead?"

The matter-of-factness of the question caught Mac off guard. There was a pause during which he considered that if he told the girls about their father it would be one less thing for Dolores to have to go through. Also, everyone seemed to be treating Mac as if he had a right to be there and make decisions, so he said, "Aye, he's dead. I'm sorry, love."

"Phew, what a relief," Shirley said. "I had a dream about him, you know. But it didn't look like him. I mean, not like he looked at the hospital all burned and that, or like he did when I knew him. No, in me dream, he looked really happy and young - 'cause he's in Heaven - just like that picture that was in the paper. But me mam never looks 'appy, does she? How's she going to look in Heaven if she's never looked 'appy? When there's nowt for God to go by? Oo, look, Sheridan's waking up."

Indeed, the baby's eyelids fluttered as if beckoning life. Mac hoped she would open her eyes, but she didn't. God came to mind, but the fisherman refused to pray for His help. There would be no point. Hadn't God already shown him how little He cared for Mac's prayers going back all those years to the time He ignored the young boy's pleas to save his father. No, Mac thought. I'll make me own promises. So he promised the newborn baby girl that she would live and that she would be all right. He would see to it. And as he made those silent promises, he squeezed her softly to his bare chest, pulling the soft blanket over her, and leaning back his head to rest.

Sitting in her mother's chair opposite, Shirley's little legs didn't reach to the floor so they swung up and under while she kept her doll warm and snug inside her cardigan, cooing to it as she had seen her mother do to Shane. After a while, though, she became bored. She jumped off the chair and wandered shyly around the room until she ended up behind Mac's chair.

Peeking over his shoulder to get a good look at her tiny sister, she said, "That used to be my blanket when I was little but I gave it to Lizzie. Do you think she likes it? Sheridan, I mean. She's ever so bonny, isn't she? Fancy her having golden hair like that an' all, like an angel. She's so little, like a baby rabbit. Do you think she likes having my blanket? I do. She can keep it forever. I don't mind. Can I kiss her? Mac? Can I?"

Coming from behind the chair, the young girl rested a small, grubby hand on Mac's large knee and leaned forward to kiss the little mite. But as soon as her lips touched the baby's forehead, she withdrew quickly and shivered.

"Oh, she's cold," she said. "Ever so cold, like Lizzie."

Chapter 24

The doctor said it was for the best, that nothing more could have been done to save little Sheridan Mary Alford. He said that if she had lived, there would have been terrible problems because her brain had been starved of oxygen. She had been too tiny to breath properly on her own. At best, he said, she would have been blind and deaf. At best, he reiterated.

When she was told that her daughter had died, Dolores released an inhuman cry then sobbed and rocked with unbearable pain. Tearing off her blouse, she scrambled to her feet and snatched the baby from Mac, who did nothing to stop her. Rocking on the bed, she held tiny Sheridan to her breast for hours thinking maybe if she could get the baby to feed she could bring life back. If that innocent little girl only knew how much she was loved by her mother, she would see that life was worth living. But the dead don't have a change of heart.

Dolores' behaviour terrified Shirley who had screamed and cried and had to be carried from the room by Mac. Though he was in no fit state to console the kicking, wailing child since his own emotions, hidden behind a frozen, stern expression, were also kicking and wailing, he held those skinny arms and legs tightly and buried her face in his chest. As he breathed in the scent of her chestnut hair, he knew that the young girl had been the first to realise that Dolores had completely, utterly and irrevocably lost all hope.

While Dolores held the baby in her arms and the tears dried in dirty streaks on her face, she had the vague recollection of her other children crying, needing her, but she had nothing left to give them anymore. Eventually, the doctor gently eased the dead baby away from her, and Dolores's arms were empty. She stared at those empty arms refusing all offers of tea and food because holding anything would take away the emptiness.

Despite her anger toward God, Dolores buried baby Sheridan in sacred ground inside a proper little polished wooden coffin, which looked so helpless and alone Dolores felt compelled to grab it and hold it, until she was dragged away from the gravesite so the coffin could be interred.

Embarrassed by the spectacle, her mother remarked, "Other people have lost babies, you know." But Dolores was already swallowed by so much pain there was nowhere for the comment to take hold.

There were two separate services; one for Jimmy and one for Sheridan. Despite the increased expense of two funerals, Dolores would not permit father and daughter to be buried together. Even after his death, Dolores didn't trust her husband. She believed his spiteful spirit had come and taken Sheridan away from her.

Though Sheridan's death followed the birth so quickly, Dolores insisted on signing both a birth certificate and a death certificate. "She did live," she insisted. "And I want it to be on record." Yet so grief bound was she that when it came to signing the latter, she could scarcely see to sign her name. The ink smudged under a deluge of tears. Holding the two certificates side by side, she thought of what should have come in between them: there should have been other certificates; school certificates, a marriage certificate and birth certificates for Sheridan's children. But there was to be none of those things of which a life is made up.

Dolores visited her dead daughter, sitting by the grave, reading over the date of the day she was born and died with disbelief that someone could have lived so little, barely a breath upon this earth. Then, it was always such a terrible, wrenching ordeal for Dolores to leave her daughter in the graveyard alone with all the other dead souls. She hoped some of them were kind and did not frighten her daughter. Perhaps, she thought, a kind mother ghost is protecting Sheridan, and guiding her tiny one to wherever souls depart for eternity. Perhaps.

The pain was unbearable. Dolores often wished she had died with her daughter, and sometimes she was angry at the doctor for saving her life. Dolores' heart ripped asunder every time she thought of the little girl child crying for her mother in the vast eternal night. With increasing frequency, she wished she could join her. She cried and sobbed and clung to the tiny gravestone for hours. Soon, she became skeletal from lack of sleep and food, appearing as if she too belonged in the graveyard as one of the walking dead - a moaning spectre only visible to those who believed in her.

Perhaps she thought denying herself all things that promote life; food, drink, love, laughter, would give her an insight into death. The pain of her loss was so great at times it eclipsed her very being. She believed there was no more light in her life. Then there were moments when she almost grasped the pain in its entirety, as if she could mould it into a ball in front of her, examine and study its meaning and therefore control it, but, ultimately, understanding and acceptance of Sheridan's death proved ever evasive and she began to believe that she would never fully recover.

"There's an 'ole in me heart and nowt to fill it," she told Prudence.

Sighing inwardly Prudence tried her utmost to urge Dolores to concentrate on the children living. Shirley had been coming to the Goodwell's for food and milk for herself, Sharon and Shane, and, truth be told, Prudence was becoming increasingly irritated by her friend's lack of responsibility toward them.

Though the children had lost their father, the finality of that loss had not yet sunk in considering they were used to long absences from him; yet, they experienced their mother's absence most astutely. Prudence could see by their eyes how alone and afraid they felt. Even Shane, who was too young to understand the import of recent events, felt his mother's withholding. He cried constantly and could not rest, even in sleep.

Mac was away for the funeral of Sheridan. He was utterly devastated and full of blame for himself. But Dolores wasn't sure what to make of his self-pity, especially since she felt the blame was all hers and hers alone, and she wasn't willing to share it with anyone. She felt older and wiser than everyone around her. She looked down on them and all their petty miseries. No one could tell her anything anymore because she had suffered the worst pain of all.

A husband was lost too, mind you, but about this she was conflicted. After all, she had wished him dead on many occasions, and what if her prayers had been answered for that so that when time came for Sheridan to be prayed for, all prayer was exhausted. She was tormented by the gypsy's warning. If only she had listened to her. Not to a living soul did Dolores reveal any of her inner torment about Jimmy, but instead she believed that God had punished her for her wicked thoughts.

Jimmy knew she had prayed for his death. Every night he haunted her. Every moment she was alone in the house he came to torment her. At night, and often during the day, she dozed fitfully. She tried to hide under the bed clothes, but when Jimmy's spirit was in the house, the room grew colder, and her head would hurt from the intense pressure of the freezing cold. She would sense his body lie down next to her - the bed giving way the same way it used to do when he was alive. She could hear his breathing, and sometimes his low, mocking laugh.

Since it was winter, the bruises on her arms were easy to hide, but one morning she woke with purple marks around her neck and so she took to wearing a scarf all day, complaining of a cold to anyone that called at the house, which hardly anyone did anymore. In all the years she had prayed for Jimmy to be gone, she had never considered that his incorporeal body would torment her from beyond the grave. He was worse dead than alive because dead he was never gone to sea; he was always around to bedevil her. She had tried apologizing to the apparition, then begging it to leave her alone but her entreaties went unheeded.

At Prudence's behest, Dolores began working at the fish shop. She hated it at first the way people came in, ordered their fish and chips and looked at her: the woman whose husband had drowned himself in the dock and who had been so grief stricken her daughter had been born too early to live. It was as if they needed to see how someone who had been through all that existed. She knew they were all whispering about her and giving each other knowing looks in the queue. Sometimes, she would spin quickly from the fryer to catch them in the act, but they were too clever for her: they would smile and nod pretending to be friendly and sympathetic, but she would only scowl back, and they, the clever things, would look surprised.

She didn't work the weekends Mac was home. Not after the time he came into the shop looking for his supper not knowing Dolores was working and had mumbled his order without once looking her in the face. Such was Mac's discomfort that Dolores had again refused Prudence's offer to move into the flat above the fish shop.

In between shifts, Dolores returned to net braiding, which she found peaceful and rhythmic. In an uncommon gesture of humanity their landlord had given them a few weeks grace period to catch up with the rent past due, but even after using all the money she had saved under the mattress, and pawning off all of Jimmy's meagre belongings and her wedding ring, there was barely enough to cover the funeral costs and medical bills let alone the rent, and that day of reckoning, when the lump sum of past rents was due, loomed closer.

Dealing with her friend's difficulties had been all-encompassing to Prudence, to the point where she had not really had time to think about Derek Stalworth's recent marriage proposal or, indeed, why she had turned him down. If only there was a quiet moment in her life when she could consider her own future. She longed for some time to take a walk in the grave yard where it was quiet, and where she could be alone with her jumbled thoughts and emotions. She was simply too tired at the end of the day, tired from caring for her mother and her siblings, from working in the shop, from worrying about Dolores, too exhausted to etch out some time to herself.

Up until the very point Derek Stalworth proposed, everything they had done and talked about in their brief courtship suggested matrimony - the actual transaction to be carried out as quickly, logically and efficiently as a business deal and the proposal itself when proffered seeming only a mere formality. So why had she said no?

Unfortunately, Derek had chosen to propose during the first pantomime dress rehearsal. He was the writer, director and producer of the Christmas pantomime, *The Princess and the Pea*, and after calling a halt during one of the scenes, he asked Prudence to come up on stage and fix the hem on the Dame's skirt. As usual, the Dame was being played by Fred the milkman who even went so far as to wear women's underwear for the part, though only Prudence was aware of that level of commitment.

So there was Fred in full costume and make-up; garish red lipstick, blue eye shadow, rosy cheeks and a blonde wig, chatting away in his gruff Yorkshire voice while Derek was on his knees holding up the hem of Fred's skirt to show Prudence, ostensibly, the fallen hem. However, when she came close enough to look, Derek span on his knees and grabbed her hands, causing her to let out a surprised laugh. She looked quizzically upon her suitor for a moment before becoming brazenly aware of the bright stage lights on her and what was about to happen in the old dance hall.

One of the mattresses, with only an actor's head, hands and feet visible out of the square stuffed costume, waddled over to remove the needle and thread from Prudence's mouth and stick it into the pin cushion she was holding.

Not only were all the other members of the cast present, including Winnie, George and Gloria, but some of the cast's family, who had been too excited to wait for the actual show, and had pulled out some chairs and watched and hooted at the rehearsal performance. Everyone had been so certain of Prudence's acceptance of the proposal that Mrs. McKenzie, who wrote and played all the pantomime songs, started to play Mendelssohn's Wedding march before she realized that Prudence had said no, which was when she hit a wrong note, the first one in anyone's memory, and promptly closed the piano lid with a cough.

All present were saddened and embarrassed by the spectacle of the rebuffed landlord down on bended knee with his head bowed; yet it was the milkman's expression that was the most terrible to bear: tears ran down his craggy face dragging mascara with them, and leaving terrible trails of black cut through thick cream foundation. From the sleeve of his blouse Fred took a white lace handkerchief and dabbed at his eyes, shaking his head. He then offered the kerchief to Stalworth who declined.

Prudence fled to the costume room which was nothing more than an old store room with a full length mirror propped on one wall and a black sewing machine on a small table on the other. All the costumes were on stage, being worn for the dress rehearsal. What was left were re-cycled fabrics scrounged from everywhere and anywhere along with bits of lace and ribbon all neatly stacked or rolled on the shelves. Prudence felt safe in that small, orderly room. After closing the door, she slumped on a chair and spun around on its wheels, slowly pulling the tape measure from around her neck. A bare bulb connected by an extension cord to a socket in the hallway burned accusingly. To escape its brilliant vision, she buried her face in her arms and cried.

There was a knock on the door.

"Prudence?"

It was Winnie and George.

"Go home you two, but don't tell Mam what happened. I want to tell her mesen."

"But I need help getting out of me costume," whined George, who was wearing a round, green costume as he was playing the part of the pea.

"Our Winnie can do it. I just need a minute to mesen."

"Can I keep mine on?" asked Winnie, who loved her pretty, long dress, with its frills around the bottom. "Gloria wants to keep hers on an' all."

Winnie was playing a princess who doesn't feel the pea while Gloria was playing the princess who does feel the pea. Upset that she didn't get the main part, Winnie gladly accepted Constable Popple's proposal that she be his magic assistant during the intermission.

"Best take the dresses off or they'll get all dirty."

"We'll be really careful, Prudence, I promise."

"No," said Prudence. "Tell everyone to leave their costumes in the dressing room. I'll see to 'em later."

After saying their goodbyes, the children's voices disappeared down the hallway.

"Stop bumping into me, George," said Winnie.

"I can't help it. It's this bloody costume."

"Oy! You're doing it on purpose."

"Am not," he said, with a shove. "Whoops, sorry."

"I'll push you over, then you'll have to roll yoursen home."

When Prudence was sure everyone had left, after the large front doors had closed shut for the umpteenth time and the quiet murmur of voices had ceased, she released her arms and sat up. The mirror would show her who would do such an awful thing to a sweet man like Derek Stalworth. Her heart was heavy with shame, and her face was smeared with tears. Why couldn't she have said yes in the moment to please everyone, then later addressed her concerns? Poor Derek Stalworth was probably the first person in her life to whom she had said no. But why?

Why the hesitation when recently, she had often thought about marrying Derek and whether he would move into the house on St. George's Road or whether he would want to remain above the pub since he had often cited security reasons for doing so. Hitherto that had been the gist of their conversations: Derek talking about what he liked about his life and the way things where, and Prudence talking about her plans for the shop and how she needed to be with her mother to take care of her. All this with no mention of marriage as such, only what had seemed to be an unspoken understanding between them.

While she thought on these things, she stabbed at the pin cushion over and over again until, "Ouch" she pricked her finger. The bleeding satisfied her. She squeezed the finger to force out more blood. I could sleep now, for a hundred years, she thought, picturing Derek Stalworth on a white charger, battling with his sword through briar to reach her. Oh but I've tortured him worse than them Grimm brothers could ever have imagined.

While she was pondering all this in the store room, footsteps approached the door. A familiar scent filled the air, but Prudence couldn't place it. Not everyone had left after all. There was a gentle knock. Perhaps Derek had stayed behind to talk to her. So sure was she that it should be him standing at the door that when she opened it she thought there must be something wrong with him before she realized with a start that it was Mrs. Bingsley, her fiancé's mother, whom she hadn't seen since his funeral, several years before.

"I'm sorry to startle you, love," Mrs. Bingsley said. "I have been meaning to come and see you for a while now, but … well, it's difficult, isn't it? Then, I saw the posters for the show so I knew you'd be here. I snuck in with the others and watched from the back. Looks like it's going to be a good one. Takes me back. Alec didn't half love choreographing the dances, didn't he? Sorry, love, you don't mind, do you? It's only that there aren't many people who remember him the way you and I do."

Here was the same Mrs. Bingsley Prudence fondly remembered. As always, the former dance teacher's dark hair was scraped back in a bun, and her large-featured face was made up expertly with red lipstick, black eye-liner and the same tan foundation. And, as always, she wore Lily-of-the-Valley perfume. It seemed to Prudence that Mrs. Bingsley looked no different to when she had first met her.

"Of course, I don't mind," said Prudence. "It's just such a surprise to see you. A lovely surprise, I mean. I wish I'd known you were in town. Gosh, I must look a rare sight. Sorry."

She rubbed her reddened eyes.

Mrs. Bingsley smiled. "It's me that should apologise. I should have waited or called at your house but it was too tempting to come in here again. I think I wanted to recapture a bit of that old feeling, if you know what I mean. The way we felt when we all performed together, making people laugh."

"Aye," said Prudence. "We've all had a lot of laughs in this old hall. We're lucky it survived the war."

"Yes, we are. What I wouldn't give to live through one of those nights again." Mrs. Bingsley smiled. "One of the things I miss most about Alec was the way he could clown around and make the children laugh."

Prudence's heart lurched. Years had passed since she had thought of Alec in that way: simply the way he was. Winnie and George had loved him. He had always delighted them with silly stories, and he had never minded having them around. It was an awakening to realise that she been so caught up in her feelings of regret she hadn't allowed the pleasant memories to filter through, and there were plenty to enjoy.

"If there's a tea urn going in the kitchen, I'll make us cuppa," said Mrs. Bingsley. "If you'd like one?"

"Aye, I would, very much. Ta. There's some biscuits an' all. You know where it is, of course."

"Yes," said Mrs. Bingsley. "I do. I still have me key to the side door, if you can believe it." She took the large brass key out of her coat pocket. "I brought it with me, but the door was open. Here, take it. I won't be needing it anymore."

"Ta," said Prudence, clasping the key. "I'll be along in a sec, after I blow me nose and collect me thoughts a bit."

"All right, love."

A few moments later, Prudence joined Mrs. Bingsley in the brightly lit kitchen. Really, Prudence would have rather stayed in the shadows to hide her blotchy face and swollen eyes, and also to hide her embarrassment that Mrs.

Bingsley must have witnessed the proposal from Derek Stalworth.

"You were always such a nice girl," said Mrs. Bingsley, stirring the tea. "I've often felt that when I lost Alec, I lost both a son and a daughter that day."

She smiled sorrowfully while her words tugged at Prudence's conscience. Prudence hadn't really thought about Mrs. Bingsley's loss in terms of the grandchildren she might have enjoyed into her old age. Alec had been her only child. After millennia of animal struggle and evolution, a bullet had put an abrupt end to their lineage. The finality of Mrs. Bingsley's loss swamped Prudence. She doubted that the count of the war dead included lost descendants.

"I'm sorry, I should have written, stayed in touch, I -"

"Oh, don't worry, love," replied Mrs. Bingsley. "I know how it is. The war, I mean. It was so hard on all of us. I wasn't the only one to lose a son. And you lost a fiancé. That can't have been easy. Your mother wrote a couple of times. Perhaps *I* should have written more. I mean, you were young when it happened. At least I was older, more... well, I was going to say 'more prepared' but I wasn't at all prepared. It was a shock, and it's still all I think about. In some ways I do feel proud that Alec fought for a good cause, against such terrible evil. I do try to believe that his death meant something, but I can't help feeling, well, sometimes angry but mostly very sad. I came across a quote in the paper. Here, I cut it out."

Mrs. Bingsley and her quotes: Prudence had quite forgotten about that side of her personality. There was a breath of comfort to be found in the way some things hadn't changed despite the years of chaos and destruction that had passed. As Mrs. Bingsley reached into her handbag, her hands seemed to pause on something but after a moment they moved on and pulled out a tiny note book stuffed with bits of paper.

"Me book of quotes. Do you remember it? I still stick quotes in here or even thoughts of me own sometimes. Then when I'm feeling really low they help lift me spirits. Makes me feel I'm not alone, and that's really important when you're suffering," she said, leafing through the book. "You know, sometimes I think people get so caught up in thinking their problems are unique, when there isn't a problem in the world that some other poor soul hasn't suffered before them. Ah, here it is. You don't think I'm daft with these, do you? It used to drive Alec mad."

Prudence shook her head. She never minded someone else doing all the talking.

Mrs. Bingsley read from her book, "Some feller, I won't even try to say his name, Her-o-do-tus something or other, said," she paused, "*'In peace, sons bury their fathers. In war, fathers bury their sons'*. It's true, isn't it? Sort of like war changes the natural order of things. Except, when I really think about it, I can't decide whether war is natural or not."

"Perhaps it's only natural as long as we think so."

"Oo," said Mrs. Bingsley. "Watch out, or you'll be finding yourself a place in my book. I daresay we all become philosophers, those of us that have lost someone unexpectedly."

As Mrs. Binglsey put away her book of quotes, Prudence realised she would never again lay eyes on the book that used to be brought out and read as a sort of grace before every meal. She missed their discussions on whatever topic was thus broached. Perhaps, Prudence thought, she would start something similar with her own family, which led her to think of Derek, and a sick feeling returned to her stomach.

"Well that's enough of that," said Mrs. Bingsley. "Our tea'll be getting cold. Am I right, two sugars?"

"Oo no, not anymore, not since rationing. Maybe a quarter teaspoon, just enough to take the edge off."

"Not tonight you won't. I brought me own sugar."

Oh, Alec's mother would have such made a wonderful mother-in-law! She was so kind, cheerful and understanding, and intelligent too. Oh, the discussions they could have had over the years. A mental picture popped into Prudence's head of how they might be, together now, if Alec were alive. The renewed sense of loss filled her with great sorrow. She imagined them having dinner together every Sunday; roast beef, Yorkshire pudding, mashed potatoes, roast potatoes, cabbage and that leek and cream dish Mrs. Bingsley made that was so delicious. Of course, there would be a wonderfully, light, steamed pudding for afters, perhaps a treacle sponge pudding or spotted dick with lots of lovely, thick yellow custard. It was years since any of them had eaten a feast like that; a feast that left them so replete the only thing to do, after the pots were washed of course, was to drift off into a pleasant Sunday afternoon doze.

But there would be no more Sunday dinners at the Bingsleys; the war had seen to that. The war had taken away Mrs. Bingsley's son, her home and her grandchildren. As a consequence, she was having to move to Leeds to be with her sister, where she would have plenty of grand nieces and grand nephews who would both ease and increase the pain of her having no grandchildren of her own.

"I was thrilled to bits when you two got engaged."

"I remember when we told you," Prudence said, a fond smile touching her lips.

Mrs. Bingsley smiled too, recalling her son's excited eyes. But then silence fell like an axe between them, the quiet made even more deafening by the large empty hall beyond. There would be no more such happy memories for them to share. Prudence poured more tea.

"Prudence, I've brought something for you, some letters."

Reaching into her black handbag, Mrs. Bingsley pulled out a small stack of envelopes held together by a scented lavender ribbon. Prudence recognized the hand-writing and

275

the ribbon as her own. Tensing, she hesitated to take them. She was about to find out whether Alec had read her final letter. Had Mrs. Bingsley read them? Hitherto, all memories of Alec had been safely locked away in a hidden room at the very corner of Prudence's mind, and only she held the key, or so she had thought. She knew then why she had made no effort to contact Alec's mother.

Mrs. Bingsley continued, "A soldier who served with Alec brought them to me, you see, along with some other of his effects. Nice lad, he had some wonderful things to say about Alec. Anyrode, I wasn't sure what to do with them. I thought you might like to have them back. Sometimes it helps us, well, it helps me. I look at the cards and letters that I wrote to Mr. Bingsley when he was a soldier in the first war, and it's nice to remember how we once felt for each other, especially when we was young. All the plans we had. We realized most of them an' all. We wanted to be dance champions, and we were …

"I hope it's not too painful for you, Prudence, love. I understand how it can be both wonderful and horrid to see and touch something that was once in the hands of someone you loved. Imagining them reading your letters, what they thought, if your words cheered them up…"

'Someone you loved'. Mrs. Bingsley's words were forcing themselves through Prudence's closed ears but, for some reason, her mind did not want to accept what she was hearing.

"And that's such a bonny ribbon you sent Alec. He must have liked that you sent it, something pretty and feminine against all the ugly manliness of war."

The ribbon felt soft and silky between Prudence's fingers. She breathed in its fragrance but didn't untie it.

"I did love him!" she cried. "I did!"

Burying her face in her hands, she sobbed.

"I know you loved him," said Mrs. Bingsley. "I know you did. And Alec knew it too, love."

Like a swan, the older woman gracefully opened her arms, and pulled Prudence to her breast, rocking the girl as she wept. Gently stroking Prudence's black hair, she said, "You know I had Alec late in life. I was forty years old when he was born, soon after Mr. Bingsley passed. Alec never knew his father."

She stopped stroking Prudence's hair, and instead held her close, saying, "I've never told anyone this, but when Alec was first born I was so afraid of losing him that I wouldn't allow myself to love him. Sounds silly, doesn't it? I mean, sometimes I think back to that first year of his life when I really thought he was going to be taken away from me at any minute, like Mr. Bingsley was, and I was so scared to touch him or hold him. Thankfully, the other Mrs. Bingsley, Alec's grandmother, loved him and coddled him then. And she didn't hold nowt against me for it, bless her. I wish I could have that year back but I can't, can I? I really should have made the most of every moment, holding him as much as I could, because you know it's not long while they don't want holding no more.

"I'd say it wasn't till he got the whooping cough, right after his first birthday, that I realized how precious he was. I tried to make up for it but then me mother-in-law said I was going to turn him into a right mummy's boy if I wasn't careful. She was right in a way. You can't really make up for the past, and that's what you have to remember all the time and live your life every moment so you won't have no regrets later on. I can't have that first year back, but I can dwell on the times when I know I was a good mother. And I know I was."

"You were," said Prudence tearfully. "You are."

"It's funny you say it that way," said Mrs. Bingsley. "Because it allus struck me that when I lost Mr. Bingsley I went from being a wife to becoming a widow, but there's no word for a woman who loses a child, is there? You don't become something else, do you?"

Closing her eyes, Prudence leant heavily against Mrs. Bingsley's chest, remembering Alec. She imagined his arms around her as they once had been. Gentle tears filled her eyes and tipped over her lower lids. But a door slamming caused her to jump up.

"Derek!" she cried, automatically, before glancing, nervously, back at Mrs. Bingsley, who only smiled.

"Sorry, you see, Derek's my ... I mean he's ..."

"Oh, you don't have to apologise to me, love," said Mrs. Bingsley. "Life goes on, doesn't it? We know that. You just have to look at this old hall and see it all dressed up with lights and the stage sets to know that. Oh, how I used to wish and wish I could have had one last dance here with Mr. B. He was the best." She sighed.

Holding her arms open as if to dance with an imaginary partner, Mrs. Bingsley waltzed a few steps across the floor, gliding effortlessly like a ghost. When she reached the door, she came to a stop, looking quizzically at Prudence.

"Well, aren't you going to go after him?" she asked.

Chapter 25

Mac's mood was sombre as he put the finishing touches of paint to the new arch that went between the sitting room and the parlour. The wall had been knocked through with sledgehammers wielded by Mac, Bert, Jake and a couple of others who had been only too willing to spend a few hours away from their nagging wives. To relieve the crowded parlour, Muriel's bed was set up in the sitting room where, from her bed, she could keep an eye and ear on what was going on with her children, as they in turn could keep an easy eye on her. The project had kept the Goodwells'

minds pleasantly busy and away from the reason for having
to have such a room in the first place. Once it was finished,
they would have to get back to that.

Muriel praised Mac for his work on the arch, but he
only half-smiled and winked in reply: his mind occupied by
the order from the skipper to find a new cook for the Ichthus. One evening, Ginger tipped over a whole pot of
shackles so the men had been served only a mug of tea and
bread for dinner. Then the Russian galley lad had to take
over bread-making duties after Ginger burned a couple of
batches, leading to near mutiny. If the cook had been a
lighter fellow he may have been tossed overboard.

Finding a new cook was not an easy task since all the
best ones were already taken, and a second rate one would
not bode well for the men's morale. With any luck, Mac
hoped, Ginger would pull himself together, and Crostaff
will have forgotten about it by Monday.

Placing the last of the clean brushes on the draining
board to dry, he whispered, because Muriel had nodded off
again, "Right, I'm off for a pint."

"So soon?" Prudence asked, who more and more
dreaded being alone with her dying mother.

"Aye. Where's Jake?" asked Mac, who fancied some
company.

"In the chippy. He works the dinnertime shift on the
weekend with our Winnie. He's getting quite good, really.
He makes beans now and this chilli thing -"

"Well, if he'd rather do lasses' work then come wi' me
to the pub, so be it. Ta-ra."

So Prudence was left alone. She wished Vivian would
hurry back from her walk with Ted. Whenever Muriel and
Prudence found themselves alone, their mother continually
discussed her impending death with things she wanted to
make sure were not overlooked. The dying mother was not
the same as the living one, whom Prudence already
mourned deeply. Prudence felt she was carrying the burden
alone. And since I'm being given all the responsibility, then

279

I might as well take it and make the decisions I think are best.

For starters, Dolores *will* be moving into the flat above the chippy. Everyone will just have to grin and bear it. When our Vivian finally gets back from her walk, she can watch Mam while I go right over and tell Dolores to put her bloody pride to rest and for once do what's easiest for her and the bairns. Where the bloody hell is our Vivian anyrode? She's been gone so long she might as well have taken Ted to the moon and back.

As she tidied up the paint brushes, Prudence glanced out the window and squinted, being pleased to see a little sunshine struggling to replace the grey.

"Dolores Alford you *will* be moving in with us," she said aloud. "And I don't want to hear no more about it."

"Over my dead body," Muriel said; her eyes still closed.

"Oo, Mam, you startled me. I didn't know you was awake. But what do you mean over your dead body? We *should* help her. Dolores is me mate. And, anyrode, if she lives above the shop, she'll allus be 'andy to help us in the fish shop. And her landlord's been pestering her, and -"

"Oh Prudence, I were only pulling your leg. 'Over my dead body' Tch! Look, it doesn't matter to me no more whether she moves in or not. I'll be gone soon enough. I can't take me old gripes with me, can I? So I might as well leave 'em here."

"Oh, Mam," Prudence said with a sigh. "I wish you wouldn't be so flippant. It makes me queasy."

"Oh, leave me be. Anyrode, while I've been lying here, I've been thinking; maybe I've been too hard on that girl. She was such a young lass when she courted our Mac, and she never had any proper guidance, did she? I wasted so much time being bitter about the way she hurt our Mac. It's funny 'ow when you're so close to death's door like I am, you wonder how you could have 'elped people more. Hanging on to all those slights, why, it seems daft now."

"You helped a lot of people in your time, Mam. A lot. Loads of people look up to you. Including me."

Muriel fiddled with the blanket on her bed before saying, "That's nice, love."

"Well, it's true."

"All right, don't go on about it, you'll make me blush."

Wouldn't that be nice to see, thought Prudence.

"Now here's a funny thing," said Muriel, sitting up. "I actually feel hungry today."

"You do! That's smashing news, Mam! What can I get for you?" Prudence asked, stuffing some pillows behind her mother's back. "Is that comfortable enough for you?"

"Aye, love," said Muriel. "The usual please."

"Fish, chips and mushy peas?"

"Aye, and throw in a pattie for us an' all, will you, love? Oh, and some of Jake's beans."

"My goodness, you are hungry, Mam."

"Aye, well, I'll only take a few bites of each, and, by heck, them beans make me fart like a sailor."

"Mam!"

"Oh, I don't mind. At least I know I'm still alive, then. And so do you."

Prudence was about to chastise once more, but then she snorted and, unable to control herself, started laughing. Muriel chimed in, and soon the two of them were giggling like a pair of naughty school girls. Prudence laughed so hard she fell onto the bed, face down, muffling her guffaws. Slowly, they recovered, wiping tears from under their eyes, and saying, "Oh dear," and, "By gum, I needed that."

After straightening her hair, and blowing her nose, Prudence lovingly stroked her mother's cheek with the back of her hand while Muriel gently rested her head on the hand.

"Me stomach hurts from all that laughing," Prudence said.

"By heck, laughter brings you back though, doesn't it?"

"Aye, it does."

Prudence checked her tear-stained appearance in the mirror above the fireplace. Thank goodness it's tears of laughter, she thought. There have been too many of the other kind.

"Prudence," Muriel said, "You are me favourite. You know that, don't you?"

"Oh, Mam, don't say that," Prudence said, blushing.

"No, I mean it. You're me first born, and that means something. You had all me love at one time, and I had all yours. For ages, it were just you and me with your dad being at sea so much. I know I gave the others more attention when they came along, but they needed it. They was allus getting into trouble. It was allus so much 'arder with them. But with you, well, you've allus been so easy, and so 'elpful. You're such a thoughtful lass. No, don't bow your head. Look up. You deserve only the best that life has to offer. Don't forget it."

A cloud flitted across Prudence's brow. She wanted to believe her mother's words as there would be no one to say them after she was gone. Feeling a chill, she slipped on a cardigan.

"Mam, I know you're worried about me being 'appy."

"Happy? No, love. But I do worry about you being *un*'appy. There is an in-between, you know - being content."

Prudence buttoned the cardigan slowly, her mind mulling.

"I'll fetch you that dinner, then, shall I? And some for me, and we'll sit and have a cuppa together."

"Aye, love. I'd like that."

Prudence opened the door to leave but was held back by her mother saying, "Oh, Prudence, the funny thing is that at the end, I think I do worry about you the most."

Prudence came to her mother's bedside.

"Don't worry about me," she said, holding back tears. "I'll be all right. And I'll make sure everyone else is all right. I promise."

Smiling, Prudence leaned forward to kiss her mother, but the scent of death was so strong on Muriel's breath that Prudence placed her lips gently on her forehead instead: the reason for which the mother both knew and accepted.

Chapter 26

Elsie Waggin couldn't have timed it better than to be in the queue at St. George's fish shop when Mrs. Edith Butler pulled her car to a screeching halt outside and came bursting into the shop carrying a sopping wet Shirley Alford. The young girl's red hair was plastered to her small, distraught face, and in her own skinny arms, she carried Shane, whose blanket was also sodden. The trawler owner's wife looked anxiously from face to face while water dripped from the children and formed a puddle at her feet.

"Prudence Goodwell!" she cried. "Which one of you is -?"

"That's me!" said Prudence, coming from behind the fish counter. At once, she recognised the wet-through girl. "Shirley! What happened! Where's your mam?!"

"Put me down! Put me down!" cried the girl, shaking herself free, then once down, running and throwing herself against Prudence, sobbing hysterically, crushing Shane between them.

"What is it, love? Calm down so you can tell me."

Taking the small, anguished face between her hands, Prudence stared into the large dew-filled eyes. Trying to catch her breath between sobs Shirley made an attempt to speak, but no words came forth. Her teeth chattered with cold.

Embracing Shirley tightly, Prudence asked Edith Butler what had happened.

"I don't know. She was like this when I found her," said Mrs. Butler, whose brown tailored suit was damp down the front from carrying the girl from the car. "I was waiting for my husband, Samuel Butler, when I saw her, in my mirror, running along the docks. The men tried to catch her but she was too fast and dodged them. She came to the car and banged on the window and begged me to bring her here. I didn't know what to do but she seemed so upset. It wasn't until she was in the car that I noticed she was carrying a baby."

Something terrible had happened. They all knew it. Portentously, an old fish odour, brought in by the girl, permeated the shop, wafting unpleasantly under the noses of all present.

"Please help him!" Shirley begged.

Carefully, Prudence removed the swaddling. The quiet infant was white-blue and drowsy. She pinched his cheek, and he let out of cry. "Shush, shush," she said, softly. "That's good." Quickly, she removed his wet things and wrapped him snugly in own cardigan. She hugged him to her chest, rubbing his chilly feet.

"Shirley, let's take Shane next door so he can get warm by the fire," said Prudence, careful to keep her voice calm. "You an' all. You must be freezing, love. We've got some dry clothes you can borrow. Winnie go get some towels and some of your clothes that'll fit Shirley. Aye, now. Mrs. Waggin, love will you fetch the doctor, please? And you, will you fetch Constable Popple? And Jake turn off the fryers and put that sign up. Aye, the one that says closed for family emergency. It's in the bottom drawer. Aye, there it is."

Only last week she had made the sign in preparation for Muriel's passing.

"There's no need to close. I can manage," Jake said, who was keen to stay busy and out of the way.

"All right," said Prudence. "Ta. Come on, Shirley. Come with me. Shane's going to be all right. He's already got a bit of pink coming back. Look!"

Though Shirley looked at the boy, it didn't seem to register with her quite what was going on. From crying hysterically, she had become quiet, withdrawn.

"We'll give him some warm milk, love. You'll see. He'll be right as rain. And you too. I bet you'd like some warm milk and a jam tart."

But Shirley didn't respond.

Edith Butler coughed to draw attention to herself. She looked so far out of place in the fish shop among the Hessle Road locals who now looked at her with astonishment as if she had suddenly appeared from nowhere. Most noted the ruby colour of her hair which was striking close up.

"Excuse me, Miss Goodwell, but would you mind awfully if I came with you?" she asked, gesturing with the calfskin gloves she had removed. "I'd like to make sure the children are all right. I don't know them well, of course, I mean I have seen them at the docks before, but I do feel some responsibility having brought them to you."

No amount of bribing with sweets, cake and warm milk could induce Shirley to talk about what had transpired. She wouldn't or couldn't explain why she and Shane were soaked through. Whenever she was asked about Dolores she would catch her breath and her eyes would grow wide with fright.

Upon his arrival, Dr. McKenzie administered a sedative to the child and within minutes she was asleep in Prudence's arms.

"The poor wee thing's in shock," he explained. "Hopefully, with plenty of rest and nourishment, she'll come around. Mrs. Butler, you say you found Shirley at the docks?"

The trawler owner's wife, who had been facing the fire to dry her clothes, turned to them.

"Yes," she said. "Or rather, I should say, she found me. I've seen the girls before. They're fascinated by the car, you see. She must have remembered, and thought I could help her."

"She is a smart one little Shirley Alford."

"Aye, it were right kind of you to 'elp her," said Muriel, who had, at first, been mortified by her own appearance, bedridden and dishevelled, beside the well-to-do lady. But her mind went off such things when she was given baby Shane to care for. She kept the boy close to her bosom to warm him up. When he became alert, he was given some warm milk, and they were all relieved to see that he was eating and would be all right.

"Did you know that my son's the first mate on one of your trawlers?" Muriel said. "The Ichthus. Perhaps you know him. His name is William Goodwell, but everyone calls him 'Mac'."

"I think so," said Edith. "My husband sometimes talks about the men. I recognise the name. 'Mad Mac', isn't it? I think that's what I've heard."

Muriel chuckled. "Aye. That's him," she said so proudly her cheeks hurt. "He's hard to miss. He's the biggest feller that ever sailed in these parts! Sorry, love," she murmured to the fussy infant. "I didn't mean to raise me voice."

"Dolores must be worried sick," Prudence said. "We have to find her."

"Is Dolores the girl's mother?" asked Edith Butler.

"Yes," said Prudence. "They've had such a difficult time of it lately."

"To say the least," commented the doctor.

Prudence recounted recent events to Edith who shook her head sadly. After further discussion, Mrs. Butler offered to drive to the Alford house to see if Dolores was there.

"That would be grand," said Prudence. "Here, I'll write down the address for you. It's not far."

She lay Shirley on the bed next to Muriel.

"I'll drive over to the docks," said Doctor McKenzie. "See if I can find oot what happened."

"Oh goodness!" exclaimed Mrs. Butler. "Would you mind letting my husband know what happened? He'll be wondering where I am! I completely forgot about him."

After the doctor and Edith Butler left, Muriel said, "Prudence, you don't think Dolores –"

"I don't want to speculate," Prudence said quickly.

"Do you think she's what, Mam?" asked Winnie.

"Mind your own," said Muriel. "This is one of them times when you should be seen and not heard."

"Not another one."

"Go help Jake in the shop," said Prudence. "And don't be cheeky to your elders."

With a heavy sigh, Winnie dragged herself next door.

Over all, the baby was fine, thankfully, being too young to understand what was going on, and simply happy to be having his basic needs met. There was a wistful smile on Muriel's face as she fed him. The bottle was almost empty and the baby's eyes were becoming sleepy. Muriel recognised that this was probably the last baby she would hold.

"They grow up so fast," she whispered to Prudence, so as not to wake the sleeping, fitful girl lying beside her. "I know you hear it all the time, but it's not till you have some of your own that you appreciate just how fast. It seems five minutes since you was in me arms like this. At the time, it's a lot of hard work, but now when I look back it was worth every minute, and it went by so fast, so fast. Oo, look at me." She sniffed and wiped away a tear. "I'm turning into a sentimental old fool. I'm sorry to say but I wish I could have lived to see more of me grandchildren born. I do hope your mother's all right, Shane, I really do."

Double checking she had the correct address, Edith Butler parked on the street opposite the Alford's house where the landlord, Victor Richardson, was busy emptying all the contents of the property onto the side of the road.

Without any ceremony or care, he was dumping all the furniture in a big pile, like a bonfire. For all its menacing history, there was Jimmy's winged chair on top, discarded with as much regard as scrap wood.

"What on earth are you doing!" Mrs. Butler cried.

"It's all shite," sneered the landlord with his customary nasal twang a result of his nose being broken on more than once occasion by irate tenants. "There's no point in saving it. Can't sell it. Probably can't give it away neither."

He looked the trawler's wife up and down. Who's she when she's at home? he thought. Maybe she was from the council and had come to investigate him.

"Victor Richardson," he said, extending a hand.

"Where's the woman who lives here?" Edith asked, ignoring him. "Aren't those her things? Look at this painting! It's actually quite good. You can't throw it away."

"If you're talking about Dolores Alford, she's gone."

"Gone? Gone where?"

"How the 'eck would I know? All I know is that yesterday was her last day 'ere. That's what I gave her, till yesterday. Last night, I put a note through her letterbox reminding her, and when I came by this morning she weren't here. At first, I thought she'd done a moonlight flit, like, but then I found this: it's my note with some money folded inside. Mind you, it's not all what she owes me. Can't for the life of me think why she left her furniture – to make up the difference in what she owes me or what, I don't know. Anyrode, it's all crap. Not worth selling. And believe me I would have sold it, if I could 'ave. Like that painting you have in your hands. It's of the bloody milkman of all people. I mean, who'd want it. It's not even bloody finished. But you can 'ave it if you want. To me, it's all just firewood. And bonfire fire night past an' all."

"Have you no heart?" cried Mrs. Butler. "She's a widow with three children!"

"Listen, I had the heart to give her six weeks to pay off the arrears. I'm not running a bloody charity 'ome here. I need to eat an' all. Same as you do. And look how she thanks me by leaving a big mess for us to clear out."

"But I don't understand why you're so sure she's gone. What if she comes back later?"

"Look, madam, these things happen all the time. I know when someone's not coming back. Go on, look for yoursen."

Unwillingly, Edith Butler believed the landlord, but nonetheless she decided to walk through the open front door hoping to find in the house some sign of Dolores or of where she might have gone. The shabby curtains had been removed, torn down by the landlord, and the daylight now allowed inside was not kind to the dismal interior of the house. The poverty was apparent. Everything about the remaining furnishings was threadbare, perhaps third or fourth hand in Edith's estimation. When she thought of her own house, of her friends' houses and their highly polished interiors, her heart became heavy with sorrow for the poor.

"And she left me with them bloody pigeons to clean up an' all," said the landlord as he took down the last of the unfinished nets hanging in the hallway. "Can't even make a decent pie out of 'em they're so bloody thin. Mind you, they'll make good target practice for my lads."

Edith Butler's soul was heavy with shame. She had never given any thought to how the widows of the fishermen managed. And the truth was, as she saw it that day, they didn't manage. What is this but poverty's end, she thought. These are British children. My children. It reflects horribly on me and on my class that we have allowed our children to live like this.

"The strange thing is," the landlord was saying, "that she didn't take any clothes, or 'ardly any by the looks of things. All the food's gone though."

"No food," said Edith.

"Not a scrap."

Nothing to take, nothing to leave.

The landlord swallowed audibly. He was steeling himself against any feelings of remorse but couldn't avoid rubbing his eyes. If he had known the tough decisions he would have to make he might never have gone into the business of tenancy. His dark-circled eyes were tired. He looked forward to the day he could retire.

"What about her family?" asked Edith. "Could she have gone to stay with them?"

"Her mam and dad live just up the street. I rent to them, an' all. I own ten 'ouses on this street. But she won't be there," said the landlord, who knew the ins and outs of most of his tenants' lives. He made it his business to know so he could tell who was speaking the truth and who wasn't when the rent was late. "Her dad's a real nasty feller, even worse than her 'usband was, if you can imagine that. No, she won't be at their house. Have you asked that Goodwell lass? The one what runs the chippy on St. George's Road. Mrs. Alford and her were right friendly."

The landlord went into the girls' bedroom to remove the bed and other decrepit furnishings. The tattered rug was so threadbare he thought it might disintegrate when he picked it up.

"Look at this," he said, holding up the mattress. "It's an old picture of Alford. I remember it were in the paper when he went missing. He weren't bad looking in his day."

"It must belong to the girl," Edith said, taking it from him. "If you don't mind, I'll take it, and the painting."

"They're of no use to me."

"That's very generous of you, I'm sure."

Edith slipped the picture into her handbag. She opened one of the ill-fitting drawers of the splintered chest by the window, rummaging through the clothing hoping to find something for Shirley to wear but the ragged state of the clothes depressed her, so she let them be.

"My daughters might like this doll," said the landlord, holding Lizzie in his hands.

290

"No, I'll take it," said Mrs. Butler. "It definitely belongs to the girl. I've seen her with it."

The landlord's eyes narrowed suspiciously.

"Hold on a minute, how come you know so much about them?"

"My husband is Mr. Samuel Butler. You may have heard of Butler Trawling and Fish Meal Co.," she said coolly, as if that settled everything, which it did since most of the landlord's tenants worked for Butlers.

"Listen," the landlord said, "if you need help looking for her, I'm more than willing to help out, once I've finished here, that is."

He wanted to clean the place so he could rent it again by the end of the week.

"No. You've done enough, thank you. Good bye."

"She'll turn up. Don't worry," the landlord called after her with forced cheerfulness. "I mean, she's got all them bairns to take care of. She'll turn up."

Dolores Alford did turn up; her dead body was spotted floating in the dock later that afternoon. Sharon's body was never found, though it was presumed she had also drowned. For decades to come all the fishermen who boarded trawlers there were haunted by the thought of that little girl's undiscovered body rotting in the depths of the dank water beneath.

"What's to become of the bairns?" Muriel whispered when Constable Popple imparted the news.

She nodded to the babe in her arms, and the one sleeping next to her, holding tightly onto the doll Edith Butler had dropped off earlier.

"They're all on their own now. No mother, no father."

"We had bacon for breakfast," said Shirley, opening her eyes but lying still, loving Lizzie.

"You're awake, love. You gave us a start. What did you say?"

"We had bacon for breakfast. I'd never 'ad bacon before. It were delicious. Sharon had four pieces, but Shane's too young. Mam said he might choke. I had two pieces. And then it were all gone. Sharon wanted more and me mam got cross. And she made us leave and I wanted Lizzie to be safe so I hid her under me bed. We didn't know where we was going."

She described walking in the direction of the docks.

"I were scared," she said. "It was me mam, her face. She were crying and she wouldn't talk to us. We was all scared. Me and Sharon held 'ands. Then when we got there me mam showed us where they'd found me dad. Then we sat on the edge while me mam stared into the water for ages and ages, rocking Shane in her arms. Shane was crying, so I said he was hungry but she didn't do nowt about it. Then she grabbed Sharon's hand and squeezed it really hard, and Sharon started crying an' all. Then I told her me bum was getting numb 'cause the dock was hard and cold but she didn't say nowt about that neither so I stood up and rubbed it and she told me to sit down but I wouldn't. I said, 'I won't!' And then she just looked at me like, I don't know, like she was really sad or mad or some'at, but then she smiled, but not like a real smile, and then she said, 'All right, Shirley. You're the only one. Go on, go find Prudence. She'll take care of you.' I didn't want to go but she yelled at me to go. Sharon was really crying and I could see me mam was hurting her hand, so I said, 'You're hurting Sharon.' And me mam said, 'She'll feel better soon. Now go, please. And don't turn around.' So I walked a bit, but then I heard a splash and me mam and Sharon had fell in," she sobbed. "Sharon screamed and I screamed and I jumped in after them. I got hold of Shane and pulled him away from me mam. Sharon grabbed me mam round her neck. I couldn't do owt 'cause I had to get Shane out. I was close to the steps. I couldn't hold him up. Sharon was screaming and splashing and me mam was pulling at Sharon's arms trying to get 'em from round her neck. I climbed up the ladder and put Shane on the side but when I turned round they was gone. Me mam and Sharon was gone. Me mam can't swim. It was me dad learned me and Sharon at Albert Ave baths but me mam would never go. She just wouldn't go!"

Sobbing, Shirley buried her face in Muriel's lap.

"I'm so sorry, love," Muriel said. "So sorry. There, you're safe now. Shh. You were very brave when your mam ... *fell?*"

The sobbing girl nodded. Helplessly, Muriel looked to Constable Popple who nodded: *fell* would be the official report since there were no other witnesses to say differently. Edith Butler inclined with her head to show that she too agreed. Prudence sat on the bed and stroked Shirley's head.

"You were a very brave girl," the policeman said. "What a terrible accident."

"Aye, very brave."

"You saved Shane's life."

A young, tear-stained face looked up, then reached over and kissed her brother's forehead before hiding again in Muriel's lap.

"I can't believe nobody saw them," Muriel said.

"It were busy," said Constable Popple. "There were three trawlers landing their catch."

"Too busy," Edith said sadly.

At the services for Sharon and Dolores, little condolence was offered to Dolores' parents for the loss of a daughter they had abused and abandoned long ago; though Prudence's heart did feel a prick of pity when the mother's knees weakened and the father's arm went around her waist for support. But Prudence turned away so they wouldn't see her sympathy.

There was also bad blood between the two families since, citing their role as Shane and Shirley's grandparents, they had laid a claim to have the children live with them. But given their dreadful history of abuse, Prudence had refused to allow it, so Dolores' father said he was going to sort it out with the proper authorities and there was nothing the Goodwells would be able to do about it.

Not many mourners attended the service. Perhaps it was because of the gossip surrounding the circumstances of Dolores' drowning, or perhaps it was out of shame for what should have been done to help her. Also, there might have been those who were angry at Dolores. Was it possible they felt let down by her death, as if their own struggle meant nothing and, as was generally believed had happened, by taking her own life she was giving the message that the struggle wasn't worth it - that there would be no better days. Hitherto, the desperate had hoped for the dawn of good fortune, at least for their children's sake, but Dolores had taken a child with her as if to say that the next generation, too, was lost.

Aside from Muriel, who was too sick to attend, all the Goodwells were at the service. Elsie Waggin was in attendance (she wouldn't have missed it for the world), along with her daughter Gillian. The two whispered comments to each other regarding the cheapness of the caskets. Prudence sighed. Yet such idiosyncrasies, people behaving in their same irritating ways, were of some comfort to Prudence. Imagine, she thought, if I went over now and thanked them for their lack of tact. I wonder what they would say.

At the wake being held at the Goodwell home, the mourners were astounded by the arrival of Dolores' landlord.

"I've come to pay me respects," he said. "I mean, I'm sorry she did what she did. If I'd known she were this desperate, like…"

Seething but polite for the sake of the occasion, Prudence quietly asked him to leave but he was adamant about staying. Witnessing his sister's distress, Mac immediately came to her aid, making a grab for the landlord's arm to guide him away, a gesture which the landlord firmly rebuked. But Mac grabbed him again, more powerfully. He was glad to have something he could hurt. All the anger and despondency he felt about the deaths of Dolores and Sharon were concentrated in the hand squeezing the landlord's upper arm. If he could only hear the bone snap perhaps then his pain would break too.

"Ow! Bloody hell! Watch what you're doing? It's easy for you all to blame me, isn't it?" Richardson said loudly. "Well, where were you lot with your reddened eyes when she needed you? Talk about closing the barn door after the 'orse has bolted. This wouldn't have happened if any of you had lent an 'elping hand. You Goodwells have the means. Everyone knows it."

"Listen, I'm warning you," said Mac, tightening his grip.

"Oh, I'll take some blame," said the landlord. "But really I gave her more charity than any of you. Six weeks in fact. Do you know how much money that is? I didn't see her living at any of your 'ouses for free."

He looked into the faces of the small gathering but to Mac specifically he said, "Tha knows, if only I'd taken what she'd offered to pay the rent, she might be alive today."

"What do you mean?" Mac seethed in the landlord's ear.

"Oh, you know what I mean, don't you, Mad Mac?" The landlord made a play to free his arm but did not succeed. "I'll admit I had an 'ard time turning her down. After all, I had quite a thing for her a few years ago. But I'm not one to take advantage -"

Maybe Victor Richardson wanted to be punched so hard that his nose broke in two places. If he did then he got his wish. Bloody and broken and lying on the ground, he didn't know whether it was Mac or God that had struck him, so damning was the blow.

"Bollocks. Me nose," he said. "You've broken it."

"Re-broken it more like," said Mac, hesitating a moment before extending a hand to his foe. The gesture was accepted, and the slight man was lifted to his feet with ease.

Since hearing about Dolores' death, Mac had vowed never to come to blows over her again. He wanted to put that part of him in the past. Yet here he was punching a man who had defamed her. But that would be the last time. He swore it. His physical threats and retaliations had not helped Dolores in any way, in fact, Mac felt, his behaviour had added only further duress to her life. Why had everything become so complicated when it had started off so simply with just a girl and a boy? There weren't only me and her in that relationship, mind. There were her mam and dad an' all, and all that they had done to her. We was already crowded. No wonder the boat sank.

"Here's a towel," Prudence said to the landlord.

"Ta, love."

Blood spread across the tea towel.

"Feel better?" the landlord asked Mac, his nasal twang even more pronounced.

"Aye," said Mac. "Do you?"

Cupping his bloody nose, the landlord looked the fisherman in the eye, then nodded.

"Aye, reckon I do an' all," he said.

Mac sighed. "You're an easy feller to be angry at. You can be a real mean bastard sometimes."

"Goes with the territory."

"Here, Bill," said Gloria Baxter, putting a cold, wet towel over Mac's hand and holding it there.

"Oh," he said. "Ta."

Looking at the beauty and warmth standing before him made his eyes ache, but within him emotions clashed. He panicked.

"I have to go," he muttered, breaking their touch.

"Where to?" she called after him. "Hold this," she said, handing the towel to whomever was standing next to her, and she ran out into the ten foot where Mac was kicking his bike into action. She jumped on the back.

"What the bloody hell are you doing?" he asked.

"Going with you," she said.

"What the bloody hell for?"

Revving the engine with his bloodied hand, Mac looked over his shoulder at Gloria, indicating that she should get off. She shook her head. His black eyes flashed.

"Leave me be. I don't want no passengers slowing me down."

"You don't scare me William Goodwell. I'm telling you, I won't move. You'll have to push me off. Take me with you. I want to see where you go. I won't talk nor nowt. Pretend I'm not 'ere. I want to ride with you, properly, not careful, because you have a lass on the back."

"Oh aye? We'll see about that, won't we?"

Her heart raced as loud as the bike engine. She felt magnificent, all powerful. Her whole body was electrified. By the look in his eyes, she knew he was going to take her with him. She knew it before he did.

Thirty minutes later, they arrived in the hamlet of Faxfleet, and parked near the grassy bank of the River Humber. Gloria was breathless from the thrill of the ride along the twisty, narrow country roads. Perhaps he *had* forgotten she was there. And she, giving up to the experience completely, had clung tightly to him letting his body and the bike direct her. It had been scary at times but she had kept her eyes wide open watching the countryside and the grey road whiz by in a blur.

Without waiting for her to disembark, Mac climbed the embankment to the path and walked a few feet along it before stopping to light a rolled cigarette, cupping his hand against the strong wind, and watching the rippled, muddy water in the wide, dangerous river flow past on its way to out to sea. He looked to his right to see where it had come from and glanced to his left to see where it was going. The continuous motion fascinated him. He wished he were the river that kept moving without purpose, without considering that it even had a purpose.

But I have been that river, he thought. I have. Moving fast, without thinking, and then owt or anyone that comes near me I drag 'em down wi' me. I don't mean to. I'm just so bloody clumsy at life. Oh, Dolores. Why did you do it? Why did you do any of it? Maybe there is only one path for each of us. I hope God can forgive you for taking Sharon with you 'cause I know I can't. Not yet at any rate. Why did you take her? I think you meant to take them all. I thought I knew you, but I didn't know what you were capable of. To feel that sad that you can't bear your children to go on neither, well, I can't imagine it.

"It's shite! It's all shite!" he bellowed at the muddy river that didn't alter its course on his account.

A whining brought him back to his senses.

"Go on, lad, I forgot you was there," he said, taking the dog from his coat and putting him on the path for a run.

Monty lifted his leg on a thistle.

Nothing's changed, Mac reflected. Not the sky nor the trees nor the river. Even me dog's carrying on like nowt's different. And yet ... she's gone. Look, there's a man riding his bike to Blacktoft. Doesn't he know she's gone? Why hasn't time stood still?

Removing her high heel shoes, Gloria climbed up through the wet grass. Tendrils of dark blonde hair had escaped their grips and were whipping about in the wind, catching in her mouth. Keeping her promise not to talk, she maintained a respectful distance. The path was stony, so she replaced her shoes while safely, she thought, observing him. He seemed deeply lost in thought and unaware of her presence, until he said, "How old are you? I mean what are you doing coming after me?"

"I'm old enough," she said with a broad smile.

"Aren't there any boys your own age."

"Plenty," she said, brushing a wind-blown lock out of her blue eyes. "But there's none like you."

He threw up his hands.

"How can a young lass like you say that? So bold like?"

"'Cause I'm more than just a young lass. Look at me. Your eyes'll tell you the truth."

Turning to look at her, he noticed she was cold wearing only a dress and cardigan. She had run after him without any thought of where they would end up. She came after me. She's not waiting to see what comes to her. He should offer her his coat, but, smiling inwardly, he didn't.

"I wish you'd talk to me like I was a woman."

"How's that then?"

"You still see me as that girl you remember before the war. And I'm not her no more. I'm a woman now."

"Maybe you remember me as the boy I was before the war. I'm not him no more neither."

"So, in a way, you could say, we're meeting each other for the first time."

"By heck, you are a rum lass, aren't you? You've got a way of talking that... Here, take me coat. You'll drown in it but it's bloody freezing out here."

The word 'drown' hung between them, but the young woman was not going to let the moment pass. She might not get another opportunity for a long time to talk to him alone, so she strove to steer his thoughts away from Dolores.

"It is cold," she said, pulling the coat around her. "I've never been 'ere before."

"It's 'ard to get to I suppose. You need a car or a bike like mine. I like to come here a lot. It's desolate, just a few 'ouses here and there, but I like being alone and watching the river. That's all there is here, river, bank and sky."

"You're not alone now."

"Aye, and I still don't know how it 'appened that you ended up here with me."

Hands in his trouser pockets and shoulders up around his ears, he stomped his feet against the cold.

"You do like me, you just don't know it yet," she said.

"I didn't say I didn't like you."

"You know what I mean."

"And what would your dad 'ave to say about it?"

"Me dad's dead. And if you mean Bert, he doesn't have a say in who I marry. He's not me real dad."

"Maybe not, but he's my real friend, and I work wi' him every day."

"He looks up to you. He wouldn't mind."

Her colours stood out against the muddy sky and river. Despite the thick wool fisherman's coat, still vivid to him were the tight olive green cardigan, ivory blouse and slim black skirt she wore underneath.

"Hold on, did you say marry?"

Her eyes sparkled mischievously, daring him.

"I did."

Shaking his head, he took a drag on a cigarette, and walked a few steps along the path seaward bound. The dog was chewing on some grass. Mac squatted to pet him.

"I know things," Gloria said. "You don't think I do, but I do."

Surprising him, she approached his back and touched him, sliding her hands around and clasping them in front of him. Feeling struck as if by lightning, he tensed when she leaned her cheek against his giant back. She had the scent of someone young and fresh, like the first crocus in spring.

"I can barely reach around you," she whispered.

Her hands were soft and white. When he touched them, she reached up and brushed his face teasingly. Closing his eyes, he let her fingers trace his dark brow, his cheeks, and his lips. It was many years since he had been touched with such inviting tenderness. The sensation was loving, as if she sought to learn his face by touch alone. Maybe, he could get used to that.

Tossing the cigarette, like old memories, into the river, he turned and pulled her close. Their eyes met, man to woman. Holding her sweet, creamy face and neck in his large hands, he stroked her cheeks with his thumbs, considering. Red lips smiled and parted, slightly. He looked away for a moment, at the river, then lifting her off the ground, he kissed her long and passionately.

"I told you!" she cried at last. "I told you!"

More gently, he embraced her, nudging her nose with his and looking into her beautiful eyes. There was a real fire there. There were no lies, no doubts. What man wouldn't, he thought. With her arms around his neck, she stood on her toes, longing to be kissed again. She wanted him, and only him. Gloria wasn't fearfully escaping anything, no this girl was fearlessly pursuing something, him. A life without broken promises? I could live with that, he thought. But it's not right, not now.

Suddenly mindful of what was waiting for them back home, he released her arms.

"Come on, love," he said. "Everyone'll be wondering where we are. We shouldn't be doing this. I got carried away. I'm not mesen today."

"Can't we stay, just a while longer?"

"No, love. It'd be best if we left now. I'll drop you off 'ome, then take Bert out for a pint."

"Why? Are you going to tell him about us?" she asked.

"About us?" He cleared his throat uneasily. "What's there to tell?"

"You kissed me."

"You want me to tell him that?"

"Not exactly. But aren't you going to ask him about us courting? I know, I know. I understand. You were in love with Dolores, and you need time –"

"Love? If that's what you think, then you know more than I do."

"But I thought –"

"I might have been, once. But me feelings changed. I ended up worrying about her more than owt else. Reckon I wanted to save her. She knew it an' all. But it were like trying to bail out a boat using a bucket with an 'ole in it."

"Are you going to try to save me?"

"From what?"

Grinning, he put an arm about her shoulders and pulled her to his broad chest, kissing the top of her head.

"No, love," he said. "You don't need saving. That's what I like about you. I think it's more like you're the one what's going to save me. But give me time to get me 'ead on straight."

She reached on her tip-toes to kiss his cheek lightly. As they began to descend the embankment, "Hold on," she said. "I have to take off me shoes again or me heels'll sink in the grass."

"No need for that," he said, catching her by surprise and effortlessly swinging her up in his arms, carrying her like a new bride.

"Getting in practice for the big day, are you," she said.

"Oy, stop that," he said.

She laughed, throwing her arms about his neck.

As they walked, she said, "Promise you won't forget me."

"Forget you?"

"When you go to sea."

"No, love. I don't think I'll ever forget you again."

"I'll wait for you," she said, and he believed this one would.

He felt so light riding home with her close behind him, like a bird in flight, soaring. It had been a struggle for him. Like that Albatross, he mused. He was surprised to feel at peace, as if all the effort of life had suddenly been washed away. He patted the hand that clung round his waist and grinned when she snuggled even closer to him.

I have a chance, he thought. For all me failings, I have a chance. Don't haunt me no more Dolores. Leave me be.

Chapter 27

"Well I never!" Muriel exclaimed when she was told of Mac's disappearance with Gloria Baxter. "I knew she made me this shawl for a reason; wanted to get her feet under the table, I see. Well, I approve. She's a decent lass. I only hope he keeps her that way."

The wake was over, as was most of the cleaning up. The gentle strums of Jake's guitar could be heard coming from upstairs. He was playing a lullaby to soothe Shirley and Shane to sleep.

"What do you mean, Mam?" asked Winnie with Yorkshire Curd crumbs falling out of her mouth. "About Gloria?"

"She means Gloria Baxter is going to end up being your sister-in-law if she gets her way," said Vivian.

"What? But she's my friend!"

"Oh, is that why you think she's been coming around 'ere, then," Vivian said. "Because she's your friend? Don't be so daft."

"Vivian Goodwell shut your gob right this minute," said Muriel. "Don't listen to her Winnie. Honestly, what's got into you today, Vivian? You've been moping around and snapping at everything that moves."

"The truth hurts."

"Stop it *now*. Bloody 'ell I almost told you to go to your room. Gloria and Winnie have been friends since they was bairns. Why, anyone would think you was jealous."

"Gloria *is* very pretty," said Prudence. "And young."

"You can stop it an' all," said Muriel.

"I'm young," said Vivian.

"Not that young," Prudence said with a smile.

"Younger than you," said Vivian.

"But that doesn't matter to me, 'cause I don't value mesen in that way," said Prudence.

"But she's *my* friend," Winnie said again. "If she wasn't, she wouldn't 'ave ..."

"Wouldn't have what?" asked Vivian.

Winnie pressed her lips together refusing to speak further. She had almost told them about losing Mac's caul.

"What is it, love?" asked Muriel.

"Nowt," said Winnie. "Nowt at all."

None of them had any concern that Winnie could be involved in anything serious, so they were about to return to their business when George said, "I know what it is," then, pushing the rest of the curd into his mouth, he said. "Everybody does."

"George!" cried Winnie. "Don't!"

"Except us," said Vivian, now intrigued. "Pray tell, dear sister, what is it?"

"I'm not telling. It's a secret," said Winnie.

"George?" Vivian asked.

"Leave our Winnie alone," said Muriel. "If she doesn't want to tell us, we don't 'ave to know."

Though secretly she knew she would pry it out of her daughter later.

"But *I* want to know," said Vivian.

"I must admit, I wouldn't mind knowing either," Prudence chimed in. "Go on our George, tell us."

Winnie groaned.

"Well," said George settling himself in the chair and reaching for a mince pie to which no one objected his taking, "What I heard was that Gloria Baxter went to our Winnie's school one day and beat up that lass what's been bullying our Winnie."

"Bullying Winnie!" cried Muriel. "I'll bloody go and give her a good hiding mesen. Well, good for Gloria. I like her even more now. Winnie love, you should 'ave said some'at. I suppose with everything what's been going on you didn't want to trouble us. I 'ope it's stopped. It better have. Has it?"

Winnie nodded. Yes, Gloria had gone to the school and beaten up Dolly Collins but, thankfully, George did not know the exact details of what had happened: that Gloria had pushed Dolly's head down the school toilet and flushed it several times while instructing Dolly to look for Mac's caul. When the bell rang, Gloria ended the torment by declaring, "If my Bill drowns on account of what you did then I'm going to drown you."

There was a knock at the front door.

"Who the 'eck is that?' said Muriel. "Honestly, there's no peace for the wicked."

"I'll go see," said Prudence stifling a yawn as she dragged herself down the hallway to open the front door.

"Mrs. Butler! What a surprise. Would you like to come in?"

Stepping into the hallway, Edith Butler looked nervously toward the parlour.

"Are the children here?"

"Shirley and Shane? Yes, but they've only just gone to sleep."

"Oh," Edith said with obvious disappointment.

"They're doing ever so well though, considering. It's so nice of you to stop by to check on them. Would you like a cup of tea? It's cold out there."

"I wouldn't want to trouble you," Edith said fiddling with the buttons on her coat, apparently reluctant to leave.

"It's no trouble," said Prudence. "Come on, come in and warm yourself by the fire. Is everything all right?"

"Yes fine except … there is rather a private matter I would like to discuss with you and your mother."

With Winnie and George dismissed upstairs, and Jake taken himself for a walk, Edith Butler settled into the parlour with a cup of tea and an audience of three women dying to know what this was all about.

Haltingly, Edith told the story of her time in Paris and how she had returned home pregnant. The three Goodwell girls daren't look at each other during this revelation;

though Vivian felt a slight triumph that she wasn't the only one, then. Edith went on to explain that she had secretly given birth to an illegitimate child who was taken away to a local orphanage by Dr. McKenzie. Not a day went by, she said, when she didn't think about her son and what had become of him. But she was always too afraid to investigate his whereabouts because of the scandal it would bring to her family.

"After the incident at the docks, Dr. McKenzie came to see me. For all these years, we'd never spoken about the baby, but I guessed as soon as I saw his face that he'd come with news about my son."

Her chest quivered, catching a sob. As she reached into her handbag for a handkerchief, Muriel and Prudence exchanged a look wondering if they were both understanding correctly.

"Oh, I know. I've heard the stories about him," said Edith. "But if only I could have kept him, his life would have been so different. And not just his; his wife's and his children's, their lives too. Instead, well, instead James lived all those years believing his own mother didn't want him."

"Jimmy Alford?" said Muriel. "You're talking about Jimmy Alford, Dolores' 'usband?"

"He was your son?" said Prudence.

Edith nodded, wiping away a tear.

"Then Shirley and Shane are your -?"

"Grandchildren. Yes."

"Well, I never," said Muriel. "You could knock me down with a feather."

Edith smiled thinly.

"If Dr. McKenzie had told me sooner, I could have helped that young woman. She was my daughter-in-law, after all. But now she's dead too, with one of ... the girls."

Edith closed her eyes, taking a deep breath to contain her emotions, while wringing the handkerchief tightly in her hands.

"If you don't mind me asking, love," Muriel inquired. "How is Mr. Butler taking all this? Does he know?"

Mrs. Butler took a sip of tea and seemed quite glad of it.

"He already knew, as it turns out. Apparently, my father had told him about the child before we married."

"Whatever for?" asked Muriel.

"To put him off, I think." Edith smiled. "The marriage was my mother's idea, and my father was embarrassed, I think, that he had let us down, financially speaking. But Sam, Mr. Butler, married me anyway, and he never let on that he knew. My father made him promise not to. To think I've been looking down my nose at him all these years, when he had greater reason ..." Absentmindedly, she stirred her tea. "He even knew who it was, that it was James. He had done some investigating, you see, finding out the surname that had been given to him at the orphanage."

"Goodness," said Muriel.

Tears filled Edith Butler's eyes. "Then he made sure that James kept his job on the Wilberforce, even though he had a problem with his drinking and his temper. He did all this," she sobbed, "for me. It's been such a terrible secret between us for all these years. But, finally, it's over. And now," she sniffed, pulling herself together. "Now, he agrees that we should bring the children, *our grandchildren*, he called them, home."

The fire crackled, spitting an ember onto the rug. Prudence used the tongs to throw it back onto the fire.

"But what will people say?" she asked.

"Who cares what people say!" snapped Vivian, standing.

"I used to care, very much," said Edith. "But I realised that my pride should not depend on appearances, but rather on *doing* what is right. And *really doing*, not wishing or hoping or intending, but doing."

307

"What about Dolores' parents?" asked Muriel. "They said they're going to get a solicitor to fight for the children."

"Don't worry. I've heard enough about them to know they'll back down when they see these," Edith said, referring to a judge's order and a cheque book she lifted out of her handbag.

"I suppose that's that then," said Muriel sitting back with her hands clasped in her lap. "When do you want to, I mean, the children are asleep upstairs."

"Oh, I don't mean to take them now. I think it's best if they get to know me, and Mr. Butler, a bit better, don't you?"

"The hair!" exclaimed Prudence. "Shirley has your red hair! We allus wondered where it came from."

"Yes," said Edith, smiling and touching her hair subconsciously. "I think she does, though mine has some grey in it these days."

Muriel started crying. "She's a real cheerful little soul that Shirley. Got her looks from her mother, but thank God, that's all she got. The poor darlings don't have owt at all in this world, save for the few bits an' bobs you was able to get from their 'ouse. No, they don't have owt, so I reckon they'll be real glad to find out they have you."

"Thank you. And thank you for your kindness and understanding," said Edith. "I'll see myself out."

Each bid farewell with a view to meeting the next day.

"If only Dolores had lived to see this," remarked Prudence after Edith Butler had left.

"This day might not have 'appened if she'd lived," observed Muriel.

"But it might have. Just another week, that's all it would have taken for her life to turn around. Why can't we see into the future?"

That night, as Prudence slipped between cold sheets, she pondered recent events. There was a lot to think about, and lessons to be learned. One thing she knew for sure was that she did not want her fortune tied to any man's, in case it turned out to be misfortune, as with Dolores who had depended on Jimmy Alford. And tonight, Prudence had admired Edith Butler's courage. No matter how much money the Butlers had, they would still have to ride out wave of gossip and disapproval.

Pushing a hot water bottle down between her feet, Prudence realised she missed the bed being warmed by Winnie now that she had moved into their mother's old bedroom. The bottle was no substitute for the heat of a human body, though it was nice to finally have some time to herself. These were the hours when she could think and do whatever she wanted and nobody would know.

It was dark in the room, and, she knew, cold enough for her breath to be visible. She sighed heavily imaging her breath condensing in a cloud above her. Moonlight filtered in between the curtains, and, soon, her eyes became accustomed to the darkness as she tried to stare into her own future, thinking of how it could go this way, if she did this, or how it could go that way if she did that.

But what good has all this thinking brought me? Look at me. I'm still lying here alone. I haven't moved an inch, night after night, day after day, for years. And while I'm waiting, whatever I'm waiting for, a bloody gypsy tries to take what's mine to give away. Get up, Prudence Goodwell!

Silently, but with great resolve, she pushed back the covers and sat on the edge of the bed, toes barely touching the floor. The bed looked so inviting, so safe. But if she stayed there, she might never get out of it. Careful not to let the wardrobe door creak too loudly, she slipped on one of her mother's faux fur coats over her flannel nightdress. Making as little noise as possible, she peaked into the bedrooms to make sure everyone was asleep. Jake and Mac were still out, though by this time 'last orders' had been called and they must be on their way home.

Outside on the cold front doorstep, she slipped on her shoes, and hurried along in the direction of the pub, praying she wouldn't run into her brother and Jake. If she did, she reasoned, she would say she was coming for them on some pretext or other, and then turn and walk back home with them. Perhaps there was a part of her that hoped it would happen that way; though it was possible they might not recognize her across the street and in the dark. Certainly, they wouldn't be expecting to see her.

"Oh no, it's Fred," she whispered, dipping into an alley when she heard the unmistakable sound of a horse's hooves - the measured, heavy gait of Samson, accompanied by Fred's soft voice.

The milkman was complaining about the UXB in his front yard again. It was his favourite topic when he'd had a few drinks.

Prudence stayed hidden until they passed then made her way on to the pub, arriving just in time to see the last of the downstairs lights extinguished. Stalworth was probably already on his way to the upstairs flat. She should have had a better plan, she thought. Or even *a* plan. What had she been hoping to do, sneak in somehow as everyone was leaving? Perhaps she should go home and rethink what she was doing. No, if she went home now she might never return to do whatever it was she was aiming to do. Gathering strength and determination again, she went around to the back of the pub to see if there was a door that might be unlocked. Alas, there wasn't. A belt and braces man like Derek Stalworth would never take such a chance, especially in a thirsty community like Hessle Road.

When a light came on in the flat upstairs, her heart leapt nervously, and her anxious eyes watched Derek's shadow shift from room to room. As he removed his tie, he came to the window and looked out. So she waved and whispered his name as loudly as she dared. But he didn't hear or see her.

She could throw a stone, but she might break a window, and draw attention not only from Derek, but from anyone else within earshot, and *that* she most certainly did not want to do. She would never live it down. To be found here, around the back of the pub, in the middle of the night would be very embarrassing, especially since Stalworth was not expecting her. Not to mention, she had no idea how he was going to react *when* he saw her. What if he was angry? He had been cordial to her at pantomime rehearsals but perhaps that had only been due to the presence of other people. Alone with her he might show his true feelings about the way she had treated him. It occurred to her that he might not want to see her at all. And anyway, what was she going to say to him when they did get face to face? She hadn't planned that part at all. It was hopeless. She would have to go home.

A quiet rustling behind the dustbins reminded her that Derek had complained about rats hanging around the pub. She loathed rats. If one darted out at her she would have to jump up onto something. With that thought she looked for an elevated position and saw that if she climbed onto the wall there, using the coal bunker for leverage, she could get onto the roof of the outside toilet and reach across to tap on the lighted window above it: if she dare, which she did. Only, she wasn't aware she had been followed.

Jetty the cat was hot on her trail, no doubt as curious as anyone else might be about the unusual circumstance of one of the family going out at this ungodly hour. With great interest, the cat watched Prudence scramble up on to the top of the coal bunker, then traverse across it to the outhouse where she managed to get a foothold and hoist herself up on to the slanting tiled roof. This spectacle was too much for Jetty to witness from afar, so the cat trotted along the top of the cold, brick wall until she too reached the outhouse just in time for Prudence's nervous shimmy across the roof to the window.

Prudence was about to tap on the glass when she felt something slither around her calves. Picturing a giant rat, she let out a terrified scream, lost her unsure footing and slipped backwards, grabbing frantically at the empty night air, searching for something to save her from the inevitable.

Then, surprisingly, she enjoyed a reasonably soft landing. But it took a moment for her to recover. Gazing up at the clear night sky and all the stars in it, there was a brief moment when Prudence felt quite philosophical. The sky was so beautiful that night, black and infinite, that she was able to lose herself in the vastness of it briefly before someone, a man, coughed underneath her. Quickly rolling to one side, she got onto her hands and knees, and was horrified to see that it was Constable Popple who had broken her fall.

"Oh dear, I'm so sorry" she said, as he sat stiffly, coughing and brushing at his uniform.

"I'm all right. How about you?" he asked.

"I'm fine. Thanks to you," she said, glad of the dark to hide her red face.

"Think nothing of it," he said standing and shaking first one leg, then the other. "I'm here to serve. Here, give me your hand. There."

He pulled her to her feet, and peered into her face.

"Prudence Goodwell," he remarked.

"Yes, Officer. It's me."

"Have you seen me 'elmet? I can't see owt back here, it's so dark. It fell off when I caught you."

"Sorry about that. Let's see."

When she stepped back to take a look, her feet kicked something hard that scooted across the concrete back yard.

"Sounds like it," he said. "Ah, yes."

Retrieving it, he put it on, slipping the strap back under his strong chin.

"I thought I heard a noise," he said. "Stalworth's been 'aving some bother with lads breaking into his cellar, so I make a point of walking this way on me beat. At first I thought it were just that cat."

"Cat?"

"Aye," he said pointing to the roof where Jetty was calmly watching the goings-on below.

"Jetty? Is that you? You could have killed me. She's allus knocking things of the mantle to see what 'appens. I suppose she wanted to see what happened to me if I fell off an' all. Well, Jetty, I'm not an ornament you know. Although I would break just as easily." Prudence talked quickly and nervously, while her mind tried to drum up a reasonable excuse for her being where she was.

I could say I were looking for our Mac. No, that's ridiculous. Why would I be up on the roof peering in through windows. Well, I can't tell the truth, can I? It would be far too embarrassing to say I'm here because I've decided to … Hold on, what exactly 'ave I decided?

A polite cough from the policeman interrupted her thoughts.

"Now all that needs to be established, Miss. Goodwell, is why you are here on these premises."

"Well," she said. "I …"

Consulting his watch, he added, "You missed last orders, you know. Couldn't you have waited till tomorrow, like?"

"I'm not here for a drink," Prudence said with an awkward laugh.

Although, in truth, right then, there was nothing more she would have liked than a tot of something or other. She could say she was following the cat and thought it was trapped on the roof. Aye, that's a good one. That would make sense.

"Well, then Miss? Was it some last minute pantomime business? Some'at you had to go over before opening night?"

How she wished she could see the officer's face. There was definitely a smile in his tone. Thankfully, they were interrupted by the unlocking of a door, and light suddenly spilling out over them from the pub.

"Prudence!" Derek cried in astonishment. "What on earth are you doing here? Is everything all right?"

She gestured with her hands open, and shrugged.

"Good evening, Mr. Stalworth," said the constable.

"Good evening, Constable Popple."

"Might I ask if you were expecting a visit from Miss Goodwell on this cold December night?" asked the officer.

"No. Yes. Well ... yes."

"I see," said Constable Popple.

The policeman looked from one to the other as the two stared at each other in silence; neither of them knowing why Prudence was there. Constable Popple coughed again, lifting them from their trance.

"Looks like my work here is done. I'll be off, then, shall I and leave you two to it?"

"I'm sorry about what 'appened," said Prudence. "I'm ever so embarrassed. Are you sure you're all right?"

"Aye. Nowt that a hot bath and a cup of tea won't fix. From now on, I think you should leave roof climbing to the professionals."

"You were on my roof?" exclaimed Stalworth.

"Well, you see," said Prudence. "Jetty was, and I ... Yes, I was on the roof."

The landlord smiled.

"Would you like a drink, Popple?" he asked.

"No thank you, Sir. Not while I'm on duty."

Tipping his hat, he bid them farewell.

"Perhaps when you're off duty? It'll be on the house."

"Perhaps," said Constable Popple before disappearing into the darkness. The landlord and Prudence watched him leave: the last obstacle to their being alone.

"Come inside. It's freezing out 'ere," said Stalworth, rubbing his hands together and ushering Prudence in through the back entrance to the pub.

"Is he a regular?" she asked. "Popple, I mean."

The landlord thought for a moment.

"You know, I can't recall ever seeing him in here."

"Have you ever seen him off-duty, then? Out of uniform?"

"Can't say that I have now that you come to mention it."

"Neither have I. Don't you think that's a bit odd?"

"'Odd' you say."

Derek Stalworth mulled over the word for a moment, then he looked Prudence square in the eye and smiled. Placing a hand on each of her shoulders he sat her down at one of the pub's polished wood tables. The brasses and mirrors gleamed. There was no mistaking the pub odour; all the beer and blood that had seeped into every crack and crevice of the wood floors over the past centuries. Stalworth noticed the bottom frill of her nightdress sticking out from under the fur coat. She was bare-legged, he noted, and her skin was soft, creamy and smooth. His eyes travelled up her legs to her face to where the black hair he had so often dreamed of running his hands through was loose about her shoulders.

"Aye," said Prudence. "To think he's been around here for years, and for neither of us to have ever seen him out of uniform, well, I do think that's a bit odd, don't you?" She was breathless.

"Oh Prudence," said Derek. "Talk about the kettle calling the pot black. Now, I'd say that being on the roof of my outhouse would be considered a bit *odd*, wouldn't you?"

"Oh that," she said.

There was a pause as she fumbled for words. She had no plan. In her mind, she pictured herself exclaiming, "I've come to say ,'Yes'!" and then throwing herself into his open arms, but social restraint kept her seated. She wished he would make a move toward her but why would he after the way she had humiliated him? She couldn't believe how much she desired his hands on her. It was all she could think about right then. But she couldn't say or do anything to show it.

"Prudence?" he asked quietly. "What is it?"

"Do you forgive me?"

She vowed not to look away as his soft brown eyes bored into hers. Then he turned his face, as if thinking. She felt sick with panic. Was he about to spurn her? Her whole being pleaded.

"Yes," he said. "I'll say 'I forgive you' since that's what you're asking. But what's to forgive? I should have known better. I shouldn't have sprung it on you like that, in front of everyone. That's not you. You're not one for surprises, though you've surprised me tonight."

Smiling, she burst forth from her seat and he from his. With strong hands gripping her waist, he held her away from his body for a moment, gazing down into her face, then slowly reaching forward he kissed her lovingly. After an immeasurable while, he stopped, he wanted to say something, but she kissed him again to silence him, pushing him further into the place where he wouldn't be able to restrain his desire.

For the sake of propriety, again he tried to prevent it, but she put a finger to his lips then guided his hands to the buttons of her coat where he fumbled and she helped him while, at the same time, removing her shoes. The coat fell to the ground and he knew she was naked beneath the nightdress. No longer hesitant, he lifted the garment up and over her head so he could see her. His eyes burned as they swept over her body, quickly, briefly, taking it all in before gathering her up in his arms, and taking her as his own.

Afterwards, they lay tight together in his bed, each enjoying the feel of the other's body and knowing there was no need for words between them. Illumination from the street light outside seeped into the sparsely furnished room bathing everything in a ghostly glow. Stalworth traced a finger down Prudence's arm sending goosebumps along her whole body.

"Prudence, there's something I'd like to ask you -"

Putting a finger to his lips, she said. "Let's just stay like this forever and not care whether it's right or wrong. I'll run the fish shop and you run the pub and we'll have our sizzling, secret affair for everybody to gossip about."

"All right," he said. "But actually I was only going to ask if you would like a cup of tea?"

"Oh you!"

Smiling in the dark where she couldn't see him, he took her hand and slid it down his body. This was his desire for her again, so soon. He kissed her mouth, her neck, and her breasts, before turning her over on her side away from him, and pulling her hips toward him, with his arm crushing her breasts and his face buried in her voluminous hair.

Then came an explosion from whence Prudence didn't know, outside or in, 'til Stalworth said, "What the bloody hell was that?" and jumped out of bed, going to the window.

"Sounded like a bomb," said Prudence, also rising and wrapping a quilt around her to keep warm.

"Aye. It did."

"I haven't heard that sound for a while. Can you see owt?"

"No."

"Talk about feeling fireworks," quipped Prudence as she stood next to him peering out the window.

"What?" Derek said, then he laughed. "Aye. I just hope it isn't... Look over there. Is that smoke?"

"I can't tell. What is it?" she asked, noticing his worried expression, exaggerated by the shadows.

Stalworth plopped down on the edge of the bed, running a hand through his hair.

"Fred was in here tonight," he said, dressing quickly.

"Fred? Oh no! I saw him on me way here. He were going on about that bomb. You don't think he finally tried to move it, do you?"

"I hope not but he were going on and on about how he was sick of the council doing nowt about it. He were right wound up, more than usual, complaining that the government ignores the working man now the war is over. He said 'im and that 'orse could have had it out by now."

"Oh, no. Fred."

"The daft sod," said Stalworth, as he tied his shoelaces. "He'd had a lot to drink, but that's nowt new. He's been saying the same thing since the war ended so none of us pays no mind no more. But it were him I thought of just then, with the explosion. Look, do you mind if I go over there and take a gander? Make sure he's all right, like? I'm hoping I'm wrong."

He stroked her hair, feeling how soft and luxurious it was slipping between his fingers.

"I'll come with you," she said. "If you'll fetch me clothes from downstairs."

"Aren't you worried about folks seeing us together?"

"Not one bit. I meant what I said. A little bird has taught me to fly."

Frowning but smiling, Stalworth bent forward and brushed her lips with his.

Chapter 28

The anguished whinnying of the horse was difficult to bear. One of Samson's back legs was missing, and he writhed in pain further crushing Fred who was pinned under him. The milkman sobbed, "I'm sorry, Samson. I'm sorry," while crying out in his own agony.

There were no street lights on Fred's road, so those by-standers with torches flashed them across the devastating scene. The dying horse shook and lifted his massive head, snorting and whinnying in terrible pain, and Fred, who had tried to calm his friend, could no longer endure the pain of his horse or himself.

"Help me!" he cried. "Get me out! I can't move!"

But Fred couldn't be rescued while the animal thrashed its remaining legs, appearing to make a futile effort to stand once more. Anyone who tried to get too close was severely kicked for his trouble, including Mac and Jake. Jake grabbed the horse's head and tried to soothe it, stroking its thick mane and speaking softly. But if Fred moved the horse started up again. And no one could bear the animal's cries.

The vet was called for but it would be some time before he arrived. People walked away, blocking their ears, unable to bear the sound. They all loved that horse. Hysterical children were pulled away by parents and walked home to beds and nightmares. Fred shouted out in pain every time the horse writhed. Murmurs ran through the crowd. "Where's the bloody vet?" "Poor Samson." "Poor Fred." Then someone cried, "That lass - she's got a gun!" The onlookers gasped as Winnie broke through the throng and, with her legs braced, aimed Jake's gun at the horse's head.

"Winnie!" cried Vivian. "What are you doing?! You haven't even got your glasses on! Jake! Stop her!"

Winnie fired but missed the horse, inducing further cries from the crowd. Terrified now, the horse jerked and whinnied, with its wild, frightened eyes darting nowhere and everywhere. He tried to stand again, but fell, crushing Fred anew.

"Somebody grab the gun or the lass'll shoot one of us!"

Big tears rolled down Winnie's face, as she cried, "I can't stand it! Samson! I'm sorry!"

"Get the gun from her Jake! Get it!" Vivian cried.

319

Winnie raised the gun again, and the crowd stood back, cowering, except Jake who had run to her side. Standing behind her, he held her hands steady. "Aim for the blaze," he said. And they pulled the trigger together.

At once, the horse was silent. Everything was silent. With expressions of utter disbelief, everyone looked from Winnie to the horse.

"Bloody hell, Winnie," said Vivian, visibly shaken. "I never knew you 'ad it in you."

"Oh Winnie!" Prudence exclaimed, clasping the child to her. "You're braver than all of us."

Winnie sobbed, wiping her eyes and under her nose. Jake took the gun.

"Please," Fred cried. "Help me. I can't breathe. He's got real heavy now he's gone."

By the time the vet arrived, Fred had been removed from under the Shirehorse. To do the job required eight men; Mac, Jake and Derek Stalworth among them. Bruised and bloody, Fred lay on the ground, spent and heart-broken, with his eyes closed, prompting George to ask, in a whisper, if the milkman was dead an' all. For his curiosity, George was rewarded with a clip round the ear.

"Show some respect," said Mac. "Bloody hell, our lass," he said to Winnie with great pride. "That took bloody guts, that did. What is it? What are you looking at?"

A new wave of chatter had broken out. Some neighbours were pointing at Fred and, despite the horrible circumstances, there were even a couple of titters: for when Fred was pulled out from under his horse, his trousers were pulled off too, exposing the red lacy, women's underwear he was wearing. Someone's torch flashed over Fred's attire, and stayed there for a moment, as if the light too was shocked, before moving on to illuminate Fred's face, which was as devastated as his garden by the bomb.

Thankfully, he was in too much shock from the explosion and the loss of his beloved horse to be aware of the guilty snickers and giggles going on around him. In fact, it wasn't until later that night when he pulled himself from the settee, from under Samson's old blanket, and went, as usual, to untie the string belt that for years had kept up his trousers, that he realized his trousers were off. The shame he felt upon realizing that some, if not all, of those present that night had witnessed his secret and were probably gossiping and laughing about it up and down Hessle Road, was crippling, almost over-riding the guilt he felt about Samson's death. He imagined himself ruined in every way, and he daren't go out for days, not even to the pub, especially to the pub. What if they shun me? he thought. I could tell 'em it were part of me pantomime costume. If only Samson were there to talk to. He never minded. Live and let live, that were his motto.

Fred sobbed. His secret was out. He had to face it: there would no more going out during blackouts dressed completely as a woman, with a wig and shoes and handbag trying to dodge the home guard or local police or men on the lookout for ladies of the night. In a way, he had been sad when the war ended taking away his freedom to roam the streets of Hull as Janice when everyone else was hidden behind blacked out windows and doors. He felt so lonely. I've allus been kind to people. I've allus done me best. I wish people would just accept me for who I am.

The next time Mac was home from sea, he heard that Fred hadn't been seen in the pub for three weeks, so he called on the milkman and, in the spirit of Christmas, asked him, "Fancy a drink?" Fred declined. "Come on," said Mac. "My shout. You've been mourning that 'orse long enough. The lads are all worried about you." He didn't even mention the knickers. Fred was so relieved. All that worrying for nowt, he thought, and thought again when he arrived at the pub where the men were nothing but cordial and pleasant toward him. Even the priest and doctor were at the bar, sharing a drink and a joke with each other. The place was so familiar and reassuring.

I am a daft sod, he thought. These are me mates. I could have been in here every night instead of at 'ome alone, feeling sorry for mesen. I should 'ave known better.

But when the landlord poured a pint of bitter for Mac and half a pint of lager for Fred (instead of his usual pint of Guinness), the milkman's heart sank. Here it comes, he thought.

Sliding the small glass along the bar to Fred, Stalworth said, "First drink's free on ladies night," sending the whole pub into an uproar of unabashed guffaws. The men burst out laughing, throwing in some wolf whistles for good measure, embarrassing poor Fred, but it was all good-natured humour meant to break the ice after what had happened. So when he bolted for the door, he was wrestled back to sit on a stool at the bar. "Sit ye down. Sit ye down. Ye daft ha'p'oth. We mean ye no 'arm."

Fred's face and big ears were bright red.

"Here you go," said Stalworth, producing a full pint of Guinness for Fred. "I were just pulling your leg. Mind you, I hope I didn't put a ladder in your stockings."

Again, the men laughed. Stalworth had given the Mary the night off. No one wanted to hear her chiming in.

"Bugger off," said Fred. "I'm not hurting nobody."

"We know. We know," said Stalworth. "But we've got to 'ave it out with you, haven't we?"

"Reckon," Fred said sulkily.

"Look," said Mac, putting an arm round the milkman. "The lads was real sorry to hear about Samson. He was a magnificent beast. A real war hero."

"Aye," the men agreed and nodded, raising their glasses.

"We got some'at for you, Fred. As a token of our esteem for you and that horse. Stalworth, do the honours, please."

The landlord nodded respectfully, then from under the bar he produced a square parcel wrapped in brown paper and tied with a piece of new string.

"Hey up, look," said Mac, flicking the string. "We got you a new belt an' all."

Fred smiled sheepishly. He didn't know what to make of the situation. Aside from the meagre Christmas tips and pies he received from his customers, no one had ever before given him an actual present. His family had been too poor to spare any money for felicity. If asked about his birthday, he wouldn't know the date. He had given gifts though, to his horse, to mark the day they met, and for Christmas, of course. And, all year long, the horse had given him the only gifts Fred had ever wanted: companionship, loyalty and devotion. He had never longed for anything more, certainly nothing material, since, as experience had taught him, a piece a string will often do.

"Well, go on, then, open it," Bert urged him impatiently.

Fred started unpicking the knot but someone's cough made him nervous about the parcel's contents. He hesitated. The cough had sounded suspiciously like contained laughter. What if it was all a big joke, and there was nothing but women's attire inside? But the package was heavy and solid; it couldn't be clothing.

Even so, sensing the men's tremendous anticipation, he expected nothing but a joke as he noisily removed the stiff paper. He was completely surprised, therefore, to hold in his hands a framed painting of himself and Samson. Some of the painting was really good; Samson's head was as graceful and handsome as it was in real life, but Fred's face was a bit clownish, and the hands holding the reins were too big, but all in all the spirit of their relationship was captured, and that was of most importance to Fred. Lost for words, he shook his head.

"Dolores painted it for you," said Mac.

The mention of her name caused some men to shift uncomfortably in their seats. Someone coughed. Another man took off his cap and others followed suit. Fred's heart swelled and he felt tears come to his eyes.

323

"Only she didn't finish it, so me and Bert had a go. I hope you don't mind. We did our best."

Pressing his lips together, Fred shook his head. Tears welled in his pale blue cataract eyes, until, finally, a single tear tipped over and slid down one wizened, weathered cheek. He tasted it at the corner of his mouth. He wished Dolores had spent the money on food instead of paint but he knew it was her way of thanking him for the extra milk he had given her at the end of his round.

"It were done from that picture that were in the Hull Daily Mail," said Mac. "You know, from the article about animal war heroes after Samson pulled that pillar down at the bombed theatre. Look, here, Dolores even stuck it in the back."

Mac was amazed himself at how freely he could speak her name now that she was gone.

"Aye," Fred said proudly. "I know that photo well."

The article was known to him by heart. He didn't need to read it again. Under his bed he kept a box of letters from well wishers that had responded to the story. When their favourite radio programs were over for the evening, Samson had liked to hear the letters read out loud to him. The realisation that Samson wasn't around anymore to hear the letters of praise washed over Fred. To quell the pain, he clenched his teeth and gripped the painting more tightly.

"I reckon she just loved that horse as much as we all did," said Stalworth.

Fred nodded in appreciation of the remark. He would never mention anything about the milk. He wouldn't want to embarrass Dolores, even in memory.

"I suppose she meant to give it to you," said Mac, beginning to choke up himself. "And she would 'ave ... after what happened to Samson .. if she was still with us, I mean."

"Aye, reckon," said Fred, wiping his eyes with the back of his hand. "Ta, lads," he said. "Ta very much. I say, lads, what's the date today?"

"December twenty first, Fred. Why d'you ask?"

"Then it's my birthday, today."

"Well, I never," said Derek. "Here, I'll write it on me calendar, along with everyone else's. Free pint on your birthday, Fred."

"I know that," said Fred

"I must say, you're not much of a Yorkshire man, passing up a free drink all these years. Are you sure you're not a red rose?"

"Positive," said Fred. "Yorkshire born and bred. I could play cricket for Yorkshire, I'm that pure."

Stalworth rubbed his hands together brusquely.

"Well, lads. I think it's time," he said.

"Time?" said Fred. "Time for what?"

Solemnly, the men stood in a row, apparently preparing to sing. Some of them cleared their throats or massaged their necks as if warming up. Fred knew what was coming: they were going to sing Samson's favourite song, the one mentioned in the newspaper article. It was kind of the lads, he thought, sort of a memorial service for Samson. He wasn't sure if he would be able to hold it together while they sang, so closing his eyes, Fred cleared his own throat ready to join in.

"On three," said the landlord. "One, two, three."

"*Amazing Grace, how sweet -*" sang Fred. But upon realizing he was singing solo, Fred opened his eyes to such an amazing sight that once he got over the shock that befell him, he laughed long and hard at the row of men bent over with their trousers down, wiggling their bottoms, all attired in a wide variety of ladies' knickers stretched to their limit (the men's wives would later threaten to kill them because each man had, out of pride, taken his wife's best Saturday night pair). Those arses, some fat, some skinny, those legs, all hairy, were a sight Fred would never be able to erase from his memory. And he was glad of it: the more good memories the better.

"You bastards!" he cried. "You rotten bastards!"

However, the men did go on to sing *Amazing Grace* for Fred and Samson, accompanied by Dr. McKenzie on his bagpipes. The deep male chorus made for a wonderful, moving sound as the men, trousers up now in respect, swayed to the music, holding their pints and not looking at each other, but staring off into the distance, misty-eyed, singing for all the dead heroes of the war.

The only regret of the night for Fred was that Samson wasn't there to share the evening with him. He missed seeing the horse's ears twitch as if he were really listening to the music. But of course, none of it would have happened if Samson hadn't died. Fred had known all those men for most, if not all, of their lives and yet it wasn't until he lost Samson that he was made aware of the high regard they held for him. When I needed them, thought Fred. They was there. Like Samson. That's the kind of friend he was an' all. The best. I could allus count on him.

The painting was given pride of place centred above the fireplace in the parlour where Fred would lay eyes on it the most. For hours on end, he liked to sit with his bottle of beer in the evening and gaze at the picture of him and Samson. It was as if the painting reached out to him, and he often fell into a doze exactly where he was within its comforting embrace.

The sleep came after he closed his eyes, which he liked to do so he could feel Samson from memory; he imagined running his hand along the horse's thick chestnut neck, stroking his coarse mane and tail. Sometimes, with his eyes closed thus, Fred would hold out an arm as if offering Samson a white sugar cube on his palm and the horse would nibble it up, and Fred believed he could hear the horse eat. Eventually he would drift off to sleep hypnotised by the sound he imagined of Samson's large mouth crunching on a sugar cube.

One morning, after falling asleep in such a manner, Fred woke with a start, stiff with sitting for hours with his arm outstretched over the side of the chair. He opened his eyes just as the first shaft of sunlight glanced in through a gap in the curtains; the thin ray pointing to a particular part of the painting and, thus, revealing something Fred hadn't noticed before. Putting on his glasses, he stood, and on stiff legs shuffled over to the painting to get a closer look.

"Those cheeky buggers," he muttered, chuckling.

For painted just above the waist of his trousers was a thin waistband of lace that could only be spotted close-up.

"Those cheeky buggers," he said again. Then he called, "Ay, Samson, look what Mac ..."

But Samson wasn't there to share in the joke, which was a pity because the horse had always exhibited such a great sense of humour; one of the best. So Fred closed his eyes tight until he heard the horse snort and paw at the ground with a great hoof as he did when he found something amusing. "Samson," he told the horse. "Look what those cheeky buggers have gone and done now. I'll bet it were that Mad Mac's idea. What do you reckon?"

Chapter 29

All the usual ribbons, balloons, festivities and celebrations of the season had come and gone for Christmas and the New Year. With it being the first Christmas after the war, there had been renewed good cheer and optimism for the year ahead, which even the dearth of the usual Christmas treats had not dampened. As fate would have it, Mac had been away for the holidays, which had saddened him greatly since he felt this would be his mother's last Christmas. However, he managed to catch the pantomime, which was enjoyed by all, young and old alike, though George wasn't sure he would ever live down playing the part of the pea: he had been in more barneys about it than anything else in his life.

Recently, the weather had been cold and miserable, yet the mood was warmed somewhat by the excitement of a planned April wedding between Prudence Goodwell and Derek Stalworth. Prudence agreed to marriage only when Derek promised she could keep running the fish shop without any interference from him, and also that she would not be expected to either live above or work in the pub. Gloria and Winnie were to be the bridesmaids, which they practised for hours on end using Muriel's net curtains. And Mac would be giving Prudence away.

But none of this was on Mac's mind as he raced the Norton along Hessle Road, incensed that Ginger had not shown up at the dock that morning, and there being no time to find another cook. Mac had waited half an hour, then sent a Runner to Ginger's house to fetch him. The last couple of times the cook was late, the Runner had forcibly kicked him all the way from his bed to the docks; but this time the cook was neither at home nor did his wife know where he was: "And if you do 'appen to find him, you can tell him this from me," she said, slapping her infamous rolling pin in the palm of her hand.

Mac scolded himself for not giving his friend the sack when the skipper told him to, but Ginger had pleaded and promised to change his ways. Serves me right for being in a good mood that day. I should have had a back up cook lined up anyrode, just in case this happened, which it did. Now my neck's on the line.

"You ginger-haired bastard!" Mac shouted as the bike roared beneath him.

When Mac had first realised that the cook was not going to show up at all, neither drunk nor sober, his mind had run through the faces of the crew, trying to remember if any one of them was known to have started off in the galley. But it wouldn't do. The thought of gathering them all together and asking for a volunteer would not go well with

328

the men or the skipper. Consequently, he had been about to resign himself to a trip fuelled by the galley lad's greasy Russian stews, when a brilliant idea struck him.

There was no time to waste; there was less than an hour to letting-go; so he speeded up into the fog, almost smashing into Fred who was turning the corner in his new motorised milk float. A Jack Russell puppy, sitting on Fred's lap, barked out of the window. "Quiet Sammy," said Fred.

Parking his bike in the ten-foot, Mac charged into the house waking his mother who called, "Who is it? That you William?" which caused him to pause on the stairs.

Using his normal, cheerful voice he called, "Aye, Mam, it's me, Mac."

But what she said next sent shivers up his spine.

"Did you forget your comb again?"

A fearful sickness grabbed his stomach, and a cold sweat broke out all over his body: his father had forgotten his comb on his last trip. Mac opened his mouth to respond but all of his words had dried up. For the first time in his life, he considered not showing up for work. Already, too many things had gone wrong.

"William?" his mother called again.

Mac shook his head, trying to shake free from the feeling of apprehension and dread that pulled at him. He continued up the stairs with great speed, taking the steps two at a time as if escaping. Without knocking, he burst in to the bedroom where he had expected to find Vivian and Jake still sleeping. But Jake was not asleep. He was smoking as he had been since the early hours, reading and re-reading the soldier's letter. Vivian had stolen the covers again, so he had woken up freezing after dreaming that he was on a frozen field lying on top of a cold corpse. When the door flew open, the American jumped up in surprise, flicking hot ash all over Vivian.

"Oy! Watch out!" she cried. "What's going on? Mac, what the bloody hell are you doing 'ere?"

"Come on, lad," said Mac. "I need you to come wi' me."

"Me?" Jake asked.

"Aye you. Come on, get up! We've got a boat to catch."

"What are you sodding on about?" asked Vivian, rubbing her sleepy eyes.

"I need him to come wi' me," Mac said as if it was obvious. "That fucker Ginger's gone awol. For good this time, I reckon."

"What's that got to do with Jake?" she asked.

Jake watched the exchange as if it were a tennis match, yet he was the ball being banded to and fro. He rubbed the dark blonde stubble on his chin.

"Cooking! I need a fucking cook. He can cook, can't he?" To Jake, "Can't you? You do it in the chippy all the time!"

"Jake can cook," Prudence spoke from behind Mac. "And he cooks for me."

She had been awoken by the commotion and loud voices. Hearing Mac's voice, she had been quick to get out of bed, out of concern, since he was supposed to be down at the docks. She wore a pink, candlewick dressing gown belted bulkily at her waist, but her feet were bare and cold on the floor, so she snuck one foot up to rub against the warmth of her other calf, and then swapped feet. Her arms were folded in front of her, ready for battle.

"Aye, well, he can come and cook for me and the lads."

"I need him in the chippy," she said.

"Sod the chippy. This is more important," said Mac.

"Sod the chippy?! Are you mad? I've got enough on what wi' our mam sick and everything. I need all the 'elp I can get. He's staying here."

"Well, it's not up to you, is it?"

"Yes it is," said Prudence. "He works for me."

Jake coughed. He felt like a slave being bartered. The idea of getting out from under the women appealed to him.

Things were even more stormy between him and Vivian since he had been urging her to come clean with her mother before she passed away, but Vivian refused, which saddened and angered him.

He said, "I've never worked on a trawler before."

"Neither had I at one point," said Mac. "Neither had anybody. There's a first time for everything. Don't worry. I'll learn you right quick. Come on, what do you say? I've got men depending on me for this. Without a hot meal three times a day, I'll have a mutiny on me 'ands. And I'm not joking when I say that. One thing's for sure, you'll get paid more than you do here. And I'll give you a decent bonus on top. Anyrode it'll do you good to hang wi' a bunch of men instead of lasses. You'll go soft if you stay round here much longer."

"I'll give you a raise," Prudence said to Jake. "It's freezing out there, Jake. At this time of year the conditions are dreadful."

"Dreadful?" said Mac. "Dreadful? Bloody hell. You don't mind me going, though, do you?"

"I do mind. I mind all the time. But you're used to it. You were born into it."

Mac scoffed. "Used to it? I got used to it because I had to. And born into it? Me father's sins, is it? You make it sound inevitable. But it's not. It takes 'ard work and guts. Not all of them whose dads did it, can do it an' all. What, you think Jake's not man enough? Did you hear that, Jake? Well, I say he is. I say he's man enough, all right. Come on, Jake! Help us out 'ere."

Jake rubbed his bristled cheeks then clasped his hands at the back of his neck while he considered.

"Don't you even think about it," warned Vivian.

"It's a bloody adventure!" Mac cried trying with his eyes to convey to Jake the excitement. "There's nowt like it on earth. We're hunters! It beats dropping a basket of chips into a fryer."

"Mac! I can't believe you're doing this to me!" scolded Prudence. "Vivian tell him!" she pleaded. "You don't want your 'usband going out there. He'll be gone for three weeks. Or more if some'at happens."

"Bloody hell," said Mac. "Some of us do make it out alive, you know. There are some retired fisherman in Hull."

"Aye, but not many," said Prudence.

The look exchanged between them spoke of their father. Prudence regretted her words, but there was no taking them back. She knew all this talk would make Mac nervous about the trip, if he wasn't already.

Said Vivian with a shrug, "Fancy that! My 'usband – the most wanted man in Hull... for his cooking. I'm right proud."

Jake cleared his throat and all eyes turned to him while he carefully folded the soldier's letter back into its envelope and placed it on the bedside table. Eyeing the letter, Vivian vowed to destroy it the minute she could lay her hands on it. She was tired of the morbidity surrounding it. Jake became so melancholy after reading it, but he refused to tell her what it was about or where it had come from. She despised that letter as much as she might a mistress of Jake's. Aye, she was jealous of it, the way it reached into Jake's soul and crushed it in a way she never could.

"I'll go," said George, joining in the fray. "I can cook."

"No you bloody won't," said Mac. "Never. Mam'd kill me."

"It's not fair!" George cried, though he had known what the answer would be. At least, he would be remembered for having volunteered. Satisfied, he went back to the warmth of his bed.

Mac turned to Jake. "Listen lad, I'll be downstairs waiting. I'll wait five minutes, enough time for you to grab some stuff. You'll find some of me dad's spare sea gear in that wardrobe. His jumpers and sou'westers and that. They'll be a bit big for you, but they'll keep you warm and

dry. Could never bring mesen to wear any of it, mind…
Five minutes. Oh, and bring some'at to entertain yoursen.
How about your guitar, then you can entertain us an' all. It
can be dead boring the first week on the way to the
grounds, then on the way back an' all. Maybe not for you
though in the galley. The cook's allus busy. But bring it
anyrode. The men'll take owt for a distraction, even old
Grandad on his spoons. Well, I'm rambling. It's me blood
pumping, doin' me head in. You'll know what I mean as
soon as you make up your mind to come wi' us."

Mac took the five minutes to sit with his mother. Her
mistaking him for his father troubled him. He wanted to
see that she was all right before he left. Tugging at his gut
was the feeling not to go on this trip but he wouldn't do
that to the men. Such a feeling of impending doom was
new to him but he put it down to Ginger's not showing up,
which was unsettling but not unexpected. These days,
upon the return of every trip, his first thought was of his
mother and whether she would be there in the parlour waiting for him. Perhaps there was some hope that she had
passed on while he was away: the only thing worse being if
it happened while he was at home.

Hoping to cheer her up, he went to the garden to pick
some snowdrops. A beautiful cluster of the white flower
had sprouted up in the raised bed by the back wall. Muriel
was too weak to walk out there herself. It caused Mac pain
to look at his father's garden so well tended over the years
and about to bloom when spring came, and knowing that
the two people he loved most, his mother and father, would
never lay eyes on it. The best he could do was take the first
signs of spring into his mother. The crocus would grow in
the shape of heart, just as his father had planted it all those
years ago. If there was a way for him to transplant the
whole heart, dirt, flowers and all, and bring it into the
house, he would, that is, if she lived long enough for the
crocus to bloom. The snow drops in his hand were so deli-

cate, whereas the pain in his heart was so powerful, yet it was the flower that tamed the pain.

By heck, you've got to enjoy things while you can, he thought. You never know when it'll be your last time to lay eyes on some'at. Surely, I've learned that lesson through and through by now.

Muriel was asleep again when he entered the parlour, not waking even when he filled a small glass with the flowers and some water. Knowing she didn't like the side table she used to get water-stained, he took the trouble of locating a crocheted doily to lay on the table first. He placed the vase where she would see them if all she could do was open her eyes, and he adjusted the flowers to make a better display.

"Snowdrops," a weak voice said.

"Aye, Mam," he said. "It's me, Mac, your son."

"Of course, Mac, my son," she said. "Mac, who else?"

Relief flooded his heart. With a grin on his face and tears in his eyes, he sat down next to her, taking her hand. Then love, sorrow and loss overwhelmed him and he took her body in his arms, the body that was so unexpectedly frail and light he almost lifted Muriel clear of the bed without meaning to. Holding her tight to his chest, he was afraid to speak.

"What's all this," she said. "I'll see you again."

"Oh, Mam." His voice was thick.

"In the next world, if not this one," she said. "Promise me, you'll believe it."

Her words crushed him. He hoped the agony in his chest was greater than the pain she felt from cancer. He wished he could absorb the pain from her like a sponge taking on water. With this thought he squeezed the weak body until she said, "Son, it's good to feel a strong man's arms around me again but you're crushing me."

"Oh, Mam," he said. "I love you. Don't leave me."

Those were words he had never spoken to another soul, and it was the first time he had said it to his mother. He felt some strength return to her and she hugged him back.

"Aye, son. I know you do."

"Stay, and I promise I'll be the son you allus wanted."

"I never wanted another."

"I mean, I won't fight no more. I'll work hard –"

"You're already there, Son. My God I wish your father could see you now: all grown up and taking good care of your mother …"

She felt him sink in her arms. If only there was a way for them to reconcile on the subject before she left the earth. Keeping his face turned away, he lay her gently back on the bed. Then he knelt at the side of the bed, holding her hand.

"Son, look at me," she said. "I want to see your eyes."

"Mam?" he asked, looking up at her with tear-filled black eyes. "Do you forgive me?"

Muriel's heart tore. Those beseeching eyes belonged to the little boy who once got in trouble for putting pike in the pond at Queen's Gardens, killing all the koi.

"Forgive you?"

Though she knew.

"For what happened to Dad. I tried to hold on. I did. I tried me best."

"Mac, love, I never blamed you. Never. Why do you think that? For all these years, that's what you've been thinking? Oh no. I feel terrible. I should have said some'at. It was me who blamed mesen for letting your dad take you. I didn't want you to go, I had a bad feeling. Then when our Vivian saw that he had forgot his comb and ran out with it, and he turned back… you know a fisherman should never turn back … I wanted to tell him to stay but there was no telling your dad owt, once his mind was made up. Oh, love, you shouldn't blame yoursen at all. You were just a boy, then, a very brave boy from what I 'eard about it. Why, to me you still are a boy, of course, 'specially with them eyes."

He grinned, met her gaze, and squeezed her hand.

"Mac, love, you must believe it wasn't your fault. It weren't nobody's fault. It's the fishing life, isn't it? It's perilous. We all enter into it half-expecting the worst. Your dad's not the only one who ever fell overboard, now, is he?"

"But maybe if I'd got a better foot'old or some'at."

Muriel gripped his wrist.

"Stop Son, please. I've told you now that I never blamed you. No one did except yoursen. I can see that now. When I think of how you must have been torturing yoursen all these years, well, it's time to stop. From now on, you can believe me an' get over it or drink and fight yoursen to more blame. It's up to you. You've got a grand life ahead of you, if only you'd allow it." There was impatience in her voice. "Life's too short for self-pity. It shouldn't have been you there alone on the deck with him. That was the mistake. I know your dad wouldn't have wanted it to be you neither. It probably tore him up proper to see you up there fighting for his life."

"If he could have held on for a bit longer," said Mac. "Crostaff came on deck, right after, he would have helped pull me dad out; if only he'd held on for a few more seconds."

"You know your dad. He held on for as long as he could, till the very last second. He only let go 'cause he had to. Come closer." She cupped his face. "Do you know who you remind me of sometimes?"

"Who?"

"Desperate Dan."

Mac grinned. "Who me?"

"Aye, in a way. You're so big and strong, like him. And I bet you could eat one of them big cow pies to yoursen an' all." Mac kissed her hand. "Poor Desperate Dan," Muriel continued, "he means well, doesn't he? But sometimes his strength's a help, and sometimes it's an 'in-drance."

"Is that like me?"

"Maybe that's like all of us. Only our strengths are different. We just need to learn how to use them wisely."

Her lids drooped briefly. It was tiring talking about human frailty and, perhaps for the first time in her life, she longed for a stuff and nonsense chat with Elsie Waggin, someone who needed nothing more from Muriel than that she lend her an ear.

Her eyes flickered open again when Jake noisily entered the parlour. Thrown over one shoulder was a hastily put together kit bag (their father's), which Prudence had, reluctantly but dutifully, helped him pack before returning to bed. He slapped the kitbag, evidence of his decision to go with Mac. In the breast pocket of the borrowed coat sat the letter, which he had remembered to bring at the last minute when he was already once down the stairs. When he ran back up to get it, he had been surprised to find Vivian weeping; the tear-stained face brightening with hope when she saw him but falling again when he reached for the letter and slipped it into the breast pocket.

"Don't go," she sniffed. "Please."

"Don't worry, I'll make it back so you'll have your free passage outta here," he said, striding toward the door.

"Don't be like that. Why won't you believe me? I do love you. Don't you love me anymore?"

Twisting the door knob to and fro, he had hesitated, before turning and saying, "The problem is, Vivian, that I don't trust you. You've lied to everybody, to me, to your family. You -"

"Must you keep making me pay and pay and pay. Go on, then. It's no use if you won't forgive me. It must be nice being the only person in the world who's never made a mistake. That's you, isn't it? I suppose it's your clear conscience that keeps you awake night after night? That letter!" she spat. "You have your secrets too!"

337

He left, slamming the door behind him.

"I hate you!" she cried.

Jake had been embarrassed to come into the parlour after his exchange with Vivian, but it appeared as though they had not heard. Mac even laughed when he saw him.

"What is it?" Jake asked, a cigarette burning between his lips.

Jake was wearing William Goodwell's sea gear, and Mac thought it funny the way the American's head was sticking out just above the neck of the jumper. To Mac he looked like a turtle ready to retract all its limbs at the first sign of trouble.

"Reckon I forgot to mention that we don't put our gear on till we're steaming off," said Mac.

"Huh?" said Jake.

"Aren't those my William's clothes?" asked Muriel.

"Aye Mam. Don't worry, he'll grow into them. Jake's coming with us as chief cook and bottle washer."

"On the Ichthus?"

"Aye, Mam, wi' me."

"But why?"

"Ginger didn't show up. Don't worry. We'll see you in three weeks."

His kissed her on the forehead.

"Not if I see you first," she whispered.

"Goodbye, Muriel," said Jake.

Spontaneously, he kissed her forehead, and she smiled.

"Take care of each other," she said. "Oh, Mac?"

"Aye, Mam."

"Take this."

She pressed something still warm from being on her finger into his hand.

"Your ring? But I'm not ready."

"No, but I am. Take it."

Muriel shut her eyes so she wouldn't see the back door be closed and them gone through it as if to a magical place from which they might never return. But her lids flitted

338

open again having caught something pure out of the corner of her eye.

"My son, my Bill brought me flowers," she said, smiling and letting her eyes close again. "He's such a good boy."

The cat, having snuck in as soon as the door opened, trotted over to Muriel and jumped up, landing almost weightlessly on her chest. Muriel smiled when she saw him - glad of the company. These days Muriel was his favourite place to be since she hardly moved and so he was sure of an undisturbed, wonderful warm nap, all day if he had the mind to. Absentmindedly, she stroked the thick black fur all the way from the top of his head to the end of his tail, and he purred with pleasure. Quickly tired, she stopped and rested her arm. The cat looked at her with expressionless eyes. His head nudged her hand.

"All right, lad. Just a bit more."

The cat felt strong and healthy under her weak, sickened hand. She drifted.

"William," she murmured drowsily. "Don't look back."

A frown briefly touched her eyebrows. Once more, her eyes opened briefly but soon closed again. With her eyes shut, she sang in a whisper:

"We'll meet again,
Don't know where, Don't know when,
But I know we'll meet again some sunny day."

Chapter 30

In the dark, early morning, the skipper was on the bridge, bracing the cold head winds. At high water, the order was given, "Stand by to let go," and the men went to their stations, some aft and some to the whale back at the front. A rope was passed to a tug boat which pulled the boat into the lock pits. Each successive lock filled with water and the Ichthus passed through each one and into the River Humber where she steamed off at twelve knots. Surveying the scenery from aft, Jake's heart raced at the spectacular sight of eight sidewinders from Hull and seven from Grimsby steaming off to the fishing grounds. There was something so powerful knowing that each boat carried twenty-one of the most rugged men in the world.

The river was terrifying; everything was black but he could tell the fast-flowing current either side of the boat. He wouldn't want to fall in. Muddy and wide like the Mississippi. I'd be sucked under faster 'n ya suck the brain out of a crawfish.

Jake followed the Ichthus crew down to the fo'c'sle, below the whale back, where the man got shifted, changing out of their shore gear and into their sea gear, thick wool jumpers and socks, and oil skins. Jake didn't feel out of place anymore in his borrowed gear. Then the men set to work, getting the Ichthus ship shape, tying down loose equipment and battening the hatches. Normally, these jobs would take about an hour, then the beer would come out but, suddenly, there was quite a commotion when Ginger was discovered sleeping under a trawl slated for repair. He had been ratted out by Monty. His snores and snorts were so loud Jake asked if a pig had been smuggled on board.

"Mr. Mate, tell your men not to mention grunters on my boat! We need fortune's favour!" the skipper roared, then he stared for a moment at the cook's hatless head, before turning, without a word, to look elsewhere.

The cook slept on as peaceful as a babe, sucking his thumb - the gentle lull of the boat acting like a cradle - as the crew gathered round wondering how best to wake him. He wasn't going to be let go lightly. Various ideas were put forth, such as dousing him with the powerful hose used to wash the fish, or crushing up a block of ice and sticking it down his trousers. Bert crouched down next to him.

"Last orders!" he bellowed in the cook's ear.

But all Ginger did was swat at him like a fly, and turn on his side muttering, "Mine's a pint."

"I'm going to learn him a lesson he'll never forget," said Mac. "Fetch me some rope with a bowline."

"You're going to hang him?"

"Aye, in a manner of speaking."

A rope, attached to the derrick and winch, was tied around Ginger's ankles. He was hauled, sliding across the deck, still snoring, to the side of the boat.

"Shoot!," cried Mac.

"Oh shite," laughed Bert.

"Come on, out me way," said Mac.

"Oy, is that any way to speak to your father-in-law?" asked Bert, who had come around to the idea.

"Leave shores matters at 'ome, Mr. Bosun."

"Aye, aye, Mr. Mate."

The crew ran starboard to watch as the cook was swung over and his head was dipped briefly in the fast-flowing muddy river. At once, the cook became conscious, coughing and spluttering, and jerking around on the end of the rope like a fish on a line. The mean laughed heartily while the winch complained.

"By heck, he weighs more than the cod end," Grandad muttered.

"You'd better hope our new deckie learner knows how to tie a bowline good and proper!" yelled Mac.

"What?" Ginger looked up at his feet. "Oy! Get me up! You bloody gits! Get me up! Friggin' hell, where am I?"

"Oy lad, pass us your gutting knife," Mac said to the new the deckie learner – a hard-looking lad with brown curly hair.

Leaning over the side, Mac made a great show of reaching for the rope, and displaying the knife to the cook.

"You'd better promise never to miss high water again, you fat bastard," he growled.

"I didn't miss it! I were the first one on board!"

"Aye, well, you're meant to be conscious when we let go."

Mac pressed the knife to the rope.

"You wouldn't dare! You ruddy mad looney! Get me up! I could drown! Come on, Mac! This isn't funny."

"It isn't meant to be funny, Mr. Duncan. What shall we do with the drunken sailor, eh? Eh, lads?"

Mac made a show of slicing at the rope.

"All right! All right!" cried the cook. "You bugger! You've made your point."

"Reel him in lads," said Mac. "I think I finally got through to the bloody sod."

There were suggestions that the cook should hang thus till they reached the fishing grounds, and that maybe he would be good bait for a big halibut.

"I wouldn't do that to an 'alibut," said Mac.

"Oy you bastards!" shouted the cook. "Hurry up! I'm freezing me bollocks off here!"

"Bollocks? I'm surprised your Mrs. hasn't knocked 'em off with her rolling pin by now. Haul!" Mac shouted, indicating with a flick of his thumb that Ginger should be brought back on back.

As soon as the cook hit the deck, none too softly, mind, a couple of deck hands came toward him with their gutting knives drawn.

"Oh, piss off you lot," groaned Ginger, flapping about like a fish out of water trying to sit up and untie his ankles. "Oo me ankles. I'm not sure I can walk."

The two deck hands closed up their knives and slipped them into their pockets. They helped the cook into a sitting position. He did look a sorry, sodden sight pulling the rope from around his legs. But Mac hadn't yet sated his ire.

"What the hell were you playing at? You almost got yoursen blacklisted. Popeye's already been after me to have you sacked."

"I know, I know. Aye, well I thought I were better off taking me chances here that at home with her indoors."

"Aye, reckon," Mac said with a grin. "When I sent the Runner to fetch you, your Mrs. was so ready to knock your block off, she almost took his instead. Reckon I should use a rolling pin to keep you in line an' all. It does nowt for me pride knowing you're more afraid of her than me."

"Aye well, I apologise. It won't happen again."

"No, it won't," Mac said firmly. "If you do that to me again, you'll be trotting the plank trussed up like the butcher's prize p–i–g with a rolling pin stuck up your arse and an apple in your mouth."

The men laughed while Ginger clenched his buttocks in protest. Jake gave him a hand to his feet.

"Hey up Yank!" Ginger remarked upon noticing who was helping him. "What the bloody hell are you doing 'ere?"

"Your job," said Mac. "Or at least he was going to. Now I'll have to find some other way for him to earn his keep."

"You brought him on here to cook! Over my dead body!" cried the cook, shaking off Jake's helping hand. "Out of my way! No one steps foot in my galley without my say-so."

Mac grinned at the disappearing, blustery figure of the rotund cook who carried the weight of indignation in each step. Seeing Ginger on board took away some of the bad omen Mac had been feeling about the trip.

"Well, lad," he said to Jake, "We don't really need you no more. So if you want to go home you could swim for it though I wouldn't recommend it. Or, we could find some'at else to make you useful. Reckon you could help out Ginger once he's simmered down a bit. I'll work it out so you still have a job and get paid, like. We allus need as much 'elp as we can get once we're on the fish. Hey up, here's Spurn Lightship. Time for me to take over the bridge."

Jake looked over as they passed the black Lightship that had 'SPURN' painted in white on the side. He could see it was a sort of lighthouse at sea. Mac nudged him.

"Helps us navigate," he said. "These waters can be pretty treacherous."

On the bridge, Crostaff told Mac. "Let her go north to two mile off Flamborough Head, Mr. Mate."

"Aye, Skipper."

While he set the watches on the bridge with the bosun and third hand, Mac sent Jake to fetch him a mug of tea. Down in the galley, the radio operator, Sparks, who had also popped in for a mug of tea, introduced himself to Jake. As they made conversation, watching the cook chop and slice pork and vegetables for a stew, Jake asked where the Ichthus was headed.

"North, I reckon," replied Sparks.

"I figured that," said Jake. "But where North?"

"Aye, well, that's it exactly, isn't it," Sparks said mysteriously, tapping the side of his long, thin nose. "Skipper'll tell us exactly where when he's good and ready, probably tomorrow morning. Keeps it to hissen, like, to make sure no one follows us. Got his favourite spots. All the Old Men are the same."

"But Popeye's the best," commented Ginger.

"Aye, and that means all the other skippers are allus trying to glean our whereabouts and what market we're shooting for on our way back."

"Why?"

"So they can get there first. Beat us to it. That's part of me job - to listen in on t' other skippers and give off red herrings about what we're up to. We're still pirates, tha knows. A lot of the old men radio using code words and say daft things to throw you off. It's a bit of a lark, really. You're welcome to come and listen in if you'd like."

344

"Gee, I'd sure like to."

Noticing the cook had turned his back, the radio operator reached for the sugar.

"Oy, I saw that, Sparks," Ginger snapped. "No extra sugar. You know the ration."

"Sorry, I lost count while we was talking," Sparks said, slipping the spoon back into the bag.

"Oh aye?" said Ginger, with a wry nod to Jake. "So," Ginger asked the American. "You reckon you can cook, do you?"

Jake shrugged. "I've done a bit, here and there. I've been helping out in the fish and chip shop."

"Oh aye," said Ginger. "Her indoors said she'd seen you there. My Mrs.'ll be right chuffed to hear you was on board wi' us, especially if she hears you was working wi' me. In fact, you're being here might save me from serious injury. She'll want to know all about it, tha knows, so she can have one over on that Elsie Waggin, like. You know how women are. Besides, I could use an extra pair of hands," he said. "Igor here allus gets dragged on deck for entertainment. He's got one 'ell of an high voice, like a lass's, and he can do that Russian dancing, what's it called, Igor? That's right, Cossack they call it. By heck, it isn't half a laugh watching some of the men have a go at it, an' all. You should try it. You need strong thighs though, and not so much of this." He smacked his huge belly. "Oy Sparks, will you send me Mrs a telegram telling her about Jake an' that, and how he's working wi' me, an' that. Aye, that's right. Oh, and order her indoors some flowers an' all. Aye, the usual. No, wait, better make it a really big bunch. Tell 'em to put it on me account. Ta, Sparks, and here's another sugar for your trouble. No, only one, you cheeky sod. Now look sharp. She'll be really mad at me this time for not coming 'ome at all.

"I'm allus getting into trouble with her indoors," the cook said to Jake after the radio operator left. "Marriage is like a see-saw, tha knows, and you have to keep it balanced. Like this see." He motioned with his hands, moving one up and one down. "My Mrs gets mad at me, I buy her flowers, then by the time I get back she's forgotten what it was all about."

He added some chopped carrots to the pot on the stove, and tasted what apparently was an agreeable sauce.

"Yeah," said Jake. "I guess I do."

"Oy, Igor, how's that dough rising. Good. Stay here Jake, and I'll learn you a thing or two about bread."

But once the Ichthus hit the open sea, Jake was in no fit state to learn anything, except that is, that he was not a natural sailor. For the next couple of days while the rest of the men were working on deck getting the nets, bobbins and otter boards ready for hauling time, Jake could often be spotted racing for the rail and vomiting over the side.

The wind was strong against them. It took twenty four hours for the Ichthus to get to Flamborough, a journey that with a good fair wind behind them should have taken only three hours.

Jake preferred to be on deck in the freezing air to being cooped up inside the mess or the galley. On the third day he was enlisted to help get the fishroom ready, but he only lasted five minutes before he ran up on deck again. He had travelled on big troop ships before and never felt ill or thought much at all about the water, but with the smaller trawler he felt every squall as if the sea was demanding attention and letting him know she was in control.

The North Sea below and the dark sky above stretched out in every direction as far as the eye could see. Sea and sky alike were carpeted with gentle swells of white-crested grey, like mirrors of each other; making the grey endless, irrefutable, and the existence of the horizon disputable. Jake had never felt more ill in his life. No longer a reasoning being, he had become a sickness; just a nauseous, retching stomach and bile-filled, projectile mouth. The end would come only if he jumped into the insensate waters that would drown or freeze him to death in an instant. But what relief that would bring. He was tempted.

His stomach rolled with the waves, puking, puking until there were only dry heaves. He was given ginger tea, but that too came spilling out of his mouth. On the second day of the illness, his arms tremored violently and his legs became too weak to support his body, so he was tied to the rail, facing forward, and told to keep his eyes on the horizon, which if his rubbery neck could lift its pounding head, he would gladly do.

Mac showed no hesitation in letting Jake know how irritated he was that his brother-in-law, whom he had brought along to cook, could not stand up long enough to measure tea into a pot. Having never experienced sea sickness, Mac believed that the cure was simply a case of mind over matter; he had no sympathy for its sufferers, even, or especially, family members. So when Jake tried sleeping to escape, with his forehead resting on the rail, he was often prodded awake by Mac who asked if he was ready to play his guitar for the lads, or help in the galley or to be on deck scrubbing, but the only reply Jake could muster was a groan, leaving Mac with nothing but contempt.

During the hours spent on his own, holding his body as still as he could with his eyes closed, Jake wondered why he had agreed to come along in the first place. Then he couldn't remember if he had agreed. Soon, he began to believe he had been press-ganged into coming on the trip, and his resentment toward Mac grew. This wasn't the adventure he had been promised.

How he longed to see and feel dry land all the way up to the horizon. He missed the dust of Texas more than ever. Anything, he would do *anything*, to feel well again. For all he had lamented the death of the German soldier, he would gladly slaughter a hundred more if only the feeling of sickness would go away. He killed again and again in his mind.

The greyness depressed him. Even the sun appeared to emit grey light, struggling in the drizzling rain to make a difference. Every now and again, when he caught the stink of the smoke billowing out of the funnel, his stomach flip-flopped with renewed vigour. He was downwind on port-side having made the initial mistake of vomiting into the wind on starboard side. The vomit had splattered on his clothes, on Mac's father's thick cable jumper that itched his neck, not helping him feel any better. The illness had so taken over his rational mind that he had no inclination to admire the way the Ichthus lifted her head over the waves so the waves rolled under her. All he knew was getting soaked by a freight train of water when her bow was beaten by a particularly massive wave. Believing he was going to die he thought of the unposted letter in his pocket and of his wife waiting for him ashore; though he couldn't decide which to regret the most.

The smallness of the Ichthus juxtaposed against the vastness of the sea scared him; he felt like an ant crawling on the skin of a giant who might swat him at any moment.

All the other members of the crew he despised with such vitriol that perhaps his brain had turned to bile. It was the men's cheerfulness and good-natured ribbing of his predicament that riled him the most. How could they walk around, looking well and cheerful, while he remained tied to the railing for hours day and night? In the end, he convinced himself it was a joke they were playing on him. It was they who were making him sick, not the sea.

Four days into the trip Jake awoke to find himself being lifted slowly up and down from his bunk in accordance with the motion of the ship, which was struggling against a head wind. He couldn't ascertain whether it was his head or his stomach that hurt. There was pain, pounding and emptiness. He felt light-headed, and believed he was floating, which indeed he was before he hit the bunk again when the ship lifted. Loneliness overwhelmed him. From out of his wallet, he pulled a black and white photograph of him and Vivian taken on their wedding day. He wished he could regain the feelings for her he had back then.

"You passed out," said a voice Jake thought he should recognise. "Yesterday. So I had you brought down here. Against Mac's wishes mind. He thought you should stay up there for the whole three weeks. Some brother-in-law, ay?"

Casting a large black shadow on the fo'c'sle wall was the skipper, John Crostaff. He wore a rain spotted sou'wester, and his blue eyes pierced the dimness from under a large waterproof hat. Fully aware he was in the presence of a superior and that he should be on duty, not prostrate, Jake immediately swung his legs over the side of the bunk and sat up. He saluted, American style, and the skipper laughed.

"Don't know your arse from your elbow, do you Mr. Huggins?" he said, offering a small silver-lidded flask with the lid off. "Here have some of this. Works wonders for me."

"You have sea sickness, Skipper?"

"Aye. Had it all me working life. For the first two year out here, when I were a deckie learner, I were just like you, puking me guts out. All the other men gave me 'ell like."

"Like me?"

"Oh, aye. And some of the others have had it, an' all," he said with a nod to the crew.

"They treat me like I'm the first."

"No. You're in good company with the likes of Nelson."

"Who?"

"Lord Nelson. A famous sailor of ours. Never mind, here. The missus brews it. If it worked for me, it'll work for you."

Taking a tentative swig, Jake pulled a face and clenched his stomach, waiting for a reaction. But there was none.

"Damn! What is it?"

"Ginger tincture. Ginger steeped in spirits."

"Ah, moonshine," said Jake, rubbing an eye with the heel of one hand. "Boy, I don't get it. Why d'ya keep coming back? If ya were sick all the time."

"Didn't 'ave a choice. I needed a job." Crostaff said. "A bastard like me doesn't have many options. Besides, I loved it. The sea has a way of calling you back. You'll see."

"No way. Not me," said Jake. "This is the first and last time you'll see me on a trawler."

"Some men say that and mean it, others say it and mean it and come back anyway. I've seen 'em all. But I reckon you've got a different life planned for yoursen. You and her. Off to America, I hear." He nodded toward the photograph in Jake's hand.

"Yeah," said Jake. "That's the plan."

"Taking the lad with you, are you?"

The ship lurched causing Jake to fall back and bang his head. Unaffected by the sudden motion, the skipper grabbed Jake's hand and pulled him up. Jake smiled weakly, rubbing the back of his head.

"I'm still not used to that," said Jake.

"Being on this boat is just like owt else, lad. You've allus got to expect the unexpected. It's part of life. If you assume smooth sailing, you'll end up falling over and banging your head all the time."

Jake nodded, massaging the sore spot on his head.

"Well, lad, it's time you was getting up to fix us some grub. That fat git needs an 'and while Igor's up top singing for the lads. Aye, I know. Reckon food's the last thing you want to think about, but there's hungry men to be fed. Just try not to spew on owt. Chew on this; it's crystallised ginger. It'll help stave off the sickness for a while."

He broke off a small piece and handed it to Jake.

"That's all you'll get," said Crostaff. "You'll have to use it sparingly. I need the rest for mesen. Well, I never said I got over it, did I? Aye, I still get queasy, especially when I see another poor sod at it. Why do you think I came down here to sort you out? 'Cause I care about you? Don't be daft. I'm not your mam. I'm your skipper. So 'urry up and get to work. You're not on the Queen Mary, yet, you know."

As the skipper's feet disappeared upwards, Jake lay down again, just one more minute, he told himself. But the bunk lurched, taking Jake's stomach with it, and the stench of dried vomit filled his nostrils. But he didn't throw up, which both surprised him and gave him hope. There were no clean clothes, so he pulled on the borrowed sou'wester and, with queasiness dogging him all the way, gingerly made his way to the galley.

Crostaff found Mac in the mess with the rest of the men applauding the end of a song by Igor. The crew, each man with a beer in his hand, begged the galley boy for more.

"Just nowt sad, I can't stand it," said one man. "Makes me think of 'ome."

"I checked in on that brother-in-law of yours, Mr. Mate," the skipper said to Mac.

"Oh aye, Skipper? By heck, I don't understand a word of this Russian lark, but it int 'alf beautiful," Mac said as Igor started up again.

"He's going to be all right," Crostaff said. "Jake."

Mac drew on a cigarette while the skipper studied that well-known face, watching the thoughts churn in the younger man's head as the brow furrowed and the jaw tightened accordingly. Crostaff assumed Mac's inner turmoil was on his account.

"I've been meaning to tell you," the skipper said, "that it's over between us."

"What?"

"That matter that's been between us."

"What matter?"

Of course, he knew to what thing Crostaff was referring, but this particular subject wasn't meant to be broached at sea, during their professional relationship. And why was the subject being raised at all when it hadn't been men-

351

tioned between them for weeks? For just a few moments, while watching the galley lad, Mac had escaped the uneasy feeling about the trip that had prevailed all morning since he had returned home to fetch Jake. But now it returned tenfold.

"Can't this wait till we're at 'ome?"

"No. Not anymore."

Crostaff pulled Mac to one side, but Mac jerked his arm free, subtly enough so the skipper could feel his irritation but not so the men could see. He couldn't allow the crew to witness any insubordination on his part toward the skipper otherwise it might ripple through the men and cause problems for himself.

"I told her," said the skipper, once he was sure they could not be overheard. "My Mrs. A while back. I told her about Vivian and, and the bairn. Aye, that's right. I thought you'd be surprised. So there's no holding it over me 'ead no more, Son."

Mac made no response.

"I planned to tell her that day Jimmy Alford were found in the dock. But some'ow the news about Jimmy's body got home before I did, and our Iris were so full of it, wanting to know what had happened and all that, that I couldn't get a word in, or so I told mesen. You know," and he paused, reflecting on the various times he had tried to tell Iris, and how each of those times he had been put off in some way by Iris taking over the conversation, talking and talking, almost feverishly about some silly piece of gossip from the school or the neighbourhood. Perhaps, it suddenly occurred to him, she had wanted to put off the revelation as much as he had.

"Anyrode, it were your Vivian that caused the telling of it. She kept pushing that bairn up and down our road in its pram. I started to dread going home. Then I was afraid to look out me own window. Seems daft now," he reflected. "but while it were going on … Well, the day came when Iris remarked that she saw Vivian only when I was home from sea. 'Wonder where she walks him the rest of the time,' she said. She knew, you know. I don't know 'ow, but she knew. Women do, don't they? They allus know. It's that woman's intuition, I suppose. Anyrode, never mind that she knew, 'cause she cried anyrode when I confirmed it. I've never heard owt like it. The way she sobbed, it broke my heart. But she weren't crying 'cause I was unfaithful to her. No, she were crying 'cause, as she said," he took a deep breath to compose himself, "because I have a son and she doesn't."

The skipper glanced around at the men but they were still enthralled by the Russian boy's alto.

"I broke my Iris' heart and for what? I know we hadn't been getting along as man and wife after we lost our son, but that's no excuse. I mean, I thought it was at the time, but all I did was hurt a lot of people. I was lonely, but so was she. Now, when I look back on it all, it seems impossible that I would do such a thing. What sort of madness was it, Mac? I don't blame you for being angry. I should have known better."

Mac glanced at him, agreement in his black eyes. He was glad of the chance to end their differences; he hadn't known how to himself. The two men had once been close.

"I can't say I would have acted any differently if she were my sister," Crostaff went on.

"She's not just my sister," said Mac. Closing his eyes for a few seconds, he paused, enjoying the smoke thick in his lungs. Slowly, he exhaled. "She was me father's daughter an' all. Imagine what he'd have done to you if.... Well, I reckon you wouldn't even have dared if he were alive, would you? But don't worry you'll not be getting no more bother from me."

Not wanting to discuss the topic further, Mac attempted to return his focus to Igor who was smiling cheerfully with voluptuous red lips and rosy cheeks as he sang a catchy folk song, in time to which the crew clapped their hands and tapped their feet. A couple of the most drunk were trying their hand, and feet, at Cossack dancing, much to the merriment of their peers. It wouldn't be long before Igor was induced to dance, which he always saved for the finale.

"I have recognised ...," the skipper began. He swallowed hard, removed his cap, and rubbed a hand through his blonde hair. "I realise the disservice I committed toward your father's memory. He was a man I greatly admired. He taught me everything. He would be proud of you, not me, if he could see us standing here."

There was a knot's pause, during which Mac released the anger he had once felt toward the skipper. With indescribable relief, the sour emotion waned from his body, draining from each limb and out through his fingers and toes. He felt clean.

"I would never have said owt to your Mrs.," he confessed.

"Aye, reckon I allus knew that, Son. But we kept up the pretence for a good while, didn't we? My guilt, your anger, maybe the fuel what kept us going through the war, eh?"

Replacing his cap, Crostaff blew out a huge breath of pent up regret, and said, "Got a spare fag for me?"

"Aye. Here, take two."

The skipper slipped one behind his ear.

"Igor roll these for you?"

"Aye, he did."

"He does a bloody good job of it."

"Aye, that and the singing."

"Maybe it'd be more efficient if we could get him to do both at the same time."

"What, while he's doing that Cossack dance an' all?"

"Aye. That would be the best use of his time, that would, rolling, singing and dancing."

"I can just picture it."

"Aye, me an' all."

It took a moment for the laughter to take them. Mac's shoulders shook as he tried to contain his guffaws, while

Crostaff coughed a few laughs trying to hold onto his cigarette. But soon the two men were laughing together without restraint, Crostaff with one hand on the first mate's back. The crew looked over, pleased with what they saw.

It was time for the boy to dance. Bert clapped and chanted, *"Dah-dah-da-da-da-dah-dah-da-da-da-dah-dah-da-da-da-dah-dah-dah, oy!"* and soon the rest of the crew joined in, getting louder and faster with each turn.

Shouting above the din, the skipper asked, "So who are you going to be angry at now you don't have me no more?"

Mac shot him a glance from under dark furrowed brows.

Smiling kindly, the skipper squeezed his shoulder. "There are other ways to feel alive, you know, Son."

"Oy!" the men hollered and clapped as Igor jumped five feet into the air with his arms and legs wide apart. They whistled as his hands touched his feet mid-air, where he seemed to hover for a second before landing. He sprung onto his hands, kicking his legs up repeatedly. Then, back on his feet, he spun and spun and spun kicking the leading leg high on each turn, before crouching and kicking his legs out in front of him.

Chapter 31

After some five days at sea, the Ichthus had entered almost complete darkness and cold off the coast of Iceland. The men would be lucky to see an hour of daylight all day. The wind whistled, causing Mac further disquiet. The sound reminded him of the old gypsy's whistling, and felt like a warning.

Still a little queasy but no longer throwing up, Jake's new battle was with the cold. He had never experienced anything like it, even when driving cattle up north in the deep of winter. But there were awesome sights; frozen waterfalls, giant icicles, snow draped mountains and glacial blocks of ice scattered on black rock beaches. All of it was new and breath-taking to Jake. He felt lucky to be a part of it and thought of little else than what was before his eyes.

He had just come up from the engine room where Mac had sent him on an urgent errand for a long 'weight'. "A really long one," Mac had said, holding his hands far apart. When Jake made the request to the engineer, the engineer had simply nodded and said, "Stand there, and I'll give you what you came for." After twenty minutes standing thus Jake thought he'd been forgotten, so he asked again for the long weight. "What?" said the engineer. "That one not long enough for you?" Then the stokers started laughing and Jake realised he'd been fooled. 'A long wait!' So far, he had found a live crab under the blanket on his bunk and, one night, his boots were swapped for a pair that were two sizes too small. What a lot of merriment that had caused early one morning while the men watched him, half-asleep, trying to squeeze his feet in, trying one boot then the other.

By now all the beer was gone, as it always was before the real work began, so the men, continually on the lookout for a new distraction, had persuaded Jake to teach them to lasso. When the time came that some of them had garnered enough skill to evoke a competitive spirit, the new deckie learner was made to run about the deck, wearing a pair of icicle horns, while each new cowboy put himself up against Jake in a bet to see who would be the first to fell the respective deckie.

"I could have been a cowboy," Grandad remarked, after surprising them all with a win. "Reckon it's better to face danger under a blue sky than a grey one."

Jake played his guitar, sometimes on his own, and other times accompanied by Mac on the harmonica and Grandad on the spoons. The men liked to sing, and Jake was happy to oblige. He treated them to some Gene Autry and Bing Crosby; White Christmas being a particular favourite. The men's voices rang sound and true, singing as they installed a new trawl, attaching the mouth of the net to the big iron balls that would roll the trawl along the sea bed over anything that was in its way.

Also singing along were the youngest deckie learners who supplied the workers with twine-threaded needles. Eager-to-please lads, the boys longed to be well thought of by the more experienced fisherman, and enjoyed the feeling of belonging during those halcyon days.

Almost to the fishing grounds, the day ended with an afternoon rain squall, treating the men to a colourful pink and blue haze at sunset. The crew retired early to make the most of their last good night's rest for a while.

The men were up at six the next morning ready for the long work days ahead of shooting and hauling the trawl. The sea was rough, tossing the boat. One minute the rail was a few feet above water, then the next it fell below the water. Jake had to fight the urge to run back to his bunk. Not that he would be safe there. During the night, he'd had a terrible experience when the boat dropped twenty feet into a trough and he had lifted up from his bunk and then landed, banging his head. There would be little sleep over the next five days, maybe two to four hours a night, until the skipper was satisfied with the catch.

Crostaff was on the bridge, Mac was on deck at the winch, and the bosun, Bert Smith, was at the wheel.

"Stand by, down trawl."

Hanging from the derrick, the cod end was swung over into the water on the starboard side astern. When the bubbles emitting from it reached the middle of the ship, Mac sang out, "Let go!" The ship stopped, and the bobbins and trawl went over the side and sank, lowered on cables, then a deckie learner clipped the otter boards to the end of the warps. The ship was brought around at half speed, and the wheel turned fifteen degrees.

"Let go your doors!"

Using the winch, Mac lowered the doors half-way. The concentration on his face was marked. He had to have a steady hand; a mistake could lead to the whole gear being fouled. The Ichthus came around the rest of the way to where Crostaff wanted to shoot along the bank at one hundred fathoms.

"Away!" yelled the Skipper.

The boat steamed steady ahead until the warps were taut. Mac went aft to check the warps. All was in order. They were towing into a fifty-mile-an-hour head wind. The skipper removed the stopper and blew down the brass speaking tube. He put his ear to it. Down in the engine room, the chief engine answered the whistle, "Hullo?"

"Shove her up to seventy," the skipper called down.

"Aye, aye, Skipper."

Crostaff replaced the stopper and paced the bridge. He became visibly anxious now that the trawl was in the water. His job was on the line. He began muttering under his breath and looking over the side. The mutters escalated into swearing the most obscene profanities known to man. The tension was so great, he couldn't stand still. The skipper scrambled up onto the gun on the foredeck and rode it like a cowboy at a rodeo; throwing his fist at the sky. Jake looked around for somebody to intervene, but the only response he received to his alarmed looks of inquiry was a wink and a quiet word from Sparks.

"It's nerves," the radio operator explained in a low voice. "Whatever comes up in that net is all on his shoulders, you see. That's how he deals with the stress. Popeye's not the only one loses it when we shoot. Hey up. Mind yoursen."

The skipper ran past, eyes darting about like a mad man. Suddenly, he stopped and looked around at everything and nothing. Frowning, his eyes rested on Jake. Then he ran to starboard and, gripping the rail, tipped so far over, it looked like he might fall into the water. Jake took a step toward him but Sparks held him back saying, "I'm telling you lad, he does this every time."

Feet firmly planted back on deck, the skipper shouted a prayer and ran on until he disappeared down below, running through the mess and into the galley where he screamed more profanity at Ginger before galloping back up and onto the bridge falling to his knees and pummelling the deck with his fists.

"Mind you," Sparks remarked, "there's them that says it's all showmanship. A dance for the gods." He looked at his watch. "We've got half an hour or more yet. Time for a cuppa. Fancy coming wi' us."

"Nah. I want to see this," Jake replied.

The skipper's prayers were answered.

"Hauling time!"

All hands scrambled on deck, coming from the fish room, from the galley, from sleep. The winch creaked and turned, reeling in the warps. Water splashed everywhere. The otter boards were first to break the surface whetting the appetites of the increasingly excited seagulls that wheeled and practiced their dives above the trawl. By the time the cod end bobbed up, the gulls were in a frenzy, diving to rob the net of its catch.

Jake covered his ears to block out the screeching. Grandad laughed. Pulling one of Jake's hands away, he shouted into his ear, "Ay lad, this is nowt compared to the summer when you have to pick the birds out of your hair. There's millions then. It's the sand eel cod tha knows, soft as owt they are, your fingers go right through 'em, and the gulls love them bellies."

The dripping cod end was full when it was swung in.

"Could be a china man," said Peggy.

"Aye, could be a hundred baskets," Grandad agreed.

Mac bent under the cod end and untied the knot, releasing the catch. Fish flooded the deck until the men gutting were up to their wader thighs in silver bodies flipping, flopping, mouths opening shutting, gills gasping, bold eyes darting about not yet knowing there was no hope. The cod end was tied up and chucked over again. The Ichthus went full ahead filling the cod end with fish from the belly of the net.

"Stop her!" cried the skipper.

At this time of year, the frigid air was colder than the North Sea, so some of the catch was already frozen by the time it hit the deck. As the gutters worked on the most recent catch, the call came to shoot the trawl again. Working in the pounds, the men tried to keep their balance as the rough sea tossed the ship about. For the veterans the motion was automatic now, dreamlike, their bodies swaying with the swinging boat; but they still kept their wits about them for surprises, of which the sea was fond. Frost snowed the men's whiskers. Snow fell in six foot drifts on the boat.

The men's hands, feet and snot slowly froze as they gutted the fish, three per minute, in the open air. What kept them going were dreams of the next cup of hot sweet tea and the next hot meal; the better the meal, the stronger the tea, the harder they worked. They also laughed and joked and teased each other endlessly as they smashed fish heads against the wood and sliced belly after belly from top to bottom throwing portside the heads and guts, which were deftly caught by the gulls before they had a chance to hit the water. The cod livers were thrown into a basket.

Given the job of hosing the fish with salt water, Jake revelled in the way the men worked in the moment without thinking of what was behind them or the terrible work that lay ahead. He wished he could join their mindset.

Once the liver basket was full it was dragged aft to the boilers where Sparks did double duty as Liver Boiler. Sparks worked carefully: dropping a single liver or spilling a drop of the rendered oil would be akin to spilling kindred blood if the men found out. The cash from the oil was shared among the crew, which made it worth enduring the appalling stench of the boiling livers. Luckily for Jake, his frozen nose had lost its sense of smell. Everything about him was frozen, from his toes up.

"All hands on deck! All hands on deck!"

All able bodies, except the engineers, were ordered to chip away ice that was building on the rigging at a rate of an inch a minute. If the boat became top heavy, it would capsize quickly, helped along by coal shifting in the bunkers as the ship tipped. Hard and bright as diamonds, the ice was already inches thick. Pouring hot water on the ice to soften it, the men then proceeded to chip, chip and chip away.

Jake climbed the rigging, chipping without gloves, wishing for the relative warmth of snow over ice, not looking down. Down was far, far, away. His ears hurt so badly from the cold, he alternated hands, one covering his ear and the other hacking at the ice. There was a wool hat down in his kit bag, but he wouldn't be forgiven for going to get it. Personal discomfort meant nothing at a time like this.

Even my eyeballs are frozen, he thought. I'll never cry again.

But he wanted to cry now; he wanted to beg someone to make it stop, but looking around at the men working to save their own and each other's lives he knew they were all in the same boat. He wouldn't find any sympathy here, and why should he? He had none to give either. The only difference between him and the rest of them was that he, Jake, would not be coming back. At least he had that to look forward to. He had never felt so far from Texas in his life. Soon he got to wondering if a place like Texas even existed. Had he ever lived somewhere that was hot, dry and dusty? He didn't trust his own memory anymore. He couldn't recall what warmth felt like.

The ice grew more and more, very fast, right before his eyes. He couldn't keep up. His chest hurt from breathing in the freezing air. Every part of him hurt. His nose and ears burned with cold as the tight, frigid air gnawed at him.

Throbbing intensely, the bayonet wound in his side felt fresh as if he was being stabbed repeatedly anew by a frosty blade of ice. The cold was a thief finding every way in to steal his peace of mind.

Working side by side with the men, hacking away at the ice twice as hard as anyone else, was Mac, keeping the crew motivated with angry shouts, bad jokes and false promises. "Come on Hardcastle, I've heard your mrs being called the ice queen and you still managed to crack seven kids out of her. Now get a move on!"

Perhaps only Mac and the skipper knew how close they were to death, but they kept tight lipped about it. By heck, the skipper thought, she's making us work for it. She is. I don't mind. The harder the toil the sweeter the fruit. Go on lass, show us who's boss. But privately he crossed himself in prayer, hoping that God was giving only a moral lesson, not a fatal one, about not taking for granted the spoils of nature's larder.

"Jesus, Jesus, Jesus." Jake prayed, without knowing he was praying, as he worked alongside the men to keep boat and life afloat.

The struggle for him was as intense as the fight with the German; same battle, different foe. This current enemy didn't have blue eyes but it wanted his life just as much. He wished he had left Vivian on better terms. All the fighting between them seemed so insignificant compared to the battle he was in now. Having her love with him would have kept him warm and given him the will to endure. Without her, there was no one left to love him, he realised. He longed to forgive her. Perhaps in America, with all the memories left behind, they could start afresh. But there would always be the boy to remind them of her deceit. But the boy was innocent. Jake had promised he wouldn't hold anything against him. The boy. Why had the skipper asked if they were taking Ted with them? A strange question. Why would he care? Jake suspected. A picture flashed in his mind of the two of them together; Vivian and Crostaff.

Sparks shouted to him, "At least we can see this ice. Black ice is worse, catches you unawares. You can't see it till it's too late. Only the boat can feel it and over she goes, groaning." He made an arcing movement with his gloved hand.

"Not with our skipper," someone else shouted. "He wouldn't let it take over the Ichthus. He never has. He's 'ad us down in them bunkers shovelling the coal to right her before. He outwits nature every time."

Said Grandad, "Don't be so daft, lad. He doesn't outwit nature. He challenges it. He shouldn't have us out here fishing in this weather. It's in'uman. I'm changing skippers when we get back. He's the only arse'ole that does this to his men. I've talked to some others. They won't sail with him. You don't see any other boats around here do you. They all went 'ome while we're out here freezing our bollocks off."

Mac shouted, "Come on Grandad, you say that every winter."

The old man bowed his head in respect of being overheard by the first mate, but grumbled, "Well, I've got a right, haven't I? Got the oldest bones on board, me. I've been doing this since before your dad were born."

A dark flicker in the first mate's eyes at the mention of his father had not gone unnoticed. Grandad longed to say, "We've a right to talk about your father. He was a great man and an even better fisherman. He was our friend. You don't own his memory." But he knew better and kept silent, though he resented being robbed of the chance to talk about William Goodwell.

"Aye well," Mac shouted. "All's forgiven, isn't it, as soon as you get paid? I don't hear you moaning once you're in the pub supping a pint. But go on then and grumble, Grandad, if it keeps you warm."

To Jake, Mac said, "Don't mind him, he says this every time. But he loves this boat too much. He's been around longer than cod, and he's starting to look like one an' all. Look at his bulging eyes, and 'ow he keeps his mouth open all the time, just like a cod."

Jake laughed.

"We've caught enough," said Grandad. "We should be on our way 'ome by now. Why does he allus have to push it."

"You're too old for this lark, Grandad. It's your rheumatism talking," said one of the Deckie learners; a strong, young lad of eighteen.

"I am. You're right. But what else is there for me to do? And don't laugh at me. Old age'll 'appen to you in good time. If you're lucky."

But being young they didn't think so. Being young they thought they would never be old like Grandad, just as he had thought so when he was their age. But only he knew that; they didn't. He remembered the old timers on the old wooden trawlers against whom he had loved to roll up his shirts sleeves to show off his young brawny arms with its tan skin and hard muscles. They'll learn, he thought. 'Tis a pity I won't be around to see it though. But maybe on that day they'll remember the old fool they used to scoff at. I hope there is an 'eaven so I can look down on them and laugh. I'll send a strong nor'easterner with my face on it for them. Meanwhile, there's the rest of me sodding life to get through. This fucking skipper. I hate his guts, which was an oath almost all the men uttered at one point or other during the trip.

When the imminent danger of capsizing was relieved, most of the men went below to warm up with a hot meal, some tea and plenty of banter. Mac stayed on watch, with Bert at the wheel. Reviving mugs of tea were brought to them by the galley lad.

Down in the mess, Jake couldn't feel his feet, though logic told him he had a pair of size tens somewhere at the end of his legs. "Watch out for frostbite," he was told by a man with eight toes. "But warm 'em up slow." So Jake rubbed his feet vigorously, holding them against a warm pan or warm mug of tea to revive them, thinking of Grandad's words, 'This is in'uman.'

As Jake pumped his cold, stiff fingers to get them working again, he thought, I don't how these men do it time after time. They're even joking now. Their bodies might be frozen but their spirit isn't. They'll never give up, just as Churchill said. They're showing me something here. I promised myself no more running away. If you can't keep your promises to yourself, then what good are your promises to anybody else?

Now it was fish for supper every night. Being part of the crew, Jake understood why Mac had been in such an uproar about Ginger not showing up. The exhausted fishermen traipsed down to the mess deck, wet, cold and ravenous. But after a meal and a mug of tea, a smile returned. The cook advised Jake, "Bread's the most important. You can bugger up the rest but the bread has to be good."

During Ginger's frequent breaks, Jake made some meals he had learned from the fish shop; fish pie, fish and chips, and his own shackles recipe wherein everything fish was thrown in the pot to wallop along with an onion, carrot, celery, a bayleaf and a little chilli powder he had brought with him. The Shackles pot was kept on the go at all times to keep the men warm, and Jake spiced his version up a bit more than the man were used to, but they claimed to like it though their noses ran and their eyes watered. Grandad complained that Jake's version of the fish stew kept him on the bog more, but Mac told him to shut up or he'd dock his pay for taking too many shit breaks.

Every night, before he turned himself in, Jake took Crostaff a bowl of hambone soup at midnight. He was nervous the first time, but after the skipper had taken a sip and nodded approval without looking at Jake, the cowboy-fisherman felt relieved, and more accepted than ever.

Sparks told Jake, "If you pleased old Popeye, then you're well in. He's real fussy about that soup. I've seen him throw it back at Ginger, but don't tell Ginger I told you that or he'll spit on me dumplings."

Down in the ice room, the layers upon layers of ice, fish and pallets were stacking up.

"Move the rest of the coal," Mac told Bert, " We need the room for more fish. After this haul, we're bringing the gear in. We're going head to wind. He's going to dodge her."

"Isn't it time to clue up and go home?" asked Bert.

If it were up to Mac they wouldn't be fishing in this weather. It was too rough and too dangerous. Fish weren't worth men's lives, in his opinion. I know I've got a reputation for taking risks, but I only do it with me own life. No one else's, he thought.

He told the men, "Skipper's orders. We're running in. He reckons there's a good lee up the coast a bit. We can get three mile in. You'll get a half day rest, Mr. Bosun."

Mac went back above deck with Monty close at heel.

"I'd rather have half a day closer to home," responded Bert, under his breath.

But to cheer up the men, Bert started to chant, and the fish room men joined in.

"When the wind is on the quarter
And she takes on lots of water
And brings her down slow
Oh, yes
The lads'll get a roger
The skippers gunner dodge her."

To Crostaff, the best part of bad weather was that all the fish would be his for the taking. On calmer days, it wouldn't take long for other trawlers to show up once the Ichthus was known to be shooting and hauling. So he relished the times the other skippers stood down and he was the only one to go on.

Disgruntled murmurings met Crostaff when he strode into the mess at dinnertime. He looked around at every face knowing that not one of them dare speak against him to his face. Yet, he wasn't looking for forced assent to his decision to go on. The skipper sought to replace the weariness on the bristled faces of his men with an enthusiasm he believed only he could ignite.

"Men," he began, "We're going ahead up around the North East coast to follow the cod."

He ignored the mutters, impossible to tell anyway where they came from because all mouths looked to be closed, lips sealed, and all eyes, silent but expressive, were on him. The skipper pulled on his pipe while he paced the floor, waiting until the men quieted, which with no agreement to do so among them, they did. Then he spoke, softly, the very softness of it commanding their attention.

"You're war weary just like my old girl, here, the Ichthus. She served in the Great War, you know, like Grandad over there." Grandad nodded his agreement. "And like most of our fathers," he paused to puff his pipe. "Then, like most of you she was outfitted for this war. You've seen her gun platform near the bow, she wears it like a medal. She's still got the oscillator on the keel and the depth charge racks to stern, she wears those like stripes she earned after every battle. She was there, D-Day and Dunkirk saving the lives of man and country. I'm telling you, she'll be recruited for the next one. What do you say Grandad, will you join her?"

The men laughed.

"No," the old man sadly. "I reckon two wars is enough for me, and 'er."

"She's brave, lads, our boat," continued the skipper. "Look at her. Waiting to go into the fray."

Pausing to re-light his pipe, he sucked hard on it. The tobacco glowed warmly, stoking the thrill he felt at reaching the point where his men were at low morale and it was up to him and him alone to renew their vigour. Before him was a captive audience that was almost, he felt, *willing* him to inspire them. Part of this inspiration would come in the form of an extra tot of rum to be added to every man's tea. And he could tell they were already appreciative upon spotting the rum bottle brought in by Jake.

"We few, we happy few," Crostaff said softly to himself, and the men strained forward to better hear him. "An extra measure of rum for all of you. Go on, Yankee. See to it. I'll make fishers of you men before this trip is through."

"Here, here," said the men raising their mugs and taking a sip of inspiration tea.

"What civilian men have experienced only recently in battle, in the wars, fighting for their lives, we have experienced every day for generations. War tests a man's fear and it tests the depths of his love for life and honour. But the war's over, which takes those other men back to their warm beds and warm wives, but not us."

Sucking on his pipe, he paced the mess floor collecting his thoughts, "War for us was but a change of command. For those other men, the passion they felt for God, country, home and hearth will lessen over time. Routine will take over and their wives' faces will become too familiar. They'll try to forget about death, but for us, we fisherman, death is our constant companion and thus our passion remains." He emphasized this last point with the saliva'd nib of his pipe.

"We fishermen are treated like dogs by the government and the trawler owners, and by any of them what doesn't know what it's like out here. Aye they treat us like dogs. Fed and beaten, told to sit and stay, told 'Come on boy,' when there's a war on. Like dogs, expected to fearlessly obey and feel nothing but an eagerness to please our masters. But this," he pointed with his pipe again, "This is the time when we're doing it for usselves, when we show them rich bastards what it is to be a man because they don't know. Oh aye, we could go home now with what we've got and everyone would be satisfied. But we can achieve glory with a world record catch. What we can do today will lift us above the rest. They'll look up to us and we down at them."

Think on that, lads, he thought, his chest swelling with pleasure at his own speech.

"All this just for bloody fish," a crew member said in a low voice.

"Just fish! You thick get!" snarled Crostaff, leaping over the tables to grab the man by the collar.

Hauling the startled fisherman to his feet, Crostaff shouted in his face, "Fish is what's keeping this country alive! Woolbottom kept fish from rationing for a reason. Jesus Christ fed the starving five thousand with fish, and we fed a nation of millions! It's the protein what gave our people the strength to go on in the darkest days of war. It's what's going to help us put this country back together through the next years too. We're helping to rebuild a nation! The more fish, the more trains to transport it inland, the more coal to fuel the trawlers, the more work for dockworkers and lasses at the fish processing factory, the more fish shops and mongers around the country. And who brings in the fish? We do! Right here!" He pointed to the floor with his pipe. "And it's up to me to find it, and I know there's more up there. Have I ever been wrong? Have I?"

Crostaff let go of the man's lapels, but so frozen in place was he that he stayed where he was with his clothes pulled up until the skipper straightened his lapels and gave him a little push back onto the bench seat.

"Allus remember, lads, that Christ chose a fisherman for a disciple. He chose you," he said, gesturing with his pipe. "And He chose me. He said, *Cast the net on the right side and ye shall find*!" the skipper shouted. "Any man who doubts me, doubts this old girl."

As he headed toward the door, he smiled to himself, but turning, he regained his serious expression saying, "So it's up to you, lads. I'm taking volunteers. All of you willing to go with me, show up for work tomorrow morning. The rest of you sods can walk the plank. And remember, your pay stops the minute you leave my boat."

The news settled heavily on the crew. They shifted in their seats and scratched their ears, waiting for the skipper to leave so they could complain. Then Jake startled everyone by asking, "How much fish have caught we so far, Skipper?"

"Mr. Mate, please remind the newest member of your flock that no one talks directly to me, except you and the engineer," Crostaff said sharply.

"Never ask the old man that question," Mac scolded Jake after the skipper left.

"But how does he know when we have enough? He's talking about the world record."

"He doesn't know, not for certain anyrode. Only I know. That way he allus wants more, you see. He'll find out when we land it, when it's counted and paid for. It's not just him, mind. None of the skippers wants to know. It keeps them 'ungry. Like a wolf not knowing its belly's full."

But we could lose everything if she tips over, thought Mac, as he had thought many times before when Crostaff had pushed them, boat and men, to the very crest of existence where death and life grabbed at them from both sides with icy fingers.

Crostaff thrived on the storm. During this time, he closed off all feelings for the men and thought only of hunting the fish. His days were spent pouring over the charts that contained generations of knowledge about the migratory routes and peculiar habits of cod shoals. He consulted his copious notes, looking for clues and patterns.

As he watched the men chip the ice off the rigging in the last light of day, he thought, Where else do men work like this? Working now to save their very lives.

In these conditions, the men hated Crostaff, hated him so vehemently they kept themselves warm by plotting his demise. It was all they could do to stand upright through lack of sleep, the biting cold, and hard work like no other, but when it was over, when they were home they were glad to be on his crew, to have survived the danger, to have stared death in the face, and to be looked upon with respect by other crews of other boats. Never let it be known that they complained in thought. In their telling of the trip, it was as if they had chosen to go on, as if they had convinced the skipper there was more fish to be caught. Yes, that's how they made it sound back at the pub.

With the worst of the ice removed, the skipper gave the order to shoot the trawl. They had found a good lee. The weather was just as cold but they were sheltered from the ferocious wind. The repaired winch groaned and creaked under its three quarter mile of cable that was threaded through two gallows, taking the weight of the trawl. At high risk of injury, the men worked between the taut warps. The tension was so great that if one of the warps snapped it would lash across the deck slicing a man in two.

Waiting for the final trawl to reveal its secrets, the skipper's stomach gripped and churned and he thought, as always, that he might vomit. Exhausted, Crostaff fell to his knees on the bridge, swearing and cursing, before curling up in a ball whimpering. But he needn't have worried, the cod end bobbed up full. Giving a satisfied nod, he poked his pipe at the net as if to say, "See there."

The winch faltered.

"What's happening?" cried Mac. "Have we got Moby fucking Dick in there or what? It's that fucking useless winch. Come on, lads, let's give it some welly."

"It's no use, Mac," said Grandad. "I think we've got some'at really heavy in the net. Several hundred pounds of some'at."

The blood drained from Mac. He grew even colder.

"You don't think it's a mine cut its mooring, do you?" asked Bert, the fear showing in his face as well.

He was too afraid to look over the side just in case he was right, but Mac did, and he saw in the near dark something round and familiar in the net, shaping the lay of the fish around it.

"Looks like it," shouted Mac. "Fuck! We've no choice. Haul!"

The wheeling seagulls were getting impatient for the fish. They dove squealing and grabbing at fish through the net. All hands were on deck in anticipation of the cod end being swung aboard but now they waited and watched the first mate, skipper and bosun confer about the mine.

"Do you think it's a live one?" shouted Bert.

"How the fuck would I know?" yelled Mac.

"What's the hold up? You ladies having a tea break or what?" Crostaff's voice boomed.

"We've picked up some'at heavy. Looks like a mine, Sir," Mac shouted close to the skipper's ear so he could hear him.

"You're fucking kidding. Christ! I'm sick of this shite. Dead bodies in me net, bits of boat, submarines. A bloody jeep. Now this! A mine! When's this fucking war going to be over!"

"Sir! Sir!"

Now what?!" Crostaff roared when a young deckie learner vied for his attention.

"It's Grandad, Sir," cried the lad. "I think he's having an 'eart attack."

The old man had fallen into the pounds clutching his chest.

"Sod it, not now!"

"Skipper, we have to bring in the mine and dump it later, in deep water!" shouted Mac. "Away from the grounds."

"I know the fucking protocol, Mr. Mate."

"Aye, Sir."

372

The skipper motioned with his arm to swing the cod end over.

"Legs bent! In case that fucker explodes. The vibrations will shake the ship and I don't want any broken bones to have to deal with. This is still a record catch. I don't want to be putting in anywhere so these bastards can have an 'oliday in a Rekyavik hospital."

"Should I tell Sparks to resume radio contact?" shouted Bert.

"Give out our position? Them bastards'll know where me best fishing is."

But he nodded his assent. There would be no hope for them at all if no one knew where they were. As it was, he knew there were probably no other boats about. Their best hope, and an unlikely one, was that there was another mad bastard skipper who had taken the chance in this weather.

The cod end swung over and was released, spilling cod over the deck and the mine with it. The sea was rough and nerves were high as the boat tossed from side to side. A couple of times it looked as though the deck might come up and hit the mine.

"Steady! Steady!"

"Jesus," someone prayed.

The mine sat before them on the deck. For a moment no one moved as if even a breath would set it off. Then the order was given to make the davit ready to crane the mine to the portside forehead where it would be held with the rest of the rubbish to be dumped later in open water three hundred fathoms deep.

"How's Grandad?" the Skipper asked, keeping one eye on the activity with the mine.

"I'm all right, Skipper," a frail voice called out. Grandad's face was pale and sweaty, despite the cold. "It weren't no heart attack. It were indigestion from that yank's shackles. You know I wouldn't die when it were so inconvenient."

"Bloody hell you gave us a scare. Get yoursen to my cabin and have some of that vodka. Aye, there's a bottle left."

Some of the men gripped their chests, faking pain.

"Oh go on, get back to work!" yelled Mac. "This isn't ladies night."

"Fuck him and his get back to work," muttered one of the crew. "While he's on the bridge with the skipper."

As the davit swung the mine, an errant wave smashed over the deck pulling the boat portside and sending the mine out over the water. Mac tried starting the winch to bring up the mine but it jammed, creaking and straining under the weight.

"She's had it!" he cried.

Fearing the mine would hit the side when the boat righted, Mac grabbed a hacksaw from a deckie's basket and scrambled forward to cut the mine free; but while sawing at the ropes, the ship rode a large swell and Mac was swung out with the mine and dipped into the water. He clung on to the rope, still hacking at it while Monty barked furiously from the deck. The first mate was waist deep in freezing water, and losing the feeling in his legs but his hands kept working and soon the mine dropped back into the water and was lost to sight behind another swell.

Grappling to retain a hold, Mac's only thought was of returning to the boat and getting warm again. He was so cold he felt almost warm again like the fine line between love and hate. He tried to keep his mind on where he was, and not think of the parlour back home in Hull and its red glowing hearth. "C-cold," he chattered to himself as he shimmied back along the hemp cable. "So f-fucking c-cold."

But as his mind flitted, searching for warm thoughts, the wind whistled cruelly like the old gypsy. The shrill whistling rode on the wind, wrapping around him like a wide gypsy skirt and petticoats, choking him, taunting him. The whistle vibrated in his ears, tunnelling into him, drilling into his soul until his bones rattled in their sockets and, nerves raw, his teeth screamed. Feeling he was going mad, he put his hands over his ears to block the haunting sound, and fell into the water.

"Man overboard!" bellowed Crostaff.

At first the skipper thought it must be a prank, as Mac had pretended to be in trouble before, but he soon realized the first mate was in real peril and would freeze to death if he wasn't pulled from the water soon.

"Man overboard!" he yelled again although the men had already gathered port side.

Bert threw a lifebelt over but it fell short of Mac who hand over hand was monkeying his way along the frozen divot cable back to the boat. It was too dark to see him clearly. He made a grab for the lifebelt but one swell took it out of reach. With great effort he pulled himself along another two feet, but his wool clothes and heavy boots hung like anchors around him. The temptress cold slowed his heart with seductive fingers, or maybe it was the old gypsy again. It was her. She was under him, with her arms wrapped around his legs, pulling, pulling. What did she want with him? His head slipped under but he pulled himself up again. Something splashed around his head. Was it her again? But he heard his name being screamed by many men, "Grab it! Grab it!"

Yet he felt so sleepy. The warm hearth of home came to his mind again, and he smiled, thinking of sharing a glass of rum with his mother. She was warm, warm by the fire. He would never be cold again if he sat with her. She would make sure of it with her mother's love. Then it was a summer's day in Pickering Park under the shade of an oak tree he sat close to Dolores who held a bowl of fresh strawberries laced with soft white cream, and sprinkled with sugar. Her lips, made red by strawberry blood, had never tasted so sweet. But no it wasn't Dolores. It was Gloria, with her creamy skin and beckoning eyes.

Arms encircled him, tighter and tighter, but pulling him upwards instead of down, and his father's voice whispered, "I'll save you. Open your eyes."

He obeyed and saw Jake at the railing holding a rope that led down to the water. Mac was surprised to see his own hands were gripping the other end. Out of necessity, they were working independently, beyond his control. Mac was being pulled along, but his dreams returned to that warm hearth. "Open your eyes," the voice cried more urgently. He jerked awake, causing Jake to lose his footing and take a step forward. At once, Mac let go of the rope, not wanting to bring Jake overboard with him. Loose again in the water, he floundered, sinking deeper into the dark sea, but then, once more, he felt himself being lifted upwards. This time Crostaff and Bert were helping Jake, hand over fist, to pull Mac back on board.

Mac came to with the skipper's flask under his nose and Monty licking his forehead. With only one eye open, the first mate snatched the flask and took a gulp or three of rum. Never had a drink been more welcome. The men laughed.

"You're alive, then, Mr. Mate," said Crostaff with a big smile though his forehead remained creased with worry.

"Reckon I am," said Mac. "Mind, it's this stuff makes it worth coming back."

"Aye. Reckon you'll do owt for a tot," said the Skipper.

"It was the Yankee kid what saved you," said Bert.

Mac opened his other eye and looked around at the group standing over him. Not used to looking up to people, he quickly found he didn't like it. Seeking the strength to get to his feet, he took another gulp of rum.

"Good job you brought him along," said Crostaff seizing possession of the flask before the rum was all gone. "Your brother-in-law."

"You should have seen 'im," said Bert, on watch for the mine in case it came back on the next swell. "He caught you just like at the pictures with them cowboys in the wild-est."

He swirled his arm above his head to demonstrate.

"Like this. He roped you like a big old cow."

"Moo," Mac said weakly, and the men laughed.

Jake held out a hand to help him stand.

"Thanks," Mac said, his teeth chattering.

"Show's over!" shouted Crostaff. "There's still fish to gut! Then we'll clue up and be on our way home, lads! *On our way home!*"

Whistling, singing, cheerfully alive, the men set to their work. The prospect of sleep spurring them on.

"It's all under control here," Crostaff said to Mac. "Come to me cabin for a minute. I've got some spare kit. Change your clothes and let's see if Grandad saved us any of that vodka."

Mac assented. He needed quiet to think about what had happened to him, and what had almost happened. He was astounded that, just like his father, he had been willing to let go and die. Erstwhile, he had never thought himself capable of surrender, at least during the war when the enemy was man. Yet when it came to the sea, he had given up almost immediately. Perhaps not given up, but given over to the sea, to nature to fate. Yet, here he was, alive because another had fought for his life.

As he recalled the night his father died, he saw his own face in place his father's as if it were he who had drifted away and faded into the black. Mac felt something inside him dissolve. A joyful realization took hold of him: for just as he had let go of the rope because he didn't want Jake to come to any harm, so had his father let go so young Mac would not be pulled overboard. He saved my life, Mac remarked to himself. It wasn't that he was giving up at all. He died fighting for my life. The knowledge of the strength of a father's love folded over him; spreading from his heart to every part of his body. Tears came to his eyes.

I want a son, thought Mac. I want a son to love that much. A son I would die for.

And he imagined Gloria, proud and smiling with a baby boy in her arms. His boy. That's going to be my life, he thought with wonder. I am a lucky bastard, I am. I don't deserve a girl like Gloria to love me. But she does, so I won't argue with it.

"Water's cold, then, is it?" said Crostaff, jerking Mac from his thoughts.

"Aye," Mac said. "I wouldn't recommend swimming at this time of year."

"Been in it mesen, a time or two."

"I reckon you 'ave."

Again, the two men looked at one another, each having something to say of a reconciliatory sort but neither venturing the actual words; instead allowing a look of understanding to pass between them as Yorkshiremen are want to do.

Back in the skipper's cabin they found Grandad dead in a chair with his eyes open and his hand around the unopened bottle of vodka.

"Poor sod, didn't even get to take a drink," said Crostaff, reaching forward and closing the old fisherman's eyes. "Least he didn't spill any. Considerate to the last, he was."

"You knew this would happen?" Mac's teeth chattered and his body shook with cold.

Crostaff held up his hands.

"I do know he didn't eat any of the Yank's shackles, so it wasn't indigestion. He hasn't been eating much of owt on this trip. It's not the first time tha knows. His daughter told my Iris he was 'aving problems with his heart. She wanted me to convince him to quit but he wouldn't have it, would he? Here, get some dry kit on."

He handed a pile of neatly folded clothes to Mac.

"You're smiling, Mr. Mate?"

"Aye, at the way that old codger spent all his time complaining and threatening not to come out with us again."

"Aye, I know," said the skipper. "Reckon that was his way of dealing with the life."

The mate and the skipper viewed the dead body.

"Well, he dealt with it," said Mac. "Here, let's cover him with a blanket. Till we bury him."

As Mac donned the spare trousers and jumper, Crostaff felt a moment of envy for the young, muscular body, but then admiration. We're like flowers, he thought, the way we bloom so beautiful before withering away. It's his turn to be young now. Good luck to him. I tried to capture some of that back with me antics with Vivian. What a daft sod I am. My Iris has put up with a lot. By heck. I'll have to find a way to make it up to her. My love. If only she knew how much I love her. I've done a bum job of showing it. Bloody men, we don't deserve any of them lasses.

Puffing on his pipe, he finished setting up the chess board, saying "You know the Russian custom, once the bottle's open we have to finish it."

Mac was sitting on the bunk pulling on a pair of dry, wool socks. Growling, Monty grabbed one of the socks and pulled on it, shaking his head as if the sock were a ferret to kill.

"Stop it you daft bugger!" said Mac. "You won't hear no argument from me about finishing that vodka, Skipper. Let me make a toast," said Mac, grabbing the bottle and pouring the shots. "Here's to Grandad!"

"To Grandad."

They tossed the drink to the back of their throats.

"By heck," said Mac, smacking his lips. "This stuff's too easy to sup."

"Aye. Pity we can't run into Vladinski and get some more."

With great gusto, they drank to everything and everyone they loved, to Britain, to the victory over Germany, to the King. And all the while they kept up a fine game of chess. Soon, the vodka was almost finished, and it was Crostaff's turn to choose the last toast. He had something in mind as he held the bottle in his hand. Deciding to go with it, he poured the last shots then, gripping his own glass, he looked deep into the first mate's black eyes. Grinning, Mac raised his glass ready.

"To William Goodwell," Crostaff said. "To your father. The finest skipper in history to ever sail the seven seas."

The smile vanished from Mac's face. For a moment, Crostaff thought he might get punched, but then tears glittered in those black eyes, like shiny new jet, as the first mate fought to regain his composure. He swallowed, and breathed deeply.

"Aye. To my father. The finest skipper - by far."

Crostaff laughed.

"Cheers!"

"Cheers!"

A sudden, muffled explosion startled the men, breaking their laughter. Monty barked.

"What the fuck was that?" cried Mac, jumping to his feet. "The mine?"

"Some'ats run into it!" cried the skipper.

"Christ," said Mac. "Well, better them than us," he added, less than a second before they were thrown across the cabin by an unseen force.

Sea water immediately gushed into the cabin, washing the little dog out-of-sight under the skipper's bunk. All power was lost and the cabin fell into darkness. The men scrambled for a foothold, grabbing each other and slipping down into the freezing water.

"It's a bubble jet!" cried Crostaff. "Split her in half! Jesus! They're dead! Anyone initspath; in the mess, the galley. Ginger! Igor! They're all dead! Ah fuck, she's sinking fast! I can't believe it! All that soddin' fish an' all. We have to get out of here!"

Up to his waist in freezing water, the skipper waded up an incline aiming to get to the deck and a lifeboat. The effects of the vodka had vanished in one wash. Table and chairs, floated by, and with it, he knew, his beloved chess set; an inheritance from his grandfather. He grabbed a piece and squeezed it in his hand. It was only a pawn but he stuffed it in his pocket anyway. Then he felt Grandad's body brush against him like a warning, *This too shall be you.*

"Mac," he cried. "Come on! We've got to get out of here or she'll be our coffin an' all!"

"I've got to get me dog!" screamed Mac, holding on to a post, not sure which way was up.

"Don't be so daft! It's drowned by now."

"Not my dog!" shouted Mac.

"You'll never find it in the black!"

But this time there was no response. There was only sea water, darkness and the deafening noise of water filling the boat. As Crostaff heaved himself forward, he felt a hand grab him and pull it up. It was Jake.

"Where's Mac?!" Jake yelled looking into the blackness of the cabin as if the whites of the man's eyes might show themselves. "Mac!"

Crostaff waved his arm about in the cabin hoping to find human purchase where there was none.

"He went to get that fucking dog!"

"I'm going to get him!" shouted Jake.

"No, you're not. And that's an order. You'll both be lost if you go down there. Find a lifeboat, Son! Think of Vivian!"

But Jake pushed him aside and dove into the dark cabin.

The crew were shouting; some injured men were screaming for help. But it was darker than night. Those that could scrambled onto the deck. There was frantic, organized activity as the men tried to launch lifeboats but they were losing hope along with their footing on the slippery, inclined deck.

Since God was the only hope left, Crostaff cried, "Please God, take me if you have to, but save my men!

Iris!" he pictured her briefly before he too slipped back into the black water-filled cabin to search for Mac.

Chapter 32

That same night, a wind howled about the Goodwell house, breathing into every crack and crevice; whistling through the rooms and disturbing the sleeping occupants. Though the ground did not buck and weave underneath the house like the North Sea under a boat, their nerves were nonetheless rattled by the wolfish ferocity of the storm outside that seemed to have the strength to blow down the thick brick walls with its next carnivorous breath.

Wailing ghostlike down chimneys, the powerful gusts extinguished fires rendering the house cold and desolate with an emptiness like a void that could at any moment be filled by something otherworldly unless the void was filled with prayer.

Prudence was tossing and turning in restless sleep like a lifeboat on a stormy sea, but she jumped quickly awake and out of bed when she heard Muriel cry out; her cold feet searching for slippers while she quickly pulled on her dressing gown.

"William!" her mother cried again.

Fear fluttered in Prudence's breast. Barefoot, she ran down the stairs with her hair loose about her shoulders, but half-way, she tripped on George's football and fell, missing the last three steps, and landing on her hands and knees by the front door while the ball bounced by her hitting the wall.

George, you bloody -! she screamed, but only in her head, typically mindful not to wake the others. "Ow!"

Each time she put weight on her foot, a pain seared in her ankle making her nauseous. She steadied herself, stork-like on one leg, taking deep breaths and leaning on the banister for support. By the time she gathered herself, all was quiet, save the wind seeming more inside than out. Softly, she called out, "Mam?" There was no reply.

Perhaps she had only imagined it was her mother's voice crying out. What she had heard was probably just the wind playing games. To make sure, she hobbled towards the dark parlour, wincing at every brief step taken by her injured foot, and cursing herself for her foolish imagination.

Embers glowed in the grate like a red warning light barely illuminating the room. But through the archway, Prudence was able to make out the sleeping form of her mother.

A sudden draft blew through the parlour and through Prudence, flapping the bottom of her nightdress and lifting her hair. Pulling her dressing gown tighter, she hesitatingly looked in the direction from whence the draft had come, and the hairs on the back of her neck stood on end. The back door was wide open and heavy rain was intruding just inside the threshold. She looked about the room, but no one had come in, that she could tell, and she had thought the door closed when she first entered the parlour. But surely she was mistaken. Perhaps, she briefly wondered, her mother had gone outside to use the lavatory, and had forgotten to close the door on her way back in. But on a night like this with a ready chamber pot under her bed?

Usually, Prudence loved the wind; she loved to watch it brush along grass and rustle through trees like a symphony. The wind was strong but transparent, sometimes powerful enough to break boughs, and turn over carts; an invisible force, like faith. But this winter wind was cold and unwelcome. It was invading her home - reaching in with icy fingers, slipping dangerously around her exposed nape like Death's scythe.

The pain in her ankle was severe but she had to use it for walking to get to the door. The walking stick her mother sometimes used was leaning against the fireplace so she grabbed it and hobbled over to the back door. A sharp intake of breath accompanied every step, but she made it, closing the door with some effort against the strong wind. She locked it and leant against it for a moment, taking a breath while she gathered the strength to hobble over to where Muriel was sleeping. She felt stupid for having fallen down the stairs.

As she limped along, she called out to her mother in a whisper, "Mam? Are you all right? Are you cold? The door was open. Did you open it? I closed it, so you'll be all right now."

The wind answered in the chimney but her mother was silent. More silent than Prudence had ever known her to be.

"Are you asleep?" she whispered so quietly even she wasn't sure if she had said it.

Unexpectedly, the fire brightened, and the flames danced and reflected off the shiny ornaments on the dying Christmas tree that no one had the heart to take down. Muriel had enjoyed making the colourful paper chains that were strung across the walls and ceiling in decoration, and she had insisted on overseeing the baking of the Christmas cake; pouring the brandy over the baked square fruit cake while she described how moist it was going to be when they ate it on the day, which it was.

But Prudence had no chance to reflect fondly on Christmas.

"Oh Mam!" she cried in a whisper.

Muriel was lying at an unnatural angle on the bed; as if she had been felled there. But even more startling were Muriel's dead open eyes staring straight ahead, over Prudence's shoulders at the back door, which, upon turning, Prudence was relieved to see was still closed. The young woman's heart beat wildly in her chest; she wondered what could have shocked her mother so.

"Oh Mam, no," Prudence said sadly. "You've gone? What happened? Why tonight?"

The expression in Muriel's wide staring eyes moved Prudence to want some live company, and her first inclination was to call out to the others in the house, but she had no voice; her throat was too dry. The gaping eyes were set as though they had witnessed something terrifyingly rapturous, perhaps as if God Himself had come to take her hand in His. The closed back door loomed ominously behind Prudence as she approached her mother whose unblinking eyes gazed into the beyond.

At least the pain in her ankle gave Prudence tangible proof of the present, without it she might have been lost to the horror of her mother's dying so suddenly, unexpectedly, but at the same time expected every day since the diagnosis.

Then I'm next, thought Prudence. I'm the next generation what's going to grow old and die just like they did. Now there's no parents, there's nowt left between me and God.

She felt frightened and desperately alone until she remembered, with some relief, that she was soon to be married and would have someone with whom to share her life, someone to grow old with, and who would care if she was well or sick, happy or sad. But not a mother, not anymore. Never again would she speak the word, "Mother" or hear her name spoken by her mother's voice ... until they met again.

A smile softened her features when she pictured her mother and father reunited in the afterlife. Would her father ask, "Cup of tea or what?" as he always had when he returned from sea? How her mother would laugh if he did. Had he come for her tonight? It was his name that Muriel had called out, twice, rousing Prudence from a restless slumber. She were still in love with him, right up until the end of her own life. Death did not part them. He were the last thing she thought of. Perhaps … the last thing she saw.

A prickling sensation rippled over her scalp, and once more her eyes turned to the back door. But whatever was carried on the wind had withdrawn from their house, and was silent.

For all the years since their father had been lost, Muriel had forbidden any of the children to lock the back door in case William returned from the sea, wet, cold and hungry and in need of a warm, welcome place by the fire and a hot meal in his belly. She had been particularly anxious about the door during the war, and kept reminding Mac not to lock it. The first thing she did, when they returned from evacuation, was to try the door, which was unlocked, as promised. And she had nodded and smiled with relief that her beloved William had not been left out in the cold.

How was it for me mam all these years? I never asked. And now it's too late. But no, I do know. I heard what she cried with her last breath. She cried his name. She's gone. The one who saw me take my first steps, who heard my first word, who fed me at her breast. She gave me life. I didn't understand it before, but now she's gone. Mother! I don't want you to go. But I'm glad you're not in pain anymore.

She studied her mother's body, her eyes sweeping over it, remembering how it had looked when she breathed, waiting for the chest to rise, but it didn't. She placed a hand on Muriel's chest, hoping to feel a breath or a heart-beat, but all was still and silent. A sob grabbed her throat and with silent, final acceptance, Prudence closed the stark staring eyes, and pulled the blanket over Muriel's face. The faint light of life that had been holding the sunken features in place was gone, only the expressionless, permanent death mask remained, and Prudence was glad enough to cover it. She didn't want to remember her mother that way.

One of Muriel's arms was dangling dead outside the bed so Prudence hid it away under the blanket, shivering at the touch of the cooling dead flesh. The finality of death tore at her heart. Her chest quivered with emotion. She closed her eyes and breathed deeply.

Satisfied that the body was completed shrouded, Prudence attended to her ankle that didn't appear to be swelling. It was just sore and she was glad of the painful distraction. Hobbling around the parlour, she managed to soak a tea towel in cold water, and hobble back to the winged chair by the fire, only to remember she should keep her foot elevated, so she shuffled a parlour chair over, and sat in one chair with her foot propped up on the other.

Watching the gentle flames catch hold of some new coal she had thrown on, Prudence recalled that her mother wished to be cremated. She glanced over at the shrouded form, then at the bedraggled Mynah bird sitting quietly in its cage.

"I don't suppose you saw anything, did you? I didn't think so. Poor thing."

She reached into the cage, attempting to stroke the bird's head but it moved away.

"Suit yourself," she said, withdrawing her hand, and leaving the cage door ajar.

Twinkling brightly in the firelight, the cheerfulness of the Christmas baubles saddened Prudence. The realisation of her mother's passing overwhelmed her. The death was no more easily accepted for having been expected. Hadn't she always held out some hope that Muriel would keep going despite the deterioration of her physical being. Since she was alone, Prudence allowed herself the indulgence of crying bitterly into sleep until first light when she was awoken by a knock at the front door.

Prudence was surprised to see the chaplain on the doorstep.

How does he know about me mam so soon? she thought, blinking against the morning sun. But at once, she realized he wasn't there because of her mother. He had to be at their house for official business. Her ankle still hurt so she held on to the door for support, not inviting him in.

Nodding calmly as if she understood everything he was saying, she listened as he told her about the distress call from the Ichthus and how there had been no radio contact since one a.m. that morning. The chaplain explained that there had been no other ships in the immediate area because of the bad weather thereabouts and when some boats did get there, there was nothing to be found, no survivors or wreckage. He didn't need to explain it was because the waters were too rough and too cold for any man to survive longer than a few minutes.

At first, she numbly took in the news, then when he finished, she could see he was watching her, waiting for a response. She shook her head in disbelief.

"You mean our Mac?" she asked, almost choking on the words.

He nodded grimly.

Again she shook her head, clinging more tightly to the door. "That's not possible. Not our Mac. He'd find a way. He would. You know him, Father."

"I'm sorry, Miss," said the Chaplain. "But we would have heard. I'm afraid all hands are presumed lost."

"All 'ands! What about Jake?" Prudence asked, scarcely able to breathe but remembering that Mac had taken the cowboy with him, and *that she had packed a kit bag for him with her father's things.*

"Jake?" The Chaplain referred to a list of names and addresses he had attached to a clip board.

"Aye. Jake Huggins," Prudence said. "He might not be on your list. He's me brother-in-law. Mac came back to get him, just before he left 'cause Ginger didn't show up at the dock. He wasn't meant to go, but they needed a cook, you see."

Referring to his list, the chaplain said, "I have a Mr. Stanley Duncan down as the cook."

"Aye, that's the one I mean. He's the usual one. The lads call him Ginger 'cause of his ginger hair, like. He didn't show up so Mac took Jake instead."

She wanted to sit down but didn't trust her legs. Perhaps it was a dream, a nightmare. She closed her eyes tight and pinched herself but the chaplain was still standing there with his clipboard. So she rested on her ankle – to feel the pain, hoping it would override the agony of loss. Yes, that was a better pain, she could control it, making it worse if she leaned on it, then making it less by lifting her foot.

With a pen as long and thin as his fingers, the chaplain made a note next to the name of the cook. "I'll have to double check with the office, of course," he said, then asked, "And who is it you said went in his place?"

"Jake Huggins. He's American," Prudence said. "He's my sister's 'usband."

"Oh aye. I've 'eard all about him, of course," the chaplain said with a nod of his head toward Hessle Road.

"Of course," smiled Prudence, although she couldn't imagine why she would smile at a time like this.

The terrible pain in her chest felt about to crush her as she thought of the other families in the community that had lost sons and father or brothers; she knew their devastation. With her mother gone too, she felt wiped out, small and insignificant in the great universe; a feeling that she should just surrender to the will of it.

For the first time she truly understood the sea's power over everything, over the men's lives, over the families' lives, over her life.

"Mac?" she said aloud, without realising it, as though evoking his name would dismiss the news. She couldn't picture him in trouble, drowning, succumbing, she couldn't: she could only see him grinning with his dog under his arm. The dog too, she thought. Gone together. But maybe they're wrong. Maybe he's all right, and that's why I can't picture it. They just haven't found 'em yet.

Then she recalled her mother crying out, 'William'. Had she been crying out for her son and not the father as Prudence had assumed? At once weak, Prudence fell against the door. The chaplain caught her by slipping an arm round her waist to steady her. He was so practiced at it now, so graceful, these women hardly felt his presence.

"You've gone all white," he said. "Can I get you anything?"

But Prudence couldn't respond; she could hardly breathe. She only stared ahead with a fearful expression on her face. 'William' was how Muriel had always addressed their father, but she had also addressed her son the same way when she was cross with him. Had he come for her, her beloved son? He would, of course he would, if there was a way. And only the dead know that. Prudence longed for the chaplain to leave so she could take another look at Muriel's expression hoping to discern from the dead features who it was she saw, or thought she saw, come for her through that door. Prudence tried to swallow back a sob that threatened to choke her.

"Miss, miss. Is there anyone I can call for you? Is there anyone else at home?"

Slipping to the floor, Prudence thought of Stalworth and how he would be there for her. He was that type of man. And thank God he wasn't a fisherman. She wouldn't lose him so easily as she had her father and brother. Her brother, Mac. Was he really dead? No, it was impossible. She thought of his grinning face. How much larger than life he was. Surely someone larger than life was also larger than death.

"Hello?" the chaplain called into the house, wary about stepping further in and catching people unawares at the early hour. "Hello? Is anybody there? It's the chaplain."

He saw a light on in the parlour and was preparing to advance toward it when a voice from up above said, "Have you come about the Ichthus?"

And there was Vivian, mid-step, half-way down the stairs with her hand resting on the polished railing. The racy black dressing gown she was wearing embarrassed the chaplain, who cleared his throat awkwardly. She took another step down, struggling to keep her legs working. The knuckles of her hand grasping the banister became white with the effort of holding on. For some reason, it was important to remain dignified.

"Yes, Miss. I came to inform your family about the loss of the Ichthus, and William Goodwell," he said, quickly giving condolences for her loss.

Her body buckled then stiffened, but her eyes remained fixed.

"I'm sorry to say it, Miss, but after speaking with your sister am I to understand that your husband ..." he paused, referring to his list. "Ah, here it is ... Jake Huggins was also aboard the Ichthus, as a substitute cook?"

Vivian swallowed, then nodded.

"Are you saying they're all lost?" she asked.

Her lips turned down and her chin trembled as she fought back the tears.

"I'm afraid so, Miss. All hands."

"But surely there must have been other boats in the area that could have picked them up," she said, almost incoherently.

"I already asked him that," said Prudence, sharply. "And the answer's 'no'. Nobody made it. Not Mac, not Jake, none of 'em. Don't you get it? It's winter. The water's too cold for anyone to survive. Even heroes have to die sometime."

She bit her lip.

"But there's lifeboats!" cried Vivian. "Surely they had time."

"They're dead," said Prudence who no more wanted to accept it than her sister.

"Well, I don't believe it. It's too soon. You, you're allus ready to believe the worst. You're only 'appy when there's bad news to moan about."

"You think I'm happy that my brother's dead?"

"He's *our* brother and he's not …," said Vivian. "They're not. None of them."

By this account, Crostaff was gone too, then. She thought of his wife, now widowed, just as she was. And Ted would never know his father. She sat on the stairs with a thud.

"I don't believe it," she said.

The chaplain felt quite uncomfortable looking from one sister to the other. People reacted in different ways to the news, of course. He had just come from the skipper's house since he always gave the news in order of rank of the crew. What a lady Mrs. Crostaff was about it, he thought. So dignified and polite. Even thanked me, and acknowledged how difficult it must be to do my job. No one ever thinks of that normally. She even invited me in for a cup of tea. Although he had declined due to the work that lay ahead of him. He had many more families to visit that day. The next name on the list was a Mrs. Bert Smith.

"I am sorry," he said. "But there are other people I have to see."

Prudence looked up at him. He extended a helping hand, which she took.

"Please convey my condolences to your mother."

"I will," said Prudence, forgetting.

"It's supposed to snow in the next couple of days," said the Chaplain, mounting his bike and pedalling stiffly away.

"Mam!" exclaimed Vivian, jumping to her feet and running to the parlour. "The news'll kill her."

Prudence didn't call after her; she was feeling relieved that her mother had not lived to see this day. She closed her ears to Vivian's cries, unable to offer comfort to another living soul.

392

Chapter 33

A gloom settled over Hessle Road. The loss of the Ichthus affected all the families in the fishing community. Everyone was either related to or at least knew one of the crew personally. Funeral arrangements were made for Muriel Goodwell, whose passing went almost unnoticed given the greater tragedy of the lost trawler: yet another casualty of war.

Neighbours offered their condolences with words and notes and gifts of homemade food. This kindness from people who had hardly anything for their own table brought Prudence to further tears. When Stalworth heard the news he had run to her and, tucking her into his arms, held her tightly to him, and over again whenever he sensed her buckling. The younger children, Winnie and George often joined them in the embrace, and Prudence, despite her devastating sadness, was comforted by the feeling of being a family with Stalworth and her siblings. They had to stick together. Even when Winnie confessed to losing the caul, the news was received numbly and without blame. Prudence felt the young girl's guilt was punishment enough.

The day before Muriel's funeral, Vivian came upon the scene of the four embracing, and felt excluded, as if the grief belonged only to them. And yet, hadn't she lost the most? Feeling despondent and alone, she took the pram with Ted sleeping in it, and went for her usual walk all the way to Pickering Road, simply, she told herself, because it was easier than thinking of somewhere else to go.

As she pushed the pram along, Vivian tried to cope with the sorrow that would overwhelm her, making her eyes hot and streaming, before she over-rode the feeling of loss by changing her focus to something normal like Ted asleep or the bus passing in the street. This time she looked at Ted's closed eyes and wondered if she would ever again enjoy such a carefree sleep.

His eyes scrunched when a snowflake fell on them. Vivian smiled and brushed it off. More flakes fell. She lifted her face to the sky and closed her eyes. Flakes fell on her face and she caught one on her tongue. The sensation was magical, and felt like a miracle. The heavily falling snow dampened the noises around her, as well as those within. Her mind felt quite clear as she walked, thinking only of the snow and how she wished Ted would wake up so he could enjoy it too. Then she arrived.

The curtains were drawn to at the Crostaff house.

Sitting on a low, brick wall, Vivian rested her head on the handlebar of the pram, staring at nothing. Time passed thus and then a voice close to her inquired, "Would you like to come in for a cup of tea?"

Before she could think of a reason to say no, Vivian found herself accepting the invitation and following Iris Crostaff up the path and through the front door of the skipper's house. Guiltily, she glanced up the stairs in the direction of where she had last been. Iris' eyes followed the young woman's gaze.

"The kettle's boiling," she said. "Let's have it the parlour, shall we? There's a fire already lit."

The two women sat at a dark wooden table laden with tea things and scones, as if the skipper's wife had been expecting company. At Iris' suggestion, Ted was placed on the rug by the fire to play with a rattle she produced from a drawer by the mantle.

"He's such a bonny lad. How long's he had that cough?"

"All his life," said Vivian, glancing over at Ted and, for the first time, picturing what he would look like as a man. Like Crostaff? With the same blue eyes and slight hook to his nose? Vivian blushed, embarrassed to be thinking about Crostaff in Iris' presence.

"Did you know," said Iris Crostaff. "That we had a son?"

"I -," Vivian stumbled, unsure of what to say.

"He was our honeymoon baby. You know what that means, don't you?"

Vivian nodded.

"He ... Thomas passed away when he was two, quite suddenly."

The bite of scone Vivian was eating, stuck in her throat as she tried to swallow it. The dry, crumbliness of it catching and refusing to do down. She hastily gulped some scalding tea, burning her throat.

"I'm sorry," Vivian spluttered, her eyes watering.

"He was always poorly," said Iris with her eyes on Ted. "From being born. His nose was always running and he never seemed to gain weight properly. Mind you, my mother-in-law always said John was a poorly baby and look how he's turned out. I mean, turned out."

The tea cup rattled noisily in Vivian's hands.

"I can't believe he's gone," Iris said wistfully. "And I'm sorry, love," she said, placing a hand on Vivian's arm, "for your losses. Your mother was always such a fine woman, very dignified, and how she managed to raise you all on her own, I'll never know."

"Aye," said Vivian, proudly. "Me mam allus found a way. She said she weren't the only one a widow with bairns to raise."

"Of course not, but even if there are others in the same boat as you, you still have to cope yourself, don't you? Look what happened to that poor Mrs. Alford. What a terrible accident. Of course people around here were saying terrible things about her for taking the child with her, and, well, she shouldn't have done that, of course, but I understand why she felt she couldn't go on after the baby died. It's very difficult when you lose a child. You see other children their age, or the age they would have been and it's so incredibly painful. After Thomas left us, I didn't want another child. I was afraid, you see. There's only so much one can take. Don't you agree?"

Vivian nodded, though she was feeling uncomfortable.

"More tea?" Iris asked, leaning forward to lift the teapot. "It's not too strong, is it? Good. There you are."

"Ta," said Vivian.

"Would you like another scone? What about the boy? Would he like one? Would you mind if I called him Edward."

"No, not at all."

Edward had been Crostaff's father's name. Vivian had chosen the name hoping it would endear her more to him.

"They're delicious, the scones," said Vivian.

Iris Crostaff smiled at the compliment.

"Yes, I can do some things a wife is supposed to do for her husband."

Again, the scone became stuck in Vivian's throat as she caught her breath at the frankness of the remark. She took another noisy gulp of hot, strong tea, fighting the urge to run from the house.

"Sorry, but with John gone now, I wish…"

Iris bit her lip, unable to go on. A tear rolled down her soft cheek.

"I just can't believe it," she said. "If we'd been able to have more children, it might have been easier for me, you understand, to see a bit of his face every day. The way it is, the loss is so abrupt."

Iris' eyes moved over to Ted. Vivian felt a tightness in her chest.

"How are the rest of the wives coping?" Iris asked.

"They're all, we're all, it's hard," said Vivian who had not reached out to any of the other wives since she felt unworthy of giving comfort.

"It's a crying shame there are no benefits for the widows."

"Aye. The women allus seem to marry another fisherman as soon as they can," said Vivian.

Iris laughed quite self-consciously covering her mouth as she did so. "I suppose that's one way around it," she said. "At least you and I have our careers so we can support ourselves. With your training, you'll do all right."

"Training?" asked Vivian.

"Yes, as a nurse."

"Oh, aye," said Vivian.

She dabbed at her mouth with a serviette. "The thing is .. I'm not really a nurse. I didn't make it past the first day of training."

"Oh," said Iris. "But I thought you stayed on to care for your mother."

"I know. Funny how it turned out really, that I had to nurse someone, me own mother after I'd been fibbing about it. Oh, I know I should have told them, but they'd only have said 'I told you so' and rubbed me nose in it. I couldn't stand that. Not again, not after... Well, no one's ever expected much of me since I had him, have they?"

She cast her eyes in the direction of Ted.

"We all make mistakes," said Iris. "We do. Besides, it takes two to tango, doesn't it? Ted's father bears some of the responsibility, doesn't he?"

Vivian coughed, reddening.

"So what did you do all that time in London?" Iris asked briskly. "How on earth did you get by on your own?"

"I was a barmaid. That's how I met Jake. Although I swore him to secrecy about it. He didn't like it, especially lying to me mam. He thinks, thought a lot about her."

Clapping her hands to her mouth, Iris let out an exclamation, "Oh dear, look what a mess little Edward has made!" Yet, she was smiling. "Oh no, Vivian, let me get it. Really, I don't mind. I'm happy to. I really am. I forgot that part. It drives you barmy at the time, but, goodness, how you miss the mess once it's gone."

Head to toe, Ted was happily covered in crumbs and jam. Vivian watched helplessly while Iris fussed over the baby wiping his hands and face clean with a white serviette from the tea tray.

"I bet you'd eat a whole plate of those scones, if I let you. Look, you've got it in your hair too. You are a proper little boy, aren't you? Full of mischief. And that smile ... why, that brings back memories."

Iris stopped her fussing and breathed in deeply. She was remembering Thomas' cheeky smile and the way he used to stand so patiently while she brushed his blonde hair into a side part. Their last morning together, the day before he died, he was on his way outside to play when he turned to look at her and smiled and she thanked him for being a good boy letting her brush his hair and blew him a kiss and he blew one back to her, kissing his hand with childish un-coordination then holding it out to her. Their eyes connected and she said his name and he came over to her with his arms held up making a little moan as if the love they had for each other had overwhelmed them both. How tightly they had held each other! Thomas with his little head resting on her shoulder while the apple pie baking in the oven filled the parlour with a warm, homey scent. It was perfect, that moment. She could remember it so clearly, even after all the years that had passed.

Although Iris had her back to Vivian, Vivian saw her touch just under her eyes. Tears, Vivian guessed, feeling guilty that she had caused someone pain.

"Excuse me, please," said Iris. "I'm being silly."

Without looking at her guest, Iris exited the room leaving Vivian to wonder how she could make her excuses to leave. Moments later, Iris returned with freshly powdered cheeks but her expression was drawn and tired.

"There," she said, as if something had been finalised.

After a moment during which neither of them could think of anything to say, Iris wringing her hands nervously and Vivian looking at the crumbs on the tray, Iris finally said, "It's been really nice to see you. Thank you for stopping in."

"Oh," said Vivian, catching her drift. "Aye. Ta. We'd best be off then. Our Prudence'll be worrying where we are. You know what she's like."

As Iris handed Vivian her red coat, she held onto Vivian's hand for a moment, saying, "You will bring him back tomorrow, won't you? It has been really wonderful to see you, to have some company. It would be lovely to see Edward again. And any time you need someone to look after him, I'd be happy to do it."

"Oh, but it's me mam's funeral tomorrow, you see, so we can't. We're having the wake at our 'ouse."

"Oh, yes," said Iris, looking sadly at Ted. Then an idea struck her. "I know, I could watch Edward for you while you take care of everything that needs to be done tomorrow. Really. I'd be happy to."

Vivian hesitated. She felt torn. Iris was so sweet, so understanding and … forgiving. Vivian felt wretched for having entertained any bad thoughts about her. Although nothing about the affair with John had been admitted, it seemed to be understood between them.

"That would be nice, ta," said Vivian. "I'll drop 'im off in the morning."

"Don't worry, he'll be well looked after."

"I know. I'll see mesen out. Ta for the tea and scones."

As Vivian paused by the front door to check her appearance in the hall-stand mirror, she noticed a letter addressed and ready for the post office. Heart beating heavily, she touched the pale blue envelope with the familiar handwriting on it, and understood everything.

Chapter 34

Mindful of her heels on the frosty path, Edith Butler made her way to the church's large wooden doors. After listening for a moment, she opened one door a crack and peered inside, relieved to see she had arrived at the conclusion of the service. The attendees were standing and returning the hymn books to the proper place, and a few were making their way to the Goodwells to offer their condolences. Prudence Goodwell had an arm around each of her younger, dewy-eyed siblings, and Gloria stood beside them. Dressed in her red coat, Vivian stood out as she talked with Father O'Brien, apparently questioning him about something he appeared uncertain about. The large number of mourners was notable. Their hearts were heavy with sorrow since the names of the lost fishermen had been read during the service.

"Mrs. Butler!" exclaimed Prudence in surprise. "How nice of you to –"

"I'm sorry to come at this time," said Edith Butler, breathless. "But I heard you would be here. I'm sorry about your mother. She was a very nice woman. But that's not why I'm here. We've received a telegram about the Ichthus."

The crowd gasped.

"The Ichthus!"

"Yes, there are survivors."

"Survivors!" "Impossible!"

"You mean Mac?" Prudence shouted over the growing din. "Our Mac's alive?"

Other fishermen's names were called out by other hopeful women.

"I'm afraid I don't know the names of any of those rescued," Edith Butler said apologetically.

A collective sigh of disappointment echoed around the stone walls of the church, but Edith hushed them with her hands.

"A list of names is going to be posted at our office as soon as possible. I'm afraid you'll have to go and see for yourselves. Mr. Butler called me at home, you see, but he didn't give any names."

Looking around at the expectant, hopeful faces, Edith sincerely wished she could give them what they wanted.

"But how were the men rescued after all this time?" asked Doctor McKenzie who was there along with his wife to pay his respects. "We were told there was no hope."

"We don't know what happened yet. We only got a bit of information, you see. It was the Wilberforce that received the message ... from a Russian Submarine."

"A submarine!" cried George.

"Why didn't they let us know sooner?" cried Bert's wife.

"I don't know," said Mrs. Butler. "I'm sorry, I wish I could tell you more but I don't know much about it, really. I can only tell you what I was told. I came to tell you as soon as I could."

"When will they be back?" asked Gloria, her eyes gleaming.

"Friday. The Wilberforce is bringing them home."

"Friday! Why that's three days away."

"You said that only some of the men were rescued?" asked Prudence.

Stalworth put an arm around his intended.

"How many?" asked Prudence. "How many men were saved?"

Edith looked carefully around the group before answering. She had been hoping not to be asked. There was excited chatter among the attendees that maybe their man was amongst the survivors, but Edith didn't want to give them false hope when they had lost their men once already. She cleared her throat.

"There was a number given but we don't know if it's accurate."

"What is it?" asked Dr. McKenzie.

"I could be wrong. But I was told ... seven."

"Seven!"

"Only seven!"

The paltry number was echoed around the group. Any brief hope that had alighted the faces of those present now turned once more to despair. If one of the rescued men was one of their own immediate family that meant that one of their friends' husbands or sons was still lost. There was certain to be more sorrow than joy since the drowned out-numbered the living. Vivian's heart sank. She had no expectation that Jake could be one of the survivors. It was his first time on a trawler. He was too inexperienced. She didn't even know if he could swim. But Mac, Mac her brother, he had to be one of the ones saved. It was impossible to think otherwise.

Silently, Prudence too felt Mac must be one of the saved. She clung Winnie more tightly to her. 'Please for our Winnie,' she pleaded with God. Reaching forward, she grasped Gloria's hand and squeezed it. The young girl's face was shining.

"Father," Prudence called to the priest. "I think we should wait to bury me mother's ashes. I think if Mac, well, I think he would want to be here, to say 'goodbye'."

"Prudence, be careful," Stalworth said.

But her glance silenced him.

"I am being careful," she said, "but I can hope with the rest of them, can't I?"

"I'll see to the ashes, Prudence," said Father O'Brien. "Just let me know when you would like to proceed. These are extenuating circumstances, after all. I'll say a prayer for you. For you all," he added to the group, most of whom were already out the door and on their way to Butler's offices, travelling by any which way they could find.

"Thank you, Father," said Prudence.

"Everything will be fine," the priest said putting a hand on her shoulder. "I'll see to it."

Prudence nodded.

"Can we come?" asked Winnie.

"No, love. You and George'd best be off home. It'll be a mad'ouse down at Butler's. Gloria, I think you should go with them. Please," she squeezed the girl's hand again.

Gloria smiled and nodded. New tears streaked her face.

"I'll go home with them an' all," Vivian said.

"Aren't you coming to Butler's with me?" asked Prudence. "To see the list? What if Jake's name is on it? Or our Mac?"

"No, I can't stand it," said Vivian. "You're right, it'll be a mad'ouse down there. I can't stand it. I can't … I just can't read those names and not see Jake's name up there. Don't you see? Anyrode, someone has to be at the house in case some people show up for the wake. I mean those that 'aven't heard."

"Jake's name could be on that list, Vivian. He had the same chance as everyone else."

"No, he didn't," said Vivian. "He didn't have the experience."

"You can't give up that easily," said Prudence.

"Willing it won't put his name up there," said Vivian. "And I won't set mesen up for the disappointment. I've already grieved once; I'm still grieving. It would be like losing him twice. Good things like that just don't 'appen to me."

Wanting to grasp her sister by the shoulders, Prudence stepped forward but Stalworth stayed her with his hand and a shake of his head.

"Best let her be," he whispered. "If Jake's name is on that list, well, then it is and she'll be happy about it, but that's all there is to it. You can't make her go."

Briefly resting her head on his shoulder, Prudence smiled up at him and her grey eyes beamed contentment. He touched her chin.

"All right Vivian, have it your way," Prudence said. "Just mind and make sure you put them breadcakes in the oven. I left me dough rising this morning. Are you listening? Good. See you soon, then."

The light coming in through the church's stained glass windows shifted, highlighting Vivian's features in a strange orange hue. She looked older to Prudence and beyond reach.

"Not if I see you first," said Vivian. "Go on, kids, run ahead. I'll meet you there. No, I've to fetch Ted on the way. No, you can't come. I want some time to mesen. Oh, Mrs. Butler has Mrs. Crostaff been told the news?"

"I assume she received a telephone call."

"If not, I'll tell her. Ta-ra."

"I can give you a lift to the office," Edith Butler quietly said to Prudence so none of the other women heard.

"That's kind of you," said Prudence looking at Stalworth.

"Go on," he said. "I have to stop in at the pub and make sure Mary opens on time. Then I'll meet you over at your house for the wake or whatever it turns out to be."

Hopefully, a celebration would be in order.

"So the wake's still on?" asked Elsie Waggin. "Everyone went to such trouble... and for your mam's sake."

"Yes, Mrs. Waggin," said Prudence. "The wake's still on."

Chapter 35

Inside one-nine-nine St. George's Road the parlour was packed with people from the funeral. When Prudence came in through the front door, her first inclination was to run up the stairs and hide, but Derek Stalworth had been waiting for her. Upon noting her sombre expression, he pulled her close. She sobbed.

"I'm sorry," he said, kissing the top of her hat.

"It were the submarine that hit the mine," she explained. "Then the explosion sank the Ichthus. They said the submarine only got damaged a bit, enough that its radio didn't work for a while. Anyrode, it surfaced and picked the men out of the water, those that it could see. It were pitch black, they say."

She shuddered imagining the fate of those that were not rescued.

"But our Jake's one of the survivors," she said brightly. "That's something, isn't it?"

"Aye, that's really something. Thank God."

"And Bert Smith."

"Oh Bert, that's good news for his wife. She's already been a widow once. Who else?"

"That Russian lad. A couple of names I didn't recognise, Yeoman and Hardcastle?"

"Aye. Good lads both."

"oh, and Stanley Duncan."

"Ginger?"

Prudence nodded, "Yes."

"Crostaff?"

"No. Poor Iris; she's lost an 'usband and a son. Hold on a minute, where's our Vivian?" Prudence cried. "I have to tell her about Jake straight away. She daren't believe he might be safe."

"Vivian's not 'ere, love."

"Not 'ere?"

"No. And no one knows where she is neither."

"What? Gone from her own mother's wake? Well, that's bloody typical, isn't it? When there's work to be done. I suppose she'll have to find out later, then," Prudence snapped. "Bloody hell, I wish I could just waltz off whenever I got the fancy. But here I am left to deal with it all on me own again."

"Not on your own," Stalworth reminded her. "Not anymore."

"No, not anymore. Sorry, love. I weren't forgetting. I were just mad at our Vivian. But Vivian's Vivian. We'll see her when we see her. As usual. Her husband's alive and she doesn't even know it. She could be feeling 'appy now instead of, instead of -

"Oh, God," Prudence sobbed.

"I'm really sorry about Mac, love," Stalworth said. "I mean, I can hardly believe it mesen. I thought, if anybody made it ..."

"I know, I know," she sniffed. "So did I. Derek, will you tell them?" she nodded in the direction of the parlour. "About Mac I mean. I don't want to go through it all again, you know, everyone telling me how sorry they are."

"All right, love."

"But have Gloria, and our Winnie and George come to the front room, so I can tell them mesen."

"Will do. I'll be discreet, then I'll fetch you a cup of tea. Fancy some'at a bit stronger in it?"

"Aye, I do, and I'm sure Gloria would an' all, and why not our Winnie and George? There should be some rum on the top shelf in the pantry on the right. That's if Mrs. Waggin didn't find it first."

Derek smiled and kissed her gently, on the lips.

"Ta. I needed that."

Her eyes were shiny with tears of sorrow and joy. She frowned, tormented by feeling two extremes of emotion at the same time, as if she should have to decide on one over the other. The front room was as frigid as ever, cold and unused. I meant to light a fire in here so everyone could come in and warm up, breathe some life into this room. What's the point of all this pretty furniture if no one ever sits on it. She walked over to the mirror above the fireplace.

Oh dear, look at me eyes. What a mess. Derek was right, I should have been more careful about getting me 'opes up.

"Help! Help!" Elsie Waggin shrieked from the parlour. "Get that thing away from me!"

Then came more shrieks and shouts from the parlour, followed by some terrible swearing. Alarmed, Prudence ran to the parlour where she saw several women dashing about, flailing their arms as if warding off a swarm of bees. At first, she could not tell who was cursing so vilely, using the most repugnant language known to man or beast. Her eyes went from one face to the next, then alighted on two boys laughing hysterically in the midst of the chaos: George and his friend, Paddy.

She was about to reprimand them when she noticed that even Father O'Brien was having a hard time containing himself. He was spitting pastry from a sausage roll while trying not to laugh. And the doctor too. His head was bent, but his shaking shoulders gave away the fact that he too was chuckling mightily at whatever was the cause of the commotion.

Pushing through the bodies collected around the parlour table, Prudence also had to hide a laugh when she spotted the poor Mynah bird mired in the dough she had left rising. It was *he* who was swearing.

"He must have been in the pantry," Derek said. "And when I opened the door to look for the rum he flew out, first getting caught in Mrs. Waggin's hair – Look."

The busybody's hair was all bedraggled and torn up. Prudence bit the inside of her lip, but that wasn't enough to stop the chuckles building in her belly, so taking a deep breath, she dug her nails into her palms.

"Then," continued Derek, "he headed for the window, smashed into it, panicked and ended up in the dough."

"Oh, poor Houdini. Well, at least he's talkin' again."

"Fuck, sod, bugger," screamed the bird. "Arse 'ole! I love you!"

"And so profound!"

By now, Prudence couldn't help it. She too was laughing uncontrollably and had to hang on to Derek for support lest her legs collapsed with merriment. Winnie couldn't help but giggle either, and Prudence felt a swell of happiness for her younger sister. The laughter spread through the room until soon the whole parlour had the giggles, but the giggles quickly turned to shrieks when the bird looked as though it might free itself and fly around again.

"That's the foulest fowl I've ever met," quipped Dr. McKenzie, sending the group into another tittering frenzy.

Prudence grabbed a tea towel and quickly captured the exhausted bird that relaxed once it was covered.

"Oh, it's my fault," gasped Prudence. "I must have left the cage door open the other night when … well, maybe the poor thing just wanted some freedom."

The bird squawked but Prudence quickly pinched its beak shut.

"Not another peep out of you, today, young man," she said. "Or I'll be washing your beak out with soap and water. I mean it. Here let's get this sticky stuff off your feet." The bird swore as she washed its feet, and everyone laughed anew. "Now, go on, back in your cage. Go on. And if you're a good boy, we'll let you out again."

Slipping his arm around Prudence's waist, Derek leant forward to nibble her ear like a parrot. Prudence laughed and pushed him away. But then she remembered all that was going on and felt she had no right to laugh. Stalworth caught her frown.

"Fancy that tot now, love?"

"Ta," she said with a grateful smile. "I can't wait to put me feet up when everyone's gone home."

Gloria linked her arm through Prudence's and leant her head on her shoulder.

"Oh, love," said Prudence. "I'm afraid I didn't get a chance to -"

"Don't worry. You would have already told me if his name was on the list."

Prudence smiled sadly. The younger children caught the exchange. Winnie slumped in a chair, and George dragged himself upstairs to look at his collection. Paddy followed.

After everyone left, Prudence started a fire in the front room while Derek made a ploughman's supper for them all with some ham, cheese, buttered bread, and various pickles. There were jam tarts for a sweet. He poured a glass of sherry for each of them.

"Ta, love," said Prudence, warming her toes near the fire. "It's nice to relax a bit, isn't it? After all that's been going on. Oo, this sherry's a bit dry but it'll do."

"Any port in a storm," said Stalworth.

Realising she hadn't seen Vivian since the church, Prudence glanced at the mantle clock. She was just about to remark that it was almost four-thirty and getting dark out when she put a few things together in her mind, and exclaimed, "Oh no, Vivian!"

"What?" a chorus of voices asked.

Prudence put down her glass, too close to the edge of the table where it fell, unnoticed, on the rug spilling its contents. She raced upstairs to Vivian's room where she found everything packed and gone. There was a note, however, addressed to Prudence in a hasty scrawl, and which read, *P.S. I wasn't really a nurse.* Clutching the note in her hand, Prudence held it to her chest with her eyes closed, taking a deep breath. Her eyes felt hot but, in the end, a smile came to the corners of mouth.

"Oh Vivian, you daft bugger, you."

Chapter 36

The Wilberforce arrived on an earlier tide than expected. Word travelled quickly around the community and, despite the cold, there was a crowd waiting to meet the survivors. People were running and slipping on the icy roads, and two wives, no longer widows, were crying as they ran to meet the docked boat.

The Butlers were there, along with a reporter from The Hull Daily Mail. Samuel Butler was telling the reporter about the compensation he had set aside for the widows and their families. Little Shirley Alford, his grandchild, so to speak, had connected the Butlers to the Hessle Road community in a way they had never thought possible. Little Shirley Alford, sitting on his knee and playing with his red bow tie, had found the soft spot in Samuel Butler. He had come to look forward to seeing her cheeky smile and spirited ways. The girl had a way of dissolving tension between people, and the devoted protection she exhibited toward her brother was incredibly moving to all who witnessed it.

Prudence Goodwell was at the docks to meet Jake and tell him about Vivian's leaving. Scanning the crowd, she spotted Gloria Baxter's eager face. The young woman was there with her mother to meet Bert Smith. I hope that look's for Bert and not because she's still hoping to see our Mac, Prudence thought. And there's the cook's wife. I don't believe it! She's got her rolling pin with her!

The crowd hushed, then cheered as the men disembarked, smiling but worn out. There was Igor, then Stanley Duncan whose rotund wife barrelled up to him, almost bowling him over. He cowered when he saw the rolling pin.

"I want to show you I'll never do this to you again," she cried, about to ceremoniously throw the rolling pin in the dock water, but Ginger stopped her.

"No," he said. "Let's keep things the way they've allus been. I don't want me luck to change one bit."

The next man to walk down the gang plank was unmistakable, head and shoulders above the rest. There was a blood-stained bandage wrapped around his forehead.

"Mac?" Gloria and Prudence cried together pushing through the throng. "Mac!"

Gloria reached him first, throwing herself into his arms and raining him with kisses. "Mac! Mac! I knew it. You're alive! Your name wasn't on the list, but I knew it! You're alive. Thank God."

"Mac!" cried Prudence, throwing her arms around him and Gloria. "You're alive."

"So everyone keeps telling me," he said, overwhelmed by the ardour. "Ladies! Ladies! Watch me 'ead."

"It's real good to see you, Mac," said Gloria's mother, though her eyes looked beyond him.

"Even better to see you Mavis. Don't worry, Bert should be along any minute."

"But your name weren't on the list," Prudence insisted. "I went to Butler's and your name weren't on it. There was Jake and Bert but not you. I must have read it ten times over!"

"What list are you on about?"

"The list of survivors! They posted it at Butler's offices."

"List of survivors? But I made that list," he said. "I gave the names to the radio operator. It doesn't make sense." He scratched his bristled chin, then grinned.

"What is it?" asked Prudence. "Are you blushing? That's a first."

"You won't believe it," he said, "but I must have forgot to give me own name."

"What are you like!" Prudence and Gloria exclaimed, pushing him between them, one on each side.

411

"It must have been this," he pointed to his bandaged head. "Reckon, I weren't thinking straight. By heck." He laughed. "I'm sorry."

"You bugger! You have no idea!" exclaimed Prudence. "Oh my God! What we just went through! You know, I kept thinking you was alive then some'at else would happen an' ... Bloody hell! I could kill you! Did you do it on purpose?"

"No, no. You know I wouldn't do that to you, or Mam."

Prudence's heart flipped at the mention of their mother. She looked away, searching for the right words.

"Well, *I* knew you weren't drowned," Gloria said triumphantly. "I just knew it. I've known for too long that I was going to marry you, William Goodwell, and no mine is ever going to get in the way of that."

Grasping Prudence and Gloria to him, he said, "It's so good to be home. I am a lucky man."

"Oo, let me go, I can't breathe," gasped Prudence.

"Dad!" cried Gloria upon spotting Bert Smith. "Mam! There's dad!"

"Where?" asked Mavis Smith, following her daughter through the crowd until they reached Bert.

"By heck, this is some welcome home," the bosun said, beaming with delight at how happy his family was to see him.

Jake was carried off the Wilberforce on a stretcher. His arm was in a sling. "Where's Vivian?" he asked when Prudence came up to him.

"Aye, where is our Vivian?" asked Mac. "Minding the shop? Looking after Mam?"

"The shop's closed for the day," said Prudence.

"What about our George and Winnie?"

"They're in school. My God, they think you're ... We'll have to go an' fetch 'em."

"What about Mam?" said Mac. "Does she think I'm dead an' all?"

"Oh, Mac," said Prudence. She needed to brace herself before she gave the news.

"She's gone?" asked Jake.

Prudence nodded.

"I'm sorry," Jake said.

"Was it because of me?" Mac asked, looking scared. "Because she thought we'd sunk?"

"No, no," said Prudence. "Thankfully, she didn't know owt about it. It was just her time to go."

"Oh," his shoulders relaxed but tensed again when he asked. "When did it happen?"

Prudence took a deep breath before answering. "Strangely enough, I think it were the same night the Ichthus went down. She called out for Dad."

"For Dad?"

"Aye." Then noticing his thoughtful expression, she asked, "Why?"

"Oh, nowt. Let's get 'ome. I'm starving and dying for a decent cuppa."

"I thought you'd want to go straight to the pub," she said with a wink over her shoulder as she walked briskly ahead.

"Don't worry, that's me next stop."

But he didn't follow.

When she felt an emptiness behind her, she turned.

"Come on, then," she said. "Let's go 'ome."

"Home," he said. "But without Mam?"

"Aye, I know what you mean. It is very different without her. Oh Mac."

She broke down when she saw the tears in his eyes. Perhaps it was the first time she had ever seen him cry. She ran back to him and they embraced. Her face pressed against his large chest. He stroked her hair as she sobbed while his own handsome features crumpled, and the tears rolled down his cheeks unchecked.

"Hey!" exclaimed Prudence when a hot little tongue licked her nose. "Monty!"

She laughed.

"You made it an' all, did you?"

"Don't tell me I forgot to put his name on the list as well! What am I like?"

"Aye, what are you like?"

Chapter 37

.

His arm still in a sling, Jake ran along the dirt path until he saw her standing on the edge of the white chalky cliffs of Dover. She wasn't difficult to spot in the red coat. The way she stood in impossible stilettos with one hip slightly higher than the other, made him smile. The sky was a clear blue, and the grass was dark green. Some of the white chalk was visible along the cliffs, and it would be all these colours he would remember most about that day.

Her striking looks meant she hadn't been difficult to find, all he needed to do was ask the next young red-blooded male if he had seen a woman fitting Vivian's description and he was immediately directed to where she had last been seen.

What a frantic race it had been to get to Dover in time. The Queen Mary was scheduled to depart that afternoon. Jake had been surprised by Mac's offer of a lift all the way down to the South of England, but Mac explained that not only had he been longing to lay eyes on the Grey Ghost but also he would like to say a proper farewell to his sister. So Jake had ridden on the back of Mac's bike all the way. He was exceedingly stiff and sore, as a result, and it was painful to walk. His head still throbbed but he had run along the cliffs anyway.

There she was, only a few feet away and completely unaware of his presence. It was Prudence's idea that Vivian would be here at the cliffs after it was discovered that she had removed half of Muriel's ashes from the urn. At first, Prudence had been furious with Vivian for not asking permission, but then she wept when she realised she might never see her sister again.

Blue-grey kittiwakes made their familiar call and flocked above Vivian as she pulled a brown paper bag from her handbag. She opened the bag, said something quietly, perhaps a prayer, and crossed herself. Then she lifted the bag into the air and shook out its contents. Grey dust blew through the air and the sea gulls became frenzied. It was a beautiful, startling moment, to which Jake was glad to have shared with his wife, though that was unbeknownst to her until she turned and saw him. Her face showed complete disbelief, even a little fear, as if she had seen a ghost. Prudence had told Jake how Vivian had convinced herself he was dead.

"Vivian!" he called. "Vivian! It's me."

She took a step back and almost lost her footing on the cliff edge. The seagulls screamed and a few people yelled out but he reached forward and grabbed her, pulling her to safety. His own heart pattered fast when he glanced down at the several hundred foot drop to the shingle shore and rocky coastline below.

"Jake!" she cried.

"Oh Vivian!"

Tears in her eyes blurred her vision, so she felt his face, and touched the bandage, making sure he was real.

"It is you! I thought you was lost."

To see her face so full of joy gladdened him but also filled his heart with pain as he recalled how he had treated her over the past few months, how cold he had been, how he had doubted her feelings for him.

"Is that why you left?" he asked.

415

"I thought you wouldn't want me even if you did make it," she said. "The way you've been."

"I'm sorry," he said.

"No, no, you had a right. I should have told you about Ted. It wasn't fair. I wish you could forgive me."

"There's nothing to forgive."

"There is. Tell me you forgive me. You must say it. I insist."

He smiled and touched her face.

"I do forgive you, Vivian. I have forgiven you. I'm in no position to judge you or anyone else. After all, I *killed* a man. Who's going to forgive me for that?"

"But that was war."

"But me," he pointed to his chest. "*I killed a man.* Call it war, call it what you will but I killed a man, a boy really, the same as me. When I volunteered, the enemy didn't have a face, but that soldier did. It was an ordinary face but filled with the most incredible clear blue eyes. I'll never forget it."

"You had to defend yoursen. You didn't have a choice."

"I did, but I found out I'm the kind of man that would rather kill than die. Could ya love someone like that?"

"I do love someone like that."

With a gentle hand he lifted her face to his, but she cast her eyes downwards. Her beauty sent a shiver along his spine. For a moment, he studied her creamy skin and wonderful red lips.

"Look at me," he whispered.

"I can't," she said.

"Please."

And slowly, so slowly, her thick black lashes lifted until her tear-filled blue eyes looked into his. Jake breathed deeply. The clean salt air washed through him. Lovingly, he brushed Vivian's cheek.

"Tell me," she asked, "that letter you're so mad about, does that have something to do with it?"

"Yes. He gave it to me, the soldier I killed. It was for his mother."

"Then you must post it. Do you still have it?"

"Yeah." He patted his breast pocket, and smiled lopsidedly. "We both made it."

"Then we'll post it as soon as we get to America. It will mean so much to her. She must miss her son."

"Miss her son," he repeated softly.

Those words sounded strange coming from Vivian.

"Oh no! Stop Ted! Stop!"

Laughing, Vivian raced over to where Ted was crawling toward the cliffs' edge. She scooped him up in her arms and lifted him above her head. The boy giggled.

"I left him over there on the blanket playing with his rattle. You didn't see him? Well, he's a little monkey, aren't you? Where did you think you were going? For a swim. Or did you just come to see me."

"You brought him even though you thought you'd be alone," said Jake.

"Aye. It's all right, isn't it? I didn't know what to do. I mean, I were worried I wouldn't be able to manage on me own (that's what our Prudence was allus telling me anyrode). But someone I know showed me that it's the little things that make a mother. So I looked at Ted, I mean properly, really looked into his face and I picked him up and held him. I know that's what you're supposed to do but it's allus been hard for me. I allus thought people was looking at me and thinking I was unfit, that I shouldn't be like that 'cause of me not being married and that. But then I realised he's not ashamed of me. I think he might even like me. I can make him laugh. Do you understand, Jake? Do you?"

Jake said nothing but embraced them both, falling in love with the girl all over again.

"Well, I'm glad that's sorted," she said cheekily, gathering up the blanket with the rest of her things. "I'm dying for a cuppa, aren't you? Do we have time?"

"For your last cup of English tea?"

"Aye. Oh, will it really be my last? I can't believe it. Hey Ted!" She sang, "*Tea for two and two for tea, Tea for you and tea for me. I mean, Tea for three and three for tea -*"

"Actually," Jake said. "It's gonna be tea for four."

"Four?"

"Yeah, a certain fella gave me a ride ..."

Until then she hadn't given any thought to how he had suddenly appeared.

"Mac brought you! He's alive! He is? I knew he'd make it. Is he really here? I can't believe it! Oh Mac!"

The fisherman was standing on Shakespeare Cliff. He had been staring for a long time at the glistening English Channel: the twenty-three mile eternal body of water that had saved them from the Nazis, and many other enemies. It was a clear day and he could see France. She was so close. An invasion by the Germans had been that close. Perhaps the channel was God's protective arm around them, around freedom, and it had been created for that reason.

"Beautiful," he said, admiring the water and then shifting his eyes to the sky. He was turning to leave when something caught his eye.

"Hold on, is that?" he exclaimed. "It is!"

The Albatross was flying close across the water on the lookout for krill. Mac grinned, and his heart filled with joy as the bird dipped its beak into the water before taking off again. By heck, look at that. We're fishermen we two, he thought, feeling a great weight lift from his shoulders. He was a free man.

Whose soul are you carrying on them wings, my dear friend?

Epilogue

The last thing Crostaff expected to hear when he opened the front door was his wife singing. Not only was she singing but it sounded as though she was singing to someone, and joyfully too. The beautiful melodic voice was so unexpected, he stayed for a moment in the hallway, with the door still open behind him, afraid to close it lest he disturb her, listening while he tried to recall the last time he had heard his wife sing, and sing that particular song.

"My Bonnie lies over the ocean,
My Bonnie lies over the sea,
My Bonnie lies over the ocean,
Oh, bring back my Bonnie to me."

Then it came to him. He hadn't heard her sing that way, if at all, since their son died. He swallowed hard at the memory: his throat feeling suddenly dry and uncomfortable. Perhaps she had gone mad after hearing the news about the Ichthus. He had heard of it happening to some women. The singing went on undisturbed:

"Bring back, bring back,
Bring back my Bonnie to me, to me,
Bring back, bring back,
Oh bring back my Bonnie to me.
Last night as I lay on my pillow,
Last night as I lay on my bed,
Last night as I lay on my pillow,
I dreamt that my Bonnie was dead."

The singing stopped abruptly, as did his breathing.

"John, is that you? I felt a draft."

He paused for a moment then, closing the door loudly, he called, as cheerfully as he could muster, "Aye love, it's me. I'm home."

Back from the dead, he thought.

He expected her to come to the door to the hallway, but she didn't. She was humming the tune now. Why didn't she come to see that he was all right? Could she really be so angry with him that she no longer cared for his welfare? The humming continued and with it the sound of the rocking chair long left unused. The sound unsettled him and he dare not take another step into the house.

"John?"

"Aye, love?"

"Aren't you going to come in here? It's warm by the fire and there's a mug of tea waiting to be poured from the pot."

He approached the door but stayed behind it.

"I heard some singing."

"We're waiting."

He opened the door slowly and his heart jumped into his throat when he saw what he saw.

"I am dead, then," he said simply.

Her eyes brimmed with tears as she rocked in the chair, and looked down at the swaddled child in her arms. Eventually, her husband came to her, on his knees by the chair and took off his cap.

Pulling aside the quilt, she said, "Look, he's beautiful. Just like his father. The same blue eyes."

"Iris," he failed to find the right words: he felt unworthy in the presence of one so gracious and forgiving as his wife.

Sobbing, he lay his head on her lap and she cradled the man and boy both, singing to them, more joyfully than before now that her family was whole once more:

"Bring back, bring back,
Bring back my Bonnie to me, to me,
Bring back, bring back,
Oh, bring back my Bonnie to me."

Made in the USA
Charleston, SC
13 July 2012